Cursed Seed

Cursed Seed

Society of Immortals

Book 1

Geralyn Wichers

Synecdoche Publishing

Edited by William McLaughlin and Giles Hovseth
Cover design by Tiffany Schank
Book design by Amanda Hovseth

ISBN: 978-1-945018-03-9

Library of Congress Control Number: 2016953614

First Edition: November 2016

Also By Geralyn Wichers

We are the Living
Sons of Earth

CHAPTER 1
Winnipeg Canada, 1990

It was the deathly scream that brought Alannah's head up, made her eyes open wide, made her stand up from the park bench before she could register a thought. She heard it again, reverberating off the bungalows in front of her, and the halfway-built concrete walls behind. A man's guttural cry. She spun around, taking in the wide, green lawn of the University.

It came again, rattling in her ears.

Alexander had just met her, was just smiling and holding out a paper cup of tea. He had the day's newspaper in the other. The wail of pain froze his wingtip shoes to the concrete sidewalk.

"Good Lord," he breathed.

Alannah swallowed hard and pointed across the grassy park to where the unfinished spires of an apartment complex rose. "Alex…"

"Yes."

Alannah set off at a jog towards it. She gave no thought to what she'd do when she got there.

Behind her, Alexander set the paper and the cup tea on the bench and ran after her.

They pulled up to the chain link fence that surrounded the gaping hole. Spires of rebar at three, six and nine foot heights.

Dead center of the hole, a worker hung three feet off the ground, suspended and skewered on three metal rods of rebar. His arms were thrown over his head, and his head tilted back. His wide eyes caught and stared into Alannah's. Workers gathered around him, staring helplessly, and one ran across the construction site toward the little office trailer and the nearest phone.

"Alex!" Alannah gasped. She gripped the fence.

Alexander shoved the rolling gate open and strode through. His mouth was set in a hard and grim line.

"We've got to cut him down, we've—" One of the men pushed his hard hat back from his clammy forehead. He caught Alexander's eye. "Hey—"

The impaled man moaned. Alannah let out a little gasp. She stood just on the inside of fence, her back frozen against the chain links.

"What happened?" Alexander pushed past them to the base of the rebar. He fell to his knees and reached up to support the man's body, and prevent it from sliding further toward the ground.

Two other men followed his lead immediately, taking up the man's dangling legs, and the weight of his trunk. "He fell off the scaffolding," one said.

"Are you a doctor?" the other man asked, from his position supporting the man's head.

Alexander ignored him. "Hey." He focused on the impaled man's face. "Hey."

The man's watering brown eyes focused on him. His hands came up and reached for the rebar through his gut. "Oh God, oh... God."

"Just be still!" Alexander reached for the waving hand. "For the love of God, isn't any help coming?" He glanced back toward Alannah. Anguish burned in his blue eyes and thawed Alannah's frozen limbs. She lurched forward, across the packed ground to Alexander's side.

Alannah dropped to her knees in the blood-speckled gravel beneath the rebar. She took one of the man's dangling hands and clutched it in hers. Blood smeared from one hand to the other.

"Shhh." She reached out with her free hand, around the worker who supported his head, and touched his shoulder, then his hair. "Just be still. Let us help you. You'll be alright." But she glanced at Alexander, and he shook his head almost imperceptibly. His blond brows pulled together, face rigid in an effort to remain composed.

Alannah looked up. The rebar had pierced the man's stomach in two places, and one had shoved through his rib cage. Blood dribbled down the ridged metal.

"Should we cut the bars above him?" The worker on Alexander's left asked.

"No, don't move him. Not on your life," Alexander said, quiet and deathly calm. "How long will it take for the ambulance to get here?"

"I don't know, minutes?" The man's face was white. "The hospital is right there." He nodded his head toward the busy road.

"Then we wait for their instructions," Alexander replied.

The impaled man groaned, weaker. "Help..." His head flopped to the side and his brown eyes met Alannah's again. He had curly hair, the color of cinnamon, plastered to his head by sweat and pressed down by the hard-hat he'd been wearing.

"Shhhh." Alannah reached up and stroked his hair. "What is your name?"

"J-Jack." His lips and cheeks were flecked with blood. "You're going to be alright, Jack. Do you have a family?"

"Y-yes—oh shit!" Jack cried out.

"No, no, shhh. Shhh." She touched his cheek. She tried not to stare at the blood pooling at the base of the rebar, the very life flowing out of young Jack.

"Dear God, save him," Alexander whispered in German.

Alannah turned her head and realized that Alexander was praying, his lips in constant motion as he supported Jack. His eyes were squeezed shut; sweat beaded on his brow.

Sirens wailed, very close.

"It's going to be alright, Jack." Alannah brushed her hand over his hair again, and his cheek. "Help is close, so close. Think of your family, Jack, be strong for your family."

One of the construction workers nearby retched. Alannah pressed her lips together.

A couple moments passed and the paramedics reached around them to support Jack's body. They slid a body-board crosswise underneath his hips. A firefighter, blond and broad shouldered, squeezed in between Alannah and the construction worker holding Jack's shoulders. He was so close she could smell diesel fuel on his jacket. "I'll take him," he said.

Jack cried out. Even the small movement of the firefighter reaching to support his shoulders dug the corrugated metal deeper into his flesh.

"It's okay Jack. We're going to get you down." Alannah squeezed his hand urgently.

"Step back, please," the firefighter ordered, "step back, ma'am."

A metallic glint—cutting tools—passed just inside Alannah's line of sight. Alannah released Jack's hand with a final squeeze and got up. She stepped back and saw the stain of blood on her hands.

Alannah swallowed hard and released Jack's hand. She dropped back a few steps, and the firefighters and paramedics closed in around Jack. She pressed her hands tight together. Sticky blood smeared between her palms.

Every cut of the tools sent shocks through the rebar. Jack's screams were fainter, feebler every moment.

"He's free." The paramedics lifted Jack onto the stretcher. The three bloody bars of rebar still protruded from his body. A trickle of blood snaked down the body board.

"Can I go with him?" Alannah jogged after them as they pushed the stretcher towards the ambulance.

"Are you family?" the medic asked without turning toward her.

"No, I—"

"Then no."

"But where are you taking him?" Alannah cried as the stretcher was lifted up through the doors of the ambulance.

"Health Sciences Center." The doors of the ambulance shut and the sirens wailed as it pulled away.

Alannah stood, staring after it. Her pulse pounded in her temples. Her hands dangled, clenched like claws at her sides. Alexander grabbed her elbow. "Alannah, you've done all you can."

She turned to look at him. His old, blue eyes stood out in his pale, young face, which sagged with exhaustion. His cheeks were wet, but his eyes were tearless now.

"Do you want to follow the ambulance?" Alexander asked.

"Yes," she said, almost inaudible. "If you will."

"Let's get the car."

"My hands," she sniffled. It wasn't just her hands. Her formerly crisp, grey slacks were speckled with Jack's blood. His life blood was spattered all over her.

"It's alright, Alannah." Alexander took one of her dirty hands in his and led her across the University grounds trudged to his car. He had a bottle of water and a box of tissue in his car. Alexander and Alannah scrubbed at their bloody hands and stuffed the crimson stained tissues into the center console.

"How will we find him?" Alannah asked softly. She was curled up in the passenger seat with her head against the window. They knew the young man's name was Jack, but they'd never asked his surname. "Do you know which building to go to?"

Alexander didn't know. They pulled alongside the massive hospital complex.

"Emergency!" she pointed. "On William Avenue. There."

Alexander pulled up at the doors and let her jump out. He took his time finding a place in the parking garage. He didn't want to go in and find out that the young man was dead. He'd outlived too many young men already, and each time he watched them go it was with deep sorrow, and yet a pang of envy. He was not going with them.

He sighed as he walked through the sliding doors, into the bustle of the waiting room. Alannah stood against the wall, near the triage desk. She had her arms wrapped tightly around herself. Every chair in the emergency room was full. Alexander slipped to her side. He shrugged out of his sport coat and wrapped it around her shoulders. She tugged it close.

"He's in surgery." She sniffled. "They told me that much. I just asked if the construction worker with the rebar was brought here." She tipped her chin toward a delicate young woman with a halo of flaxen hair, who sat between two older women. All three had their eyes squeezed shut, their hands clasped tightly. "Do you think that's his wife? She just came in."

Alexander felt a sharp burst of pain, and turned his head away. The privilege of dying carried with it a steep cost for those left behind. He knew what it was to be left behind.

Alannah leaned against his shoulder.

They waited for three hours, Alexander leaning against the wall, Alannah leaning on him, snuggled up in his jacket, until a nurse came out and called out "Mrs. Krause?"

The blond woman opened her eyes.

Alexander took in the nurse's face, and saw resignation, mixed with abject weariness. She said something to the young woman.

"Oh God!" she screamed. Then higher, disbelieving, "Oh God no!"

Alannah turned and looked at Alexander. Her face drooped, eyes dead. "Alexander."

He laid his hand on her shoulder. "Let's go home."

∞

"I'll cook something." Alannah dropped her leather satchel on the little kitchen table and turned to the refrigerator. She swung the door open and stared in. The grey-green light spilled out into the dark kitchen.

"It's alright, Alannah." Alexander sagged in the doorway and flicked the kitchen light on. "I'll have toast. You're exhausted. Take a bath, put on clean clothes, and go to bed."

"I won't sleep anyway." Alannah rubbed her eyes and sniffled. Her arms and legs felt leaden but she knew if she stopped moving... sat down... shut her eyes... she'd hear Jack's groans again and feel the splat of sticky blood on her hands.

She yanked a carton of eggs out of the fridge and the half-full jug of milk. "I'll make crepes. Sweet or savory?"

"Alannah," Alexander said as he took a step into the kitchen and laid a hand on her shoulder, "it is alright to mourn over death. Death should always hurt, as something contrary to the original order of creation."

Her face contorted. "Well, that doesn't mean anything to me right now."

"Alannah..."

She spun around, away from his grasp. "Sweet or savory?"

He sighed, defeated. "Savory. I... suppose you want me to make myself scarce?" Instead of waiting for an answer, he turned and left the room. A moment later his light footfalls ascended the stairs.

Alannah yanked a crockery bowl out of a cupboard and began to viciously crack eggs into it. She whisked them so hard that they began to splatter out of the bowl, onto her top. She glanced down and saw the creamy yellow egg yolks, juxtaposed with burgundy, dried blood. The whisk dropped from her hand onto the tile floor, and fell to her knees beside it. She wheezed out one, strangled sob. Then they came relentlessly. She cried so hard it hurt. At some point she realized that Alexander was sitting beside her, his back against the splattered, white cabinets.

She raised her head and pushed herself up slowly. She rubbed at her eyes and felt a smear of eggs transfer from her fingers to her eyebrows. "Ugh. Maybe you should just have toast," she said with a wobbly attempt at a smile.

Alexander leaned his head against the cabinet doors and smiled back. "I can finish the crepes, dear Alannah. Take a shower."

He was so calm, but Alannah had been Alexander's friend for more than fifty years, and lived with him for forty. She could see the strain in his face, the haunting in his eyes. Alannah settled herself beside him and touched his knee. He was in loose gym shorts and a white t-shirt. He'd probably been heading out for a run. "Are you alright, Alexander?"

"I'll live." Alexander stood and reached down to give her a hand up.

Alannah held up one shaking hand and let Alexander hoist her to her feet. "I should take something for my nerves. I'll... I'll live too." She attempted a smile again, then leaned toward him and kissed his cheek. "Call me when the crepes are ready."

She trudged up the stairs to the second floor, down the long hall to her bedroom. The light was still on in Alexander's room, the door half open, like he'd bolted down the stairs when he'd heard her crying. That would be like him. She reached in to turn off the light and saw a sheet of paper lying on the bed. It had five, small pencil portraits, one in each corner and one in the center. Alannah switched off the light and closed the door. She knew whose portraits they were. The five loves of Alexander's life, all gone.

"Oh Alexander." She sighed as she slipped into her own bedroom.

She'd just put on a clean pair of pants and a soft sweater, when a thought occurred to her: an accident like this, in a well-populated area like the University grounds, would make the news. She hadn't looked for a media presence. She'd had her eyes on Jack. What if her face had made it onto the news screen? God knew who might see it eventually.

Alannah's chest tightened. She began to pant. "Alexander!" she called out. She stumbled back toward the staircase. "Alexander?"

"Yes?" Alexander appeared at the bottom of the stairs with a spatula in his hand and wide eyes.

"What if this made the news?"

"It likely did," he said calmly. It wasn't an irrational question, not for Alexander. Immortals lived with their heads down and their eyes open. Publicity was an invitation for trouble, for people to try to delve into their secrets.

Rationality had little to do with it for Alannah. "What if... if we made the news?" Alannah could feel tears welling up again. She gasped for air. "What if my face is on the news, Alexander?"

"Sh-sh-sh." Alexander bounded up the stairs to meet her and gripped her arms. "Breath, Alannah, breath. There were no reporters, and they would never film so close to an accident such as that."

"But, but," Alannah whimpered, "are you sure?"

"I never saw one reporter, Alannah." Alexander cupped her cheek. "Come sit down in the kitchen. The news will be on at seven. I'll check. I won't let anyone hurt you, Alannah."

He held both of her shoulders and made her march in front of him, down the last few stairs, across the hardwood floor into the kitchen. He sat her down at the little table under the window and set a plate of crepes in front of her. "Did you take any medication yet?"

She shook her head, mute, and forced herself to breathe deeply, like she was actually calm. A modicum of reason returned. Just enough to be angry with herself. Alexander set a glass of water and a pill in front of her and glanced back at the clock on the stove. "I'll take my plate to the TV. The news will be on in a bit."

Alannah tossed the pill back and swished it down with a third of the glass of water. She heard Alexander turn on the little-used television set in the living room, then the squeak of one of the easy chairs.

Alannah looked down at the crepes in front of her, filled with sautéed onions, ham and cheese—melted, but beginning to congeal. She cut off a rounded corner with her fork and placed it tentatively in her mouth. It was delicious, and she was suddenly hungry. She shoved in another bite, and then another.

"Alannah?" Alexander's voice came from the living room in a strange, strangled pitch. "Alannah can you come here?"

Her thread of calm snapped. She stood up. She was out the kitchen door before she realized that she had her fork clenched in her shaking hand. She stopped behind Alexander's chair. He stared at the screen in front of him, playing the tail end of a news clip, with a picture of the Health Sciences Center Hospital in the background, and a young, male reporter with a serious face in the foreground.

"...doctors pronounced him dead, after he went into cardiac arrest on the operating table and could not be revived. Two hours later, doctors say he woke up, seemingly unaffected by the incident."

The camera cut back to the newscaster in the studio, whose perfectly made up face and professional composure couldn't quite hide her disbelief. "Are doctors giving any more details at this time?"

The screen cut again to the reporter. "Well, Sandy, at this point they have no explanation but the family of the construction worker is calling it a miracle of God."

Sandy moistened her lips. "Well, Gord, I certainly wouldn't disagree with that."

Alannah blinked at the screen as a clip began to play, an interview with a stunned construction worker, twisting a pair of gloves in his hands.

"He's alive, Alannah," Alexander said softly, "Jack is alive."

Alannah walked over to the other wingback chair and dropped into it. Her heart throbbed in her chest. Jack, alive. The angelic wife with the halo of blond curls, not a widow. Was it really a miracle of God, as Jack's rejoicing family proclaimed? She glanced at Alexander and met his eyes. They both suspected that something very different was at play, something they both knew well.

A few minutes passed before either of them spoke.

"He's one of us, isn't he?" Alannah said finally.

Alexander didn't answer, only ran his teeth over his bottom lip. His hands lay on top of his knees, fingers drumming slowly.

"He came back to life, unaffected," said Alannah.

"I know, Alannah, I know." Alexander sighed. "I only hope... I only hope that it isn't true. I'm glad that he lives, but I do not wish this curse upon him."

Alannah sat silent.

"I am duty-bound to find him, and find out now." Alexander stood up stiffly and set his half-eaten plate of crepes on the little table beside him. "Tonight let his wife hold him and rejoice that he is alive. God knows it's what I would want if I were him."

CHAPTER 2

Dresden, Germany. Present Day

"Should immortals have the right to die?"

A laugh burst out of the young man's mouth. Across from him, the young woman grinned impishly.

"An oxymoron, no?" she said. "Humor me. What do you think?'

He rubbed his hands together at this, the fourth or fifth of these questions they'd traded back and forth across the little bistro table all afternoon. Around them now, the tables began to fill up with patrons, on their way home from work and errands.

His date was a woman young in appearance, with a long, silky brunette ponytail and a dark blue scarf wrapped with apparent carelessness around her slender neck. Her fingers drummed on the side of her mug of beer. She had a tiny tattoo of a spreading oak tree on her wrist, which she touched absently every now and again. The man had the same mark.

"It's not fair." He laughed. "In order to remain consistent in my arguments, don't I have to say yes? I've been arguing for freedom of choice all afternoon."

"And so convincingly," she said snidely.

"Hey! You've been playing devil's advocate. I know you agree with me."

She grinned, and her eyes glinted. She downed the last of the beer, swiped the foam off her upper lip, and set the mug down with a bang. She raised her eyebrows at the man. "Well?"

He felt a prickle at the back of his neck. He didn't know why. He pushed away from the table and stood up. "Let's walk," he said.

When he'd paid for their drinks, they stepped out onto the cobblestone street. The sun just peeked over the edge of the roofs of the old, yellow-brick buildings. A church bell tolled out six times.

"Such heavy conversation," the woman said. She tucked her hand into the crook of his elbow and gripped his arm. "I promise you, this isn't my typical first date conversation material."

He laughed. "Should I be honored or concerned?"

"I'm impressed. I thought I'd have long since scared you away." She tipped her head back and smiled up at him. "Where do you live? Are you taking me there?"

"Shall I?" the young man wondered what that meant. "It's on Ausburgerstrasse. It's not far."

Her hand on his arm tightened. "Let's go there."

"Alright." He didn't mind, not at all. His little flat was only two rooms, plus the toilet, and most of it was taken up by easels and canvasses, splattered with paint. He'd had women in there before. The tortured artist ambiance was practically an aphrodisiac.

"But you never answered my question." She rested her chin on his shoulder and dug it into his flesh.

"Well," he said slowly, "I personally don't know any others, but I hear many of us attempt suicide."

"Mhmm."

"If a person doesn't want to live, then they shouldn't have to. But that's... that's theoretical, right?" He hadn't done the reading he was supposed to, on their history and law and such. He'd skimmed the basic points—it seemed death would be a basic point. There was no mention of death in the laws. It seemed like a given, in an immortal society. You couldn't outlaw something that doesn't exist.

She tilted her head to the side, chin still pressed into the soft muscles in his shoulder, and hugged his arm. She just let his question hang in the air. He couldn't tell if he'd answered right or wrong.

The young man turned onto Ausburgerstrasse and led her through into a little alley and up three narrow, concrete steps. They paused in front of the black, metal door.

The woman released his arm and turned to face him. "Do you want to live?" She gazed at him frankly.

"Of course," he said, fighting the urge to squirm under her gaze. Instead, he shoved his key into the lock and jimmied it back and forth until it opened. "Are you coming up?"

She followed him up the skinny little staircase, three flights up to the top floor. As he fumbled for his key in the dingy hallway, her hand came down on his arm. He looked up as the key slid into the lock.

"Um," she said. "I..."

"Yes?"

She grabbed his face and kissed him.

The shock was gone in an instant. He wrapped her up with one arm, tangling his mouth with hers and fumbling to open the door with his free hand. They crashed together into the flat. He kicked at the door.

"Ohh..." she sighed. Her hand strayed to his neck and pressed against the throbbing vein there.

"Hmmm."

Suddenly he felt a prick, then a burn in his neck.

"What the—" he tried to twist to look, but her arms restrained him.

"Shhhh," she breathed in his ear, "it's going to be okay." Her voice dragged in his ear, lower and lower like a bad recording.

His eyes focused over her shoulder on an abstract painting, all splashed with blood red. The whole apartment tilted slowly. He fell.

∞

"No, don't touch his hair."

Something whined by the young man's ear, barely registering in his foggy mind.

"I said don't touch it, Jordan!" the same shrill, female voice said.

The whine stopped.

A hand stroked his hair, and the woman said, "I like it."

"But I need to attach my electrodes—" a male voice grumbled.

"Oh God!" The young man snapped wide awake. He bucked against the hand and struggled to sit. The room, bright white concrete, spun. He fell back, gasping.

"Hey, hey." The hand stroked his hair again. The woman's face came into focus above him. Her dark hair was in a braid now, wrapped in a coronet across her brow. She held his head firmly. Her lean arms were bare, exposed by a tight, white tank top. She smiled at him, as if nothing were amiss. "Everything will be fine."

"What do you want from me?" The young man jerked away from the electric razor that the man with a soft, round face and wire glasses brandished at him.

The woman slapped it away. "Freedom of choice," she said in a hard voice, "you are about to help me exercise it." She leaned in close to his ear and said, "There was an immortal that died, you know. No one knows how he did it, no one but those three bastards we pretend are Lords over us." Her voice became a whisper. "Don't you want to know how he did it?"

"How?" he asked in a strangled voice. He meant to say no, but he couldn't, not looking into her glaring, glinting eyes.

She sat back abruptly. "I changed my mind. Shave his head."

"How?" the young man cried.

She stood up. "I don't know. We shall have to find out, together."

"Hold still," Jordan said. The razor whined and came down roughly, sloughing away his dark curls.

The young man twisted. The razor nicked his ear.

Jordan slammed his elbow into the young man's face, into his eye socket. The young man cried out.

"Inject him now," the woman's cold voice came from across the room. Her footsteps approached. "This is two-hundred milligrams."

A syringe loomed over the young man. He gasped and rolled away.

"Hey, none of that. Hold him, Jordan!"

Jordan's weight fell heavy upon him as the man straddled him and pinned his arms. The young man struggled, but his slight frame could hardly budge the man. Jordan's fist slammed into his face. "Stop! You are goddamned immortal. Stop struggling."

"This won't kill you." The woman bent over him. The syringe pricked his neck. "Not permanently. It's only a baseline. We have much more interesting things to try."

"Don't!" The young man lay limp. "Please don't. I haven't done anything to you. Don't hurt me."

"Shhhh." Her breath brushed his throbbing face as she bent low over him.

The needle pierced his neck. Heat flowed through it into him. The young man's eyes opened wide. "No—" died on his lips, and he was gone.

CHAPTER 3

Present Day

"You know you're back in Winnipeg because of the fucking potholes." Jack gripped the slick vinyl handle over the half-ton's door as the truck clunked over another pit in the pavement.

His mouth tasted like cigarettes and stale coffee. His legs were cramped from twenty hours in the truck. He licked his lips and grinned at Brian, in the driver's seat.

Brian, quirked a smile around the cigarette that dangled below his scraggly moustache. He pulled the stubby smoke out of his mouth, flicked it out the window and said, "I'm gonna pick up gas, else I won't make it to the North End."

As Brian pulled the truck up to the gas pumps, Jack turned around and fished for his backpack in the backseat of the extended cab. Brian opened the door to a gust of cold, moist air. Jack jumped out of the other side. His bag bumped against his side. "I'm going to be a moment," he called in Brian's direction, "I'm going to clean up for my lady."

The gas-station bathroom smelled like they'd tried to cover up the piss with Pine-sol. Jack stared at his scruffy face in the cracked mirror. He hadn't shaved in months—half because it made him look older, half because when Mary Rose wasn't around, he didn't give a crap how he looked. He'd shave it, so when he kissed Mary

Rose he didn't leave her flower-petal skin whisker-burnt. That would be evidence, and Clarissa was now old enough to know what whisker burn looked like.

Although today, hiding from his own daughter didn't depress him. As his beard fell into the sink, Jack could only think of getting Mary Rose in his arms. He swabbed the sink out with a brown paper towel, and inspected his clean face. "You look like hell, man," he said to his reflection. He looked skinny, with dark circles under his brown eyes from driving through the night. A weekend with his wife would put him back to rights.

When Jack jumped up into the truck again, Brian grinned at him.

"Holy shit, Jack, you look you're in high school."

"My woman likes my baby face," Jack grumbled, "I'll look thirty when I'm fifty, I guess."

Jack already was fifty-two, and he didn't look a day older than when he was twenty-five. Brian was twenty-five, and none the wiser that Jack *wasn't*.

Jack switched on the country station and turned his face toward the window. Brian stared straight ahead and drummed his fingers on the steering wheel. Jack could feel a low burn of excitement building in his belly.

Fifteen minutes later, Jack stood on the sidewalk outside Mary Rose's little blue bungalow. He dragged his suitcase to the edge of the concrete steps and bounded up onto the welcome mat.

Jack's knuckles rapped against the flimsy glass pane. He could hear his own fast breathing. Five houses down, a little girl drove her tricycle in the opposite direction, but there were no peering faces as far as he could see.

He knocked again, and heard light footfalls inside. The door opened, and there stood Mary Rose.

"Jack," she breathed, through a radiant smile. She yanked him in and shut the door.

She pulled his face down toward hers. Their lips seared together, and their bodies slid together like two puzzle pieces. Finally Jack broke off the kiss, leaning back to see her without budging her from his arms. She reached up and touched the nick on his cheek.

"Let me guess," she said, stroking his smooth jaw, "you haven't shaved since I saw you last?"

He grinned. "Almost."

"You need a haircut."

"I was waiting for the best."

"I'll cut it after dinner." She stood on tiptoe to kiss him again then just stared at him, scrutinizing his face. "You look just the same, Jack."

He pressed his lips together and looked past her blue eyes to the laugh lines, fanning out from them. He slid his hands down to her waist. "You're still as beautiful as the day I met you, Mary Rose. You know that."

She smiled and fluttered her lashes. For a moment she looked the schoolgirl in spite of the greying at her temples. Jack laughed.

"I have fresh bread," she said, "June brought it to me, but I didn't let her stay for tea. She was almost irate." Mary Rose disentangled herself from his arms and took his hand. "The water is on to boil. Let me get you some real food."

"Oh, I haven't had that in months." Jack sighed and laid his hand on his flat stomach—still thin in spite of the crap food the camp passed off as meals. "But you know what else I haven't had in months?" He reached for her again.

She batted away his hand and ran, giggling toward the kitchen. As he caught up to her, Jack swore he saw a hint of darkness in her eyes. He frowned, but pushed it out of his mind. He leaned against the fridge and watched her fly around the little kitchen, watched her graceful hands flick the dial on the stove and turn up the element, pull the coffee from the cupboard, open the oven to peek inside. A savory, beefy aroma washed out and over Jack. He sighed.

As the coffee began to drip into the carafe, Mary Rose turned, smiled at him, and sidled over to drop a peck on his lips. She slipped her arms around his waist and pressed her face into his flannel shirt. He felt her shake. Was she crying? He pushed her away to see her face. She was laughing!

"You left a pair of underwear here last time. Did I tell you?" Her blue eyes snapped and sparkled with humor. "You made me lie to my daughter, Jack! I told her they'd come in the bag of rags I bought at the thrift store." She chortled again. "Good thing they were frightfully thin. I threw them out."

Jack snorted. "The ones I got on now won't be any better, sweetheart." His eyes fastened on the fan of laugh-lines around her eyes—so many of them now, and the silver strands in her golden curls.

She's getting old, Jack.

Every time Jack saw her he was reminded that she would leave him, and he fought desperately to keep that knowledge at bay. In the early days it had been so much easier to deny. He came home from the oil rig in the Gulf of Mexico only once every three or four months. Clarissa would go to a friend's house and he'd sneak in. They'd flirt and kiss and make love like a couple of teenagers sneaking around behind their parent's back. They still did. Their passion burned as hot as it ever did. It was just that Mary Rose's beautiful body was growing softer, taking on lines, sagging here and there. His was as wiry and smooth as it had been on his wedding day.

Mary Rose caught his eye and opened her mouth as if to speak. Instead, she shut her lips and remained silent. Her eyes lost their luster. She turned around and returned to the kitchen counter. "I'll pour you coffee," she said. "I need to mash the potatoes."

When she turned around again to put his coffee cup on the little kitchen table, she was smiling again.

They didn't linger long over supper. One minute Jack was swallowing his last bite of apple pie; the next Mary Rose slid onto his lap and wrapped her arms around his neck. Her mouth came down hot on his. Her small fingers fumbled with the buttons of his flannel shirt.

Later, as the August sun set, turning the white walls gold and orange, Jack settled on the couch by the window. The blinds were up just enough for him to see into the backyard where the swing-set stood. He'd built it for Clarissa on her first birthday, three years before he left them. The wooden seat dangled, crooked on its chains.

"She doesn't use the swing much anymore," Mary Rose said softly. She stood beside him, wearing his baggy flannel shirt and carrying two mugs of fresh coffee. She set them both on a card table and sat down between his knees. Jack leaned her back against him and took the mug that she offered him.

"But she sat on it last time she came home," Mary Rose said wistfully, "she really does love her new place."

Jack smiled wryly and sipped his coffee.

"I'm glad you suggested buying that place for her," Mary Rose continued, "she and Lyla found another roommate, and with the rent she's collecting, Clarissa will have a tidy little income for herself while she's in school. She'll be... she'll be well provided for." She trailed off and stared at her knees. Jack couldn't see her eyes, but something about her tone of voice sounded off.

Jack rested his chin on her shoulder. "You miss having her in the house?"

"Yeah." Her delicate brow furrowed. She didn't look up. "June's been hinting about moving in together. She's been so lonely since Patrick died."

"That would make this a little tough," Jack said softly, "she'd be harder to sneak around on than Clarissa."

"Hah!" Mary Rose smiled again. "I told her no, anyway. We're both too old and stuck in our ways to move in together." She paused. "It's hard to believe my baby is twenty-five. I mean, of course she's out of the house. She's a strong independent woman, and I'm lucky to have her." Mary Rose sighed heavily.

The sigh hung in the air like the last strain of a sad song. Those sighs had come so frequently over the years. Jack had learned to pretend they didn't exist. It was too late for his daughter to know him now. She believed he was dead.

All these years he'd watched Clarissa grow. He'd seen her chubby pink cheeks diminish, and her baby teeth fall out, and her skinny arms and legs take on feminine curves. He'd even watched her with her first boyfriend, lounging on the trampoline in the backyard.

Clarissa had rebuffed the punk's attempts to kiss her.

"Good girl," he'd said.

He'd fixed her bike on a week when she was at summer camp. He'd paid for her braces. He was paying for her college tuition.

Meanwhile, Mary Rose had taken a hairdressing job and pretended to move on. She spurned all of June's attempts to set her up with a new man. Bless her, June. She was a good friend. But Mary Rose was a loyal woman.

Jack knew she was lonely. He was lonely, so lonely that sometimes it drove him halfway to madness. He'd never cheated on her. He drank, oh boy, did he drink. In those first days on his own, he'd drink more than a man could survive. He'd done stupid things, but she'd always been his only one.

He stroked her face, and her narrow, swan-like neck. She sighed and leaned into his hand. "And I'm so lucky to have you, Mary Rose," he said.

He looked up and saw tears well up in her eyes. She pulled him in and buried her face in his neck. "I'm an empty nester, Jack. My baby bird has flown."

Jack stroked her back and said nothing.

Mary Rose still had the bed they'd bought when they were newlyweds. That night, with her nestled against him in it, Jack didn't want to fall asleep. It was childish, maybe, but he struggled to keep his eyes open. He could sleep when he was alone. He just wanted to hold her, feel her breath, feel desperately happy, desperately melancholy, anxious. It was the depth of *feeling* that he only knew from one other place: the edge of death.

Jack had died too many times to count.

The first time, he was twenty-six, ten stories up on the scaffolding of an apartment building construction site. He'd dropped a tool and lunged for it. The wind caught him at just the right angle of off-balance and sent him plummeting onto the spikes of rebar below.

He hung, impaled two feet off the ground, screaming in agony until they cut him down. Then, despite the best efforts of the firefighters and medics, he bled out on the operating table. He'd slid into death like a dark, slippery tunnel. One moment the world was blinding white light and searing pain, and then he lost his white-knuckled grip on life and fell down, down, down into darkness. He'd never felt so scared, he'd never felt so *real.*

An instant later he awoke, shrouded, about to go to the morgue. He'd been dead for two hours. Inexplicably he was alive, whole, unhurt.

He could recall the details as if it had been an hour ago.

∞   ∞   ∞

Pain hit him the moment he woke up.

He couldn't explain how, but pain had shot through him like his brain still thought he was impaled upon the steel bars.

Jack's eyes and mouth opened at the same time. He sucked in his first breath and cried out. His hands scrabbled across his chest and found only cool, bare skin—smooth, unbroken skin—but he kept slapping at his chest like the bars would be there. He turned his head frantically back and forth, half blinded by fluorescent lights.

Why was he so cold? Where were his clothes?

"Where am I?" Jack tried to shove himself upright but his arms collapsed out from under him. The gurney shook and rattled under him. "What happened to me?" He clutched at his chest again. "What happened to me?"

The door popped open. A nurse, young, pretty, chocolate brown skin and curly hair, walked in and saw him. "Oh my god!" Her hands clapped to her mouth. She spun around. "Help! Someone! Come quickly!"

A few seconds later an older nurse skidded in. Her round, motherly face drained of all color. A doctor burst through the door, nearly piling on top of the two nurses. They all stared; Jack at them, they at him.

"What happened?" Jack wheezed. He struggled, trying to sit.

The two nurses rushed to his side. "No, no, lie still. You're badly hurt, you're..." The motherly nurse touched his chest. "Holy Mother of God, what happened?"

The doctor pushed the younger nurse gently aside and rolled the sheet down to Jack's waist. He stared at the unbroken skin, his eyes wide, sweat beading up on his pale brow. "Mr. Krause, how do you feel?"

Jack licked his lips. "What happened?"

"How do you feel?" The doctor insisted, "Does anything hurt?"

"N-no." Jack shook his head weakly. "I'm s-so cold."

The older nurse drew the sheet back over him. "Janelle," she said to the younger woman, "get us a blanket."

The young nurse ran from the room.

"The wife is on the way," the old nurse said softly to the doctor, "I have to meet her before she gets here, I need to..."

"What are you going to say?"

"That her husband is alive."

Two minutes later, the young nurse was back and wrapping warmed blankets around Jack's shivering body. The doctor, meanwhile, kept pressing his icy stethoscope to his chest and poking at his skin like the wounds would reappear. Jack lay trembling. Why wouldn't anyone tell him what was going on?

"Jack!" Mary Rose threw herself through the door and onto the gurney. Their heads bumped together. She clutched at his face, weeping, kissing him. "Jack, oh Jack."

Mary Rose called it a miracle as she cried over him and held him on the bed in the hospital room. He was weak, dazed, frozen with fear. Strangely in that moment, he wasn't grateful to be alive. The unsettling thought lingered: he'd seen death and death had rejected him.

They kept him overnight for observation. Doctors, nurses—heck, every damn employee of the hospital—kept peeking in on him. Finally, Mary Rose got out of the hospital bed and screamed at them to leave them alone.

Then somehow, someone in the press got his number and started calling them at home, looking for an interview. Jack knew he couldn't hide in his house. He was perfectly healthy, and he needed the money. He returned to work for all of three days until a reporter tracked him to the job site. So Jack got a job working at a feed mill well outside of the city.

He moved Mary Rose, pregnant with Clarissa, to a modern bungalow in a quiet residential neighborhood near the University. Still, a couple months later, after Clarissa was born, a camera crew caught him in the garage, fixing up his old pickup.

"Are you Jack Krause?"

"Yes...?" He stood slowly, wiping his oily hands on a flannel rag.

"I'm Peter from Unsolved Mysteries of the Beyond. Can we talk to you about—"

"Get off my yard." Jack had brandished a tire iron at them and chased them off his driveway, but inside he wasn't angry. He was terrified.

By then, he knew something was wrong with him.

∞   ∞   ∞

Mary Rose shifted in his arms, lifting Jack from his reverie for a moment. She smiled sleepily at him and lay her head back down. A moment later her breath grew deep and even. It was a good thing she couldn't divine his thoughts. She knew how he'd defied death over and over.

And that was one of his greatest regrets. She had been the one to find him, the first time he blew his brains out, in the basement of this very house.

It hadn't been like it was now. Now he was a hundred percent convinced he'd wake up. Then he wasn't sure. He was a scared kid, trying to make sense of what was happening to him.

He knew something was wrong. The feeling had been building since the day he'd died and resurrected.

∞   ∞   ∞

It was September of ninety-two. The night before, he and Mary Rose fought about it. He didn't even know why they'd fought. "It wasn't a miracle, Mary Rose. Something is wrong with me. Wrong with me! Look at me!"

Her tear-filled eyes focused on him. Her lip trembled, but it only made him more feverish. He tore at his hair. "I'm twenty-eight years old and I swear I'm as baby-faced as I was when I was twenty. I haven't even put on weight—"

She tried to take his hands but he yanked away. "Jack, that doesn't mean something is wrong with you."

"No, you don't understand! I just..." He couldn't explain the madness creeping, slowly over him. He kept dreaming about dying, the slide down into death, the release, and then a detail he hadn't remembered on the day it had happened: a sharp rebound upward toward a bright light. He'd been spit out. "Something is wrong with me, I'm not..."

"There's nothing wrong with you, Jack!"

"No!" His hands clenched in the air. There was no way to tell her that he wanted to try again. He didn't want to, he needed to! The thought ate at him like corrosive acid.

That Saturday morning, while Mary Rose was out grocery shopping with little Clarissa, he'd gone downstairs, sat against the cement wall of the unfinished basement. He stuck a pistol in his mouth and shut his eyes. He squeezed his eyes tightly shut as his finger slid inside the trigger guard.

For a moment, the only sound was his ragged breathing. His fear-fueled bravado had vanished.

Do it, he thought, *It won't kill you. It won't kill you.*

What if it does?

I have to know! I have to—

The gun shook in his trembling hands.

He pulled the trigger.

He felt that same euphoric release that he'd felt on the operating table, rocketing down toward death. He floated in warm darkness, weightless for a moment. Then all feeling vanished.

He woke, cradled in Mary Rose's arms. He rocked back and forth in her grasp, in time to her agonized sobs. Her head was flung back, mouth open, eyes squeezed shut.

"Jaaack. Jack!"

He opened his mouth and tried to form her name, but nothing came out. He licked his lips. "Mary Rose."

She only sobbed harder.

"Mary Rose." He pushed his palms against the cement floor. It was slick with his blood, and his hand slid out from under him. He fell back. She went absolutely still.

"Mary Rose," he whispered, "I'm fine."

They stared at each other, motionless. Then she drew back her hand and slapped him.

They fought, oh did they fight, for the next six months. He hated himself for it, but he was so scared, so confused. He'd hurt himself, and she'd scream at him, but he couldn't seem to stop it. Every time he hoped it might work, and feared at the same time that it would.

It didn't help that another magazine reporter called them.

"I'm not a goddamned circus freak!" Jack screamed into the phone. He'd hung up, panting, and turned to wide-eyed Mary Rose.

"What am I going to do?" he cried, "it's only going to get worse! I have to get out of here."

With tears in her eyes, Mary Rose finally agreed. Together, they made a plan for him to disappear.

Jack drove his dilapidated Dodge pickup two hours into a secluded area of a provincial park, all geared up like he was going fishing. He pulled onto a dirt road where no one would find the truck for hours, even days. Then he undid his seatbelt and accelerated until the old truck's engine screamed like a wild cat. One twist of the wheel sent the truck into an ancient pine tree, and him spinning through the air.

When he woke up, he didn't have a mark on him. The truck was still burning.

Jack met Mary Rose at a gas station just outside of the park. They kissed and clung to each other desperately. She handed him a backpack with the money and clothes to remake himself, and walked away. The authorities would sift through the burnt out truck and search the park for his body, but he'd never be seen again.

∞   ∞   ∞

He had to stop thinking about that. Jack sighed and tried to focus on the present, on Mary Rose in his arms.. He cradled her a little closer and pressed his nose into her mussed-up hair. She smelled like sweat and apple pie.

He'd given up killing himself, just like he'd given up drinking—for her. He didn't need to think about that when he was holding her. He didn't need either of those things.

Jack dozed. The next moment he woke to Mary Rose sitting bolt upright up in bed.

"Wha—"

Her hand clamped over his mouth.

"Mom?" a sweet but insistent voice came from somewhere in the house.

"I'm here!" Mary Rose called, "give me a second." She threw her legs of the side of the bed. "Get in the closet!" she hissed to him. She scampered, naked, across the room and jerked her terry-cloth bathrobe from the hook on the back of the door. "Where is your bag?"

"Under the bed." Jack grabbed his pants, shirt and boxers and dashed for the folding wooden doors. Mary Rose was already out the door, tying her robe around herself.

Jack leaned against Mary Rose's clothes in the dark closet, breathing hard. He heard her say, "Sorry baby, I was just getting into the shower. I, uh, didn't think you would come this morning."

"I'm going shopping, but I left my sunglasses." His daughter's voice was just on the other side of the wall, in the hallway. "Um... is everything okay?"

"Yes! Yes. I was just startled." Mary Rose's laugh was sheepish, but natural.

"And you're alright?" Clarissa's voice held hesitance, mingled with some note Jack couldn't place.

Jack shut his eyes, drinking in the tones of her voice, the knowledge she was *right there*. Right on the other side of the wall. It hurt like hell, worse than a stab wound—and he knew what those felt like.

"I'm okay, baby. Don't feel guilty. Go shopping and enjoy yourself."

"Okay," Clarissa said with a sigh, "text me if you need anything. I'll come for lunch tomorrow, 'kay?"

Two minutes later, the closet door opened. Mary Rose stood there, with a red face.

Jack laughed, more harsh and hurt than humorous. "Holy shit, that was close."

Mary Rose's face crumpled. She pulled Jack out and sank into his arms. Her face pressed into his chest, and his chin rested on top of her head. He felt her quiver, and knew this time it wasn't laughter. He wrapped her arms around her.

"There I go, lying to her again," she said into him. He felt moisture on his skin.

"It hurts me too, you know. It's just got to be this way."

She didn't move.

"Mary Rose."

Silence. He felt a tear trickle down his chest. Anger prickled in his gut. "It hurts me too, Mary Rose!"

She pulled back suddenly. "I know. I know it does." She wrenched her arm from his grasp and swiped at her eyes roughly. She opened her mouth and shut it again, and then just stood, looking at him. Her forehead was all twisted up, and she looked all of her forty-eight years.

"What?" Jack said, after fifteen or twenty seconds passed in silence.

"Jack..." She bit her lip. "Jack, I've got to tell you something."

He dropped his arms from her waist. The look in her blue eyes froze him in an instant.

She stepped toward him. "Jack." She laid her fingertips along his jaw and forced him to look into her eyes. "You know how last time we talked on the phone I said I was going to the doctor?"

"The abdominal pain," Jack rasped.

"He did a lot of tests and..." she blew out her breath. "I have cancer, Jack. I have pancreatic cancer, and it's advanced."

He wasn't sure how long he sat there. After a couple of minutes, Mary Rose stopped waiting for a response. She wrapped her arms around him. He didn't move.

"Jack," she said after a long time had passed, "Jack, I'm sorry."

"Sorry?" He gently loosed himself from her grasp and brushed past her. He began to pace. "God, Mary Rose. What does this mean?"

Her breath shuddered. "It means I might... I'll probably die, Jack."

"Well, they're going to treat it, right?"

"Well," she said slowly, "they will try."

"Try?" Jack cried, "try? Can't they do surgery?"

"They can't. It's spread too far." Mary Rose blew out her breath and raked her fingers through her pale hair. "I'll start chemotherapy in a week and a half."

"And that will get rid of it?"

She gazed into his eyes. "That will...extend my life'."

"Extend life? To hell with extended life!"

"Jack?"

He pulled away from her hand. "Why didn't you tell me? How long have you known?"

"Two weeks," she said in a small voice, "and I'm sorry I didn't tell you. I just—I just wanted to have one more happy reunion, like old times."

"Fuck old times!" Jack turned away from her and pushed past her into the living room. He felt like he'd taken a bullet to the center of the chest. The air was punched from his lungs.

She's going to die.

"Jack, I've always been dying." She said from the bedroom door. "Since I was born I've been dying, and I'm not afraid of it.".

"It's not true! It's not—" he picked up the first thing his hand found, a ceramic knick-knack bird, and hurled it toward the kitchen. It crashed against the wall and shattered on the linoleum. The sound brought him to his senses. He turned around slowly, and saw his wife's white face. "Mary Rose—"

She came to him, slipped her arms around his waist again. She choked and pressed her face into his chest. "Oh Jack, I'm so sorry." Mary Rose began to cry in earnest, body shaking with tears. But Jack was too stunned, too numb to cry. He sank with her to the floor and curled up around her. They lay on the battered carpet in silent misery. The dying, and the undying.

So it was. It was twenty-six years ago, almost to the day, they'd realized something was wrong with him. Fear had driven him away from them. And since then, Jack had waited for the day he'd really be alone.

"Don't do it, Jack." Mary Rose stood in the kitchen door and looked at him, with her bottom lip sucked in and her hands clasped in front of her. "Tell me you won't hurt yourself again because of me."

Jack said, "I won't hurt myself."

"Call me soon."

"I will." He spun around and plunged out into the rainy morning. He'd made it a hundred yards before he realized he hadn't kissed her goodbye. But she'd already closed the door when he looked back. In some ways, he suspected they were both glad to get away from each other. She'd tried so hard—he'd tried so hard—to pretend that this was a normal weekend together. She'd cooked, poured wine and told him stories about Clarissa. They'd made love again.

And the whole time, all he wanted was a bottle of Jack Daniels and a bullet to put through his brain.

He had a pistol, purchased in not exactly legal fashion.

The bullet wouldn't kill him, but he knew from experience that it would do what fatigue couldn't: make him sleep for a couple hours. It would draw him to the brink of hell, and hell would spit him right back out on the earth to live... live and live and live... while Mary Rose died.

Don't. You've been clean for so long; for her sake don't do this.

He would skip the bullet.

He caught a bus back to Pembina highway and bought a bottle at the Liquor Mart. With the brown bag stashed in his backpack, he checked into a Holiday Inn.

The Jack Daniels sat on the nightstand, with the light shining through it. Jack stripped off his shirt and jeans and lay down in his boxers on top of the bedspread. A pocketknife fell out of the jeans as he tossed them across the room.

You said you wouldn't do it.

The image of the knife slashing across his wrist sent shivers through him, the blood spilling hot, and the searing pain as he fell deeper and deeper into darkness. And that infinitesimal moment of release just before death spit him back out again.

No one could understand what that felt like.

Jack tipped his head back, squeezed his eyes shut, and reached for the bottle. No, he said he wouldn't and he wouldn't—not today, not that.

He woke up the next morning with whiskey dried to his face, and the last bit in the bottle spilled all over the floor where he'd dropped it. He picked his cell phone up off the nightstand, and through blurred eyes, dialed his boss.

"I'm not coming back."

CHAPTER 4

"Good morning, and welcome to German and German-Jewish History." Alannah hefted her satchel and shut the car door with her knee. She muttered under her breath, "Good morning, I'm Professor Alannah Krueger. Welcome to—damn!" Her travel mug—empty—had slipped from under her arm and bounced on the cracked asphalt. "No good," she said. She kicked the cup forward and swiped it up. "It sounds so frightfully dull. Just say—" She sucked in a breath through rounded lips. *Breathe, Alannah, breathe. It's just another class, just another class... In a totally different building.*

She didn't know this building. She didn't know the people in it. That was the thing turning her stomach.

"Good morning, Alannah," a male voice said behind her.

Alannah squeaked. The coffee cup flew from her hand again and rattled its way under a parked car.

"Sorry, so sorry!" Miles Corder bounded to pick it up. He dropped to his knees beside the silver Civic and came up with the offending cup in his hand, and two damp patches on his knees.

Alannah laughed sheepishly. "No, I'm sorry Miles. I'm a wee bit edgy this morning."

"Yeah, me too." He grimaced as he handed back the travel mug. His blue eyes were apologetic behind his tortoise-shell glasses.

"I'm a veteran, I shouldn't be..." Alannah blew out her breath. "First class today? How are you feeling?"

"It'll be alright." Miles sighed. "How do you like your new office?"

"It's fine. It just takes getting used to, is all. A shorter drive."

"True," Miles said with an agreeable nod. He held the door of the Fletcher Building open for her. He went to the left, and she to the right.

Alannah licked her lips and tried the door of the lecture theatre. Locked. The anxiety began to rear its head again. She put her bags down, and hunkered beside them. With shaking hands, she opened a side zipper pocket on her purse, pulled out a bottle, and shook out a gaba tablet into her hand. She swallowed it dry, and leaned her head back against the wall and smiled wryly.

Ten years ago, when she'd taught her first class, Alexander drove her to the University and walked her up to the classroom. It was a little like she was in kindergarten. Today, she sort of wished he'd been there to do the same, but he was an ocean away, in Germany.

The gaba would kick in. She'd just have to put one foot in front of the other until the panic in her chest melted away.

Alannah opened her eyes and pulled out her phone to call security so they could send someone over and unlock the door.

"Good morning." Keys jingled nearby.

Alannah looked up to see a janitor in a grey work shirt walking toward her.

"I'm sorry," he said, still flipping through his ring of keys. He looked up and smiled, a smile that didn't quite meet his dark-circled brown eyes. "I should have unlocked this for you already, but I got my buildings mixed up. They all look just about the same, as far as I'm concerned. It's only my second week here."

"Oh, it's fine," Alannah said, "I just got here." She stood and put a composed smile on her face.

He slipped the key into the lock and held the door open for her. "Do you need anything else, since I'm here?"

He looked about the same age as her students—tall and lanky, patchy beard, rumpled, cinnamon colored curls. The guy looked like his weekend had been a heck of a bender. His eyes were slightly bloodshot in his pale face, rimmed by dark circles.

"No, no, I'm fine." Alannah pushed the door open. She walked down the ramp toward the bottom of the lecture theatre. As she swung her bag onto the wide, stainless steel and particleboard desk, her phone dinged.

Alexander. *Dear Alannah, thinking of you on your first day of classes. I know you must be anxious. Just know that you are cared for. I'll see you again soon.*

A lump swelled in Alannah's throat.

Dear Alexander, her white knight and protector. Alannah brushed at her eyes. Calm seeped into her, more from Alexander's text than the gaba.

Her composure lasted just long enough to boot up her laptop— new laptop, to compound things—and realize that she was going to have to figure out how to hook up the projector to it. She examined each end of the wires, which burrowed like a great electronic worm into the desk. None of them looked familiar. She laughed helplessly.

"Okay, okay." Alannah pressed her fingers to her temples. "I know this. Miles told me."

Footsteps by the door made her swing around, hoping it was Miles. It was the janitor, sneaking the recycling bin out of the door.

"Um, hey," she said—a little high, a little squeaky. He was young. He'd know.

He glanced up. "Yeah?"

"Um, do you know how to hook up a Macbook to the projector?" Her breath came quickly again. Her face flushed hot. "I didn't know they weren't the same as... as the other computers."

He stepped into the doorway. His brow furrowed. "Well, I can try."

"O-okay. Or I could just call tech..."

"You could." He left the blue recycling bin by the door and clomped down the aisle with heavy strides.

"I don't see why computers can't just last forever," he said with a sigh as she slowly typed in her password. The janitor bent over beside her, but at a reasonable distance. She'd limped the old one along as long as she could, until the fear that it would crash mid-lecture eclipsed the fear of going into a computer shop.

"Yeah, true eh?" He picked up the cables from the projector and scrutinized the ends. Then he peered at the laptop.

"None of the plugs match anything you have," he said. He ran one hand over his hair, making it even more disheveled.

"Oh!" Alannah picked up her satchel and fished around in the bottom for the white cord Miles had given her the previous day. "I think this is some sort of adapter that's what Miles—Professor Corder—said."

"Oh." He squinted at both ends of the short white cord, shoved one end into a port on the laptop, and the other into the long cable from the projector. "Does your laptop just recognize it's plugged in, or do you have to start a program?"

"I don't know."

He glanced up and smiled wryly at her. "We may both be out of luck then, Professor."

Alannah found herself smiling back.

They bent their heads together by the screen and stared. Nothing happened. The janitor yanked the cable out of the laptop and plugged it back in. A message box popped up, giving her the option to configure the projector.

"Nice," the janitor breathed, "I am a tech genius and I didn't even know it." He looked up and smirked. "Or, they're just making these things for dumber and dumber people—me of course, not you." He straightened up. "Anything else, Professor?"

"No that's-that's it, I think."

"Alright. Have a nice day, Professor." He started up the steps. As he reached the top, he looked back. "Hey, what class is this?"

"I... um..."

He grinned. "Tell me you know at least that much."

"German and German-Jewish history," she said, lifting her chin.

He raised his eyebrows. "Cheerful. Maybe I'll eavesdrop sometime." He raised his hand in a wave and disappeared out the door.

"Hmmf." She smirked as she sat down in the chair and began to open the files for her presentation. "Cheerful yourself."

He looked familiar, didn't he?

No he didn't. Don't you freak out again.

I'm not going to freak out. I'm fine.

Maybe he had been a student, once. He looked about the right age. She straightened. Well, he did and he didn't. Actually he reminded her of Alexander in a way—young at first glance, and then older at second. It must have been his eyes.

She rubbed the tattoo on her wrist, a delicate, black rendering of an oak tree.

Did you see one of these on his wrist?

And she'd had a look at his wrists, protruding from his rolled sleeves as he'd worked at the computer.

Stop being paranoid. He's just a janitor. He's not looking for you.

Her notes opened onto the desktop.

"Good morning," Alannah whispered as she scrolled down the page, "I'm Professor Alannah Krueger. Welcome to German and German-Jewish History. As some of you may know, this is a topic that is close to my heart."

Yes, that would do.

∞

As the last students filed out of the lecture theatre, Alannah plopped down at her desk and stared up at the door. It was only eleven-thirty, and she was burnt out. The youngsters staring at their computer screens, covertly playing solitaire and checking their social media accounts, couldn't know how real this history was for her. She hadn't lived through the seventeenth century, but Alexander had. Later on she'd deliver lectures on World War 2, and pretend that she wasn't hearing the bombers roaring over Berlin, rattling the windows of her adoptive family's little house, sending them running for the bomb shelters. The distant booming, getting closer and closer, then filling the peaceful residential neighborhood with flame.

Alannah sighed. The hard part of the day was done, but she still had a few hours of work up in her office. She'd run down to the Starbucks on Pembina highway, and get a proper coffee before she got started.

Alannah wasn't thinking of the janitor as she rolled out of the parking lot, but as she paused at a stoplight on University Crescent, she glanced over and caught sight of three apartment buildings. The sight of them, familiar though they were, brought back a sharp memory.

Oh...

Maybe I'm seeing things.

That's why the janitor looked familiar.

Jack, the construction worker, impaled on the rebar of those very buildings, who'd died and rose again within hours. He'd had the same light brown, curly hair. And how could she forget his brown eyes? She'd stared into them, watching the light ebb away.

I'm seeing things. It wouldn't be the first time.

Alannah licked her lips. The light turned green, and she rolled through the intersection. Maybe she was seeing things. But then, they'd never found Jack. Alexander's scruples had kept him from immediately confronting the young construction worker about his deathlessness. When Alexander finally decided to find him, Jack had disappeared.

If it really was him, Alexander would want to know, even if he was across the ocean at Castle Schwalenburg in Germany, the headquarters of their community.

In the lineup at Starbucks, she texted him. "I have a question. Can I call in twenty minutes?

"About to go into a meeting. Urgent?" He texted as she was shoving her wallet back into her handbag and sidling over to wait for her coffee.

"No," she texted back with one hand, but it came out "Np." She backspaced, only to do the exact same thing and delete it again.

"Goodness," she muttered.

Another text popped up before she could send her garbled message. "Call me after work."

That would be almost midnight, Dresden time. Alannah frowned. She wanted to text back, "Since when are you a night owl?" But that would be far too much to manage on the tiny glass keyboard. She texted, "K" and took her venti macchiato from the barista.

She stared at the apartment buildings again as she passed by. She needed another look at the janitor.

Back at the University, Alannah purposely took a circuitous route through the building, sipping her macchiato as she went. Just before she reached the spiral staircase up, she caught a glimpse of a rolling garbage cart crossing the hall behind the stairs. A moment later, the janitor came into view.

He smiled when he saw her. "All is well with the computer, Professor?"

She wrinkled her nose and smiled. "Fingers crossed, knock on wood." She conjured a mental image of the young construction worker: the blood flecking his lips and cheek, his wild brown eyes, his clutching hand on hers.

Maybe...?

"Knocking on wood never worked for me," he said as he pushed the cart toward her. The dark circles under his eyes seemed darker now. "I'm Jack, by the way."

Jack. It was him! It must be.

Alannah swallowed her excitement. She felt the burgeoning pressure of anxiety in her chest. What did she do? "Um... I'm Alannah."

Exactly how did one ask this sort of thing? Did you just blurt, "Are you the same Jack that died in a construction accident twenty years ago, and then resurrected? Are you immortal like me?" Goodness, the very thought made her nauseous.

So she instead she asked, "Are you new here?"

"Yeah."

"How do you like working here so far, Jack?"

His face fell. He shrugged and glanced down at his gloved hands. "I've had worse jobs."

His face tightened and he turned to walk on, then paused. His whole face darkened. "Ah, who am I kidding? It's a shitty job with shitty pay."

Alannah flinched, and he must have seen it, because he frowned and said quickly, "Sorry. I didn't mean to go off on you like that."

"It's alright," she said quietly.

"Anyway," he said and shifted his weight as if he was about to leave, "if the computer dies, let me know. Apparently I'm good at fixing these things." His face relaxed into an impish smile, and he walked away, towing the garbage cart behind him.

Alannah frowned and stroked the back of one finger across her chin. *I think that is him*, she thought, *and if it is... well, I've never found one of us before. What do I do?*

When Alannah got home, she microwaved a plate of leftover spaghetti Bolognese and sat down at the little kitchen table. She texted Alexander "I'm home" and propped the phone up against the salt and pepper. She had her mouth full of beef and tomato when phone rang and flashed a picture of Alexander on the screen. She slid her finger over the icon, and soon the screen filled with Alexander's merry blue eyes.

"Good evening," he said.

"Ooooh, look how long your hair is getting!" Alannah leaned in. "I should've used this video chat earlier."

Alexander turned his head to show off the tufty knot of blond hair at the nape of his neck. A few gold strands flew around his face, probably from his habit of digging his fingers into his hair when deep in thought. "Can you believe that the other Lords have both cut their hair? I have to keep growing it to dissent."

"You rebel, you."

Alexander laughed.

"Your accent is stronger again, too." Alannah grinned at him as she shoved aside the paper sandwich bag.

"I haven't had to speak English for a week," he said. His face blurred as the background swirled. In a moment it focused again. He was sitting on a sofa. "I force Cyrus to speak Deutsch while he's living with me."

"Cruel, Alexander, very cruel." At least he didn't force her. Her German was pushed back into the furthest closet in her mind. "Where is Cy now?"

"I can hear him in the other room. He's talking to Idina. She's in England on official business and he couldn't go with her." His face wrinkled in slow motion as he rubbed his clean-shaven jaw. "There's been a bit of an incident. It's going to keep me here for a couple more days. One of us has gone missing."

"Like, left without explanation or *missing* missing?" Alannah swallowed hard.

"He hasn't been heard from for two weeks. His name is Marcus Koenig. He had a history of not communicating well with Idina, so at first she wasn't alarmed. But he's failed to answer all phone messages and emails. He hasn't been seen at his flat—she's worried about him. I just want to stay until this is resolved."

"So, Cyrus is looking for him?"

"I passed this one to Daniel." Alexander rubbed his eyes and stifled a yawn behind his hand.

"You haven't been sleeping?"

"Ehh," Alexander shrugged. He stifled another yawn. "How can I sleep well when one of my own is missing? You know that."

They both paused and looked away from their respective screens.

"Say, uh, Alexander..." she began.

"Say, Alannah." He looked up again and gave her a bleary grin.

"Do you remember that young construction worker—the one who fell on rebar?"

Alexander shifted and squinted at the screen. "Remind me."

How could he forget that scene? "It was maybe twenty-five years ago. They were building an apartment block near the University. He fell on rebar, right through his chest and stomach. We were right there."

"Yes." Alexander sighed. He kneaded his temples. "Yes, yes. He died on the operating table and came back to life. His name was Jack." Alexander leaned in closer to his phone and his face got larger. "Why?"

"Well," Alannah ran her teeth over her bottom lip, "I saw someone today who looked like him. I think it's him."

"We were never able to talk to him."

"No."

Alexander rubbed his temples and the bridge of his nose. "Can you take a picture?"

"I guess I could get one with this funny new phone." Alannah bit her bottom lip. She glanced around the kitchen. The entire wall behind her was a testament to her photography skills; a collage of frames, pictures of places she and Alexander had been together. But none of them had been taken with the little smart phone. She'd only opened the camera on accident. "Exactly what excuse will I give?"

"Good point," Alexander said.

A distant voice, over the phone, broke her thoughts. She heard a distant, male voice call, "Alexander, wo bist du?"

Alexander glanced off to the side. "In here, Cyrus."

The same voice said, nearer, "Talking to Alannah, I see."

Alexander grinned. "Hey, I didn't say you could speak English."

"Hi, Cyrus," Alannah called.

"Gute nacht, Alannah." Cyrus's voice was right next to the voice, and three dark-skinned fingers waggled in front of the camera. "Hello from Idina, fairest of lawkeepers."

"Hello Cy, " Alannah said.

Alexander shifted in front of the screen, and for a moment Cyrus's handsome, dark face appeared. He waved and disappeared. Alexander settled back against the sofa again.

"When I get back, I'll come observe him. If this Jack is one of us, it is high time he was brought into our society." His face wavered closer to the screen. "Are you holding up alright?"

"Yeah. Well, at first I thought... well, he had that look like one of us and I panicked for a moment, but—" she waved her hand. "No tattoo. I could try—"

"Build a rapport with him, if you feel you can," Alexander said gently. "Don't worry too much. I'll look into it as soon as I get back."

Alannah sighed. "Alright. And you should get some sleep. Take a good stiff drink of Schnapps. Daniel will find your Koenig."

"He always does." Alexander gave her a weary half smile. "Alright, I'd better let you go." He leaned toward the camera, about to hang up on her, when a silver chain slid out of his collared shirt, and something swung past the screen—a little glass vial, all encircled with ornamental silver.

"Why are you wearing that?" Alannah gasped. She felt her heart clamp up in her chest. "Why are you wearing that?"

Alexander caught it and stuffed it back into his shirt with a guilty look. "Daniel released it from evidence today." Alexander sighed. "It's empty, Alannah. It is."

"Throw it away!" Alannah's burned with tears. She swiped at her eyes and knocked over the phone. "I never want to see it again!"

"Alannah," Alexander's voice came, tinny and distant, from the phone's speaker. "Alannah, I'm sorry."

She didn't wait for him to say anything more. She slapped at the phone and managed to hang up on him. She clapped both hands to her chest, against her pounding heart.

The phone rang, persistently. Alannah's hand was shaking too hard to touch the 'ignore' button. She got up and tottered out of the kitchen as a memory enfolded her. She saw a cold, wet body, lying beside a claw foot bathtub in a Dresden apartment.

"No, come back! Come back. Jurgen, come back!"

Alannah clapped her hands over her ears so she wouldn't hear her own cries, echoing across forty years. She sank down against the wall in the hall.

It was all my fault!

"Stop. Stop it." She whispered. *Breathe. In through the mouth, out through the nose. One, two, three, four.*

In the kitchen, her phone went off again.

"Everything is alright." *In through the mouth, out through the nose. See? Everything is fine.* "Everything is f-f..." She dropped her head into her hands. She was so tired. Just so tired of this. Tired of living in Winnipeg like an exile, far from the companionship of other immortals. Tired of anxiety attacks, medication and breathing exercises. Tired of guilt.

She was immortal, right? Surely in a life that long she could overcome it.

Alannah lifted her head. She was alright. Winnipeg was far from Dresden, so she was rarely forced to think of what had transpired there. Alexander had chosen the little Canadian city because it was obscure but central, an ideal beachhead for an immortal community in Canada. Alannah hadn't cared where she went as long as it was far from Dresden, far from Zoran, and Jurgen's grave.

She, Daniel, and Alexander had packed up, flown to Winnipeg and settled into the house on Wellington Crescent. Once Alannah was settled in, Daniel flew back to Germany. He never returned. Forty years later Alexander's Canadian community had yet to materialize, and Alannah had become accustomed to being alone.

CHAPTER 5
Prague, 1560

Alexander lay with his face to the wall, and his arms wrapped around his pillow. He'd awoken like that, and lingered for just an instant in blissful half-sleep, before coming to reality. He was alone, cold, and stiff in the narrow pallet bed in the one bedroom of his cramped, Prague home. In his dream he'd been in a massive canopied bed in Castle Katlenburg snuggly wrapped up with Idonia, her cheek on his chest and her silky brown hair tickling his chin.

He felt he was a truly pathetic soul, to wake up with only a pillow in his arms.

The cold finally drove Alexander off his pallet and to the hearth to push together the last, faintly glowing coals. He lay a few sticks of kindling on the embers and blew until thin tendrils of smoke began to curl up, and a feeble flame licked at the dry wood. A moment later, the fire crackled to life.

He leaned back on his heels and spread out his cold fingers to catch the faint warmth. Dawn had yet to shine through the tiny window beside the door. He felt cold all through, from his fingertips, to an icy spot right between his lungs. On the little brocade footstool at his elbow, his Bible beckoned him to take up and read.

Alexander swung the kettle onto the fire, and picked up the large, leather-bound volume. He plunked down on his chair and opened the Bible across his knees, but he didn't read. He was still memorizing the details of the dream. It wasn't a new dream. He'd been having it for a couple hundred years now, and each time it was just as precious.

He shut his eyes. The tip of his tongue ran over his teeth. He sighed. "Ahh... God, how much longer?"

It was bitterly cold that day, no birds sang in the scraggly little tree outside Alexander's door. The wind nipped at his ears and nose as he hurried through the murky morning light toward the little Carolinum Protestant Academy, clutching at his cap.

He stumbled a little as he ascended the stairs into the hall. He passed two fellow professors, in dark robes and close-fitting caps. He nodded to them with a smile. One turned his head entirely, and the other smiled stiffly and didn't meet Alexander's gaze.

Alexander pursed his lips and stamped his cold feet a little as he marched into the classroom. Twenty-seven young men milled about the lecture hall. Their conversations, raucous with the enthusiasm of youth despite the frigid morning, echoed off the high, stone, walls. The weak winter sunlight shone down in pale rectangles, undulating as the young men milled about.

Alexander smiled. His body may have ached from weariness, but he could not help but feel lighter in their presence.

He slipped along the edge of the classroom and ascended to the lectern before they could take notice of him. "Good morning," he said.

The din didn't falter.

"Good morning," he boomed.

A few men turned. The conversation hushed. Benches scraped, bags opened, and parchments slapped onto the long, bench desks. Alexander leaned over the mahogany lectern and watched them assemble. His eyes rested on one student in particular. A slight, young man with a shabby jacket and a profusion of dark curls escaping from his cap. The young man looked up and caught his gaze. His eyes were so dark, nearly black, bright with intellect.

Alexander smiled ruefully to himself. *What impossible question shall you trouble me with today, young Zoran?*

"We will take up where we left off yesterday," Alexander said as the room fell silent. "In the book of Hebrews, as you will recall, we were discussing the temple and its elements as a type, or picture of the heavenly realm. I will read—" He began to read, in Latin. "Et omnia pene in sanguine secundum legem mundantur: et sine sanguinis effusione non fit remissio. And in almost all things are by the law purged with blood; and without shedding of blood is no remission..." He continued on until he read, "And as it is appointed unto men once to die, but after this the judgment—"

"But sir..." Zoran's hand waved in the air.

Alexander paused then said, "Yes, Master Kosar?"

"But sir, why does it say that it is appointed for men once to die?"

Ah God. Alexander tilted his head. "I do not take your meaning."

"Sir, what of Lazarus?" The lad's eyes gazed brightly up at him. "He died twice."

A smile twitched about Alexander's lips. "Indeed."

"And the widow of Nain—her son. I imagine after the Lord raised him from death, he died again. He is not alive now. So he died twice as well."

"Yes, well," Alexander said, "the Lord can raise whom he pleases, but as a general rule all of us die only once. It is not the intent of the passage to commentate on—"

"But it does say that." Zoran leaned forward in his seat. "Are the Scriptures not inerrant?"

A prickle of annoyance went through Alexander, mingled with slight interest. "Are you jesting, Zoran, or do you have a serious issue to take up?"

Zoran dropped his head, but a twinkle remained under the hood of his dark lashes. "Forgive me, Sir."

Alexander sighed softly.

At the end of his lecture, as he stepped down from the podium and the young men dispersed, he caught sight of young Zoran lingering in the back of the room.

Alexander tucked his notes into their leather case, and put the case under his arm. "You are about to ask another vexing question, Master Kosar?"

"I meant no harm."

"Perhaps," Alexander said. He narrowed his eyes at the young man. "But this is now the fourth day you've asked odd, even impertinent questions. Do you trouble your other teachers so? Or is it because of my youthful face?" He turned sharply, and began to march away.

Zoran's footfalls clattered after him. "Indeed, your youth, now that is a mystery to me. How came you to this teaching post?" Zoran walked at his elbow, peering into his face.

Alexander felt a cold prickle on the back of his neck. "Five and twenty is old enough to complete a fair amount of schooling if one is intelligent and starts early. Excuse me, Zoran."

But Zoran kept up with Alexander's stride, down three steps, and around the corner to the Carolinum's small library. Alexander paused in the doorway. "Excuse me, Zoran."

"Your superiors think you a very odd man." Zoran gripped his elbow. "I've seen how they avoid you."

Alexander's face flushed hot. "I am an odd man, but that is my own business. Good day, Zoran." He threw off Zoran's hand and strode into the library. This time, Zoran left him be.

Alexander dropped onto a hard, high-backed bench, and wiped the back of his hand across his forehead. It came away moist with sweat. Was this it, then? Would he leave his students and move to the next city now? He'd begun to feel comfortable, and seen the signs that a few of his fellow faculty members were finally thawing toward him. He had pupils that he liked: looked up to him with admiration.

"Damn you, Zoran," he whispered. "What did I do to make you wonder?" He'd been so careful. Maybe that was the trouble—too careful. But it was difficult not to be distrustful after what had happened in Zwickau, two years before when a plague of smallpox had swept through his neighborhood. Against his better judgment he'd offered his assistance to a widow and her children, only to catch the disease himself.

The widow he'd saved was the one to nurse him, watch him succumb to the smallpox, and resurrect without a scar by the morning. By that afternoon she'd had soldiers and churchmen there because obviously he must be a sorcerer.

Ah, that's what he got for caring for the widow and the orphan.

"And now?" Alexander kneaded at his temples. Go to another city immediately or find a way to get rid of young master Kosar?

In the lecture the following day, Zoran remained silent. He watched Alexander with a keen gaze, head tilted to one side, but silent. When the class adjourned, a couple of the young men stayed back to speak to Alexander. Mid conversation, Alexander realized that Zoran still sat at his bench.

He shifted uncomfortably.

When the two lads dispersed, Zoran still sat there. He got up and approached Alexander.

Alexander turned his back and began packing up his notes.

"Sir," Zoran said slowly, "I wanted to apologize for my unseemly conduct yesterday."

Alexander licked his lips and closed his leather-bound portfolio. "Have I offended you in some way, Zoran?"

"No," Zoran sounded forlorn, "no, not offended. On the contrary, I sense we may... understand each other."

Now Alexander turned slowly. "Forgive me, Zoran. I do not know how you came to that conclusion."

"I want to tell you a story, Sir. Perhaps then you shall change your mind."

Alexander regarded him—frayed collar and cuffs, faded cap, pale, thin face. His black eyes held a strange, haunted expression.

Alexander felt his heart relent. He sighed. "Fine. Walk with me. I've fasted all day, and am hungry. Come to my lodgings with me and tell my your story."

"Why are you fasting? It's not a—I didn't miss—" Zoran hurried after him.

Alexander stepped down into the street. The cold air blew down his collar, causing him to wince and pull his coat tight. "No, it isn't a holy day. Have no fear. It is only that I forgot to eat." The last of his words were obscured by a cart, passing by over the cobblestone street. Zoran hurried alongside him, clutching at his coat.

Alexander steered the younger man off the wide street onto a smaller, cramped street. They stood against the stone wall of the nearest building to let a horse and cart, loaded with bricks, pass. Grit blew off the back of the wagon, into Alexander's face. "In here." Alexander led him into the rooming house, and paused to request food from the housekeeper.

They soon sat down to eat. Alexander poured wine into Zoran's cup and sat down on the bench, across from him. "Where do you come from?"

"I am from the city," Zoran said softly.

"Your family?"

"I have none, not anymore."

"I'm very sorry," said Alexander.

"How came you to this school?" Alexander tore off a piece of bread and popped it into his mouth. His empty stomach twisted, something between protest and anticipation.

Zoran looked up, bread poised to his mouth. The keen expression had returned. "I have always wanted to be a scholar," he said," but I was born desperately poor. I have worked many years as a laborer, that I might study as I wish."

"Ah." Alexander washed down the bread with a gulp of wine.

"But as to how I came to *this* school, it wasn't my original plan. I'd intended to leave the city."

"What made you stay?"

Zoran tilted his head and narrowed his eyes. "A long story, which I shall not tell now. About the passage yesterday, sir..."

Alexander swallowed his mouthful of meat and picked up his cup. "Yes, Zoran, what troubles you so about it?"

Zoran's eyes narrowed, an odd expression, nearly eager, but almost apprehensive. "Sir, that is the story I wished to tell. Several years ago, I experienced a mystery, something that makes me question this passage."

"Go on." Alexander's wine glass had been poised to his lips, but he set it down and folded his hands.

"When I was sixteen," Zoran said, "I worked as an apprentice bricklayer. We worked, one day, at a building site not so far from here. The night before it had rained, it was muddy, the ground was very slippery. As I crossed the site, carrying my tools with me, I had to dodge out of the way of an oncoming wagon. My feet slipped, and I fell beneath the wheels."

"Good heavens."

"I was crushed under the wheels," Zoran said quietly, "I have no memory of what happened in the interim. I woke up, hours later, bearing no injury at all. I'd been laid out for burial."

Alexander drew in a breath. A hot flush crept down the back of his neck. "What mean you by this? You nearly perished?"

Zoran leaned closer and said, very softly, "Sir, I believe I actually died. The longer I live, the more distinct the memory becomes. It felt as if I was dangling over a bottomless pit, holding on desperately to not fall. I lost my grip and plunged into the pit. I fell downward for only a moment, and then I was flung back upward toward a blinding white light, and then I awoke."

Alexander's heart throbbed in his ears. Heat crept up the back of his neck.

"There is more," Zoran whispered, "for that was nearly twenty years ago when I was a lad of eighteen, and since that day I haven't aged a day, not as far as I can tell."

Alexander looked up, into Zoran's earnest, obsidian eyes. The heat vanished, and cold crept through him like a cold wind. It couldn't be. "H-how old are you?"

"I am thirty-seven."

"You have a young face. It means nothing."

"Means nothing?" Zoran mouth twisted. "Means nothing? It means a great deal to me. I lived through it. I haven't aged. I am as young as I was when I was twenty."

Alexander drew in a long breath before saying, "Why are you telling me this, Zoran? Are you trying to confess something to me? Are you a sorcerer?" Why would anyone tell him what he'd never told a soul?

"No!" Zoran threw up his hands. "I am not a sorcerer. Where would I learn sorcery? I am an uneducated laborer, the son of a laborer. If it is sorcery, it isn't my fault."

It can't be. He can't be immortal.

What if the young man were just acting, what if he *knew* about Alexander himself, what if he were attempting to draw him out, his intention to pounce?

"Sir," Zoran said softly, "I fear that I cannot die, not at all."

In the silence, the church bell began to chime.

"I do not know what to say," Alexander began, slowly, grasping for his thoughts, "dear God, I know not what to say."

"I am not a sorcerer," Zoran said then looked up and smiled weakly, "but I fear this means I am a damned soul."

Alexander swallowed hard, for he thought the term 'damned' was quite applicable, given that Zoran, now thirty-seven, could barely appreciate the sentence that immortal life could be. After a moment he let his breath whistled out of his nose. "Why do you tell me this? You have other professors, why do you tell me this?"

The humor left Zoran's eyes. "Sir, with respect, I have reason to believe you understand me."

The words were like an ice bath down his neck. "What do you mean?" Alexander demanded.

Zoran's voice dropped lower, "Perhaps it is only a sense I have, but I think it rather odd that a man who appears so young, can clearly have so much learning, and so much experience. Sir, by looking at you I'd think you younger than I. But it isn't that. It's the references you make to the past. The way you guard yourself from us, Sir. I've heard the other professors talk. I've listened to them often. They say you came with excellent credentials, but no references, and no friends, out of nowhere. There are rumors that you are not who you say you are."

Alexander's stomach twisted, never mind that this was the sort of thing he was accustomed to hearing whispered.

"They're rumors I fear to hear about myself. So, Sir," The emotion returned to his voice, "if you do—if you are, Sir—"

Alexander sat silent, frozen in indecision. If the lad was lying, how convincing of a liar he was! Alexander's voice was caught in his throat, just above his throbbing heart. "I..."

"Sir," Zoran's voice trembled.

Finally, Alexander met his eyes. "You are insane, Zoran. You are absolutely insane. You need help, spiritual help."

Zoran leapt up. "I am not crazy, sir! I have been looking for other people as myself since I knew what I was. I am not mistaken, not about me, not about you. I will prove it." He reached into his threadbare jacket and pulled out a short dagger.

Alexander gasped.

Zoran pressed the blade to his own neck. The blade just nicked the skin, drawing a thin crimson line.

Alexander reached slowly toward him, across the table. "Zoran, do not harm yourself."

"It won't hurt me. I'll return to life in but a few hours." Zoran's obsidian eyes sparked, but he was not crazed. It was a keen, calculating light.

"Zoran!"

The knife bit deeper.

Alexander flung himself across the table. His hand clamped around Zoran's wrist. They crashed against the cold flagstone floor. The knife hovered between them, Zoran pushing, Alexander pulling.

"Don't!" Alexander cried, "I believe you." His arm trembled against Zoran's strong pull.

Zoran smiled calmly. "Do you, Alexander?"

"I—"

Zoran yanked his hand down, out of Alexander's grasp. The blade sliced across his throat before Alexander could even move. Blood spurted.

"No!" Alexander grabbed at the sliced flesh, frantically trying to stem the flow. Zoran's eyes gleamed for a moment, then went dull.

"Oh, God!" Alexander leapt up, about to dash out into the street for help. But a thought came over him.

There was no saving Zoran. To run out in the street, covered in Zoran's blood, with a dead man lying on his floor. Who would come? And what questions would they ask?

Zoran had killed himself to prove his immortality. What if it were true?

Alexander sank back slowly onto his heels, gazing at Zoran's white face. He had to hide him for a few hours. He had to know if the man would come back to life. At very least, it would buy him time to figure out what to do with the body.

Alexander drew back slowly and got up. He pulled off his jacket and folded his sleeves back. He went to his bed and took his blanket back to the table. He rolled Zoran's body onto the blanket, wrapped it up, and dragged him into the bedroom. He went back into the other room and began to scrub at the blood with hot water from the kettle.

An hour later, Alexander's arms ached from scouring the floor, and his bloody shirt smoldered in the fireplace. He tiptoed into the bedroom and crouched down beside Zoran's body. Zoran lay exactly as Alexander had left him, wrapped in the blanket like a corpse for burial. His face poked out of the grey fabric, white as wool.

If he were to resurrect, how would it look? Alexander had only seen Adolf Hardwin come back to life, after his horse had tumbled down a precipice and crushed him.

Gingerly, he pulled aside the blood-blotted blanket, exposing Zoran's neck and chest.

"Oh!" Alexander pressed his hand to his mouth.

The bloody slash across Zoran's neck had closed. All that remained was a thin, jagged, pink line, and as Alexander stared at it, he had to blink and tell himself that too wasn't fading before his eyes.

Oh, Father God, I do not want him to die, but I do not want him damned to this unending life.

Alexander scrubbed at his eyes and turned back to the closed wound. Yes, it had faded some more in those few moments. Alexander pressed three fingers into Zoran's neck. The skin was cool to the touch. Alexander held his breath and tried to hold perfectly still. Not a hint of a pulse.

"Oh, Zoran," he breathed. "Come on."

The church bells pealed out five timed, vibrating through Alexander. "Come on, Zoran." He jammed his fingers deeper into Zoran's skin. Nothing.

He squeezed his eyes shut.

Then, like the lightest raindrop against his skin, he felt a beat, then another, then a weak but steady throb. A moment later, Zoran drew a shallow breath.

"Oh God!" Alexander cried. He clasped Zoran's cool face, not as cool now. The warmth of blood met his fingertips. "Zoran!"

He didn't realize how long he'd bent over Zoran, one hand pressed against the steady pulse in his neck, one over his mouth feeling his breath. The bells chimed six. As the last chime pealed forth, Zoran's eyes fluttered open. Alexander snatched his hands away.

"Sir," Zoran croaked, "have I convinced you?"

"Zoran, for the love of God!" Alexander clenched his hands in the air. "Why would you do such a thing?"

Zoran lifted one hand and dropped it back to his side. His head lolled to the side, but he smiled. "I was right. You are immortal."

"How do you know? Zoran, how could you?"

"You didn't go for help."

"It means nothing!"

Zoran pushed both hands against the floor, trying to sit. Alexander hurried to support him.

Zoran licked his lips. His face was still pale and strained around the eyes. His dark eyes bored into Alexander's. "Be truthful to me, Sir. I beg of you, tell me the truth. I've just given you my dearest secret. Why would I tell yours?"

"Do you have any inkling what might happen if someone knew what you are?" Alexander choked.

Zoran nodded. "Of course. That is why I am dead to my family, that neither I nor they might not suffer from my condition. But sir—"

"You are thirty-seven. Maybe you think this is a novelty, a lark, escaping death." Alexander leaned close, close enough to see that a spark had kindled in Zoran's eyes. Zoran knew where he was going, already. "Zoran, I am telling you, if you tell anyone what I am there will be hell to pay for me!"

"You are!" Zoran cried out. His face crumpled, and he began to weep. "You are!" he sobbed.

"Yes," Alexander said, strangled by fear and sudden emotion. His chest ached from anxiety.

Zoran lifted his wet face. "I knew there must be. I knew I couldn't be the only one. Why are we like this? Do you know? Are there more?"

"Please, Zoran, you are weak. Lie down on the bed."

"How can I lie down?" Zoran's streaming eyes glinted, but his head drooped. "I have been looking for you for twenty years!"

"I am not going anywhere." Alexander gripped Zoran under the arms and hefted him bodily onto the pallet. "Neither are you. God in heaven, what shall I do with you? You are covered with blood. You cannot go marching out there..."

Zoran struggled up onto his elbow, but his arm collapsed. "Are there more of us?"

"...and I have already ruined one shirt, and have no other coat..."

"Sir, are there more?"

"... I shall have to send you out wrapped in a blanket." Alexander sank down on the floor beside the bed and put his head in his hands. "Yes, Zoran, there are more."

"I knew it!" Zoran cried. Fresh tears spilled down his cheeks.

Alexander felt a great thickness grow in his throat. He turned his head, toward the shuttered window. Outside, a man's voice called out harshly and another answered. Footsteps clattered by the door. "How many?" Zoran asked, brushing at his eyes unashamedly.

"Only two others," Alexander said while digging his fingers into his hair. He swallowed hard. "And we thought ourselves alone too. Zoran, have you been out of Bohemia? Have you been to Saxony?"

Zoran shook his head. "No, no, I have not been fifty miles from this city."

"I was born in Saxony. The three of us were immortalized because we drank of a fountain. Do you know what I speak of?"

"A fountain?" Zoran shook his head, his eyes full of foreboding mingled with excitement. "Fascinating. A fountain? You drank?"

"Yes, a spring we found in a cave. We all drank of it—three of us, a hunting party. The next day my best and oldest friend, Adolf's horse fell and crushed him beneath it. It was just like your own accident. We carried him back to the home of the other of us, Lord von Schwallenburg. But before we could lay him in the ground, he returned to life unscathed. Within ten years, we all realized we had hardly aged, and thus it began."

"And thus it began," Zoran echoed, eyes distant, "but I didn't drink—not of that fountain, and I have not aged since I was just old enough to be called a man. And why?"

"I do not know."

Zoran whispered to himself, "I knew I could not be alone. I knew it!" He palmed his eyes, but his hands slid down to his sides. His eyelids slid shut.

Alexander did not answer, wondering at the strange numbness in his chest. How could this be? Another human confined to eternal life? How horrible it would be if there were many of them!

"Master Alexander," Zoran said weakly, "if I could trouble you for some food I would regain my strength."

"Of course," Alexander said, "of course." He got up and went into the other room. He hung the kettle over the fire and got together the remnants of their meal, what hadn't been pushed off the table in his struggle with Zoran. He carried it back to Zoran and helped him sit up.

Zoran, propped up against him, began to eat, one small bite at a time.

"Tell me now," Alexander said, "the long story of how you came to this school."

Zoran swallowed, and blinked at him. "Ever since I found my family, I've been looking for others of us. I've been all over the city with my eyes and ears open, listening for rumors and legends."

Alexander shifted Zoran's weight. "Rumors?" *Dear God, not about me.* In the other room, the kettle began to hiss.

"Stories about people who never died, Sir."

"Did you hear such stories?"

Zoran shook his head, his mouth full.

"But how did you find *me?*" asked Alexander.

"It's an odd thing." Zoran's face had flushed with color. "I suppose you don't remember this at all. I came to the school to inquire—I did want to go to school—and we bumped into each other in the hall. You only spoke a few niceties to me, but I just..." Zoran shrugged. "It was an inkling, only an inkling."

"Ahh." Alexander felt relieved and disconcerted simultaneously.

"I wouldn't worry too much," Zoran said softly, "I was looking. Anyone who wasn't would just think you were eccentric and aloof. But what brought you to this school?"

Alexander smiled ruefully. Aloof? Eccentric? Not the worst he'd been called. "Obscurity. It is a matter of immortal life that you cannot stay in one place forever. I suppose you've already realized that."

"But where are the other two of us?"

The kettle began to boil furiously in the next room. Alexander got up and prepared the kettle. He let it steep, and carried a steaming mug into the bedroom. Zoran leaned against the wall, eyes narrow in thought.

Alexander said, "One is at Castle Schwalenburg in Saxony, and the other is in Italy. Next year we will come together in Saxony again. It's our habit to meet every decade or so, and to stay together for about a year before dispersing again."

"Can I come with you?" Zoran took the mug from his hands.

Alexander hovered one hand, but Zoran seemed capable to hold it on his own. "Of course."

Zoran took a long, slow sip of tea. "Of course, I'd meant that as soon as I completed my schooling I would move on to another city. Before I met you, I'd begun to think that I'd never find

61

another like myself here. But I thought, perhaps in another city... have you looked?"

Looked? "No." Alexander had never searched for more immortals. Adolf Hardwin had, or at least he'd mentioned it in his letters, but Alexander had not.

Zoran's brow furrowed. "But why not? What if there are many of us?"

Alexander raised an eyebrow. "God, I hope not."

Zoran stopped, mid sip from his tea mug, and frowned at him. "But why?"

"Because I wouldn't wish this on a dog, Zoran!" Alexander stood and paced away from the table, toward the fire. He crossed his arms tightly across his chest. His head hurt from the questions, and from the concept. He'd never expected to find any more like him, but now that he had, didn't it follow logically that there could be more like him? Wandering over the earth, exiles in their own world?

"But why?" Zoran asked softly, "with time, all things must be possible. I see this extension of life as a chance for a son of a pauper to become something much more. A person could amass almost infinite knowledge, and wealth, as well."

"You are so optimistic," Alexander breathed, in a tone which was almost a laugh.

Zoran looked up sharply. His tea splashed in the cup. "You are not?"

Alexander's lip curled. "I am too old to be optimistic, Zoran. I've fled too many cities, I've seen too many people die." Ah yes, wasn't that the trouble? That he feared that Zoran was about to be crushed the weight of his long life, as he himself seemed to be. "Who would want to be trapped in this body of death forever?"

Zoran's dark eyes flickered. He lowered his gaze to the cup of tea in his hands. "This cannot be so," he said. "Sir, you are a man of God. How can you not have optimism?"

"In this world you will have trouble, the Scriptures say."

"But take heart!" Zoran's voice rang, "that's the next line. Sir, where is your faith?"

Alexander jerked. "Mr. Kosar, if you desire to hurt me that is exactly what you must say to me."

"I'm sorry," Zoran breathed.

"I will not deny that you may do better than I." Alexander's shoulders sagged. He sat down beside the bed. "This is a great deal to take in Zoran. Yesterday, I thought I was alone in Prague."

"Ahh..." Zoran sighed, and in a soft, caressing tone said, "Ahh... I know."

∞

"What's the worst thing that's happened to you as an immortal?" Zoran asked.

The church chimed eleven bells. The fire was just glowing coals in the hearth. Alexander got up and stretched his muscles, stiff from sitting for hours. He didn't answer Zoran's question at first, just prodded the coals together with a chunk of firewood and laid the wood carefully across the embers. Sparks flew up the chimney.

Zoran sat at the table, relieved of his bloody shirt, now dressed in Alexander's spare shirt. His face was flushed with excitement. There was no hint of the violence that had passed before. "Alexander?" he prodded.

"Are you expecting a story about being burned at the stake for sorcery?" Alexander asked as he turned around. He smiled, wearily. Zoran's eyes burned bright with curiosity, even after hours of incessant questions.

"Have you?"

Alexander picked up the teapot and glanced inside. There was some left, yet. He split it between his and Zoran's cups. "Two years ago I was run out of Zwickau because I failed to die of smallpox— I did die, mind you." He set down the teapot and plopped onto the bench. "I just didn't stay dead, and when I woke back up there wasn't a pock mark on me."

"Good Lord!" Zoran grinned, as if this were all great fun and hadn't involved a week of agony.

"But that isn't the worst."

Zoran's fingers drummed on the table and he wiggled in his seat. "Go on."

"The worst was abandoning my family." Alexander gazed at Zoran's unlined face. "There is no good way to explain why your husband and father looks only a few years older than his eldest son. Eventually people start asking questions. Eventually you realize that you provide more pain to your family when you are with them than if you are away, so you realize you must go away."

Zoran frowned, but the light remained in his eyes, as if his mind were still whirling at tremendous speed. He hadn't truly heard Alexander. He didn't understand.

"Did it not hurt you to leave your family?" Alexander asked softly.

Zoran shrugged and said, "No, not really. I knew I'd never be anything much while I was with them."

Alexander was dumbstruck. He stared at the flickering lamp light on his hands. No wonder the lad didn't resent his eternal life, then.

"I mean to study the natural sciences, if I can," Zoran said. He drained his lukewarm tea and set the cup down with a bang. "There must be an explanation for this. Haven't you wondered?"

"Of course I've wondered," Alexander said absently, still stuck on Zoran's dismissal of his family, "though I hardly think a natural explanation is—"

"Oh, there must be," Zoran said, "there will be. I'll have much time to study it, after all."

"True." Alexander rubbed his eyes.

But knowing why cannot change a thing, can it?

CHAPTER 6
Winnipeg, Present Day

"There are a few of you who still need to send me your book reports. Four pm is the cutoff, you have half an hour to email them to me. Chop, chop." Alannah's words were just about lost in the shuffle of chairs and book bags as the students trekked out of the lecture theatre. "I'll look forward to it," she muttered once they were all out of earshot.

Alannah shook her head and smiled blearily as she gathered her notes together. They'd had a lively discussion going today, with two highly opinionated sides, both awfully young-sounding.

"Can I sweep up?"

Alannah jumped. Her notes fluttered down onto the desk.

"So sorry professor." Jack gave her a sardonic smile. He took two steps down into the lecture hall, dragging his janitor cart behind him. "Chop, chop and all that."

"I've kept you waiting." Alannah returned his smile shyly with the phrase *build rapport* in her head.

Jack swiped at his nose. "Ahh... it's okay. I'm just keen to get out of here. I have an appointment to get to."

Alannah began picking up the sheets of notes again. "I'll be out in a moment, but go ahead." She rubbed her eyes and yawned. "Coffee would be nice," she mumbled to herself.

"For you and me both," Jack said as he snatched an empty water bottle from beneath one of the long row-desks.

Alannah laughed sheepishly as she shoved the sheaf of papers into her computer bag and uncoupled the charging cable. That was something they could build commonality on. "I do have a Keurig in my office. I could have a cup for you in two shakes."

"What's that?" Jack raised his head and rumpled his cinnamon colored hair with one gloved hand. His eyelids sagged.

"It's a coffee-pod-machine-thing," Alannah said and quirked her head to the side.

"Descriptive." Jack's nose wrinkled. He picked up his broom and slouched back up to the highest level of the lecture theatre. He began to brush out the dust along the edge of the wall and sweep it toward the bottom of the room.

"Well? Would you like some coffee? It isn't quite Starbucks, but it's not half bad." Alannah swung her bag over her shoulder.

He glanced up, genuine surprise written in his wide eyes. "Yeah, sure."

"How do you take it?"

"Black."

In her office, Alannah sat on her desk while the coffee jetted into her spare coffee mug. There was something wild in her that wanted to ask, "Hey, are you Jack Krause?" But if he was anything like she had been, he would rigorously deny it if it were true. If he wasn't, well, she'd be royally embarrassed.

She stuck around in her office long enough to gather up her empty lunch bag and a few things she'd need later, then screwed the cap on the travel mug and hiked down the stairs to the lecture theatre. Jack was just scraping the last of the debris off the floor into his dustpan. He straightened, and she handed him the coffee mug.

"Thanks, professor." He grinned wearily at her.

"No problem." Alannah stepped up onto the second level of the theatre. "Just leave the mug in my classroom sometime. No rush."

He waved to her as she slipped through the door.

The next afternoon her half-open office door swung wide with a loud squeak, and Jack's curly head poked in.

Alannah gasped.

"Hah! Found you. Does open door policy apply to janitors?" He gave the door a little test swing. It groaned. "Geez, I should grease that," he said. His face was no less weary, but a great deal less mopey than the day before. He glanced around her office and took in the faded, particle board desk, the book shelf piled two rows deep, and the collage of photographs on the cabinet doors.

Alannah stood up and shut her laptop. "I don't see why not," she said, "in regards to either the open door policy, or the greasing."

He walked in and placed the travel mug on the desk in front of her. "Thanks," he said, and walked out.

Alannah smiled. *There, I'm doing it Alexander. Are you proud of me?*

The next day, she didn't talk, nor 'build rapport' with Jack. She only spotted him from the door of the lecture theatre as he pushed the buzzing floor polisher, and he looked just as tired as before. She'd leaned against the doorframe and followed him with her eyes until he disappeared around the corner.

If that was Jack Krause, did he still have that pretty blond wife?

Though she exchanged pleasantries with him a couple times after that, her questions always died in her throat and he never offered information.

She got her answer the following week. She had decided to have a break from grading book reports, and took her camera out of the desk drawer. The leaves were just beginning to turn. She wanted a few snaps of the foliage, because in Winnipeg the beautiful colors didn't last long.

Alannah hiked from the Fletcher building across the staff parking lot. She cut across the broad, green park toward the Victoria Hospital with her eyes on the grove of trees surrounding it, all fledged in yellow, orange and gold. She caught sight of a bright splash of cobalt—a blue jay! But as she swung up the camera and scanned the branches, it was gone. She took a few wide shots, and then wandered among the trees, snapping close-ups of the brilliant leaves.

Alannah broke out of a hedge into the hospital parking lot and skirted around the front of the hospital. Alannah tripped over a curb, and when she'd steadied herself, she glanced up. Ahead, a lone figure perched on the wooden back of the bench, feet on the seat, shoulders hunched. The cool air blew a tendril of blueish cigarette smoke over his shoulder. For a moment, he turned his head and she saw his hollow eyes, the dark smudges under them, the patchy stubble. He dragged on the cigarette, and tapped it casually against the back of the bench.

It was Jack.

Alannah paused, gripping the camera, wondering if she should approach but her stomach tightened up like a clenched fist.

But before she could decide to spur her feet forward, or to flee, Jack glanced back. Their eyes met for a moment, he turned away again.

Say something! Alannah put on a smile even though her breath caught a little. She gestured at his cigarette. "Those things will kill you, y'know."

"Bet they won't." He turned his head just enough for her to see a glint in his eye. His lips twitched and he smiled. "Good day, Professor. Are you stalking me?"

Alannah flipped her coffee curls over her shoulder and hefted her camera. "Taking pictures."

"At the hospital?" He turned his head all the way toward her this time. He dropped the cigarette onto the bench-seat and ground it under his black leather boot. "You have a thing for human suffering? Gets you off?"

Alannah flinched. "No, I..."

"Sorry." He looked down. "Just a joke."

She sighed. "I'll forgive you—if I can take your picture." She held up the camera.

He raised his eyebrows. "What the hell do you want a picture of me for?"

"Photographers don't need reasons for taking pictures." A little grin formed on her lips. Her anxiety had, for some reason, fled. She did want a picture of him for her collection—immortal or not. His would be a striking, but somber portrait with those dark circles under his troubled eyes, and the beads of moisture in his curly hair.

His eyes twinkled, though he didn't smile. "Don't flirt with me, Professor. I'm a married man."

A hot flush came over her. "No, I wasn't, I didn't—"

The corners of his mouth twitched into a little grin. "Fine, take my picture. I don't care."

"I don't have to, I just—"

"No, go ahead." He raised both hands, cigarette clamped between two fingers. "What do I do?"

"Just-just put down your hands and look at me like that again." She framed him in the lens.

"Okay," he said, "say something stupid so I can."

"Ahh..." She snapped the shutter three times in a row, capturing the smirk on his face—his pale face with the dark circles under his eyes, the hard edge to his mouth.

"Why are you here?" she asked as she lowered the camera.

Jack pressed his lips into a thin line. "My wife is here. Chemotherapy."

"Oh God!" And she meant it. "Jack, I'm—"

"Don't say it," he said sharply. His sneer turned to a glare. "Don't say you're sorry. I don't want your pity 'cause it doesn't do shit."

"That's not what..."

"Oh no? You what, 'understand' because you've had a wife dying of cancer?"

Alannah bit her lip. "Jack, my adoptive parents are dead, and my real father is in jail, so..."

His face, in its ugly rictus, froze and slackened slowly. He steepled his hands and rested his chin on them. "Sorry."

"But I didn't have to watch them die, so I... I guess I don't understand."

"How did they die?" he asked in a low voice.

"A house fire," she said, "I was very young." By house fire, she meant they'd been bombed by the allies, and by very young she meant twenty-three. Alannah climbed up on the bench and sat like him on the back.

"What about your real mom?" Jack asked.

"Never met her."

"Oh."

There was a long silence, Jack continued to take long drags of his cigarette, and after a few minutes, Jack got up and walked back towards the hospital, not saying a word.

As she watched Jack go, Alannah mused that technically she shouldn't have met her real father either.

∞   ∞   ∞

"You know I'm not to see you," Zoran said to her when they first met, in the Schwalenburg library with the golden light falling through the high windows, "but you've grown into such a lovely young woman. You can't blame a father for greeting his daughter, can you?"

She smiled. "I suppose not."

His darkly handsome face grew slightly shy. "I'm hosting a discussion tomorrow night at a friend's house. Martin Bertholette. Do you know him?"

"A little." Only as far as she'd met him while acting as Alexander's assistant.

"Would you... would you do me the honor of coming?"

His tone was so wistful, and she, orphaned from her mortal parents, had only felt the slightest reluctance to say yes. "Well, I don't know. If I'm not needed here..." She wouldn't be needed. It was only that she'd heard quite a few scandalous stories about Zoran.

He nodded and smiled. It lit up his black eyes like gemstones, and Alannah already knew she would go.

The next evening she stood, with butterflies in her stomach, on the doorstep of Martin Bertholette's house in a quiet, residential neighborhood. Martin's wife, Camille, ushered her in.

"You came!" Zoran greeted her in the hall with a kiss on both cheeks.

Alannah laughed nervously and straightened her jacket. It had taken her a ridiculous amount of time to get dressed and do her hair, like she'd been preparing for a date.

Zoran guided her by the shoulder into the sitting room, packed with extra chairs. Two men stood shoulder to shoulder in the kitchen doorway, holding coffee cups.

"My dear, this is Christopher Bertrand," Zoran said.

Bertrand had a round, doughy face and wire rimmed glasses. He made an expression that was not quite a smile, just an uncomfortable upturning of the lips.

The other was slender, with long, dark hair caught back in ponytail. He disentangled his long, tapered fingers from the handle of his cup, and set it down just inside the kitchen.

"Hello." He extended his hand to Alannah.

"My daughter, Alannah," Zoran said, his tone warm with pleasure, "Alannah, Jurgen Zeigler."

"Daughter?" Jurgen's whole face brightened to sun-like proportions. He pumped her hand up and down. "Good Lord, Zoran, is it really? How wonderful to finally meet you. Wonderful to meet you!"

∞   ∞   ∞

Alannah sighed and cut off the memory there. She jumped off the bench. And so all the trouble had begun. She'd walked right into it, really. And now here she was, in Winnipeg.

∞

"You will see, within the text, a brief version of the wandering Jew myth." Alannah pressed the button, and a garish caricature appeared on the screen beside the translated text. "The Jew Ahasuerus is cursed to wander, undying, after refusing to aid the dying Jesus Christ. The writers then parallel this to the entire Jewish race, which seems, accordingly, cursed to wander—"

Alannah's phone buzzed in her pocket. She batted at her pocket in annoyance.

"They say, 'His nomad soul finds nowhere rest, everywhere he's just a pest.' Once again, we circle around to the pervasive idea of the Jew as not necessarily dangerous, but disgusting."

Alannah paused. Her phone vibrated again to remind her of the text. She slid it out of her pocket and laid it on the desk. The screen lit up, illuminating a text from Alexander, "Just landed in Winnipeg. I'll stop by at lunch."

For the rest of the class, despite the serious subject matter, Alannah had to keep wiping the smile off her face.

When class ended, and the students were filing out, Alannah snatched her phone up and texted, "All done. Where should I meet you?"

A moment later, the phone buzzed. "I'm here."

Thirty seconds later, as Alannah stuffed her laptop into its case, she heard light footfalls at the classroom door. She lifted her head. "Alexander!"

"In the flesh." He grinned as he marched down the aisle between the long rows of tables.

Alexander's straight blond hair had gained a little length from when she'd spoken to him on video chat. It was much like it had been fifty years ago, neatly tucked back in a ponytail. He looked every inch the European gentleman in his white shirt, slim pants, and sport coat. He had a wool jacket tossed over his arm. She held out her hands, and he dropped his jacket onto one of the chairs so he could grab them both. He leaned in and kissed her on both cheeks.

"You look well, dear Alannah," he said as he released her hands.

"I look the same!" She tugged at his hair. "I like this, Alexander."

"The more I grow it out, the more pressure I release from my brain."

Alannah chuckled.

"Can I buy you lunch?" Alexander asked.

"Yes, please!"

As they exited the classroom, with Alexander carrying Alannah's bags and Alannah carrying both of their coats, she caught a glimpse of a curly, brown head and a grey work-shirt.

"Classes are going well? Which one was this?" Alexander asked, once they were seated in the restaurant. He opened his big, leather-bound menu but didn't look at the page.

"This was German and German-Jewish history." Alannah shrugged. "I like this class. Medieval History is a bit tedious this year. I was thinking I could recommend Miles Corder for it next year."

Alexander's ageless blue eyes focused on hers. "So, this year will be your last year at the University, then? You'll move on?"

Alannah's stomach twisted. She opened the menu and pretended to browse through the salads.

"Alannah."

"It's not that simple," she said quietly.

"Yes, I know it isn't," he said, "but have you given thought about where you're going next?"

"I-I..." She didn't want to tell him that she felt nauseous even thinking about it. "Not really."

Alexander looked down at the menu. "The reason why I ask," he said quietly, "is that I had thought to sell my house here if you will no longer need it. But if your janitor is one of us, I may need to keep my post here a little bit longer."

"Then I could stay…"

"Yes, but not for long," he said firmly, "Alannah, I know it isn't simple, but if you desire to keep your freedom and privacy you must move on, even if it isn't far. You've been static for too long. As your overseer, I cannot allow it."

Alannah bit the inside of her lip and jutted her chin out.

"Change will be good, I promise you," Alexander said.

"Change? My foot," she muttered, "don't preach change to me just because you changed your hairstyle. You're the man who is still hunting for the same woman after nearly a hundred years. Is your next change to give up on Cosima, Alexander?" It was a low blow, meant to wound. She saw Alexander's eyes flicker, and he looked down.

"Was that really necessary?" he asked softly.

"I'm sorry," Alannah mumbled. She gulped from her water glass and looked away. She felt like a teenager in the presence of her parent.

"You're right in a way," Alexander said, "I'm not the person that I was when she knew me, thank God. I try not to hope in rekindling our love. I hope only to make the many apologies she deserves." He looked up at her, and kneaded his bottom lip with his teeth. "I loved her too long to give up. Is that so wrong?"

"No," Alannah said in a small voice. "I'm sorry."

Alexander gave her a weak smile and looked away for a moment.

"I'm sorry I'm such a burden to you," Alannah said. She turned the sweaty water glass around and didn't meet his gaze.

"Alannah," Alexander reached over and stilled her hands. "I've said it before, you are no burden."

He'd said it before, but in her weakest moments she'd always disbelieved him a little. He blamed himself for her very existence, didn't he? Alexander thought himself too duty bound to ever leave her in the cold.

A tear dropped from her cheek into her water glass. She was immortal, though, wasn't she? One day she'd overcome this. She'd be brave. Maybe then she'd be able to pay him back.

"I have a picture of him—Jack," she said, wiping at her cheek. She dug in her purse for her phone. She'd developed her roll of film in the little darkroom in Alexander's basement, and then scanned Jack's photo onto the computer.

She tapped her way to the photos and brought Jack's face onto the screen. The portrait was exactly what she'd hoped. She'd captured him just after he'd said something snarky—the glint in his eye, the wry twist to his lips, all in an attempt to mask the darkness in his eyes and the weary droop to his face.

"Ahh..." Alexander leaned over the picture and rubbed his chin. "He might look a little older."

Alannah traced the hard line of Jack's jaw with her eyes. "He looks so tired that it takes some of the youth from his face. His wife is in cancer treatments."

"Ahh..." Alexander's shoulders drooped. "I believe you, Alannah. I do think this is Jack Krause. If his wife is ill, this may not be the time to contact him. Or perhaps it is exactly the time to contact him. If she should die—"

Alannah could guess at Alexander's thoughts. Thoughts of a wife whose face six hundred and some years had not erased from his memory.

CHAPTER 7

Jack drove up the street by Mary Rose's house just as Clarissa's silver hatchback was pulling away from the curb. He parked five or six houses down and waited for her to disappear, then he picked the little bag off the passenger seat and walked to the step. The step was newly cleared of the light dusting of snow. He wondered if Clarissa had cleared it, or if Mary Rose had ventured out into the brisk December air.

It took two or three minutes for the door to open. Mary Rose smiled beatifically up at him. Her eyes shone like blue glass beads in her pale face.

He shut the door quickly against the cold, and kissed her like always, holding her fragile frame against him like he could pass his strength through their skin and clothes. "I brought you something," he said into her ear, "it's an early Christmas present."

She laughed as he handed her the paper bag. She propped it against her sweater to open it up. "Oh, how pretty!" She pulled out the headscarf, in a rich pattern of indigo blue, purple and white. "Help me put it on." She fumbled at the knot in the scarf she wore, but finally just slipped it off.

His chest clamped at the sight of her bare scalp. He folded the scarf into a triangle and wrapped it around her head. "It's long," he said.

"Oh, sometimes I wrap them twice." She reached back and helped him adjust it. She looked in the mirror by the door and giggled. "It seems I've finally imparted my good taste to you, my love."

He leaned his chin on her shoulder. "You look lovely." *But so pale and so tired.* "How do you feel?"

She sagged against him. "I've been so tired, Jack. I haven't been able to keep food down for a couple of days."

"Did you try again today?"

"Yes, Clarissa made me eat some soup. So far it has stayed down." She looked up and met his eyes in the mirror. For the first time, he saw fear there. Jack felt a tremor go through him.

"Jack," she breathed, "I need to talk to you. Come sit." She led him by the hand to the couch. Instead of sitting to face him, she waited for him to sit, and then sat down between his knees. He wrapped her in his arms and leaned back.

"You're so nice and warm." She sighed, snuggling into his chest. A moment passed without speaking.

"Mary Rose..." he began.

"Yes, yes." She swallowed hard and blew out her breath. "Jack, I think... I think I need to discontinue my chemo."

He jerked and almost sat up, but her hand on his arm restrained him.

"Listen," she said softly, "Jack you know how sick I've been. The treatment isn't going to save me. We've always known that. I think it's time to stop kidding ourselves."

His breath shuddered out, and his mind swirled in an ever-accelerating vortex. Options. He needed options. But after ten minutes, he knew the answer. There were no more answers, and he had no right to ask his wife to suffer on just to keep her a little while longer.

∞

Jack sat on the ripped vinyl chair in his kitchen, sipping whisky and turning his pistol over every few seconds. The green-grey fluorescent light gleamed dully on the short barrel and the silencer.

He had three bullets, sitting in a line in front of him.

You said you wouldn't do it.

"Damn it, Mary Rose!" He jumped up. The chair wobbled and toppled with a bang. He turned and kicked it. It slammed against the fake wooden kitchen cabinets. "Damn whoever made me this way! You want me to watch her die and not try to follow her?" He picked up the pistol and popped the magazine out of it. He pressed the cartridges one by one into it and slammed it back into the gun. He stomped toward the other half of his bachelor suite and ripped the blanket off the bed. He spread it out flat in a square in the middle of the room. Then he sat down on it, stuffed the gun in his mouth, and pulled the trigger.

His head roared with white-hot pain as he fell toward death.

He woke up lying in his own blood and brain matter, splattered on the blanket and flecked on the wall behind him. The red numbers on the digital clock said it was ten at night. He had been out for three hours. He'd been lucky. No one had heard the shot and called the cops.

Jack got up slowly and walked toward the kitchen. Dying and resurrecting had undone all of his drinking. He didn't bother pouring. He tipped back the bottle of Jack Daniels and let the liquid fire pour down his throat into his empty stomach. Before long, his head felt a little bit sideways. He sagged against the counter and turned on the faucet. He rinsed the blood off his palms, and then off the whisky bottle.

He stared at the drawer where he kept his butcher knife. It was a good, sharp knife. It would be a nice, long death. Long enough for him to really feel like he was dying.

"You said you wouldn't do it," he slurred. He sighed and tipped back his head. He picked up the gun. "I'm sorry, Mary Rose." He didn't even bother to move. He pressed the gun against his temple and pulled the trigger. As he fell toward the floor, he heard the crash of glass. The white light in the back of his head was growing brighter and brighter. Jack smiled.

Walking into work the morning after killing one's self never felt normal. Jack always had this vague sense that people could see that he was different. But that morning, Jack didn't give a crap if he looked different or not. His pulse beat like a hammer in his temples, sending ribbons of pain down to the base of his neck. It wasn't the bullets. It had been two in the morning the second time he woke up. He was too weak to get up, but too charged with adrenaline to sleep. He lay on the floor until he could stand, and finally got into bed at three-thirty. Two and a half hours later he woke up, put on clothes and came to work. He had left the shattered window as it was, bullet hole or no bullet hole.

He walked around the university like a zombie, and in all honesty he was nearly the definition of one.

At four, Mary Rose texted him to say that Clarissa was over, and so was her friend June. Jack just drove home after work, via the McDonald's drive-thru. As he was about to shove the keys into the lock, he heard heavy footfalls in the hall and looked up. His landlord, a paunchy man in his fifties (hell, about his age), stood there.

"Jack Gerhardt?"

"Yeah." Jack transferred the paper bag of fast food to the other hand and turned the door handle.

The landlord took a step closer. "What the hell happened to your window?"

Ah, shit. "My window?"

"Your neighbors told me they heard shouting, and then a crash late at night."

"Are you sure that wasn't my TV?" Jack asked. He had no TV.

The man's face turned bright red. "Your window is shattered and you're telling me that they heard your TV? I've already been in your apartment to look around. Your window has what looks like a bullet hole in it. Two or three cabinets are smashed. Listen. You have two options. You pay for the window, and you move out or I call the cops, and you move out!"

Anger burned through Jack's belly. He dropped the fast food and stepped toward the landlord with his hands balled into fists. The man paled, but he fished a phone from his pants-pocket and brandished the shiny screen at Jack.

"Don't you dare," he said.

"How much for the window?" Jack growled.

"Three-hundred bucks."

Jack pulled out his billfold and began extracting the fifties he'd withdrawn for Mary Rose. He let them flutter one by one onto the floor. Fifty. One hundred. One-fifty. Two. Two-fifty. Three. The landlord's eyes followed each one toward the floor.

"I'll have my stuff out by tomorrow," Jack growled, "and you can keep my fucking TV."

There would be no need to tell Mary Rose, Jack thought as he piled his few things into his suitcase and backpack. In fact, he might forgo the apartment altogether. It wouldn't be the first time.

Alannah gave him a funny look the next morning, and soon came walking out of the lecture theatre with her Advil bottle.

"Jack, do you have a headache again?" As she spoke a man came walking up behind her.

Jack looked past her at the guy leaning against the door—a slender man in a suit with blond hair in a knot on the back of his head. His blue eyes were intent on Jack.

As Jack's gaze passed between Alannah and the stranger, something sparked in his mind.

I've seen him before. No, I've seen them—together—before.

He flashed back instantly: slipping, falling, falling, falling, the white hot pain as the rebar punched through his chest.

And then two faces, a man and a woman hovering over him.

Jack reeled back a little. What the hell? Had the bullets actually scrambled his brain this time?

"No, I'm fine, Professor," Jack said slowly. He nodded to the man in the doorway. He felt his hands begin to tremble, and stuffed them in his pockets.

"Oh." Alannah glanced back. "Sorry, Jack. This is Dr. von Katlenburg."

"Alexander." The man stood up straight and held out his hand.

But if they are the same people, then they haven't aged either.

Jack shook himself slightly and shook the offered hand. "Yeah, hi. I should be going, sorry." He started to walk away, but he heard the clatter of high heels behind him.

"Jack." Alannah puffed up beside him. "Jack. How are things going... with your wife?"

He stopped and turned to glare at her. "She's dying, Alannah. She's dying, and I just got evicted from my apartment."

Her face flushed. "Oh. Oh, uh... Does she need a place to stay? Do you need a place to stay?"

"No!"

"O-Okay." Her dark brows pulled together in confusion.

Two hours later, he dragged on his cigarette by the front door of the building. The nicotine didn't help his headache or the pain in his chest. The sun shone down with a bleak, brittle light. It hadn't raised the temperature at all since it rose. All he could think of was that blond guy, and the professor, and this picture he had in his head of hanging from rebar, an upside down face wreathed in brown curls, and a soothing voice. He just couldn't quite get the picture to focus.

The clumping footfalls made by snow boots came up the sidewalk. Jack glanced over and saw blond curls, bursting from a pink toque. He turned all the way. It was Clarissa.

It was too late to hide. He nodded to her and looked away.

"Hi," she said softly as she approached.

"Hey." Panicky thoughts reeled through his head. He didn't think Clarissa had ever seen him so close. She'd never think that... she'd never recognize him, would she? God! She was beautiful like her mother.

She looked him right in the eye. There were dark shadows under her fringe of blond lashes. "Hey, uh, do you know where Professor Miles Corder's office is?"

"Take the first staircase on the left, and then follow the hallway until just before it turns."

She smiled weakly and passed through the door, which he still held open. "Thanks."

He watched her walk away with her shoulders slumped and felt bile rise in the back of his throat. Jack ground his cigarette under his heel and was about to turn and walk back into the building, when the door opened on creaking hinges.

The blond guy, Alexander von what's-his-name, emerged. "Ah, Jack. Sorry to disturb you."

"S'okay." Jack grabbed the door before it could close entirely.

Alexander moved as if to walk on, but paused. "Jack, if I could ask a question..."

"Yeah?" Jack turned back and swiped at his bleary eyes with his free hand.

"This will sound terribly forward, I know, but..." Alexander paused, kneading his bottom lip with his teeth, "did you ever hear of that construction worker who fell on rebar, near here? He appeared to die in surgery, but miraculously survived?"

Jack stared into the man's blue eyes, his air cut off.

Shit.

Alexander just stood there, waiting for an answer.

"I, um, I might have seen that on the news," Jack forced out as casually as he could, "when, uh, when was that?"

"It was more than twenty years ago." Alexander held his gaze steadily.

"Well, I would have just been a kid," Jack said. He wished he'd kept the cigarette lit. "So, I don't know why the hell you're asking me about this." He heaved the door open and was about to go inside.

"I was there," Alexander said casually, "it's the sort of thing no one forgets."

Jack blinked at Alexander's face. He didn't look old. He didn't look all that young. "Great," he said, and shut the door in Alexander's face.

What the hell is going on?

Jack jogged down the hall in case Alexander followed. He slipped into the janitors' closet and leaned against the door, panting.

How was he there?

A wild thought occurred to him. *What if he's like me?*

It's not impossible. If there's one of me, why not two?

Alannah was the woman who held my hand.

It can't be!

"What the hell is going on?" he whispered to the racks of cleaners and the mop buckets. *Is this some sort of joke? Is he a news reporter finally caught up to me?*

He couldn't skip town, not with Mary Rose a little worse every day. He could quit his job, he guessed.

Jack pushed himself off the door and paced the four steps across the room.. "Shit," he groaned, "what am I going to do?" He could feel a tension headache radiating up his neck. He thumped both fists against the only clear spot of wall. "What am I going to do?"

He spent the last couple hours of the shift watching over his shoulder for Alannah or Alexander, nauseous with nerves. But neither appeared.

Jack bought a bottle of bourbon and parked his worn out Corolla in the packed Wal-Mart parking lot, where he'd slept for the last few nights. People milled back and forth, hoods up against the cold wind, pushing carts of Christmas presents. Jack sunk down low in his seat and took a bracing sip from the bottle.

His phone battery was pretty close to dead. He'd forgotten to charge it at work. Jack texted Mary Rose the whole scenario.

He finished with, "What am I supposed to do?"

Jack locked the screen and took another sip. His head hurt so bad from thinking.

The phone dinged. "As him what he meant." Mary Rose's text was garbled, like she'd been hurrying, or shaking, "If there's—" Jack squinted at the words and guessed to what they said. If there was someone else like him, at least he wasn't alone.

"What if he's trying to trick me?" he typed.

A long minute passed.

"You know how to hide," Mary Rose's text said, "Jack, I'd feel so much better if I knew you weren't alone."

Jack tipped his head back. She was probably right, but she said it like it was so simple. He put the bottle to his lips and took a long slug of the bourbon, and then another.

The next morning, Jack avoided Professor Krueger's lecture theatre until he'd cleaned absolutely every classroom. Her room was dark and deserted. He pushed the garbage cart in and began picking up the stray water bottles, candy wrappers, and paper scraps from under the rows of chairs. Every time he bent over, the pressure in his head became nearly unbearable.

He'd made it halfway down the sloped theatre, when he sensed a presence behind him.

"Are you okay, Jack?"

He straightened. It took a moment before his vision cleared, and he saw Alannah standing in the doorway, her loose curls backlit by the fluorescent light in the hallway.

"Fine," he muttered. He eyed her. She stood there, kept looking at him.

"Did you ever..." he began, hoarsely. Fear clamped off the words.

Just ask. Ask for Mary Rose.

"Did you ever," he began again, "hear about the construction worker who fell on rebar around here? He died on the operating table and came back to life?"

To his surprise, Alannah's eyes filled with tears. "Yes Jack," she said softly. "I was there."

∞

"So how did this happen?" Jack's voice still carried a ring of stunned disbelief.

Alannah wrung out the dishrag and hung it over the side of the sink. She turned back to see Alexander answer. The smell of cabbage soup and warmed-up bread still lingered in the air. Alexander and Jack sat with coffee cups in front of them. The green digital numbers on the stove said 9:34.

Alexander folded his hands and leaned his chin on them. "If you are looking for justice to be served on the perpetrator, I fear you will be disappointed."

Jack's bloodshot eyes narrowed. "I don't really give a crap about the perpetrator. That don't change anything. But what the hell happened to you and me?" He ran his fingers through his curly hair and made it stand up even more wildly on end.

"That is generous of you, since the culprit sits right in front of you," Alexander said softly. His shoulders sagged.

"Holy shit!" Jack stood up. His fists doubled at his sides. "What the fuck did you do to me?"

Alexander held out his hand beseechingly. "I did nothing directly to you, Jack. Let me explain, and then I can beg your forgiveness."

Jack dropped his hands, but they remained balled up. He stood, regarding Alexander with dread etched into his face.

Alexander blew out his breath. "You've heard of the fountain of youth?"

Jack scowled. "Yeah, maybe."

"It isn't a myth. It's real. Those who drink of it find eternal life, and relative invincibility."

"What?" Jack's voice cracked. "A fountain? Where? When did I drink from it? I grew up in Winnipeg! North end Winnipeg!"

"You didn't." Alexander sighed. "I did. Three of us, a hunting party, drank from a fountain, which we had never seen previously and found several years later that we could neither die nor age. By then, all of us had sired children. The immortality is passed down by bloodline. It skips most generations but picks the odd unfortunate soul to grace with everlasting life."

"So you're my grandpa?" Jack pressed his palms to his eyes and wobbled across the room. "This doesn't happen here," his voice came muffled from behind his hands. "I'm from Winnipeg. This doesn't happen here!" He spun around, his face contorted. "So what, Clarissa might be?"

"Probably not," Alexander whispered.

"Her kids might be?"

"Perhaps, but probably not." Alexander's head hung. Alannah stepped forward to lay a hand on his slumped shoulder.

Jack's mouth hung open, gasping. "No, it's not true. It's not—" He jerked into motion toward the door.

"Jack," Alannah said softly, "Jack, please sit down. Please let us talk about this."

Jack had almost reached the front door. He glanced back over his shoulder. All feeling had drained from his face. "My life has been hell for twenty-six years and you want to talk about this?" He yanked the door open. "My wife needs me. I've got to go."

The door closed behind Jack. A moment later, his car coughed to life outside. It hurt for Alannah to think he was probably spending the night in it.

"Alexander," Alannah said with a sigh.

Alexander stared down into his coffee cup. His face was flushed, drooping with sadness. "Ah dear God. Another poor, cursed soul," he whispered. She didn't think it was to her. "It's my fault."

Alannah bent down and wrapped her arms around his shoulders. "No, Alexander, it's not your fault."

He sighed, touched her cheek, but said nothing.

"What will we do?"

"We'll keep an eye on him." Alexander took a tentative sip of his coffee. "If I'm not mistaken, he will soon need us very badly. I'll not abandon him."

CHAPTER 8

Cotton ball flakes of snow tumbled past the overhang, lit up by the orange light in the grocery store parking lot. Jack leaned against the cold brick wall and took a long drag on his cigarette. His fingers were numb on the paper.

As Jack ground the cigarette under his heel, his phone buzzed in his pocket. His heart lurched. He fished for it in his pocket, but his fingers seemed unwilling. Finally the phone made it out of his pocket and he saw the number. It was Mary Rose.

"Jack," her voice was almost a whisper, like it had been for a week now. "Jack, will you come please? Clarissa is gone for an hour or two. I told her June was coming. Jack, I need you."

"I'll be right there," he choked out.

He sped through the slippery streets. The hospital hallways were dimly lit, and only a few nurses paced here and there. Jack blew past everything into Mary Rose's room.

"Jack." Her voice was an airy whisper from the bed.

He bent over her and brushed his mouth across her bloodless lips. "Mary Rose."

Her face was as pale as the pillowcase. She said something, but even with his face so close to hers he didn't understand. When had this happened? He'd snuck in to see her two days before, and she'd been weak but not like this.

She licked her lips and tried again. "Hold me, my love."

Jack gulped and kicked his boots off, under the bed. Gingerly, he climbed up beside her. The bed creaked and shifted as he pulled her into his arms. Her head lolled against his chest as she settled against him, like they were back in their bed in their house.

A nurse came by and poked her head into the room. She didn't bat an eye. Mary Rose had told the staff the Jack was a close friend, and by now the nurses probably thought he was *that* kind of friend and that was why Clarissa didn't know about him.

"Jack, it won't be long now." She tilted her head just a little. He adjusted himself so she could look him in the eye. Her cloudy blue eyes were filled with tears, and moisture burned under his lids, too. "Jack, I'm not afraid to go, but..." She sucked in a shallow breath. "But I am afraid to leave you."

"Mary Rose—"

"Jack, you... try to hide it from me, but I k-know."

"I'm sorry."

"Don't apologize to me." She sank back down and shut her eyes. "I'm sorry, Jack. I'm sorry I have to leave you."

He kissed her sunken cheek, and his tears spilled over onto her pale skin. "I love you."

"You've been good to me," she breathed. "Please, Jack. Please be good to yourself." Her throat convulsed. Tears squirted from the corner of her eyes and she sank more heavily against him.

"I will." Jack fought to keep himself steady, fought to keep the sobs down. He lay, listening to her breathing. It was so shallow. Her eyelids palpitated but didn't open.

Half an hour passed. Jack heard a nurse in the doorway, but no one came in. Ten minutes later, Mary Rose sighed and turned her head. Her lips parted, and a soft, rattling breath came out.

"Mary Rose?" He bent over her. "Mary Rose." She didn't seem to be breathing. He held his fingers over her pale lips, but felt nothing.

"No. No." Jack cradled Mary Rose's face. "Nurse! Nurse! No, Mary Rose, don't go. Please don't leave me here."

A nurse rushed in.

"She's not breathing!" Jack rocked back and forth, Mary Rose in his arms.

The nurse bent over them both and pressed her stethoscope to Mary Rose's chest. "Hold still, Sir. It's alright," she said gently, "it's alright."

"Mary Rose," he moaned.

And then, in the hall he heard a soft, feminine voice that was so much like Mary Rose's. "Mom?" Clarissa appeared, framed in the doorway, "Mom!" she dashed in, toward the bed. Her eyes lit on Jack. "Hey! Who the hell are you?"

"I—" Jack rasped.

The nurse lifted her head. "I'm very sorry. She's—"

"What?" Clarissa cried.

Jack was frozen with panic and disbelief, but only for an instant. He disentangled himself from the blankets, and Mary Rose and launched himself from the bed. He took one last, wild look at Mary Rose's face and shoved past all of them.

He skidded to a halt outside the door, but no footsteps followed him. He only heard a wail:

"Mom!"

Jack stumbled past the desk into the parking lot, around the corner to his car. He reached for the door handle and bashed his numb fist against the cold metal. He yelped, and hit it again, and again until the skin split. Slowly, he sank to his knees and put his head in his hands. He felt the hot blood smear.

"Mary Rose," he groaned, "M-Mary..." He tasted bile, gagged, and vomited onto the snow. He heaved, until there was nothing left.

∞

It was three-thirty in the morning when the doorbell woke Alannah. She sat up in the dark bedroom, disoriented.

She heard Alexander's light footfalls come past the door, and recede. The doorbell jangled again, and then she heard Alexander say, "Jack?"

Alannah jumped out of bed. Her feet tangled in the sheets, and she almost fell face first into the door. She steadied herself and grabbed her robe off the hook on the backside of the door. She got the robe tied just as both feet touched down on the landing in the foyer.

Alexander was shutting the door behind a drenched, shivering, shoeless Jack. Jack looked up at her. His eyes were dead.

Twenty minutes later, Alexander had Jack in one of the stuffed chairs and was laying logs on the embers of the fire he had made the evening before. Jack slumped with his head in his hands.

"I hope you didn't need your beauty sleep," he said in a hollow voice.

Alexander brushed his hands together and stared at the embers. "I told you to call me if you had need of me." Smoke began to curl from the underside of the logs. "Alannah, I left my sweater on my chair in the kitchen. I suspect it will fit Jack."

She brought him the soft, hooded sweater. Alexander handed it to Jack, who pulled it on over his damp t-shirt. Jack wrapped his arms around himself. His lips quivered with cold, fatigue, or grief.

"Should I bring... tea?" Alannah glanced over her shoulder, toward the kitchen door.

"Yes, good idea," Alexander said. He grabbed her hand as she passed by. "Let me have a moment alone with Jack," he said softly.

Alannah flicked on the element under the kettle and watched it begin to glow, very red and bright in the dark kitchen. She sagged against the counter and tried not to listen to the low murmur of

Alexander's voice. Alexander could well understand Jack's grief right now. He should be the one to speak—if there was anything that could be said.

The water boiled, but she switched if off and waited for fifteen minutes, before letting it boil again and pouring the water over the tea bags. She carried a tray and three mugs of tea into the living room. Alexander had switched on the lamp. He sat in the wingback chair across from Jack. Jack leaned against the brocade back of his chair, with his gaze away from the door.

Jack lifted his burning eyes toward Alexander. "Prove it. Prove it to me that you're immortal. You haven't given me shit to hang on to. Prove to me you're not lying."

Alexander said, grimly, "What do you want me to do?"

"It's not complicated." Jack clenched his hands around the carved armrests of the chair. "Do you have a knife?"

Alannah sucked in a breath, but Alexander's face remained perfectly calm as he said, "There is a whole selection in the kitchen. But drowning was always my preference. You know you're drowning for a good long time. Sometimes you'll rebound and wake up under water and drown all over again."

Jack's face contorted.

Alexander pressed on. "How about jumping off a cliff. Have you tried that? A word to the wise: dive head first."

"Alexander!" Alannah clutched at her chest and felt tears well up in her eyes.

"She hasn't tried it," Alexander said. "Alannah has never tried killing herself."

"Figures," Jack growled.

"That makes her stronger than the both of us," Alexander said. He narrowed his eyes at Jack. "It takes more strength to live, as it takes more strength to believe than to scoff. I'm not going to slash my own throat, Jack. Stick around a little while, and I'll prove this to you. I am immortal."

Jack's rigid face twitched, and he squeezed the armrests. His jaw clenched and jutted forward. "This is great, just great." His breath shuddered out. He slammed one blood-smeared fist on the chair. "This is just... just..." He put his head down into his hands. His shoulders heaved.

CHAPTER 9

Alannah scrubbed at the crusted eggs on the cast-iron frying pan. Jack lay in one of the spare bedrooms upstairs. By now, hopefully he was asleep. They'd fed him, and Alexander had invited him to stay.

She swished the dishrag through the soupy water. Her head ached with weariness, the result of going to bed late, and being startled awake at three in the morning. And she had a lesson to plan.

The question, as always: was it right for her life to go on as normal when another's life had crashed to pieces?

Alexander's voice came into earshot. He paced past the kitchen door, phone to his ear, speaking in rapid-fire German. She caught just enough to know he was speaking to one of the lawmen in Dresden, and based on his language choice, not Cyrus. She caught the words 'Koenig' and 'missing.'

"Is that Daniel?" she wiped her hands on the dishtowel and hung her head out the door.

Alexander looked up and nodded.

"Say hello from me," she whispered.

Alexander nodded, and continued his conversation.

Alannah drained the sink, then tiptoed upstairs to get her laptop and notes. Jack's door was closed, the bedroom silent. She slipped past, into the library. She put in ear buds, and let Mendelssohn's 'Songs Without Words' sooth her. Her notes on German Jewish immigration to Winnipeg certainly wouldn't.

"Alannah." Alexander poked his head into the library fifteen minutes later. His phone was still in his hand. "I just got off the phone with Daniel."

Alannah looked up from her computer screen and pulled her ear buds out. "And?"

"Marcus Koenig is still in the wind, and Daniel is running out of places to look."

"So, you need to go back to Dresden?"

"No. Well, yes." Alexander frowned and walked all the way into the room. "Not now. I can't leave, having just found Jack. But..." His face twisted. He sat down in one of the armchairs. "It goes deeper. Daniel searched through Koenig's phone and email records, and in doing so he made a rather disturbing discovery."

Alannah swallowed hard.

"May I borrow your laptop?" Alexander asked with a weak smile.

Alannah got up and handed him the silver computer.

"Stay here. I want to show you something." Alexander settled the computer on his knees and opened the browser. "Daniel discovered that Marcus Koenig was subscribed to a private blog in the deep web, written by an anonymous source but clearly immortal." The page loaded, a simple black backdrop with bold, white words across the header: *What is the point of immortality, if not to live free?*

"Oh, God," Alannah whimpered.

Alexander's face tightened. "So Daniel is not wrong, then. That is a direct quote of Zoran's?"

It was a direct quote. It was nearly Zoran's motto. He'd repeated it at every meeting he'd held. It was there, in one form or another, in all of his writings. Jurgen had said it. Christopher and the others had said it. She'd said it too.

"These are Zoran's writings?" she squeaked.

Alexander waved one hand helplessly, "They can't be. Zoran has no Internet access in Schwalenburg, and his letters are closely monitored. Unless they are excerpts from his books, and someone else is posting them."

"I'd probably recognize them then," Alannah choked. She pressed one hand to her tight chest. "Alexander, I can't—I can't—"

Alexander slammed the laptop shut. "I'm not asking you to read them, Alannah. Daniel is already analyzing them. I was just wondering..."

Alannah slid down onto the floor beside his chair. "Oh God, one of them has taken him."

Alexander got out of the chair and knelt in front of her. He took both of her hands. "It's more likely that he's one of them, Alannah. Daniel thinks a few of them might be reforming their society. Do you have any inklings—even gut feelings—of who might still be loyal?

Alannah shook her head slowly, fighting back burning tears, fighting her accelerating heartbeat. *In through the mouth, out through the nose. One, two, three, four.*

Alexander stroked her hand. "I'm so sorry to upset you, Alannah. I just needed any information I might get. If you think of anything...?

Alannah drew in a long, breath. There. She was calm again. "Yes," she whispered, "I'll think about it."

Alexander sat beside her for a few more minutes, until he seemed quite sure she was alright. Then he left, and she picked up her laptop to return to her lesson notes.

Wisely, Alexander had closed the browser.

Alannah settled into the plush chair and put Mendelsohn back on, but the lecture notes swam in front of her eyes, mingled with the sentence: *what is the point of immortality if not to live free?*

She wanted to see the blog. She'd know if they were really her father's words. She would. She had to know.

Alannah tried to Google the tagline, but the blog did not appear on the search list.

"I have to know," she said aloud. "What if they are reforming the group? Then what?" She shut the laptop and stood on wobbly legs.

She found Alexander in his study, downstairs. "I want to read the blog," she said. "Maybe I'll recognize who wrote it. I need to know."

∞

The beauty of immortality is the ability to reinvent oneself an infinite number of times. You likely agree with me, but there are those who do not. There are those long-living persons who are crushed under the weight of their years. They have not the mental fortitude to reinvent. They can only live in the regret of the past, and they long for death. Generally, I know such a man or woman on sight, and believe firmly that they should be given what they desire.

Alannah licked her dry lips. Her neck and back ached from sitting on a little wooden stool at the corner of Alexander's desk all afternoon. Alexander had gotten up, but she stayed. She couldn't help it. She hadn't told Alexander yet, but she could practically hear her father's voice through the words on the screen. They brought her to a memory of sitting in the back corner of a little Dresden cafe, coffee and beer untouched, while Zoran spoke.

∞   ∞   ∞

"If a person is not fit to live for a thousand years, why should he live?" Zoran punctuated this with a slap on the table. Alannah jumped and glanced around to see if anyone had noticed Zoran's outburst, but Zoran ploughed on.

"In a mortal life, death is the natural interrupter of all downward trends. There is no sound argument for why immortals who want to die should not be given what they desire."

Jurgen leaned in with bright eyes, but Alannah shifted uneasily. "Papa—" he loved when she called him that "—forgive me, but you keep referring to giving the suicidal what they want. But that isn't possible. There's—"

"But there is!" Zoran jabbed one finger at her. "Your Lord Alexander just hasn't told you. There is a way to die, and the Lords know it. They keep it as their most treasured secret."

Alannah gaped at him like a fish on dry land.

∞　　　∞　　　∞

Alannah stared grim-faced at the screen, fighting the panic the memory brought. Death. Zoran's greatest obsession. The blog was rife with the ideas of immortal death, and immortal life—his second greatest mania, the idea of producing immortal children. He'd done that one. That was where she came from. But that wasn't good enough. He needed to be lord of death as well.

She should have walked out of that cafe then and there, but she hadn't.

Alannah scrolled through the rest of the article, barely skimming the contents. She didn't need to read it. She already knew what it said. But as she moved the mouse to click the browser shut, her eyes lit on a single comment at the bottom of the article. It was anonymous: *I heard that Zoran found the way to kill us, and that he killed Jurgen Zeigler. How did he do it?*

The comment was dated almost two months ago. There was no reply. A cold tingle skittered down Alannah's spine.

CHAPTER 10

Jack dropped the suitcase on the bed and reached for the zipper. He paused and shut the door. He pulled three t-shirts, two pairs of jeans and a flannel shirt out of the suitcase and laid them in a stack on the bed. Underneath, wrapped in a white undershirt, lay the pistol, the silencer still screwed into the end. Jack picked it up and stroked the short barrel.

"Well, what now?" he said to himself.

His head hurt so bad, like a hangover from hell, but he hadn't touched a drop. His eyes felt like they were on fire from crying; there wasn't a tear left to moisten them.

Mary Rose had talked about this, about 'cutting him loose' to do whatever he pleased.

"I don't want to be cut loose," he had said.

"You could travel," she had said with light in her eyes. "I can see you doing it—just taking a backpack and going to the airport. You could go anywhere and stay there as long as you'd like. You're that kind of person, Jack. You could survive anywhere."

That had resulted in the biggest fight of their marriage, and now that he looked back, Jack was even sorrier than he had been when he had returned and groveled before her the day after.

As it was, the Gulf of Mexico was the farthest he went, and work was *almost* all he ever did. He'd drank, sure. He pulled many a death-defying stunt. But he had always known he was a married man. His money had gone to them, and his love had gone to them.

And now?

I still don't want to be cut loose. Jack laid the empty pistol against his forehead and shut his eyes, feeling the cold steel circle against his skin. Oh to be numb, even for a few minutes.

But Alannah was just across the hall in the library, and Alexander was downstairs, puttering around the kitchen, pale-faced and bleary eyed. He couldn't disturb them any more than he already had. Not today.

He laid the pistol down inside the suitcase and zipped it back up again. He slid it under the bed, and sat down on top of the mattress. It would keep.

∞

Jack ambled into the library with a cup of coffee in one hand. He stood in the center of the room, on top of the Persian rug, and cranked his head around to see all of the bookshelves. "What are you reading, Professor?"

Alannah, headphones pumping out classical piano, didn't look up. She only noticed him when he knelt down behind her computer and peeked over the screen.

She gasped.

Jack gazed at her with a shadow of a grin. "Alexander has made coffee." His voice had some hoarseness to it. "What are you doing?"

"I'm working on my lesson. I should have finished it yesterday." Thirty-six hours had passed since Jack appeared on their doorstep.

"Ahh..." Jack gulped from his coffee. His eyes were still bloodshot, but his face had regained some of its color. His cheeks were ruddy beneath the dark stubble. He rubbed his chin absently.

"Do you need anything?" Alannah reached to shut her laptop, "Do you–"

"Don't go to any trouble for me," he said roughly, "just let me be normal for an hour or two, got it? You've got to make your lesson. Life goes on." He straightened, paced across the room, and leaned against the hearth of the cold fireplace. His lips pressed into a thin line. He was silent.

Dutifully, Alannah tried to return to her work, and succeeded for about five minutes. She heard Jack pad over to the bookcase and slide a book from it, but she didn't look up.

"Damned if this isn't the biggest house I've ever been in," Jack said in a much more steady voice, "Alexander is loaded, isn't he?"

"Yes," Alannah said toward her keyboard, then corrected herself, "that is to say, I have no idea as to his net worth. All I know is that he is very generous with his resources." She glanced up.

"And you are what?" He scrutinized her.

"I am just his friend," Alannah said firmly and with a hint of annoyance.

"Hmm." He slipped the book into the groove where it belonged.

"Alexander is a good man, and deeply religious."

Jack glanced over his shoulder. "Are you?"

"I was raised to be."

He raised one eyebrow. "Yeah, I know what you mean." Jack sat down in one of the wingback chairs by the fireplace. "So... you teach. What does Alexander do?" He took a gulp of coffee and leaned his head against the backrest.

"He's..." Alannah realized that they'd never explained anything about immortal society to Jack. She pressed her lips together and frowned. "Well..."

Jack's dull eyes took on a little twinkle. "That complicated, eh?"

Alannah breathed a laugh. "It does take a little explanation." She closed her laptop and sat up straight. "Listen, I don't think we told you this, but there are quite a few of us. Almost four hundred."

His blasé expression didn't waver. "Okay."

"Alexander is one of the three original, most ancient of us. We call them Lords. I guess you could say that they're governors of our society."

At this, his eyes narrowed. "Society? That sounds awful cloak and dagger. Should I be scared?"

"If you're picturing robes and rituals, you'll be disappointed. The society is merely for the protection and the good of the immortals. It's—" Alannah rubbed her palms together over her laptop. "It's like a tiny, secret country. There are laws, and programs, and—"

"Taxes?" Jack rolled his eyes and took another sip of coffee. "Dang it, am I going to have to pay taxes?"

"No, no taxes. The Lords pay for all of it, and they can afford it."

"Aw, how nice of them," Jack muttered. "So, you're going to make me join?"

"Well, not make, but... Now that we know you're here, and you know we're here, we're going to watch you."

"Good luck with that," Jack said into his coffee cup. He slurped the last bit and set it down on the delicate wooden end table beside him. It quivered. "I managed to lose you for twenty-six goddamned years."

Alannah's face fell as she said, "Yes, and I'm so sorry. Alexander wanted you to have a few more normal years, and then you disappeared, and—" She looked up just in time to see him flinch.

"Normal, my ass." Jack rattled the little table again with the flat of his hand. "In the meantime, I've passed my ticking time bomb genes on to my little girl. You'd think you guys could've at least warned me. I wouldn't wish immortality on a dog, and now some of my grandbabies might turn out to be little resurrectors like me."

"I'm sorry," Alannah stared at the flat silver top of her computer.

Jack relaxed against the chair and lolled his curly head toward her. "Well, sorry doesn't fix anything, does it?"

"I guess not," she said, almost inaudible. "They'll watch her too."

Jack's forehead wrinkled. "Who will? She's my little girl. Who will watch her?"

"Umm..." The wheels in Alannah's mind began to turn. "Let me show you. Stay here."

She had a stack of file boxes in her walk-in closet, crowding her shoe rack. They were organized by year, going back to a half-empty box labeled "1935-1945". Those were the most precious pictures; they were pictures taken with the Leica camera that Papa Krueger had given her for her birthday in 1935.

She slid out the box "1970-1980" and carried it back to the library. Jack lounged in the wingback chair and regarded her with curiosity.

Alannah set the box on the floor and sat down beside it. She pulled out a photo album from the early seventies, from when she'd just arrived in Canada, and flipped through the cardboard pages until she reached the black and white photo she was looking for.

It was Daniel, sitting astride his old Triumph motorcycle, staring out at the Albertan Badlands. He held his helmet casually in front of him. The spot behind him on the motorcycle was vacant, because that was where she'd sat—all the way across the prairies, with Alexander riding ahead of them like a modern knight on a steel horse.

She felt Jack's presence as he knelt and looked over her shoulder.

"That's Daniel Gunther, one of Alexander's lawkeepers—we usually just call them keepers. The Keepers are sort of like police, and intelligence agents, and immigration officers all in one. They watch over us and make sure we're safe. They look for new immortals too."

"What's he doing in the Badlands? There are some of us there too?"

"We'd just come to Canada. We were touring the prairies."

Jack glanced at her and gave her a teasing grin. "Oh, you were, eh? What's he to you? Are you together?"

A twinge of heat blossomed in her cheeks. "We saw each other for quite some time, but that's over now."

Jack's smiled faded. "Oh."

"But he's a good friend, and he's a good man," Alannah hastened to say—hastened to defend Daniel, even though she really, really did not want to talk to Jack about him. She turned a couple more pages to a photo of Cyrus Fontaine, and his wife Idina. They couldn't have been a more opposite pair, Cy with his chocolate-brown skin and mild brown eyes, next to Idina's porcelain complexion, fiery red hair, and even hotter temper. "They're both keepers. Cyrus will probably look after you... I mean, if you join us."

Jack appeared to mull this over for a moment. "And they're all based out of where?"

"Dresden, Germany, or nearby. Schwalenburg Castle. I have a picture here somewhere..." Alannah flipped back toward the beginning of the book, but all she could come up with was a shot of her laughing into the camera—probably held by Daniel—astride a motorcycle in the castle courtyard. She sighed. She couldn't remember what they'd been doing, but she wished she could go back there again.

Jack rubbed his chin. "My Dad was from Germany. He came over when he was a kid. I guess that makes sense, if I caught this from Alexander somehow." His body drooped. "We never went back. Dad did, during the war. It messed him up pretty bad. Kinda doesn't make me want to go there."

Alannah shrugged. "You don't have to. I don't."

"Good." Jack got back into his armchair and rubbed his eyes. "I'm going to have to move on, I guess. I just—I just don't..."

"No one's asking you to make a move now," Alannah said gently, gazing up at his weary face, "you're welcome here until you're ready to go."

"Thanks," he said with a sigh.

"Alannah?" Alexander's voice came from the stairs. "Can I speak with you for a moment?"

"Yeah, just a moment," Alannah called. She glanced at Jack as she stood up. "Sorry, I'll be back. Please, um, please don't look through these."

"Yeah, sure." Jack held up both hands.

Alexander drew Alannah into his office and sat down behind his big, oaken desk. The dark circles under his eyes were almost as pronounced as Jack's. "Daniel has interviewed every known friend of Zoran's in Germany. Only two said they knew about the blog, but they didn't know who was posting. They received an anonymous email with a link. That's all." He paused. "One of them admitted that she'd talked to Marcus, but she hadn't seen him in weeks."

Alannah pressed her fingertips to her eyes. "So, now what?"

"Daniel tried to trace the email, but it only led him to an account on a library computer—it was a local library. It's someone in the area."

And you wanted me to move out of Winnipeg. A twinge of anger burned at the back of Alannah's throat. "Someone is lying."

Alexander nodded. "Daniel is going back over every letter Zoran has received, looking for any clues, but—" he threw up one hand. "God knows, maybe they aren't even connected, but I can't shake the idea that they are. It's too much of a coincidence. It's..." He glanced up. "I-I don't know why I'm telling you this. I don't want you to worry."

"Are you going back to Dresden?" Alannah asked in a small voice.

"Will you be alright? Do you trust Jack?"

"I think so." She trusted him at a distance, anyway. That was a lot more than she could say for others.

Alexander laid both hands down on the desk. "I'll book a flight for next week, and I'll cancel it if you feel uneasy. Be honest with me, Alannah."

"I will."

CHAPTER 11
Stuttgart, Germany, 1628

"Alexander!" Zoran burst into Alexander's empty classroom with a roll of parchment flapping in his hand. Icy air and a whiff of rank smoke swirled in with him. "Alexander, a letter from Adolf Hardwin in Florence, he's found a—" He skidded to a stop and swung his gaze around the room. It was a long, narrow chamber filled with hard wooden benches. There were only two high, narrow windows, and no light came through them now. Alexander sat at a plain-cut oak desk off to the side with a lantern beside him. He was wrapped in the folds of his wool cloak against the chilly November air.

"Good heavens, Zoran." Alexander stood up, banging his knees on the solid oak of his desk. He pressed his hand to his heart. "Look first, shout second. These are dangerous times!"

Zoran's black eyes sparkled in the lantern-light as he drew near. He brandished the parchment at him. "Alexander, Adolf has found another immortal—two other immortals, and one is a woman!"

"What?" Alexander snatched the letter away from him. His eyes fell on the heading: *Greetings, dear Alexander in the name of our Lord...*

"You scoundrel! You've read my letter!"

"Well," Zoran said while shrugging his shoulders, "the seal was broken, and I saw my name, and..."

"Good heavens." Alexander sighed. "Why should I bother reading it? Summarize it for me, Zoran." He laid the letter aside as if he didn't intend to read it.

Zoran practically quivered with excitement. "Forgive me, Alexander. Please read it—forgive me."

"I do. I do." Alexander sank into his chair and tilted the letter closer to the lantern. Adolf already knew that Zoran tended to read Alexander's mail. In his last letter, Adolf had offered to thrash Zoran. Good-natured Adolf, thrashing Zoran like a small child. The mental picture brought a smile to Alexander's face, which he hid behind the letter.

"Second paragraph!" Zoran bent over his shoulder.

...My careful observation has finally paid off. Last year, I began business dealings with a merchant of the city, one Giovanni Ardovinni. As I befriended him, various clues caused me to view him with suspicion, stories that did not add up to his apparent youth, and a lack of all family...

Alexander scanned through Adolf's description of how he'd befriended Ardovinni and became more and more suspicious. He could hear Zoran's breath vibrating behind him.

He glanced back. "Zoran, please."

Zoran took a miniscule step back.

Alexander's breath had begun to quicken also.

Finally, I posed the question to him and was rewarded by an affirmative answer. Not only this, but there is a woman who lives with him like a sister, one Cosima Di Gaspare. She is also immortal. They are both dear people, and have become my friends even in this short time. Young Zoran will appreciate me mentioning that Ardovinni is the great-great grandson of my second son, who moved to Italy almost two hundred years ago.

"Oh my God." Alexander pressed his cold fingers to his mouth. He held the letter away from himself, as if it carried a foul odor. "Two more! How many of us cursed souls are there?"

"Well, if there are two, there are more." Zoran folded his arms across his chest and paced across the front of the room in front of the lectern. "Relatives. Ah, why did I never think of that?" He continued muttering to himself, passing out of earshot of Alexander.

Alexander stared at Zoran's back for a moment, then at the letter.

I have informed Frederick that we will travel to Schwalenburg within six months. Will you come there also, my friend?

Ah, he wanted to. Alexander hadn't seen Adolf in nearly ten years, sweet amiable Adolf. No wonder he'd charmed his way into finding two more immortals.

"Zoran, Adolf is bringing them to Schwalenburg," Alexander said. He folded the letter and put it inside his jacket.

Zoran's back remained turned, slightly hunched.

"Zoran?"

"I never thought to wonder if I were your relative," Zoran said without turning. "Do you know if any of your family came to Bohemia?"

"No," Alexander said softly, "I know many are still near Katlenburg, but they could be anywhere by now. I suppose they could be in Bohemia."

"I'd have to return to Prague." Zoran paced toward the door. "I don't care to, at the moment. It will have to keep."

They fell silent, and in the interim rain began a faint tinkle against the two narrow windows. Alexander shivered and pulled the folds of his cloak he'd tossed aside when he'd stood up back around him. "Will you go up to Dresden with me?"

"Of course." Zoran turned around. His eyes sagged down at the corners. "There were two witches burned today. Did you know it?"

Alexander nodded. "I did. The lads were talking of it this morning."

"That's the smell in the air." Zoran clapped his hands softly together and tilted his head back toward the windows. "One of them was a young woman, practically a child. Blond, and blue eyed."

"Good heavens. You watched?"

Zoran eyed him. "I've seen most of them. What if one of them doesn't burn up?"

"Zoran!"

"Well, what if they don't?" Zoran jabbed one hand toward him. "Who better to be suspected of witchcraft than a woman who seems a little too young? What if one of them should have died and didn't? These days, that person would be sent straight to the torturer and sentenced to death on witchcraft."

"Yes, and—"

"Which is why you stay in here. Agh!" Zoran crossed his arms across his chest and kicked at the paving stones beneath him. "Come home, Alexander. It's just as cold in this classroom as it is out there, and I can see that you aren't actually studying anymore."

"No, I'm not." Alexander looked up at him, bleary eyed, and smiled. "My young students are scared. You would be ashamed of them, Zoran, not asking any vexing questions, barely making a peep."

"These are mad times." Zoran held out his hands. "Come home, Alexander."

"Fine. I am coming." Alexander stood and tucked the letter inside his jacket.

One step out the door, and sleet drove into their faces. Alexander threw his cloak up around his head and leaned into the wind howling down the narrow channel of walls.

After ten minutes of walking, they broke out of the confines of the houses, into a flagstone-paved square. Alexander paused. He could just make out the shadowy outline of two charred stakes, surrounded by low heaps of ashes. He tasted bile, turned his head, and walked on.

"Wait a moment." Zoran laid a hand on his shoulder, bringing him to a stop. He wandered closer to the stakes, glancing down at them.

"What are you doing?" Alexander hissed. He glanced around the shadowy square but no one was lurking in the darkness. The ashes had been abandoned to the elements for the night.

Suddenly Zoran dropped to his knees next to one of the heaps of ash.

"Zoran!" Alexander's heart hammered. What was the man doing? If he was seen digging in the ash!

Zoran's hand went out, into the ashes. He yelped a little and wrapped something in the folds of his cloak.

"Zoran!"

Zoran slipped back to his side and motioned for him to walk on. He wiped at his dripping face with his free hand. "I found something." He opened one fold of his cloak, but all Alexander saw was the faint gleam of silver.

"You are mad, Zoran. Mad."

Zoran ignored him, and steered him around the corner. They walked in silence up to their doorstep.

The still air inside their house was cold, but felt warm compared to the sleet. Zoran knelt beside the cold hearth and set to work sparking a fire while Alexander shook out his cloak and lit a lantern.

"Now, what the devil did you take from the fire?" Alexander turned on Zoran.

Zoran set back on his heels and extended his hand toward Alexander. A silver chain dangled from his fingers, and something glassy gleamed in his palm. "It was still hot."

Alexander picked it up and held it to the lantern. It was a little glass vial, long and narrow like a lily petal and enfolded in intricate vines of silver.

"Is there anything in it?" Zoran placed a gnarled chunk of wood on the fire and turned to Alexander.

Alexander flipped it over. There had been likely been a little cork stopper in it, but it was gone now. He held the opening to his eye. It was filled with flecks of ash, and a dark stain. "Is that blood?"

Zoran held out his hand, and Alexander gave the vial over.

"I don't think..." Zoran squinted into the opening. "Oh, good heavens, it likely is. Perhaps the woman was a witch after all. That's probably why they burnt it with her."

"Throw it out."

"It won't burn." Zoran's lip curled. "No, I'll keep it. I don't care if the devil lives in it."

"Oh goodness, Zoran."

Zoran hung the chain around his neck and returned to tending the fire.

∞

"Alexander, welcome. Welcome, Zoran." Frederick von Schwalenburg stood at the entry of his personal chambers, the faintest semblance of a smile on his narrow face. He gazed at them with eyes as pale as a winter sky. "Adolf is within with Master Ardovinni, and our lady will arrive shortly."

Alexander held out his hand, and Frederick gripped it fervently.

"Welcome," Frederick whispered again. "Ten years is too long, my friend."

They walked together into the wide chamber beyond the door. Light spilled in white lines from the high, slit windows just above the entry. It formed bars of white and black, like an ethereal portcullis. Alexander stepped carefully over it, and gazed around the room. A fire leapt and danced upon the hearth, for though it was a warm spring day, the chill had yet to completely leave the thick stone of Schwalenburg Castle. Two men sat by the fire on padded settees. Their conversation paused. One of them, with light brown hair hanging in curls to his shoulders, and a moustache of the same hue, turned around and smiled brilliantly. "Good day, Alexander, young Zoran."

Zoran, approaching his one hundred and sixth birthday, grinned and doffed his wide hat, with its stylish ostrich plume. Alexander, bare-headed, smiled and said, "Adolf, it is so good to see you."

Adolf Hardwin stood and embraced him. "You look well."

"As do you."

Adolf gripped him tightly. "Come meet Ardovinni, and soon, our Miss di Gaspare." He leaned in close and added, "Frederick has his eye on her."

"Hah!" Alexander burst out, louder than he meant to, and Adolf laughed.

"Come." He swung Alexander around by the elbow. "Alexander, may I present Master Giovanni Ardovinni of Florence."

Ardovinni stood and extended his hand. His dark head just reached past tall Adolf's shoulder. His deep brown eyes stared into Alexander's without flinching. "A pleasure, Sir," his voice was soft, musical, with a faint steel edge.

∞   ∞   ∞

"He's enormously wealthy," Zoran said as the coach rattled up the road toward Dresden.

"What, did you write Adolf?" Alexander asked.

"You didn't?" Zoran stopped peering out the smoky glass window and turned toward him. "I thought maybe you'd be interested in the lady."

"Of course not!" But how could Zoran know that? Alexander had never told him of the sacred dreams he dreamt, of being with Idonia again.

"Well, then, let us leave her to the other men."

"Let them ply their charms on her," Alexander replied stoutly, "I have no plans."

"Pfah!" was Zoran's reply.

∞   ∞   ∞

A soft knock sounded at the door. Adolf and Ardovinni turned toward the door, and Alexander did so slowly.

Von Schwalenburg cleared his throat and said, "Sirs, may I present to you Cosima Di Gaspare."

She swept in, and paused in the doorway. Her deep crimson skirts filled the space around her, and her dark head was bent, momentarily occupied by safely passing them through the door. For a moment all Alexander could see were her silky curls, cascading in ringlets down her neck. Then she raised her head, smiled hesitantly, her lips poised to greet them. She lifted her eyes and met Alexander's.

Alexander found himself arrested in her gaze, the deepest ebony pools. She smiled. He could almost hear her say, "I see you, Alexander von Katlenburg."

Alexander blinked, and glanced away. When he looked back, she was already approaching, and the men were coming forward to greet her.

Adolf Hardwin drew Cosima into their circle. "Miss Di Gaspare, allow me to introduce you to these two men. This is Zoran Kosar."

Zoran smiled and bent over to kiss her hand.

"And my good friend, Alexander von Katlenburg," Adolf said.

Alexander bent over her hand, all thought of speech stolen away.

"A pleasure," Cosima said, her voice musical in its Italian accent. She looked up at him, found him still speechless, and a little grin played across her full lips. She moved on.

A gentle cuff rattled his head. Alexander gasped, and found Zoran grinning at him. Zoran shook his head ever so slightly and rolled his eyes.

∞

"We did not speak of the witch hunts nearly as much as I wanted," Zoran said as they walked along the silent corridor toward Alexander's chamber. The torches on the walls cast flickering light across his face. His expression was nearly impossible to read, but Alexander thought he saw amusement in his eyes. *Now* what amused him?

"Indeed," Alexander said. He pushed the door open and entered his apartment. He was incredibly weary from avoiding the gaze of Cosima Di Gaspare. Why did she seem to be watching him every time he looked her way? Did she find something offensive in him that she should peer at him like she was parting bone and marrow to look into his thoughts?

And worse, where had this ache of *wanting* come from?

Doggedly, Zoran followed after him. Alexander paused before the fire, which must have been recently stoked by a servant for it burned brilliantly in the small grate.

"If Adolf would marry her, what if they should have children?"

A great jolt went through his chest, but he said calmly, "Why do you ask that? Indeed, what if they should?"

Zoran raised a brow. "I've always wondered. I suppose we've never had cause to ask this."

Alexander sat down on the ornately carved wooden bench by the fire and leaned his head against the cool, stone, wall. "I have had cause to ask that, Zoran, I do assure you. It is only now that we have cause to fear it. Now that we have..." he trailed off.

"Fear it! No, I did not say to fear it, I only wished to know what our course of action would be." Zoran perched across from him on an upholstered chair. "I suppose if there is any mortal we can trust to keep our secrets, it should be our child. I think we shouldn't fear, not in that aspect. Only that they should almost certainly perish long before us, but for if the Lord should return."

"You've never had a child, or you would fear exactly that."

"I would risk it," Zoran said stoutly.

"I doubt Adolf would." Alexander lifted his head, and surveyed Zoran. Zoran, played with his hat, pulling the ostrich plume through his circled fingers over, and over. "But you shall have to hunt, and hope there are other immortal women, if you wish to have progeny."

"Progeny," Zoran mocked, "what a horrible word, how academic. Children. I would like to have children." He paused, "I don't suppose we could just immortalize them?"

"Certainly not."

And Zoran, who knew very well what Alexander thought of immortality, did not argue this time. There was a long, pregnant pause before Zoran said, softer, "I shall hunt, I suppose, but I am not yet ready to marry and tie myself to a family. That is why I have no intentions to pursue our immortal lady, not when there are older and more deserving men before her. But children, Alexander, why not have children, even mortal ones?"

"Because I have stood before the graves of my mortal children…" Alexander sighed, "and the only pain greater than parting with them in death was parting with them when they had so much life yet in front of them." He got up, and pointed his feet toward his bedchamber in the hopes that Zoran would take the hint and depart. "But," he added, "I would also not disapprove of Adolf's marriage, not when so much happiness, companionship, and mutual encouragement should come from it. She is a good, pious—"

Zoran burst out laughing. "Listen to you! Was piety and companionship what passed through your mind when Miss Di Gaspare put her pretty hand in yours?"

No, it certainly hadn't.

Upon his refusal to reply, Zoran sneered. "You are such a good, suffering servant, Alexander. If there were any time for me to impart optimism, let it be now! For all the other men shall pursue her, except perhaps Ardovinni, whom I suspect may prefer the sort of love as between Achilles and Patroclus—"

"Slander not, Zoran." Alexander held up his hand. "Whatever gave you that idea?"

"Oh I've seen a few things. For instance, he has lived with the lovely Miss di Gaspare for ten years and not married her." Zoran rose, his face twisted in playful annoyance. "Very well. I'd hoped to regale you with further stories, but it seems you are not well tonight. I will see you in the morning."

Alexander retired to his bedroom, but felt no relief at Zoran's going. He knelt beside the bed. The stone floor bit into his knees, but even this couldn't erase the limpid eyes, and silken curls of Cosima Di Gaspare from his mind.

∞

The instant Alexander stepped out of the school door, away from the happy noise of the youths within, and down into the street, he felt a strange prickle of unrest. He stood for a moment, listening, wondering what this feeling of foreboding was. The shops along the narrow street had a few customers. A man marched by, pulling a handcart with bundles of cloth upon it. A strong whiff of smoke, mixed with roasting meat, and mingled with the faint stench animal dung rose up to greet him. Everything seemed aright.

But in six months in Dresden, Alexander had never quite relaxed, nor felt at home.

He tucked his satchel of books a little tighter under his arm, and sauntered into the street toward home. The diminishing evening sun peeked over the tops of the tightly packed buildings, warming the back of his neck.

Subconsciously he listened. The feeling had not abated.

The road turned upward in a long hill. As Alexander started up it, he heard the clash of angry voices. Bystanders glanced about with wide eyes and drew off the path. When he'd travelled another few yards, a crowd crested the hill ahead him.

They were armed with every sort of makeshift weapon—sticks, hay-forks, spades, iron pokers and long knives. They dragged, in their midst, a young woman. One of her sleeves was torn nearly completely from her dress, and the bodice had a large and immodest rent in it. Her blond hair flew about her in disarray, and her eyes were wide with terror. Alexander heard among the angry clamor, 'Witch!'

They were almost upon him. Alexander, scarcely thinking, cried out, "What is the meaning of this?"

The crowd paused before breaking upon him.

"What is the meaning of this?" Alexander shouted louder, emboldened.

One ruffian, in soiled and patched clothes of a workman, took in Alexander's scholarly dress. "Sir, this woman is a witch! If you are a man of God, you will join us."

"Is this so?" Alexander turned and stared at the trembling young woman.

She made no reply.

"Is this so?" he boomed.

She jumped, and shook her head violently. Her face was salt-streaked with dried tears.

The crowd broke into raucous disagreement with her. They gathered themselves up as if they would rush past Alexander, and no doubt toward their murderous destination.

Anger surged in his breast. "Stop!" Alexander held up both hands. "What is the evidence of her witchcraft?"

Their voices were so numerous and discordant that Alexander could not make out any of the words.

"One at a time, good people!"

One of the men gripping the prisoner spoke up. "Sir, two days ago three houses were razed to the ground by a fire, and all within perished, except this woman who we found unharmed among the ashes. She started the fire knowing her witchcraft would save her!"

Tingles skittered down Alexander's spine. He was frozen for a moment.

Coincidence.

Or...?

Do something!

"Be that as it may!" Alexander cried out, with all the volume he could muster, "Do you not have wise magistrates among you who can hear your case? This woman, witch or no, is the daughter of a loving mother and father. Can we call ourselves followers of Christ if we do not give her a just hearing? If you have a case, then make it, but take her before the officials, and whom we submit to according to the Holy Scriptures. If you fear God, then you shall have no cause to fear this woman, witch or no." He pushed his way past the crowd's spokesperson, and seized the young woman by the arm. With his free hand, he unclasped his jacket and wrapped it around her, covering her bare shoulder and exposed skin.

Alexander realized he was shaking with wrath. Out of the corner of his eye, he saw two soldiers of the city standing off to the side, eyeing them. Emboldened, he pulled the woman out of the crowd. "As it is, I shall take her from you. You have punished her quite enough. Disperse, I charge you in the name of God."

The faces around him were more than disgruntled. They were murderous. The two soldiers stepped forward. Their weapons remained sheathed, but they fingered the handles and reached for him and the young woman as if to whisk her off before anything further could transpire.

"Awww, sir—" the spokesman began. He was poised on the balls of his feet, and his eyes darted toward the two soldiers. The crowd clamored around him again. Alexander saw some of them with stones in their hands.

"People," Alexander said, "disperse peacefully. I charge you, by heaven. Do not spill blood for sport, or out of fear. Trust God!"

The man dropped into a flat-footed stance. "Alright, but if I set eyes on her again, I swear by heaven and earth, the city shall have one less witch."

Two or three of the crowd dropped their stones to the pavement, and in duos and trios, they walked away.

Alexander looked up to the soldiers, nodded to them, and together they hurried the young woman up the street, away from her assailants.

"What shall we do with her, Professor?" One of the soldiers asked, taking in Alexander's scholarly dress.

"I sincerely doubt that she is a witch." Alexander surveyed the shivering young lady. "There is a deacon nearby. I will take her there, and let his wife care for her, for Satan shall quake in their presence."

He turned the young woman down a narrow side street, away from the soldiers. Beneath his grip, her arm was trembling. The wind blasted down on them, but even coatless, Alexander did not feel cold. He'd begun to feel the rapid pound of his heart and the cool breeze on his flushed cheeks. What had come over him? He was quite far removed from his more martial days. Yet flinging himself into the fray had felt right. He'd been itching for battle.

He indeed did lead her toward the deacon's house. The deacon's home, whose son he had taught, would be a safe place for the girl if she were just an ordinary, unfortunate wretch. But first...

Alexander halted her and pulled her into the shelter of a doorway. He turned her around and gazed into her tear-streaked face. Her lips pressed into a firm line and her brows drew together tightly over her button nose. Her sky-blue eyes darted around, as if searching for an escape route.

"Well?" Alexander said gently, "what is your name, miss?"

She sniffled, gulped, and said toward her feet, "Sophia Karlstan, Sir."

This name pinged in the recesses of his mind and settled down in his memory. Karlstan. His own name.

"And, how did you escape death in the fire?"

She met his eyes then. Her forehead creased deeply. "I don't know."

"But what happened?" Alexander prodded gently.

"I-I don't know. I was trapped by a falling beam and choked upon the smoke until senseless. Next I knew, I awoke, and it was morning and cold, and I was perfectly well."

He couldn't say for sure, but it seemed death had spit her out—she'd rebounded, as Zoran would say. Alexander said, "God preserved you."

"Yes," she said with little emotion. She blinked, and looked down again.

"Did your family perish in the fire?"

She shook her head. "I was rooming there, for I have no family. Sir—" she said quickly, earnestly, "I do thank you for saving me from the mob, but from hearing my story, do you not think I am a witch?"

"No," Alexander said.

A great gust of wind blew past them, throwing up dust in their faces and passing right through Alexander's thin doublet, chilling his skin. He planted his hand against the brick wall next to him, pondering how to continue.

Sophia pulled his jacket tighter around her shoulders and looked up expectantly. Tears streaked down her cheeks again.

"Forgive me." Alexander shook himself. "We are not far now. Let's walk on." He took her elbow again and led her out of the doorway. The sun had dropped behind Dresden's roofline. "Tell me, has this happened before?"

"What?" he felt her jerk.

"Has it happened before, Miss Karlstan?"

"No." Her shoulders hunched. Alexander glanced over and saw her whole face drawn into a deep frown. He could sense the great rush of thoughts through her head.

"Why do you ask me that?" she said in a low voice. She stopped in place and wrenched her arm from his grasp. Her slight form poised, like she would take flight down the narrow street.

Alexander felt his heartbeat pick up. He glanced up and down the street. The only other occupant was a woman, sweeping her front stoop. She was well out of earshot. "Because," he said slowly, "I have... heard of similar experiences."

She blinked, but she said nothing.

Alexander peered at her with interest that would have been indecent in any other scenario—taking in her apple blossom skin, smattered with freckles. She had a fresh, girlish face that was pleasant, if not beautiful. Somehow, his mind made itself up.

He gently propelled her into motion, his mind whirling. He couldn't bring her to the deacon's house now, but Schwalenburg was too distant for him to take her, with her clothes torn, weary, perhaps taken directly from the smoldering ruins of the burnt house. There certainly was a strong whiff of smoke to her.

Giovanni Ardovinni's house wasn't far. Alexander had yet to know him well, but he was an immortal, and an ally.

"Come this way," he said.

By the time they'd reached the right street, the sun had sunk behind the rooflines and Alexander felt his lack of jacket. Ardovinni's house was a yellow-brick building recessed slightly from the street, with two stone lions guarding the wrought iron gate. Alexander pushed the gate open and ushered Miss Karlstan through.

The servant who opened the door, stared wide-eyed at Miss Karlstan for an instant before gaining his composure.

"Is Master Ardovinni in? We are in need of assistance," Alexander said. His teeth began to chatter.

The young man's eyes widened again. "No Sir, but Miss Ardovinni is at home." He glanced behind him. "Who shall I say..."

"Alexander von Katlenburg." Alexander stepped forward, pushing Miss Karlstan. "Please, it is cold."

"It's alright, let them in," a musical voice carried down the stairs behind the servant. Deep purple skirts appeared on the landing, and a moment later Cosima Di Gaspare descended. Her dark eyes settled on Miss Karlstan, widened, then found Alexander's. "Oh dear," she said. She hurried toward them. "Master Alexander, what has happened?"

Alexander found his voice had vanished.

Cosima looked up into his face, then grasped Miss Karlstan's shoulders. "How cold you look, my dear. Has there been an accident?"

Miss Karlstan gained command of herself. "In a manner of speaking." She glanced at Alexander with confusion in her eyes, and a clear demand for an explanation.

"Umm, Miss Ardovinni, this is Miss Sophia Karlstan," Alexander choked out, "I believe she is the newest member of our number."

Cosima's eyebrows rose. "Oh! You are most welcome, Miss Karlstan."

"Miss... Ardovinni is as you are," he said gently to Miss Karlstan. "As am I. We have escaped death, and time."

"Prove this," she said immediately, wrenching herself from Cosima's hands. "Sir, I have escaped far too much trouble today to be trifled with."

"I cannot prove it," Cosima spoke before he could, "not without great harm to myself. What I will tell you is that I am seventy years old, but since I was a young woman I have ceased to age. I have felt what it means to slide down the chute of death, only to find it a loop that spits me out exactly where I began. I am as best we can tell, immortal."

Tears streaked down Miss Karlstan's dirty cheeks. "How horrible. How-how—"

"How old are you, dear?" Cosima asked gently.

Sophia sniffled. "I am seventy also."

Cosima gathered her into her arms, torn dress, borrowed coat and all. "Now, at least, you are not alone."

∞

It was very late. Alexander sat alone in Cosima's drawing room. He heard the door, across the house, open and boots clatter on the marble tiles in the entry.

The servant must have greeted the door, for Alexander heard two voices conversing in quiet Italian.

"Alexander." Ardovinni appeared at the drawing room door and bowed slightly. He was dressed in dusty travelling clothes. His boots were spattered with mud, and his dark hair gleamed damp in the light of the wall-sconces. "I trust you have been given all manner of hospitality? If not, I shall swiftly put it to rights."

Alexander gestured to the remains of the tea-tray sitting on the ornate little table beside him. "I have been well cared for. Thank you."

Ardovinni nodded stiffly. "Excuse me a moment." He backed out of the doorway, and a moment later his light footfalls ascended the stairs.

Alexander began to doze.

"Master Alexander," a gently amused voice brought him to.

Alexander lifted his head, and jumped to his feet. Cosima stood before him, smiling. Her ebony eyes were agleam by the candlelight.

She seated herself across from him. "Please, make yourself comfortable again, Sir. I was nearly loath to disturb you."

Alexander sat, though without slouching as he had before. "How is she?"

"Resting." Cosima sighed. "I was able to question her a great deal more, as only one woman to another can. You are right, of that I am sure. She is one of us." Her eyes rested on him, unblinking, shining with a light he couldn't place. "She told me what you did for her."

Alexander was torn between dropping his eyes in modesty, and wishing to stay forever with her eyes on him like that. He felt like strength was transferring from her gaze, into him.

Instead, it was she who looked away. "She is your relative. Giovanni is willing that she stay with us for a few days while she recovers, but he looks to you for your opinion."

"Relative?" Alexander gasped.

"She is a Karlstan," Cosima said simply.

True. It was, at least, a thin thread of connection. "A-and Miss Karlstan? What does she say? Does she wish to stay?"

"She consents."

"Then I suppose I could have no objection." Alexander leaned back in the chair. Relative? What could that mean for him? Certainly, he could offer his protection, in a way, though he was but a single professor of theology, who currently only rented a house and owned no land. "What shall I do?" He breathed, not meaning to say it out loud.

"Do?" Cosima said, gently.

Alexander glanced up. Heat suffused his face. "I have money. I can provide for her. If she is my relative, I must care for her, but..."

"Ohhh..." Cosima sighed. "Truly, Sir, though she will need protection, she is her own woman. She has made it this far. Give her credit. But—" she held up her hand to stop him from responding "—if you are asking me as the only other known, unmarried, immortal woman, perhaps an arrangement like mine and Giovanni's should suffice. He is like a brother to me, and so we act as if that is what we are."

Ah.

"But it is late." She slapped her armrests lightly. "I have had a servant make up a room. You are weary. It is all over your face. Do not refuse our hospitality, or you shall offend two Italians."

Alexander laughed helplessly, his mind still whirling. "Very well, and thank you."

∞

"Your relative?" Zoran's eyes lit up. He leapt out of his seat by the window and paced past Alexander's desk.

Alexander crossed his arms behind his head and leaned back against them. He watched Zoran, the myriad expressions passing rapidly across his face, his hand grasping at his dark curls, the other occasionally making a small gesture like he was about to speak.

He paused in the small rectangle of sunlight, which fell through the high, slit window in Schwalenburg's wall. "Did she drink of the fountain? Did you ask?"

"No, it was hardly the place."

Zoran resumed motion again, hunching over. His black brows drew together, on either side of a deep crease in his forehead. "I have a theory," he said.

Alexander did not ask "What is your theory?" for he knew Zoran would tell him.

"What if, " Zoran said, raising one finger and turning slowly to face him, "once a body has drunk from the fountain, the water flows in his blood and, therefore, when he produces—what is your word, Alexander?— *progeny*, the water flows in their blood as well."

"But none of my *progeny* were immortal, Zoran." Alexander raised an eyebrow.

"Well, that is difficult." Zoran caught his bottom lip between his teeth. He stood in the sunlit spot again. The light cast weird shadows over his face, and threw his obsidian-black eyes completely into shade. "But here is Miss Karlstan, who with a little effort, we could prove to be your relative. And Ardovinni has traced his ancestry back to Adolf Hardwin. Indeed, he said so himself when I interviewed both him and Miss Di Gaspare. I wanted," he continued at Alexander's incredulous look, "to know if they had drunk from the fountain. They had not, to their knowledge. Of course, there could be other fountains," he mused toward the floor. "In my mind it is either that, or that it is somehow passed from generation to generation."

"How terrible!" Alexander stared at him in horror. "To think I may have condemned my offspring to this fate."

For once, Zoran did not contradict his use of the word 'condemn'. He shrugged. "I shall continue to search. May I interview Miss Karlstan?" he asked, hopefully.

"Give her time to rest and collect herself," Alexander said. Miss Karlstan still stayed at Ardovinni's house, where she and Cosima had become fast friends.

Zoran barely seemed to hear him. He stood, in the shaft of light, rubbing his palms slowly together, deep in thought. "By bloodline," he said slowly.

CHAPTER 12

Winnipeg, Present Day

"Are you going outside?" Jack asked.

Alannah paused in the doorway and glanced back at Jack. Her coffee-colored curls spilled out from under her cherry-red beret and framed her wry smile. "No, I only put on my coat to complete my outfit."

"Could you bring me a newspaper?" Jack jammed his hand in his pocket and pulled out a handful of change.

"It should be at the end of the driveway," she said with a smile. "Just a moment. I'll bring it to you."

A couple minutes later, she poked her head back into the entry and tossed him the newspaper, rolled up in a plastic bag. "Cheers," she said, and shut the door.

Jack carried the newspaper up to his bedroom and spread it out on the bed. He rifled through it until he found the obituaries.

There she was. It was one of the photos he had in his wallet: Mary Rose and Clarissa in big sun hats, on the beach at Bird's Hill. Their blond curls mingled in the breeze and they were identically pink-cheeked, laughing. Jack's throat closed as he ran his finger down the text to where it said, 'predeceased by her beloved husband, Jakob (Jack) Krause'. Underneath, the date and time of the funeral.

"Are you leaving us?" Alannah's face appeared in the kitchen door. She raised her eyebrows and smiled hesitantly.

"No, uh... I need to get some proper clothes for the funeral," Jack said. He gripped the door handle a little tighter, one foot already on the front step.

"Okay." She came all the way out of the kitchen, into the hall. "Umm... would it be okay if I accompanied you to the funeral?"

"Uh..."

She frowned thoughtfully. "I could be part of your disguise, or something. I just... I just don't want to send you alone. It doesn't seem right."

No, it didn't seem right. But Jack had planned to get a bottle of whiskey afterward and enough painkillers to take him out for a good, long time. It was the cleanest way he could think to do himself in. He was a guest, after all.

When he didn't reply, she tilted her head to the side and scrutinized him.

Jack sighed. "Did Alexander put you up to this?"

Alannah smiled and shook her head. "No, that isn't his style. Alexander is much better at giving people their space."

Jack pictured walking in with her just slightly ahead of him, just in case any of his family was there. She was a relatively attractive woman. Maybe she would draw some of the attention, lest his recent beard not be enough of a disguise.

"Alright," he said, "you may... accompany me."

He hadn't actually planned to buy new clothes, but he drove past the liquor store to the men's clothing store and bought a new suit. Then he went back to the liquor store and bought a bottle of Jim Beam.

The next morning, they drove to the church in Alannah's ten-year-old BMW. "Alexander's hand-me-down?" Jack asked with a weary attempt at a smile.

"No," she said. "It's mine, fair and clear. I really wish you'd stop making those sorts of remarks."

Jack pressed his lips together and made no reply. Every bit of him wanted to force her to spin the car around and head out of town. He didn't want to see Mary Rose's body lying in a box. He didn't want to see Clarissa, the living image of Mary Rose, with his eyes to remind him that she was his even though she didn't know it, or remember much of him.

Alannah laid a hand on his wrist, between the sleeve of his coat and his leather glove. Her fingers were cold.

They were just on time to slip into the back pew before the funeral started. Jack pulled off his gloves and stared at his hands. That same picture from the obituary was in a gold frame at the front of the church, the one with Mary Rose and Clarissa, grinning under their beach hats.

"Jack," Alannah whispered. She gripped his elbow. Everyone stood, and she brought him with her. Six pall bearers stepped through the double doors, and there was the golden oak casket, wheeled along on a shiny metal cart. The box was far too big for Mary Rose's tiny frame. Jack choked and looked away for an instant. But he had to look back, and he steeled his spine.

That's not you. That's not you. You've gone to heaven and left me here.

Clarissa walked in on June's arm. Jack couldn't breath as she passed by him with her eyes on the casket. She'd pulled her blond hair back in a severe bun, and the dark circles under her eyes mirrored the ones he'd worn for months now.

My little girl.

Jack choked, but he did not cry. His tears felt frozen, somewhere deep in his chest. If he was in the front with the family, he could have been the grieving husband he was. But he was in the back, an observer.

He didn't hear the sermon, or the eulogies. Not really. He came out of his stupor for a moment when Alannah pressed two tissues into his hand. He automatically reached to swipe at his eyes, but his eyes were dry.

He wanted an empty room, and a bottle, and a gun.

They bolted the moment the family procession disappeared through the double doors and the funeral director motioned that everyone could file after them. Jack yanked the BMW's door open and slunk down in the seat.

"Are we going to the burial?" Alannah asked softly as she slid into the driver's seat. Her hand hesitated on the door without closing it.

"No." Jack squeezed his burning eyes shut. He couldn't take this anymore. He didn't want to see her body put in the ground. He wanted to hurt himself, in privacy.

But he couldn't, could he?

Alannah swung the driver door shut and let out a long, controlled breath. She turned to look at him. "Let's drive around for a bit," she said.

By the time they ended up in a Starbucks across the city, his tears had frozen in their ducts, and a tired sort of calm had come over him. His pulse throbbed behind his eyes like a bass drum as he stood behind Alannah, staring at the menu full of fancy coffee.

"Black coffee?" Alannah glanced back and smiled at him. Her eyes were bloodshot too.

"Yeah."

"Okay. Go sit. I'll get it."

She sat down a few minutes later and set a paper cup in front of him. Eyes shut, she breathed in the steam from her cup and smiled. "I think they spray coffee-scented room spray in here. I need to get some of that."

Jack eyed his coffee warily, but it seemed to be plain and black like he always took it. "What's that?"

"A caramel macchiato."

"A what?"

"Coffee mixed with copious amounts of sugar and milk. I probably gain five pounds every time I drink one but..." she sighed, "the day seemed to call for it."

"Does it have alcohol in it?"

"No." Alannah propped her chin on her hand and tipped the cup to take a sip. Foam dribbled down her cheek. She swiped at it. "I'm more of a comfort food person."

"That's okay, I guess."

"You've never been in a Starbucks?" Alannah asked. "I hadn't either, until a couple years ago. You know, every few years I have to reevaluate what a thirty-something, single, female college professor should be doing. Starbucks seemed like a good place to start." She waved her drink. "I'm putting off acting like the little old lady I am."

Jack passed his hand over his face and slumped down a little. "I guess I'm well on my way to being a crotchety old man," he said wearily.

"Hah." She poked her cup in his direction. "You're probably the youngest of the immortals, Jack. Don't start whining about being old until you're at least two hundred... or so Cyrus tells me."

"Well... damn."

Her dark eyes came up to meet his. "That sounded pretty insensitive given... given the circumstances. I'm really sorry, Jack."

She seemed to give up on polite conversation then, and set to sipping her macchiato with greater speed. Jack pressed the heel of his hand against his forehead and shut his burning eyes.

"Headache?" she asked softly.

He nodded.

"I have pills in the car."

"I should just buy my own," he muttered into his hand, "headaches may be par for the course for the next few days." Depending on if he broke down and used the gun or not. Jack dropped his hand. "I keep thinking 'now what?' I mean, what the hell am I supposed to do? She's been my existence for more than thirty years. We-we weren't together much."

"Clarissa doesn't know you're alive?"

"No. We thought it was best, and... and we did rethink it at one point, but it seemed a little late then." It had been Mary Rose who had fought for Clarissa to know her Daddy, and knowing his drinking, self-destructive self, he'd fought equally hard to keep his little girl in the dark. When he'd gotten clean, it really had been too late. "She don't need me. She's got a house that's all paid for, and a tidy sum in trust for her. She's got Mary Rose's family to take care of her, and June, who has practically been a second mom. She's a smart girl. She'll be alright." He looked up. "But what about me?"

Alannah reached out and touched his hand, but Jack pulled away. His voice trembled, and tears began to prickle behind his eyelids. He fought to hold them back. "On the night she died, she begged me not to hurt myself any more. But I'm not that strong."

She bit her lip. "No judgment here, Jack. I've never hurt myself in that way, but I've done some stupid things. Still living in Winnipeg after forty years is one of them. But..." she blew out a breath, "but I can't seem to leave. I feel safe here, and the world is a big scary place."

"A damned howling wilderness," Jack said.

∞

"Jack. Jack!"

Jack jogged himself awake. The car was lit only by the streetlights. They were parked in Alexander's driveway.

"Jack!" Alannah hissed. "The door is open."

"Hmm?"

Alannah grabbed his wrist. "The front door is open!"

Jack sat up straight and peered at the oak front door. It stood open about six inches. "Is Alexander home?"

"No. He's-he's away on business." Alannah's voice rose higher.

"I think I came out of the front door when we left." Jack tried to recall the first few hours of the day, but it all swam together. He pushed the car door open and stood up. The icy breeze ruffled his hair and blew through his open jacket and thin dress shirt. The door wobbled in the wind. "Stay here."

The door turned soundlessly on its hinges. The foyer light was on, but the rest of the house was completely dark. He listened. It was silent.

Jack flicked on the hall light and circled through the kitchen, where he pulled a chef's knife out of the block. He eased the pantry door open and stood back. Silence. Just the throb of his own pulse in his ears.

His dress shoes made no sound on the carpet stairs as he ascended to the second floor. He narrowed his eyes at each door, all shut. He dropped the knife on his bed and pulled the suitcase from underneath. He slipped the gun out and popped a magazine into it.

Jack took a deep breath, and stepped out into the hall.

A search of each bedroom proved fruitless. At the door of the Library he paused and felt for the light switch. And as he did, he heard a low moan inside.

Prickles skittered up the back of his neck. It came again, a deep, ghostly sigh. Jack raised the gun and flicked on the light.

Nothing. The stuffed chairs stood side by side. The books were in perfect order. Jack stared at the fireplace a moment, until he heard the moan again.

He laughed under his breath. It was just the wind.

He left every single light in the house shining, and jogged out to relieve Alannah's fears. He slipped the pistol into his waistband and tossed his jacket back over it. "Alannah?" he called as he turned the corner.

She didn't reply.

"Alannah? The house is..." he trailed off as he came up to the car.

Alannah had her phone pressed to her ear, and was sobbing into it. "Alex, but-but..."

He heard Alexander's voice barely audible. "Alannah. Alannah, shhh. Listen." Even through the tinny phone speaker, Jack could hear the calm, soothing tone. "Zoran is in prison. I saw him there only a couple months ago. He can't hurt you again. He's in prison."

"But... But..." Alannah pressed her hand against her chest and seemed to try to reign herself in.

"Call Cyrus if you want to. He can tell you. Zoran is in Schwalenburg..." There was a long pause. "Is Jack there with you?"

"He's checking the house."

"Alannah," Jack whispered.

Her head spun toward him and he saw her white face. The phone bounced out of her hand onto the floor.

"Alannah?" Alexander's voice came from under the seat of the car.

Alannah drove for it, came up clutching the phone, and pressed it to her ear, gasping out, "No, no I'm here. Jack's here."

"The house is fine," Jack said. "Maybe I just left the door open, because I didn't see anything amiss."

She sucked in a deep breath. "Did you hear that, Alex?"

His reply was garbled, but sounded like an affirmative.

"Okay. I guess—I guess I'll go."

She tapped the screen to end the call, and turned to look up at Jack. Tears shone in bright streaks on her face, illuminated by the interior light of the car.

"It's okay, Alannah," Jack said gently.

"Yeah." She shoved the car door closed and followed him into the house.

When Jack had turned the deadbolt on the front door, he glanced at her. "I'm going to change, otherwise I'll stick around. Okay?"

She nodded without making eye contact and pulled a tissue from her coat pocket. "I probably overreacted. I'm sorry."

"Don't be."

Jack slipped upstairs to his bedroom. As he unbuttoned his dress shirt, he stared at the kitchen knife. It glared up at him, bright silver. Oddly enough, he didn't feel like using it, or the gun pressed against his back. But once the adrenaline receded, it was likely that the day would wash in again: Clarissa's pale face, and the big wooden box for Mary Rose's petite body. It would crush him to remember.

Be good to yourself, Jack.

I will.

Jack pulled on his jeans and flannel shirt. He opened the drawer of the bedside table and pulled out the amber bottle of whiskey. He paused and placed the knife inside.

When he padded down the stairs in his sock feet, Alannah was sitting at the table in the kitchen with her head pillowed on one hand, a sheaf of small papers clutched in the other. When Jack got a little closer, he realized they were photos.

She straightened as he sat down across from her and set the gun and the bottle between them. Alannah's eyes grew big as plates.

"Protection against brigands," he said, thrusting his finger toward the pistol. "Do you drink this stuff, or only caramel whatcha-ma -call-'ems?"

"Maybe." She sighed, laid the photos face down on the table, got up and switched on the element under the kettle. "I'll start with coffee and work my way up." She opened a cupboard and passed him a mug. "Want something to eat? We kind of missed supper."

Jack glanced at the clock. It was eight. How long had Alannah driven around while he was asleep? But he wasn't hungry. His stomach still felt all twisted up in knots. "I'm fine."

"Okay."

Jack cracked open the bottle and poured an inch in the bottom of the white, porcelain mug. He lifted it and breathed in the fumes.

"You won't be much good to me if you're hammered," Alannah said.

"If I'd planned to drink myself into oblivion, I would have stayed upstairs." The chair scraped over the tiles as Jack turned toward her. "I thought your nerves might need a little help, what with our little break-in. Is anything missing?"

She shook her head as she pulled the coffee pot down from the shelf.

"Who's Zoran?"

Alannah jerked toward him.

"Yeah, I could hear Alexander," Jack said. "Alannah, is there something I should know?"

Her voice came out clipped. "He's my father."

"Father?"

"Listen, I don't see how it's relevant at the moment. You heard Alexander. He's locked up"

"Alannah, you were pretty damn excited—"

"Well, he's not supposed to know I'm here, alright?" Alannah slammed her coffee mug down on the table and snatched the photos up. She shoved them into the pocket of her jeans. "I came to Winnipeg to get away from him."

"But he's in prison. Why would he—?"

Alannah glared at him.

"Yeah, fine." Jack held up both hands. "There's the gun, if I ask again." Jack took his first sip of the Jim Beam. It scalded, sweetly burning, down his throat. He sighed and glanced up.

Alannah slapped off the stove element and held out her cup. "Oh, screw it." She plunked down across from him, took a sip of bourbon and choked.

"Smooth." Jack eyed her.

"I don't really drink." Alannah coughed again.

"Yeah, I see that."

"I have an anxiety disorder." Alannah looked up like she'd just confessed some terrible sin. "I had a nervous breakdown many years ago."

"Damn, I'm sorry." Jack sipped his bourbon and licked his top lip.

She made an attempt at a smile. I'm a basket case, you can just say it."

Jack wriggled a little. "I'm sure you have a reason. My dad wasn't exactly Ward Cleaver."

"I've no idea who that is." Alannah lifted the cup gingerly to her lips and grimaced as the liquor hit her throat.

"Leave it to Beaver?" Jack asked.

Alannah shrugged.

"Never mind."

She lifted out of her seat a few inches and pulled the photos from her back pocket. She laid them down in a thin, curved stack on the table. The top photo was a faded snapshot of a young man leaning against a stone wall, vines snaking all over it. He grinned, all teeth showing, but his eyes were dark, almost dull. Jack squinted at it. Was it a trick of the light, the fading of the photo over time? But there was a familiarity to that look. Jack had seen it in the mirror.

"That's Jurgen Zeigler," Alannah said. She touched the photo and tilted her head.

"Where is he now?"

"He's dead." The words came out empty. Alannah tipped back her cup and downed the liquor. She coughed, but held out the cup.

Jack poured her two fingers and wondered if it was, perhaps, a bad idea. "What happened to him?"

Alannah stared down into the mug. "I don't really know. All I know is that Zoran killed him, and it was my fault."

Jack blinked. "I kind of doubt it."

A flush crept up Alannah's neck. "Well, I doubt you know much about it."

"You did say that Zoran killed him. Doesn't sound like your fault."

Her throat worked, and tears began to well up in her eyes. "You can't ever understand, Jack. You can't."

"Alright, alright. So I can't. God knows I haven't lived long enough to understand a woman's—Ah, shit."

She was crying again.

Jack got up and peeled a round of paper towel of the roll on the counter. He handed it to Alannah and leaned against the counter while she dabbed at her eyes.

"I'm sorry," she whispered. She hiccupped, and took a hasty gulp of bourbon only to cough and sputter.

Jack leaned forward, pulled his mug over, and poured it down the drain. "You should go to bed, Alannah. It's been a long day."

"For me? What about for you?" A fresh tear rolled down her cheek.

His mind was going hazy, his head hurt, eyes burned. But it was all fatigue and sorrow. "Yes, but I am perfectly sober." Jack leaned forward and helped her out of her chair. "To bed, Professor."

CHAPTER 13

"Alannah?"

Alannah snapped awake and upright, and the shock of sitting up and set off an explosion in her head. "W-what?" She was on the sofa in the living room, and the drapes were shut, just cracks of light shining through. There was afghan over her, and she was in her jeans and sweater.

Alexander bent over her, smiling in bemusement. "What a night you've had, I see."

Alannah sighed and licked her sandpaper lips. "Umm..." *Jeez. He buried his wife yesterday and you're the one getting drunk?* "When did you get in?" She blinked and blinked as if that might clear her head. It did not.

"Just now." Alexander's lips twitched with suppressed merriment. "Alannah, did you assist Jack with that liquor bottle in the kitchen?"

"Don't laugh at me." Alannah swung her legs off the sofa and unwrapped the afghan from her ankles. "I haven't drank since the late sixties, and I won't do it again. Jack had more."

"Somehow I think Jack can hold his liquor." Alexander turned slowly and let out a cavernous yawn. "I'll make coffee."

"Did you drive through the night?" Alannah cast the blanket aside and stumbled after him into the kitchen.

"Just set off at five with..." he yawned again and flicked on the element under the kettle, "with Timmies' coffee in hand, since soon I'll have to return to the uncivilized wilds of Germany where they have no such thing."

"Morning." Jack appeared in the doorway. His face was almost as pale as the white paint on the walls, with deep dark smudges around his eyes. Despite that, his eyes lit on her and his mouth quirked into a little smile. "Well, Professor?"

"'I'm fine," Alannah muttered.

Alexander leaned against the stove and gazed at Jack. Jack didn't meet his eyes, but turned to fish in the cupboard for a mug.

"I'm sorry I wasn't here for you yesterday," Alexander said softly. Behind him, the kettle began to hiss. "I thought you'd be in better hands with Alannah."

"That's alright," Jack said to the coffee cups. His shoulders formed a hard line, shutting Alannah and Alexander out.

Alannah looked down at her fingers. It wasn't that hers were better hands; it was that Alexander could feel Jack's grief too deeply for words. He couldn't bear to see Jack's grief, and yet he couldn't truly bear to be away either. That was likely what had made him get up before it could really be called morning, and drive back to them in the dark.

"Would you like breakfast?" Alexander turned and pulled the coffee pot from the cupboard, along with the beans.

"Yeah, I guess," Alannah said.

The kettle hissed and sputtered. Alexander turned the knob on the grinder and it began to whine, sending little needles of pain into Alannah's head.

Alexander reached into the next cupboard, and tossed her a bottle of painkillers. He had a tiny smile at the corner of his mouth, again.

Jack took his black coffee and shuffled out of the kitchen without another word. When he'd gone, Alexander leaned forward and squeezed Alannah's shoulder gently. "Is it still alright if I fly out tomorrow?"

Alannah rubbed her eyes and reached for her coffee cup. "I'm not afraid of Jack. I'll be okay. What about him?"

Alexander squinted past her, toward the kitchen door. "Once again, I honestly think yours are the better hands to leave him in."

Alannah took her first gulp of coffee and grimaced. Alexander had made it strong enough to peel paint. "But are you going to make him join our society?"

"I want to send Cyrus to check on you. I'll return to Dresden to assist Daniel, and free him to come here soon. Adolf has lent me one of his keepers, also, to search for Koenig." Alexander worried his bottom lip with his teeth. "Good Lord, do you know we've never had someone gone for so long? Not since..."

"Cosima?" Alannah looked up at him over her coffee cup.

Alexander's jaw tightened. "Yes, since Cosima."

She could hear the unsaid half of the sentence, *and she was never found.* Cosima Di Gaspare had vanished without a trace almost a hundred years ago, shattering Alexander's heart.

"You were convinced that Giovanni Ardovinni knew where she was," Alannah said carefully, rubbing at her temples with thumb and forefinger. The painkillers were beginning to do their magic, reducing the hammering in her head from jackhammer volume to rubber mallet size. "Have you... asked him about Koenig?"

"I'm still convinced he knows where she is," Alexander whispered, then said in a stronger voice, "Ardovinni is abroad, and has not been in Dresden for two years. There is nothing to connect him, except perhaps a small connection to Zoran. That is all. No, Alannah, I do not suspect him. He is cunning, and capable of making anyone disappear, but he is not a bad man."

Alannah did not argue. She barely knew the Italian, nearly as old as Alexander, fabulously wealthy, infinitely connected. But

Alexander never, ever spoke badly of him because Ardovinni had been Cosima's closest friend and protector.

"Listen," Alexander said then cleared this throat roughly, took a sip of coffee, and continued, "yesterday there was a new blog post, a discourse on Vonegut's *Slaughterhouse Five* and his view of time."

Alannah prickled with dread and morbid curiosity. She gripped the coffee cup against the trembling in her hands.

"I lent Zoran that book before I left," Alexander said. "It is his blog, with someone else posting for him. He is reaching out to his followers again, somehow. Daniel is already interviewing the staff at Schwalenburg." He sighed, laced his fingers behind his head, and leaned it back, eyes to the ceiling. "Daniel thinks Marcus has just gone, tired of being accountable to a keeper, but I cannot shake the feeling that they are connected. I must go to Dresden. You know that Zoran hates Daniel and won't speak to him. I must speak to him myself." He dropped his hands, and turned to her. Somewhere upstairs there was a dull thump. They both glanced up, then heard Jack's footfalls pad across the floor.

Alannah's breath quivered. She stood stock-still. "You'll send Cy here?" She didn't want to be alone, then, not even across the world from her father.

Alexander nodded.

"Th-then I guess you'd better go." She swallowed hard. She had Jack in the house now, and he had a gun. She would be safe.

∞

Monday morning, Alexander caught a taxi to the airport and had flown out before Alannah and Jack were ready for their separate jobs.

Jack wasn't sure he should go back, but he didn't know what else to do. With Alannah out of the house, it would only be a matter of time. He would hurt himself.

Jack wandered around the Fletcher building by habit, picking up the garbage, polishing the floors, fixing a plugged toilet, almost like he wasn't the one controlling his limbs.

So little time had passed, but the world seemed completely different. Jack paused and blinked. Probably because Mary Rose wasn't in it. He'd been blown off his moorings.

∞

"I trust by now you have practically memorized your syllabus," Alannah said with a smirk, looking over the darkened lecture theatre and the sea of laptops. "So, you will know that next week your first paper is due—based on topics of medieval history before 1100 CE."

Out of the corner of her eye, she saw the door open and a figure slip in. She caught a glimpse of his face as he sidled to the second row and sat down at an empty space. It was a young man with short blond hair, dressed in a dark, collared shirt and a high-collared wool coat, which he was just unbuttoning.

Whatever she was about to say fled. *He looks so familiar. I've seen him before. Who is he?* She strained to see his wrists to look for the spreading oak tattoo, but he had his hands folded in his lap.

"As I was saying..." she searched for her scattered thoughts, "the paper will be on topics before 1100. I am pleased to report that for our second half, which will cover post-1100, my friend..." she faltered.

Stop it! Get yourself together.

"...my friend Dr. Alexander von Katlenburg will be guest-lecturing on topics of the Protestant Reformation, Martin Luther, and his influence on modern Germany."

Was she just imagining that he'd lifted his head as she'd said Alexander's name?

Alannah launched into her lecture but her eyes kept skittering over the face of the stranger. The other students were taking notes, or nodding off, or by their eye-movements, playing Solitaire. But he had his chin propped on his hand and never seemed to break focus. As she neared the end of her notes, she glanced at him again. This time they made eye contact. He had eyes of deep ebony, oddly paired with his fair features.

He lifted his chin in a slight nod, and smiled. His eyes gentled, but the smile didn't reach them. It made him handsome, and it reminded her of something—of what, she couldn't fathom.

Alannah's hands trembled as she clicked to the final slide but she steadied herself and concluded the lecture. "Your papers are due at 4:00 next Monday," she said as the classroom filled with the shuffle of chairs and the muffled clicks of closing laptops. She reached over to grab the remote to turn off the projector and snuck a peek at her mystery student. He was caught up in the current of students, staring at her.

"Alannah?"

She jumped and swung her head around to see who spoke.

"Here." She looked up and saw a man with coffee-brown skin standing against the far wall, waving. His teeth were bright white in the dim rear of the class. "Hello."

"Cyrus!"

"It is I," He sauntered down the stairs of the lecture theatre toward her.

Alannah saw the stranger pause mid-step, glance between them, and slip toward the door. He passed by Cyrus as he came down the aisle. Cyrus glanced toward him and nodded in acknowledgement.

Alannah grabbed Cyrus in a hug as soon as his feet landed on the floor level of the theatre. Her face mashed against his wool coat. He smelled like winter air and cologne.

"Good to see you too." Cyrus extricated himself from her grasp and eased her back so he could look her full in the face. His black eyes narrowed. "Is something wrong?"

"No, no." Alannah bit her lip. "I'm just being paranoid. I—"

"Let me decide that. What is it?"

"A man came into the class halfway through. He wasn't a student, and I don't think he is faculty. But he looked familiar. I've seen him before. And he was watching me, and I think when I mentioned Alexander he reacted strangely, and..." She paused and sucked in a breath. "I'm just being paranoid. He could be anyone."

"Where is he now?" Cyrus asked. His eyes flicked to the doors of the lecture theatre.

"He was just leaving as you were coming in. The blond man with dark eyes."

"Right." Cyrus let her go and rubbed his smooth-shaven chin. "He did look familiar."

"I was hoping that you wouldn't say that."

"Alexander told me that you were concerned that someone had broken into your house."

"Yes, I know Zoran is locked up and you probably saw him yesterday." Alannah sighed. "I'm overthinking this and I'm paranoid."

"It's quite alright, Alannah."

"Did your plane pass Alexander's over the ocean?" Sneaky Alexander. He hadn't said Cyrus was coming *that* soon.

"Something like that." Cyrus grinned impishly. "The ticket was available, so I snatched it up."

"Are you going to talk to Jack? I'm not sure he'll be open to that." Alannah bit her lip and thought of how Jack had hauled out his bottle of booze the previous evening and drank alone—she was too scared to drink anything more than coffee now. All Sunday his emotions seemed under tight control, too controlled.

Cyrus shook his head. "No, I'm going to stay at a hotel and stay out of sight for the present. I'll observe from a distance for a couple days and do some work for Alexander from the hotel. If you see this stranger again contact me. If Jack gets out of line—"

"He's been fine."

"But you are a single woman, living with a single man who is in a vulnerable place. If you are concerned, call me right away. Alright?"

"Alright." Alannah grabbed his hand and squeezed his hand. "I'm so glad you're here, Cyrus."

He grinned. "It's my pleasure. Idina is still away, and Alexander makes me speak German because I'm terrible at speaking German, and I'm tired of speaking German."

Alannah giggled. "The tyrant."

"Will it raise any suspicion if you go out for a drink with a friend after work?"

Alannah walked behind her desk and pulled the charging cable out of her MacBook. "Jack minds his own business when told to."

"Well, then he's well trained."

"I'll text him and let him know I won't be home."

∞

Jack parked his car in the driveway and lit up a cigarette. He left his lunch kit hanging by its' strap over the side mirror and walked back down the long driveway onto Wellington Crescent. The smoke from his cigarette puffed out into the cold, clear air, illuminated as he paused under a streetlight.

A silver car purred by. As it passed it slowed, and Jack saw the woman in the passenger seat stare.

Jack glared at her. "I'm not a fricking bum."

Yes you are. You're mooching free room and board off of Alexander with no plans to move on.

Jack took one last drag and ground the cigarette under his foot even though it was only half done. "I am a bum, damn it."

He turned around and yanked the lunch bag off the mirror as he passed his car—the late-nineties, rusted out Corolla that had no business on posh Wellington Crescent. He jammed his key into the brass lock and slammed the door behind him.

Jack tossed the bag on the counter, then paused in the doorway of the kitchen. He turned and began emptying the containers and miscellaneous pieces of paper and plastic from the lunch kit. Alannah would mind a mess. He took a shower, cold, to make him numb.

"Where are you going to go?" he asked his pale reflection in the mirror, after he'd gotten out of the shower. "What are you going to do?"

Jack walked into the bedroom with his t-shirt in his hand. He grabbed the bottle off the nightstand to bring downstairs, but paused. He opened the drawer and saw the kitchen knife lying in the bottom. Instantly he felt an ache in his gut, the need to end it all for just a few hours.

Alannah won't be home until later.

Not the knife. Too much mess.

The pills?

He shoved his hand under his mattress but his hand brushed against the cool polymer grip of the pistol. Jack pulled it out and hunkered down beside the bed with it cradled in both hands.

"You said you wouldn't," he mumbled. He could feel a clammy chill in his hands. He reached under the mattress and pulled out the magazine. The brass cartridge at the top of the mag winked in the incandescent light. His breath shuddered.

Just once. Just once. Just this once. It was like a mantra in his head.

Jack slammed the bottle down and stood up. The amber liquid sloshed against the sides, contained by the glass. Pressure mounted inside his head and he gripped the mag in one hand and the gun in the other.

The bathtub would contain the blood, an easy clean up. No one used that bathroom. He could patch a hole. The exterior wall was brick. The bullet wouldn't go through.

He laid his phone on the edge of the tub and leaned against the back of the tub.

Do it. Do it.

He shoved the barrel in his mouth. His finger trembled on the trigger. He hadn't been scared of this for ages.

Do it.

He pulled the trigger.

CHAPTER 14

"It's been a long few months," Cyrus said, pushing his stool back from the high pub table. He speared his final, crusty french-fry in the little metal tub of ketchup and popped it in his mouth. "It was my one hundred and twenty-first wedding anniversary last week, did you know that?"

"Really?" Alannah smiled as she wiped her fingers with her paper napkin.

"I spent it alone. She was in London. She's still in London, trying to get papers together to help one of the women there transition to a new identity. The woman isn't having any of it, though she's been there for almost twenty-five years..." Cyrus trailed off and glanced up at her apologetically. Alannah had been in Winnipeg for forty.

Alannah made a face. "When will you force me to move on?"

"Oh," Cyrus said and winked at her, "that's Alexander's job. Most certainly his job." He frowned and gazed off toward the window, where snowflakes were chasing each other sideways in the wind. "But aren't you lonely? There's only you and Alexander—well I guess there's Jack now too."

Alannah shrugged. "That's just par for the course. I'm immortal."

"Daniel is finally seeing someone else. Did you know?"

"Is he really? Who?" To her surprise, that didn't set off any twinges of sorrow at all. She was glad, genuinely glad.

"Anastasie. It wasn't a surprise to any of us, having watched them dance around each other for years. I told him to man up already. He knew very well they'd be happy together."

"So he is then? Happy?"

Cyrus nodded.

Oddly, it felt like a burden lifted. She'd always felt like Daniel was collateral damage in her own disaster. The memory had often returned to her.

∞   ∞   ∞

"I wish you wouldn't see that man."

Alannah jumped and spun around. Zoran stood, tucked into the narrow gap between two buildings, gazing at Daniel's broad back, receding down the sidewalk with spring in his step. Had he been watching them? Her face grew hot. She wouldn't have put so much passion into their goodbye kiss if she'd known.

"Hello Papa," she said softly, leaning in so he could kiss her on both cheeks.

"I wish you wouldn't see him," Zoran said again. His obsidian black eyes shone murky.

"But..."

Zoran tucked her hand into the crook of his arm and led her to walk down the sidewalk in the opposite direction Daniel had gone. "I don't doubt that you like him, my dear. But I am thinking of the future. Only yesterday we were talking about a future with immortal children."

She remembered, and she'd been dreaming of a having Daniel's baby when she'd spoken of it.

"Do you think that man would ever allow you to have a child?"

Alannah glanced over her shoulder, but the bend in the street and the high, brick-faced buildings had erased Daniel from sight and the foot-traffic had closed around them. "Well, not now, because it's illegal, but if it were legal, then..."

Zoran's lip curled. "Daniel is Alexander's man, through and through. It doesn't matter if we the people force their hand. Daniel will never voluntarily father a child. Think of that."

And, as if that was just another inane topic, he moved on and left the words to eat like a cancer at Alannah's thoughts.

A week later, in front of Jurgen, Christopher, and the rest of his inner circle, he said, offhanded—"You can never truly be one of us, and kiss the enemy."

He might as well have slapped her.

"Daniel..." She stood in the doorway of Daniel's office at Schwalenburg. She couldn't look him in the eye, just stared at the desk behind him. She'd been sitting on the edge of that desk when he'd first kissed her. "Daniel, I have to talk to you."

She told him, "I don't think we should see each other anymore."

Daniel's face went white, then livid red. "Why?" he asked in a choked voice. "Why? What did I do? Let me make it up to you."

"I just... It's not you. I've changed. I can't—" She couldn't look at him, because if she looked at him she would relent, and to Zoran that would be the highest form of weakness.

In the end, when Zoran would be exposed for what he was, Daniel would be kind, even tender to her. But their relationship could never truly be mended.

∞

Jack woke up with his forehead pressed against the cool porcelain edge of the tub. He was cold all over. His bare chest and arms were speckled with goose bumps, but clean of blood. Jack reached back and to feel the back of his head. His hair was sticky, but his skull was completely intact.

"Why are you checking?" he said thickly, "it always grows back. Everything always comes back." He picked up his phone, smearing blood over the glass, and pressed the button to wake up the screen. It was only eight. He'd been out for an hour and a half. A quick rebound. In fact, there had been no release to it. It had just been utter blankness. He felt no relief at all.

Jack stood up and turned on the shower. It turned scalding hot on his icy skin. He swore and cranked on the cold. Blood and brain matter ebbed in crimson rivulets down the drain while he scrubbed the gore out of his hair. He turned and fingered the bullet hole. It wouldn't be the biggest mess he'd patched. He should go to the hardware store right now and take care of it before Alannah was the wiser.

But his limbs were like lead. Jack turned off the shower and sat down in the tub. He stared at his soaking wet jeans through bleary eyes. The throbbing was starting behind his right eye.

"Why did you do that? Why can't you just keep your word?" He pressed his fingers to his eyes, but behind the lids he saw Mary Rose's face, pale skin and bluish lips.

Be good to yourself.

You said you would.

Jack choked and pounded both fists against the side of the tub. Funny thing was, he just wanted to do it again, and again, and again.

And then he heard the door slam.

In an instant, Jack was galvanized to leap from the tub but his foot slipped on the blood and water. As he plunged toward the porcelain he stuck out his hand to arrest his fall. He landed, and felt a sickening pop. His arm gave out. Jack would have screamed, but his teeth snapped shut on his lip. Blood filled his mouth.

Jack spat blood out and lay staring at the cherry-red spots. "Shit. Oh shit." He coughed, and a light spray of blood coated the white floor of the tub. He reached up with his good arm and tried to get a firm hold the tub. As he did, he knocked the pistol onto the floor. The pistol. If he shot himself, he'd wake up and his arm would be mended. Otherwise, it would mend at the normal rate.

"Jack?" Alannah's quavering voice came up the stairs along with her footfalls? "Jack?"

He couldn't let her see that. Jack hauled himself into a sitting position and answered through gritted teeth. "In here, Alannah. It's okay. I just slipped in the tub." He sucked in a shuddering breath. "I-I think I broke my arm."

"What?" Her voice was right at the bathroom door.

"Wait. I'll... I'll come out." Jack managed to stagger to his feet and climb out of the tub. He looked around frantically. There was still a rim of red around the drain, and the gun! He shoved it into the garbage can and yanked the shower curtain shut. Every movement shot shards of pain through him.

He stared down at his sopping jeans, soaked with both water and his own blood. "Uh... just go away for a bit. I'm coming out in a towel."

"Wait, what?"

Jack opened the door a crack. Alannah's pale face was right there. She gripped her cell phone in one hand. "I slipped and my arm is broken."

Both of her hands flew up to her mouth. "You're bleeding."

"I bit my lip through when I fell." Jack cradled his arm. The pain was mounting near to pass-out levels. "C-can you take me to the hospital?"

"Yes!" she grabbed the door, and then seemed to think the better of it.

Jack gritted his teeth. "Just go into your room for a moment. I'm going to forgo the towel when I come out."

She went from white to red in an instant. "I'll go back down and get my coat on. Yell if you need me."

As soon as he heard her footsteps recede, he lurched out of the bathroom.

Just undoing his fly sent pain rocketing though him. Somehow Jack managed to get into a pair of flannel pajama pants. He grabbed a zippered sweater and his wallet and stumbled down the stairs with his arm clamped against his side. "Can you..." he said to Alannah, who stood in her coat and boots in the entry.

"Yes, yes of course." She slid his good arm into one sleeve of the sweater. She didn't meet his eyes as her fingers touched his bare arm, and then chest as she draped the rest over his shoulder and zipped it. She wrapped his parka around his shoulders. "The car is still warm. Let's go."

Jack was shivering by the time Alannah had him seated in the emergency room. She wrapped him in a thin, knit blanket, still cool from the trunk of her car and sat down beside him to wait. They were told it wouldn't be long.

"I should have brought the booze with me," Jack muttered.

"You weren't drinking, were you?" Alannah said under her breath.

"In the shower?"

"I was just going to offer you breath mints."

"Have *you* been drinking?" He turned to scrutinize her.

"No, we just went out for burgers."

Jack laughed. "What kind of date is that?"

"I never said it was a date. And mind your own business." Alannah pressed her lips together and stuck out her chin.

"Fine, then I won't ask you how it was."

She harrumphed. "It was lovely. A nice change from your company."

"Well damn." Jack shifted in his seat and shuddered as pain wracked him afresh.

Alannah ignored him until the nurse called his name. She reached out to help him up.

"I'm fine." He shrugged off her hand and stood up.

An hour later, Jack returned, sporting a cast.

"Are you still peeved at me?" Alannah asked, later, as she slid into the driver's seat.

Jack smiled at her and leaned back against the headrest. His eyelids drooped. His good hand clutched his casted wrist. "I'm too doped up to be mad at anyone, sweetheart."

She raised one dark eyebrow and slid the key into the ignition.

"Clearly."

CHAPTER 15

Hohnstein, Germany, 1629

"Here we are, playing maiden aunt and protective brother, no?" Cosima's silky voice at his elbow made Alexander's heart leap in his chest. She smiled up at him, eyes gleaming, then turned to watch Adolf and Sophia walking ahead of them through the little garden behind Alexander's house in the little village of Hohnstein.

The sun streamed slantwise in gold and red through the trees, burnishing Sophia's knot of curls and Adolf's corn-silk hair. Songbirds kept up a sleepy serenade in the hedge. Their heads were bent together, Adolf's head slightly turned so Alexander could see the rapt smile on his face. He'd plucked a rose and held it to Sophia's nose. She giggled.

Alexander sighed, and Cosima laughed.

He looked up in surprise.

"Are you a romantic, dear Alexander?" Cosima tilted her head toward him. Her ebony curls slid off her neck and over the smooth skin exposed by the modest swoop of her collar.

Alexander lifted his eyes and laughed softly. "Romantic? Oh, I don't know, is it romanticism to think of eternal love?" He felt heat creep around his neckline, leaving a trace of sweat for his blond hair to stick to.

"It's a sensible thing to think of," Cosima said in a hushed voice, her brow furrowed as she watched the couple. "I think we have to think of it now. Zoran has scoured all of Dresden searching for more of us, and has moved on to the small villages. I'm not a mathematician, but I believe we have half chances of finding more women. And what then?"

"Frederick swears he won't remarry." He tilted his head. A sweet-spicy aroma of lavender tickled his nose, tantalizing him. He pressed on, "And knowing Frederick, he's as good as his word. Frederick is a rock island, let all waves break on him."

"Pfah!" Cosima tucked her hand into the crook of his arm and led him to walk forward. "There is no such thing, and Frederick shall know it in a hundred or three hundred years. I would rather admit it now, and be happy."

Alexander's heart quickened, even if she probably meant nothing much by it. They walked along, well behind Adolf and Sophia, between the rose bushes and the sprawling tomato vines. He glanced down and realized that Cosima was barefoot in the loose soil. His eyes fixed for a moment on her dusty toes, then he smiled and looked away. He was a moment late.

"I was a daughter of the country, and the vineyards," Cosima said softly, "forgive me if I am unseemly. Sophia's garden is so lovely, and it reminds me of my childhood."

"No, no," Alexander breathed, "I rather wish I could join you, but if Sophia saw she'd scold. She does take such good care of me, and I've been ill of late."

"I thought you looked a little pale." Cosima touched his shoulder to stop him and examined his face with serious, ebony eyes. "More walks in the garden, dear sir. I order it, since Adolf has come to distract your sister from your care."

"Ardovinni is good to lend his sister, then," Alexander said with forced lightness. His breath had quickened again.

"Well, Ardovinni wanted the house for other means—Oh!" Cosima's face flushed red, the first time he'd ever seen her blush. "Heavens, forget I said that."

Alexander swallowed. "Of course."

Cosima turned her head sharply, and walked on, her delicate toes digging into the dirt. Alexander followed after her, and after a moment she raised her head. "If Sophia marries, shall you stay here alone?"

"No, I shall return to Dresden. I came here for Sophia's safety, but Adolf shall keep her quite safe." Alexander shrugged his shoulders together and swept his gaze around the garden—the trailing grape vines, the tomatoes, the roses, and the small but stately country house. "The country life suits me well, but I want to teach again."

"It will be good to have you in the city again." Her hand slid into the crook of his arm again.

∞

"We are six souls. How can we make so much noise?" Alexander shouted in Zoran's ear. How the noise echoed in the little country house.

At that moment, Adolf Hardwin was standing at the head of table with his cup raised. Sophia gazed up at him, her flushed face every bit as flowerlike as the Alpine rose garland on her head. His voice rose and fell, but was completely incomprehensible.

Alexander laughed. He felt happy, deeply happy for Adolf, the happiest he'd felt in weeks. His mind was clearer, too, than it had been in weeks.

"I shall make equal noise at your wedding!" Zoran returned. He tossed back the contents of his goblet with one gulp and pulled the decanter toward him. He glanced at Alexander, then past him. His black eyes sparkled in the light of the blazing candelabras.

Alexander followed his gaze down the table. Cosima sat two seats down, across from him, speaking with great animation to Giovanni Ardovinni. She looked up, caught his eye and smiled confidentially.

Zoran cleared his throat and stood. "I shall take air." He winked at Alexander.

A moment later, Cosima got up, walked around, and sat down beside him. She tilted her head toward him. Her sweet floral scent brushed across his nostrils.

If I could but see that face every morning, waking should be a joy, and not a journey from one blackness to another.

Had it been three months? Four, since this darkness had descended over his mind? Since that time, he'd fought to keep his head up, to keep functioning, despite overwhelming sadness for most of the day. He didn't understand it, but at least the responsibility for Sophia's wellbeing had now passed out of his hands.

"You've yet to speak to me, Alexander. Are you well?" she whispered in his ear, her whisper louder than Adolf Hardwin's shout moments earlier.

He turned his face toward hers, lips an inch from her silken cheek. "I am well. Don't I... look well?"

"Well..." she said as her eyes dropped, "you have very dark circles under your eyes, Sir. Have you not been in the garden as I ordered?"

Alexander relaxed against the high, wooden back of his chair. "Ah..."

"So, I ask again," she said gently, "are you unwell?"

"I've slept poorly."

Her only reply was a soft exhalation, and the blink signaling thoughts passing rapidly through her mind.

Alexander tipped his goblet to his lips but found it empty.

Cosima's fingers closed hard around his arm. "Walk with me," she said softly, "please." She pushed her chair back.

She led him across the great room, through the kitchen door into the dusky garden. Alexander thought he saw Zoran out of the corner of his eye, but when he turned, there was no one there.

They'd shut out the laughter of the banquet. The only sound, the song of the birds cooing in the hedge. The mid-summer evening air felt refreshingly cool, and rich with moisture. Alexander turned slowly around, tipped back his head and breathed it in. "It will rain."

Cosima's fingers kneaded his elbow ever so gently. "In time."

They stood in the center of the courtyard, side by side, and watched the crescent moon peek out above the crown of the boxelder in the corner of the garden.

"Alexander," Cosima said softly, "you are still sleeping poorly?"

"Yes."

She turned and looked up at him. "Bouts of melancholy as well?"

Alexander nodded and looked past her.

"Sophia has talked to me," she said in an undertone, "in fact, we spoke of it last night, as soon as you were out of the room. Be plain with me, Alexander. Aren't we friends?"

Alexander blinked, about to brush her off. Instead, the words burst from his mouth unbidden. "Lately, I've often been too depressed to even get out of bed in the morning. It comes and it goes all day long. First I am a ghost and then I feel more or less myself, but with an unclear mind. For three months, maybe four, I've felt like I've been almost a shell of a person." He dropped his gaze and allowed himself to meet her eyes again.

She lifted her hand and rested her warm palm against his jaw. "I'm so sorry, Alexander. And does Zoran know this? Adolf?"

"Only if they are as perceptive as you." Her touch had stolen the breath from him. "Surely they've guessed."

She held his gaze, narrowed her eyes, and dropped her hand. "What have you done?"

"Done? I don't know, I've confessed everything I can think of—"

"No, no, Alexander!" She laughed breathlessly. "Dear Alexander, I am not asking you to make confession to me. I am asking if you've seen a physician?"

He blinked. "No. There is no physician in Hohnstein."

"And Dresden is less than a day's travel," she took on a gentle, chiding tone, "what if they could help you?" She pressed her palms together and gazed at the moon.

Alexander pressed his fingertips together. "I'm very... reluctant to see a physician. I'd rather not have too many questions asked, you understand."

After about a minute's pause, Cosima blew her breath out in a shuddering stream. "Can I tell you something in confidence?"

"Of-of course."

"Giovanni knows a physician, whom he trusts—trusts intimately. Do you understand?"

Alexander stood very still. The boxelder rustled. A thrush chirruped.

"He wouldn't ask questions, if you won't." Cosima gripped his shoulder. "Stay here a little longer. Don't come to Dresden. I'll go and send the doctor here. Perhaps Zoran would stay and keep you company."

Alexander's head drooped toward hers. He longed to rest his cheek on her dark crown of hair.

"I'll ask him," she said softly.

∞

"It does seem a bit odd to take the bride's bedroom." Zoran eyed the four-posted bed and Sophia's blue damask window curtains. "But, I need plenty of space to work. I brought all my studies with me."

"I'm quite sure Sophia won't think of it, which is good because she would mind." Alexander sighed and smiled. "She made this house so beautiful."

Zoran plunked down on the bed and laid a fat, leather-bound portfolio beside him. "You ought to keep it, and perhaps put a wife in it."

Alexander laughed without humor and turned to go.

"I am serious," Zoran called after him.

Alexander returned to his own room, two doors down the hall. He pulled aside the curtains from the canopied bed and threw himself down on it. The sun shone full across his face. He shut his eyes and sighed.

Keep it and put a wife in it.

Cosima's ebony eyes and creamy skin floated in front of his face and set off an ache in his body.

"No, no, no." Alexander sat up. "You're a shell of a person, in your own words. What's there to give her?"

Zoran and Alexander took supper the way they used to, in their days in Stuttgart—across the table from each other, and each with their own book. Zoran's book was his own two dog-eared journals.

"I'm four generations back on Sophia's genealogy now," he said, his goblet dangling from his fingers. "I'll get no farther, I think."

Alexander did not glance up from his St. Augustine. "And then?" he asked, absently.

Zoran poured wine into his glass in a jeweled stream. He tapped his fingertips against the cup and gazed into the fire. The flames reflected, dancing in his eyes. "When was the last time you were at Katlenburg?"

Alexander started and looked up. "Nearly three hundred years since I've laid eyes on it."

"Would you..." Zoran began, hesitantly, "would it offend you if I went there and poked around? Looked in their archives?"

"No, don't!"

Zoran's eyes opened wide.

Alexander was arrested for a moment by the violence of his response. "Forgive me," he stuttered, "forgive me. I meant—"

"I could start elsewhere, I suppose," Zoran muttered. He dropped his gaze to his hands, but a moment later peered at Alexander from under his eyebrows. "But would you go there... perhaps?"

"No, I—" Alexander broke off and sighed. How did he explain this to the young man, who didn't give a damn that his family had run him out of town? It wasn't that he didn't want to see Katlenburg again. Hadn't he haunted those halls nearly every night for a few hundred years? Wandering down the halls, into the nursery, kissing his daughter's rosy cheeks, into his bedchamber, lying down beside Idonia and smelling her lily-petal skin.

He swallowed hard and turned away. He could not return, like a stranger, to his home.

"Forgive me, Alexander. Here you are unwell, and I've upset you." He got up, took his books, and padded from the room carrying his wine glass.

Alexander pressed the heels of his hands into his eyes for a moment and let out his breath.

A few night's previous, he'd dreamt he lay in bed, and when he'd reached for the warm body beside him, he'd seen Cosima's face instead of Idonia's. Was it a sign that his past was finally passing over, like the end of a violent, August storm? Or was it grievous sin for him to want her. Should he confess, over and over again? He knew not. He was so confused. Surely to travel to Katlenburg would break him.

∞

Alexander stumbled into the house, unmindful of the water dripping from his rain soaked cloak.

"Alexander, is that you?" Zoran's voice echoed down the corridor.

Alexander shook his head, desperate to clear the fog from his mind. Even the cold, driving rain couldn't make him think straight.

"I've put together some supper." Zoran appeared at the end of the hall.

"I'll clean up." Alexander shrugged off the sodden cloak and let it drop.

"The food has long since been put away." Zoran walked toward him. His feet were bare, soundless on the stone floor. He picked up the cloak and slung it over a nearby chair. Only then, Alexander realized the house was half dark.

"I'll bring it out again. I've been working on the family trees again. I've incorporated what Cosima gave me..."

Her name brought Alexander's head up, but Zoran had trailed off.

"It's bad today," Zoran said. "Isn't it?"

Alexander nodded.

"Listen," Zoran said as he leaned against the chair and fingered the dripping hem of Alexander's riding cloak, "I don't know why Miss di Gaspare's physician hasn't yet come, but I've had a thought."

"What?" Alexander's head drooped down.

Zoran said, very softly, "That to die and to be reborn cures all physical ills and injuries. Perhaps it could cure illnesses of the mind."

"Suicide is a sin." Alexander felt a level of clarity return. He lifted his head.

"Yes," Zoran agreed and laid his hand on his shoulder, "but it isn't suicide. You know you won't die."

Alexander pushed past him, toward his bedroom.

"Alexander, don't you know it hurts me to see you this way?"

He ignored Zoran. His thoughts churned with the idea of death. Dear God, why had Zoran said that?

"I'll have dinner brought to you," Zoran called after him.

Alexander dropped onto the bed in his dark room. He pressed his icy fingers to his face.

...cures of physical ills... you know you won't die... cures all physical ills... dying and being reborn...

"You're a pathetic soul, Alexander," he muttered, "God help you." He lifted his head, blinking in an attempt to adjust his eyes to the darkness.

"You're not afraid of death are you?" He dug his fingers into the bedcovers. His mind wandered around the room of its own accord. He had no sword or dagger, but he imagined the little path from the gate by the boxelder tree in the garden, that led down toward the river. There was a high point on the banks not far down, where he might jump onto the rocks below.

"Why are you thinking this?" Alexander cried, "you've never thought of this before?"

"Alexander?"

He sensed Zoran's presence behind him. Zoran stepped forward, placed a tray beside him, and stepped back.

Alexander didn't really hear him. A moment later he shook his head, and came out of his reverie. "What?" he said. The room was empty. He smelled meat and savory vegetables. He looked down, and saw a tray of food beside him on the bed. Alexander reached for the tray. His fingertips brushed the plate. He felt a sharp pain, then a sticky drop rolled down his palm.

Alexander's breath caught. His hand scrabbled over the tray and found the slick handle of a carving knife. His errant fingers had caught the razor edge of the blade, and now his warm blood smeared over the ivory hilt. Alexander picked it up. Zoran had placed it there, and not because he needed it for his meat.

He lifted it, pressed the point against his chest.

"You won't die," he said. His hand trembled. "What if this fixes you?"

Alexander's breathe shuddered. What if it did fix him? He couldn't live like this anymore, but if he were well, perhaps he'd have something to give to Cosima. Perhaps he would have the strength to move on. The point of the knife bit into his skin.

Alexander set his jaw, squeezed his eyes shut, and drove the knife into his heart.

∞

"Alexander."

Alexander sat up. White light blinded him. His head cleared. He fell back onto soft pillows.

"Oh, *dear God.*" The voice went from soft, to harsh, muttered Italian.

Alexander shook his head, squeezed his eyes shut, and opened them.

"Cosima," he squeaked.

Her deep brown eyes gazed down into his, sparking with anger. "Zoran!" she said in a low voice, "I shall never entrust you to him again."

Heat flushed into his face. Alexander pushed himself into a sitting position, clutching the blanket to his bare chest. He'd been moved to a different room—Zoran's room, stripped of his bloody shirt.

Cosima glowered over him, dressed in traveling clothes. She smelled of road dust and lavender.

"Am I well?" Alexander felt under the blanket to where the knife had pieced him. He felt only smooth, unbroken skin. His mind felt heavy, thick like he'd emerged from a deep sleep. Perhaps he had.

"Time will tell." Cosima's forehead had a deep crease in it. "Get up, Alexander. Come eat something and regain your strength. I suppose I can send away the physician, ah—" She dissolved into a stream of Italian and strode from the room.

Alexander waited until her strident footsteps had receded from the room before he rolled from the bed. He stood a moment, wondering if his legs would hold him. He was weak, but his knees were solid. His mind felt clear now. He blinked at the sunlight through the window.

"Clothes," Zoran said from the doorway. He threw something into the room with a soft thump.

Alexander glanced back. Zoran wrinkled his nose, shook his head, and departed.

Cosima's here. It occurred to him and hurried his fingers. He stepped out of the room and hurried down the hall to find her.

"Eat." She ordered him to the table. He ate.

"Drink."

He drank.

Zoran was absent throughout. He poked his dark head into the dining room at one point. Cosima snapped her fingers in his direction. He left meekly.

"Walk with me." She drew Alexander's arm toward her and led him outside into the garden.

"You are angry with me," he said as they stepped into the sunshine.

"No." There was a hint of petulance to her tone. She scowled and poked her toe at one of the tomato plants. "I'm angry with damned Zoran."

"He did nothing."

Cosima paused and squeezed his arm in a tight grip. "I know an idea planted by Zoran when I see it."

Alexander's heart accelerated, recalling the knife on his plate. "What if it succeeded? What if my mind is well?"

"Is it?" She looked up at him, an unmistakable gleam of hope in her eye.

"I don't know yet." Alexander took a step forward. They walked up to where the hedge bound them in, turned and began to pace the other direction.

"You sent the physician back?" Alexander asked finally.

"You're right. I don't want him asking questions," she muttered. "I am too late anyway, I see. I never dreamed you would take so drastic of a measure, seeing as you are a man of God, and suicide..."

Alexander pulled away from her hand. "Is it suicide if I cannot die?"

"I don't know!" She threw up one hand. "You are the scholar and the doctor of theology. I'm an undereducated Italian of the court of Florence, and before that a girl of the Tuscan vineyards. The Bible has *hardly* been in my repertoire until lately."

This hit like a stab wound, more painful than the knife that had pierced his heart. "You wound me."

"Better wounds of a friend than kisses of an enemy, no?" Color was high in her cheeks. She didn't look at him—took a few short paces forward, then turned and paced back, past him. "I found out that I was immortal on the bed of suicide, Alexander. Imagine waking up and realizing you've experienced all the agonies of death by poison, and you're exactly where you started. Sometimes you must learn not to fear life, Alexander. Oh!" She flung both hands up, then crossed them impulsively across her chest and hunched her shoulders away from her.

Alexander turned away. Guilt constricted his chest. "Why should I feel guilt? I feel well. What if this were God's provision?"

"Can you find this in your theologies?" she asked sharply.

His heart throbbed with pain. Of course, of course he couldn't. He was already repentant, if it was not too late to be repentant. "Forgive me, Cosima."

She turned and brushed her hand across his shoulder. "I am not angry at you, Alexander. I only care for you."

Alexander dropped his head again, unsure if he should feel guilt over the happiness welling up within him.

Her fingers gripped his shoulders. "Let me care for you, won't you Alexander?"

He looked up, felt tears burn in his eyes, and could not answer.

CHAPTER 16

Winnipeg, Present Day

The pain medication had worn off when Jack woke up in bed, wearing just a pair of sweatpants with the covers laid neatly over him. He had no idea how he got there, but he remembered the instant he tried to move his wrist. Jack reached up and touched his swollen bottom lip with one finger and felt two stitches. "Great."

He reached out with his broken arm, paused, and then pushed himself up on his good arm. He scanned the room for his jeans but they had vanished. Jack got out of bed and stumbled into the hall.

"Jack?" Alannah's voice came from down the hall. The bathroom.

"Shit."

She emerged. Her jeans had wet spots on them, and she was wearing bright yellow rubber gloves. Her jaw was clenched. "Jack..." Her hands clenched at her sides. She reached back into the bathroom and pulled out his pistol. It dangled from her fingers.

"I, uh—"

"Don't make excuses." She stomped toward him. "I found the bullet hole. The bloody jeans were a dead giveaway, anyway."

"If you're going to lecture me, at least give me my pain medication first." Jack spun around and headed back for his bedroom. "You do have it, right?"

Alannah bolted after him. Her socked feet slid on the hardwood as she skidded in front of him. "No you don't." She brandished the gun at him. "You told me yourself. You swore to your wife that you wouldn't harm yourself anymore."

"You think I want to do this?" His voice came out higher pitched than he'd intended. "You think I'd break my word to my wife if I had a choice? I do this because I have to."

"Have to?" Alannah drew back. "What, the gun just jumped up and shot you while showering? Because I totally understand. I bring my gun into the bathroom all the time."

Jack shut his mouth so tightly that his split lip throbbed.

"Maybe you don't have a choice whether you die or live forever," she said, "but you are not a victim, and don't you dare play that card on me. One day you're going to have to wake up and decide to live instead of always trying to die. You're going to have a long life so you might as well do something worthwhile."

"Like what? Take pictures? Hide in Winnipeg because I'm afraid to leave? Teach university for eternity?"

She blanched. "That's not fair. I have a reason to be scared."

"And I have a reason to be depressed. Leave me alone, alright?"

Alannah whirled around and ran down the stairs with the gun still clutched in her hand.

"Didn't your Mom ever tell you not to run with guns?" Jack called after her. "They're liable to jump up and shoot you."

∞

Alannah stumbled into the kitchen and put her head down on the counter, pillowed on one arm and the gun shoved far away. She sobbed so hard it felt like she might vomit.

What are you going to do, call Alexander? He'd say the same thing if he wasn't a kind man instead of a son of a bitch like Jack.

Alannah lifted her head and pressed her hand against her mouth to stifle her cries. "Why do I always care for the broken ones?" She banged both fists against the countertop. "What about me attracts them?"

She had a sinking feeling about him. That constant darkness in his eyes reminded her exactly of Jurgen, and look how that had ended.

∞   ∞   ∞

"Did you do it?" Zoran made a grab for her hand as she rushed through the door of the flat. Behind him, in the kitchen, someone was laughing. It struck her as terribly unfair.

"Yes." Alannah looked up at Zoran.

"Ahh..." He smiled. "You've been wise, dear, though now it may ache."

Alannah nodded. She could feel tears flooding to her eyes. "I'm s-sorry—" she pushed past him toward the bathroom.

When she emerged, drying her eyes on a scrap of toilet tissue, Jurgen was outside, leaning against the wall.

Alannah moved to press past him.

Jurgen held up one hand, and offered her a juice glass filled with amber liquid. "It's rough. I'm sorry." His dark eyes held hers gently, full and soft.

Alannah took the glass and pressed her lips very, very tightly together. Her breath shuddered, trying to escape.

"You are very brave, and very dedicated." Jurgen's articulate brow creased. He touched his slender fingers together. "Take a drink. Perhaps today living shall be hard, but it will get easier. I promise." He smiled, a sad, weak smile.

"You're very sweet," she whispered. She took a little sip. Even holding the glass to her lips caused her eyes to water. "Oh dear," she sputtered.

He grinned. "Easy now. A bit much?"

She coughed, nodded, handed it back. Jurgen tipped his head back and poured the liquor down his throat. "That too gets easier, as does going on living." His smile faltered. He looked down. "After all, if Zoran succeeds, we won't go on accumulating these pains forever. He'll put an end to them, if we want."

It took her a minute, after rejoining the group, to realize that Jurgen was speaking of death.

Just over a week later, Alannah was having dinner with Zoran in his flat while the wind slammed the rain against the windows. Zoran was uncharacteristically quiet, after appearing before the court of Lords that afternoon. He swirled his wine in his glass and gazed out the window. The apartment was dark, but for the little wrought-iron chandelier over the table.

Alannah ate a few bites of the ratatouille she'd prepared and nibbled at the crusty roll. Alexander had asked her not to appear in the session, though she usually took notes for him.

Zoran's plate of vegetable stew had congealed. Alannah sighed, and pushed her chair. As she leaned to pour more wine into his glass, something thumped against the door. A strangled voice called out, muffled, "Zoran?"

Zoran came out of his stupor in an instant. He leapt up and opened the door.

Jurgen slumped through the door into Zoran's arms. Jurgen was soaked through. His body trembled. "It's not..." his voice slurred, "s'not working."

"What's wrong?" Alannah stood frozen with the wine bottle still in her hands.

"Help me," Jurgen whimpered.

Zoran slipped his arms under Jurgen's armpits and dragged him into the dark sitting room. He laid him down on the French provincial couch. "Bring the blanket from my bed," he said softly to Alannah as he eased Jurgen's feet up onto the couch.

Alannah set down the wine and bolted toward Zoran's bedroom. When she returned, Zoran knelt beside Jurgen, holding his hand in both of his. She tucked the knit blanket over Jurgen's wet form and fell to her knees beside Zoran. Jurgen's eyes were shut. His breathing was labored and slow.

"He's overdosed on painkillers," Zoran said quietly, "but not nearly enough to kill him."

Alannah went cold all over. "What will we do?"

Zoran picked up something from the floor beside him, and held it out to her: a syringe.

She recoiled.

"He'll be alright." Zoran set the syringe down and adjusted his grip on Jurgen's hand. "I've helped him along. He'll return to us in a few hours."

"Why?" Alannah's voice squeaked.

Zoran was silent for a minute. Outside, a fresh onslaught of rain clattered against the windowpanes. A gust of wind shook the building. "Alannah, you've only been with us a few years. Perhaps you've yet to meet an immortal who wanted to die."

"But we can't!"

"I know," Zoran soothed. He let go of Jurgen with one hand and gripped her wrist. His thumb brushed a slow circle. "It doesn't stop some from trying. To some, to live forever is an unbearable thought. So it is to Jurgen." He brushed Jurgen's damp hair away from his forehead. "This isn't the first time he's come to me."

Jurgen's breaths came so slow and shallow, Alannah had to strain to hear them. She peered at his chest, waiting for the next one to come. Her stomach roiled. Tears prickled in her eyes.

Ten minutes later, Jurgen stop breathing entirely.

"There," Zoran released his hand and turned to lean his back against the couch. "A few hours of peace for him."

"This can't be right," Alannah said in a small voice, "there must be something else we can do for him."

Zoran drew a deep breath through his nose, "Jurgen is addicted to pain pills, Alannah. This is his fourth overdose this year."

A long silence passed between them, as she digested this.

"Every time he dies," Zoran began again, "his body forgets that it needs the medication. Every time, Jurgen hopes that he'll be able to leave the drugs behind." He paused, blinking as thoughts passed behind his eyes. "He's nearly two hundred years old. He was a clergyman in his mortal life, and now he is an addict. Alexander always told me that death was the natural interrupter of evils, but he fiercely denies us any possibility of death."

∞　　　　∞　　　　∞

A door slammed upstairs. Jack's heavy footfalls came down the stairs, and Alannah sighed. It was no longer inconceivable to her that someone would want to end their life, but unlike Zoran, she didn't want to assist Jack over and over. She wished there was something she could do for him, but as with Jurgen she was lost and helpless.

"...Yeah, I fell in the shower. Stupidest fluke thing." Jack laughed with unnatural brightness into the phone. "Okay, yeah, light duties or something. Thanks." The house went silent, and then the front door opened and shut gently.

Alannah stared at the gun, and at the rubber gloves she still wore. She stripped them off and tossed them into the sink. She contemplated what to do with the gun, whether to call Cy and have him take it.

But that would obligate Cyrus to look into the whole matter, and as much as Alannah hated Jack at that moment, she wasn't ready to turn him in and she just didn't know why.

No, no she did.

He'd go, and then she'd be alone, and having him there made her feel oddly safe.

Alannah shut her eyes tightly, but fresh tears still squeezed out, and down her cheeks.

An hour later, Alannah sat in the library with a cup of tea and her lecture notes. Her eyes burned and her gut ached from crying, but she was keeping a steely calm.

The front door slammed, and Jack ran straight up the staircase. As he passed by the library, she heard him pause. Alannah glanced up, and met his eyes for just a second. His brown eyes were meek now. His face had lost its ashy hue, now ruddy from the cold air outside. But Jack said nothing, and kept walking. He had a bag in his hand, with the Home Hardware logo emblazoned on the side. She could hear him thumping around in the bathroom.

The notes swam in front of Alannah's eyes. She sighed and squeezed her eyes shut for a moment. Really, there was no reason why he should get to her like that. She turned the page. Moving on.

Forty-five minutes passed. Alannah's stomach growled, reminding her it was noon, but she stubbornly kept her eyes on the page.

"I fixed it." Jack's hoarse voice came from the doorway.

Alannah looked at him over the papers. "The bullet hole, or your life?"

Jack grimaced but planted his feet and stayed in the doorway. "What will you do with the gun?"

"I'm not giving it back."

"I'm not asking you to, but you can't just throw it in the dumpster either."

Alannah held the notes over her face again. "I'm not an idiot. I'll figure it out."

"I'm..." He sighed. "I'm going out."

∞

It was far too cold to be sitting on the ground, and one wasn't supposed to sit on graves, but Jack lingered with a cigarette in one cold-reddened hand. He sat on top of the frozen mound of earth, staring at the little marker where the gravestone would eventually go. Mary Rose lay six feet beneath him. He could almost picture her, like the night of their wedding—lying back against the cushions in a pink gossamer nightgown. Jack shut his eyes and summoned the memory: her trusting blue eyes and her silken skin.

"You shouldn't have done it, Mary Rose," he said to the pile of dirt, "you should have married a nice young farmer, like your daddy wanted." Good lord! He'd given Mr. Loewen, a respectable and religious man, a heart attack when he'd come home with Mary Rose the first time. Jack had gotten earful enough to scare the fear of God into him, or at least the fear of Mary Rose's daddy.

"Too bad I turned into a hard-drinking, self-destructive freak anyway. Too bad I left you lonely and made you cry." He took a drag on his cigarette and blew the smoke up into the sky, toward the dull winter sun. "I'm so sorry, my love. I can't seem to stop. I just... Alannah's got my gun now, and I'll try my darnedest, but..." He took a deep breath and sniffed back the snot that threatened to dribble down his lip. "I've got to find something to do with myself, something to make of myself. I've got to get out of here. Any ideas?"

The wind bit at his cheek. The cemetery was silent, and so was Mary Rose.

"Crazy. Crazy is what I am." Jack stood up and felt his knees creak from cold and stiffness. For a single moment he felt all of his fifty-two years.

∞

Jack swore at the mop and yanked at it, but the orange strings had wrapped tight around the chair leg. The chair skittered toward him and teetered on two legs before clunking back onto all four. Jack put his foot up on it and tugged. The mop came free.

He rested his chin on top of the mop stick and gazed morosely at the streaky, wet floor. At this rate, it would take him all day to clean all the classrooms. He wasn't nearly coordinated enough to mop with one hand. "Light duties, my ass."

Jack dragged the mop pail into the hall and pushed it along to the next classroom. He fumbled with his keys at the door, and as he found the right one, a taut, feminine voice called out, "Hey!"

Jack jumped and turned.

Shit.

Clarissa stood there, with both arms wrapped around a stack of textbooks. Her curls were piled on top of her head and spiraling around her face. "You. I've seen you before."

Jack swallowed. "Uh, I doubt that." He jerked the door open and kicked the mop bucket through it.

She advanced two steps. "You were at the hospital."

"What the hell are you talking about?" He tried to back through the door after the mop.

"You were in the hospital room." He couldn't see Mary Rose in her face, that moment. He saw himself. "Who are you? Why were you there when my mom died?"

His only instinct was to get away; his only emotion, fear. "What the fuck are you talking about," he said, "and who the fuck are you?"

Her face flushed cardinal red. Her eyes dimmed with doubt. "I'm..."

Jack took that moment to push past her and around the corner. He yanked the first door open. It turned out to be a storage closet. He stood trembling in the dark among the jugs of cleaners and the mops. He gripped the door handle.

"Hey!" her light footsteps pattered by the door and kept going. "Wait. Please!" Her voice broke. Jack felt it like a fist to the gut.

My little girl. I'm so sorry.

The hall fell silent. She had gone. Jack jammed his broken wrist against the door and gasped with the agony. Black spots wobbled in front of his eyes. He slumped against the shelf, nearly dislodging the containers of industrial cleaner.

Half an hour later, Jack walked into his boss's office.

"I quit."

He didn't look the man in the eye. He turned and left before his boss could respond.

He bought a weak cup of fast-food coffee and drove deeper into the city, sipping it, wishing it were booze, and hoping that some sort of clarity would come over him.

My little girl.

Got to go, got to run.

Mary Rose!

She's gone. I should be too.

Alannah.

She never wants to see me again. I should grant her wish.

But where?

Jack parked in front of the bank and chucked the last of the coffee out the window into a dirty, grey snow bank. Maybe the answer would come to him.

He waited in line, shivering because he was wound up so tight. The bored looking woman didn't ask any questions, personal or otherwise, when he asked for the contents of his bank account in cash. *I guess no one gives a crap when you only had about six hundred bucks to your name.* He'd been giving everything he was making at the University to Mary Rose. Six hundred bucks would get him across the country, and that was about it.

Jack walked out of the bank with his life savings in a letter-sized envelope. He blew out a deep breath as he walked from the bank into the cold wind. He was so tired. He wanted a drink, and he wanted death.

No, he wanted that instant right before the rebound. That release, that suspension between life and death before he rocketed back to the present.

"No," he said as he started the car.

He made it halfway home before turning around and heading back to the liquor store.

I'll just take the edge off. I won't do anything. That doesn't matter, does it?

Alannah has my gun.

He could come up with something else, no problem.

"No," he whispered to himself as he pulled the bottle of amber liquid off the shelf and walked toward the checkout.

I'm leaving tomorrow. That makes up for it, doesn't it? It means I'm moving on. Maybe I won't need to do this anymore.

"No," he said, a little more forcefully as he slid into his car. His hands shook on the steering wheel. *Don't do it. Don't.*

CHAPTER 17

As Alannah unbuttoned her coat she paused and listened to the wind howl and shake the house. She shuddered.

Wait.

It was too quiet.

Jack's car was collecting snow in the driveway, but there wasn't a light on in the house. Alannah stood still and held her breath. She didn't hear a footfall or a creak.

"Jack?" her voice squeaked. Alannah eased out of her boots and tiptoed up the stairs. "Jack, are you home? Please talk to me."

His bedroom door was open three or four inches, and a wide beam of light spilled out onto the floor. It was the only light upstairs. Alannah paused and peered through the crack.

"Jack?" she whispered. No answer. She pushed the door open.

"No! No, no, no." She stumbled back and clutched at her mouth. She tasted bile and smelled cold, coppery blood. "Oh Jack!"

Jack lay, sprawled across the bed, his arms flung out. Blood pooled on top of the covers, and splattered the wall behind the bed. His blue t-shirt had three huge slashes, right across his torso. His eyes were half shut, face slack.

She ran to him. Alannah's socked feet and jeans soaked up blood as she dropped to her knees beside him. She grabbed his wrist and pressed her fingers to the vein there, but all she felt was cold, wet skin.

"Jack, wake up!" She grabbed his face.

Suddenly she wasn't seeing Jack's wax-paper eyelids and bloodless skin, but Jurgen's white face, grey lips, and bedraggled, wet curls. She was sitting beside Jurgen on a puddled hardwood floor, crying for him to wake up.

"No, he's going to wake up." Alannah swallowed hard. "He's going to wake up." She pulled back his riven t-shirt and hardly saw skin for the blood. Her stomach heaved. "Wake up, Jack," she said through her teeth. Her hand hovered, clenched, over his stomach. She touched his cold skin and wiped away the blood. There were no cuts, only indistinct indents of freshly grown flesh. Jack's body had already rebuilt itself; inside, the blood was regenerating in his veins. His heart was not long from restarting. He could wake up at any moment, could be hours, and could be seconds.

Alannah felt choking sobs well up from her gut. She splayed her bloody hands out, stared at the crimson streaks on her skin, and wept hot, bitter tears. "Oh Jack," she cried softly, "Jack, Why do you have to do this?" No anger came, not like the poisonous rage she'd felt when she'd found the pistol stashed in the garbage can, buried beneath the tissues. She felt no wrath for the spoiled bedding, and the stains that would be left upon the walls.

She'd known agony, but she'd never done this. She'd never disemboweled herself, not even in the depths of the nervous breakdown, and the guilt after Jurgen's death.

Alannah tried to wipe her tears on the shoulder of her sweater, but salty tears and snot dripped into her mouth and finally she gave up and used a clean corner of the bed sheet. She fell back on her haunches and felt calm begin to return in spite of the gore surrounding her.

"I can't let this go on." She picked up Jack's limp hand and stroked his calloused fingers. "I don't want to be alone, but I can't keep you here anymore. There has to be a way to interrupt this evil, without death."

She left Jack to wake up lying in his own blood.

Alannah spent half an hour under a hot shower. She went in fully dressed, and watched Jack's blood run in burgundy streaks among the tiles. She did not look into his room when she passed by, wrapped in her warmest sweater, and soft tights.

Downstairs, Alannah mustered the appetite to eat a slice of toast. She sat down with a book, and a mug of coffee to wrap her cold hands around. Her bloodstained jeans and sweater were in the laundry room, soaking to see if they could be salvaged. She guessed not. An hour, maybe an hour and fifteen minutes had passed.

Half an hour later, she heard a floorboard creak softly overhead, and footfalls move toward the bathroom. Alannah looked up briefly from the page that she hadn't turned in ten minutes.

Her coffee had gone cold. Alannah padded to the kitchen and dumped it out. She switched on the element under the kettle and leaned against the stove, relishing the tiny bit of heat radiating from the stove. Upstairs, Jack crossed the floor again. She heard a light thump, followed by another.

Alannah blew out a breath. What would she say to him?

She was on the couch with her second cup of coffee half-done, when Jack's heavy, hesitant footfalls descended the stairs.

"Alannah?" His raspy voice rung hollow in the stairwell.

"In the living room." Alannah set down the coffee. In the time that had elapsed since she'd heard him wake up, she'd yet to prepare an opening line. Maybe it was better that way.

His face peered around the corner. Jack was barefoot, and was clad in the flannel pajama pants he'd worn to the hospital the other day, and a black t-shirt. His arms were wrapped across his torso. His cast was gone. Rebounding took care of that too, apparently.

"I cleaned it up," Jack said hoarsely. His bloodshot brown eyes skittered across her face. His shoulders were rigid.

She tried her best to keep her eyes soft. She patted the couch beside her. "Come sit, Jack."

His body slumped, and he dropped onto the couch beside her like his bones had gone to jelly. "I'm so sorry, Alannah. I'm so sorry." He raked his hands through his curly hair. "I can't tell you how sorry I am."

Her opening line came to her. Alannah picked up his hand in one of hers. "I wanted to tell you that I understood." She paused and bit her lip before continuing. "But I remembered what you said in front of the hospital when I took your picture."

He coughed a laugh and swiped at his nose. "I don't remember. I guess I was probably a jackass."

"You said pity didn't do shit."

He smiled.

Alannah let go of his hand and laced her fingers together in her lap. "So, I won't tell you that I understand because try as I might, I don't understand what drives you to try to die, over and over again. But I won't judge you," she said gently. "I'd like to think that you have a good reason."

He passed his hand over his face and sighed. "I'd like to think so too." He sighed. "I used to tell myself it was my Dad's fault."

"He abused you?" Alannah asked.

Jack shook his head. "He was a war vet. He married my Mom in England after the war. Both of them must have seen terrible things, they never talked about the war. He had his army gear all locked up in a box, and I only knew it was there because I picked the lock. He walloped me good when he found me trying on his stuff." He laughed and swiped at his nose. "He was a drunk, but he wasn't a mean drunk. He'd disappear for a while, probably pass out somewhere. And finally, when I was twelve years old, he shot himself. I found him behind the house, with his brains blown all over the wall."

"Oh!" Alannah pressed her hand to her mouth.

Jack squeezed his eyes shut and scrubbed at them with his fist. "So, it made sense that I'd do the same thing," he said, finally, "I am my father's son. Mary Rose's Daddy said as much when I asked for her hand. And I swore to that man that I'd never break her heart."

"I'm sorry, Jack."

"Don't be." Jack sat up straight and looked her in the face. "It isn't my Daddy's fault that I'm the son of a bitch I am. I'm my own person, and now I'm a damned addict. I'm a deathaholic." He laughed bitterly. "It was better that me and Mary Rose couldn't be together, otherwise I would've done exactly what I swore to her daddy I wouldn't do. And it's better that my little girl doesn't know that I'm alive. She don't need me in her life."

Alannah put her chin in her hands and stared at the curtained window, across the living room. The window lit up as a car passed by on the Crescent.

"I see him sometimes," Jack said, "my Dad."

"See him? How?"

"As I'm dying."

"Jack," her voice came out rough and hoarse, "don't take this the wrong way, but... but I'm sending you away."

He didn't react, just looked at her.

"One of Alexander's lawkeepers is coming for you—my friend Cyrus. He will take you to Dresden."

Jack's face thawed. His brow furrowed, but she saw no anger in his eyes. "He's going to force me to join your little cult?"

"He's going to prevent you from continuing this way," she whispered, "I can't let you do this anymore, Jack. Not when I can prevent it. But, I'm telling you this to give you the chance to get away, if you want it. Cyrus will come in the morning."

He swallowed hard. He was silent for a long moment. His eyes flicked back and forth beneath his lashes.

"Jack?" Alannah touched his arm.

"I'll go."

"With Cy?"

"Yeah, I'll go with him. I was planning to leave anyway. At least now I know where I'll go."

"Thank you, Jack."

He stood up slowly. "I might have to leave in these." He indicated his flannel pajama bottoms. "I've wrecked my clothes."

"We'll find you something," Alannah said.

"I've probably ruined your mattress. I'll pay for it. I promise. In the meantime... I guess I'll sleep on the couch."

Alannah yawned and stood up. Without warning she'd become very, very tired. "Use Alexander's bedroom." She touched his arm. "Jack, I'm not trying to get rid of you. I..."

He extricated himself from her grasp and smiled, a weak semblance of a smile. "Yeah, yeah you are, but it's okay."

Alannah smiled.

She didn't really sleep that night. Every time she dozed, she would dream flickering images of Jack lying in his own blood, and Jurgen's lifeless, face on a wet tile floor.

CHAPTER 18
Hohnstein, 1629

Alexander turned away from the door as Cosima and her maidservant strolled down the road toward the town of Hohnstein with their shopping baskets over their arms. He smiled and rubbed his jaw where she'd brushed her lips across his skin.

Zoran stood and leaned up against the wall in the hallway. His brow furrowed in deep creases. His lips were puckered in a petulant frown. "Well now, may I come out of confinement for the day?"

"Sorry?" Alexander lifted his head.

Zoran laughed, wrinkled his nose, and followed after Alexander into the kitchen. "I mean, may I bring my books back out to the table and may I laugh without that woman glaring at me for daring to make a sound. I have things I want to discuss with you, but she won't let me within a stone's throw of you."

Alexander lifted the lid of the teapot and sniffed inside. The tea was gone. "You know why."

"I meant well, Alexander. Truly! Yet she shuns me!"

Alexander turned and laid his hand on Zoran's shoulder. "I know, Zoran. I do. She knows that also. I don't know why you couldn't just apologize to her and grovel a little. You would probably be best of friends by now."

Zoran's lip curled. "I do not grovel. Never."

Alexander drew a deep breath, and poked the coals together in the fireplace so he could hang the kettle to boil. He'd noted how reticent Zoran had been over the past few days, and how Cosima's hackles rose whenever Zoran approached. He hadn't broached the topic with either.

When Alexander had hung the iron kettle over the fire, he turned. Zoran stood, arms crossed.

"I'm not a great scholar of women," Alexander said slowly, "but I've been married, Zoran. Groveling can be very effective."

"I will never grovel before that whore," Zoran growled.

The blood rushed to Alexander's face. "What did you say?"

Zoran's face reddened. He said, deliberately, "I said, I will not grovel before that *whore*."

Alexander leapt forward. He gripped Zoran's collar and slammed him up against the brick hearth. "Say that again, and I'll throw you out of my house!"

Zoran grimaced and tried to wrench himself away. Alexander pinned him with both arms, his pulse throbbing in his temples.

"It's true." Zoran grunted. "She was a courtesan in the high circles of Florence. She is no woman of virtue, Alexander. Don't be fooled by her fine face and form!"

"Fine face—" Alexander dropped Zoran and stepped back panting. "Who told you this?"

Zoran still glowered like a child who'd been denied his favorite toys. "Surely you know I interviewed her for my genealogies."

"She told you *that*?"

"I did some research!"

"God, Zoran! Have you no decency?"

"Decency? Why do you think I'm telling you? You can't marry a fallen woman!"

Alexander tore at his hair. He shoved Zoran aside and paced past him, toward the door. His stomach twisted into a sailor's knot when he thought about nameless, faceless men putting their hands on Cosima.

Alexander turned and jabbed one finger at Zoran. "You need to go. You need to take your damned genealogies and leave."

"Alexander—" Zoran scowled and raised one hand in an impatient gesture.

"Get out! Go to Schwalenburg and stay there until I send for you."

The kettle began to steam and spit behind him. His mind was doing the same, bubbling over frantically. Zoran was lying. It couldn't be true.

"Get out!" he cried.

Zoran's face blanched, then burnt scarlet. "I'm not your servant to be sent and called for at will. I'll take my leave, but I'll go where I want." He spun and stomped into his bedchamber.

Alexander twisted around and yanked the kettle away from the heat. He bolted out of the cottage, toward the edge of the village and the open fields. He needed to think. He needed to pray.

After walking for nearly an hour, his head had cleared a great deal. He sat down on a large rock on the edge of a stand of trees, and cradled his head in his hands. Around him, the wind played music with the leaves and soothed his aching temples.

So, Zoran said Cosima had been a courtesan. Perhaps it was true, perhaps not. And if it was?

She wasn't a courtesan now, was she?

Oh, dear God, you had Hosea marry a harlot. If she is repentant, there can be no wrong to it, can it?

Marry?

He could put off his thoughts of marriage till later.

Alexander stood and licked his dry lips. Even from Zoran, this felt like a dirty blow, meant to wound. Could Zoran actually be jealous of his attention? Truthfully, he'd all but ignored the young man for the past few days, and God knew he never asked much about Zoran's dearest project—the genealogies.

Alexander sighed, and felt a pang of regret. How swiftly would Zoran leave?

He jogged across the field, toward the house. When he arrived, panting and slick with sweat, the house was dark and silent.

"Zoran?" he called softly.

No reply.

Alexander wiped his forehead on his sleeve. Too late. Perhaps it would be better to let Zoran's ire cool, and then they could talk again like friends. Now he had to compose himself and prepare to speak to Cosima.

In the kitchen, he pushed the last few hot coals together and laid a log on them. He bent down and blew on the embers until tendrils of smoke rose from the underside of the wood.

He hung the kettle over the fire before it had really begun to burn and dropped into one of the wooden chair by the long, table. His head drooped.

"Alexander?'

Alexander jerked upright to see Cosima swing the spitting and steaming kettle off the fire. Her maidservant was just setting a basket of produce on the table beside him.

"Was I asleep?" His voice came out raspy.

"Quite." Cosima smiled at him. "This isn't the most comfortable place for a nap, dear man."

"I—"

She glanced around, located the teapot and began measuring out the tealeaves.

When Alexander made no more attempt to speak, she glanced back at him. She smiled but a line appeared between her eyes. "What is it, Alexander?"

"There is something I need to talk to you about," his voice pitched upward like a question.

She blinked, looked down at the teapot, and walked around the table to stand in front of him. "Leave us, Lucia," she said to the maid. The young woman tiptoed from the room.

Cosima took his hand and pressed it behind her palms.

A hot flush crept up the back of his neck. "Cosima, I've... I've heard some accusations against you, from your past."

Her dark brows pulled together in a moment of confusion, then she sighed. "Oh. Oh, I see." She dropped his hand. "From Zoran, damn him. He told me he knew."

"Is it so?"

Cosima dropped her eyes to the flagstone floor. "Was I a courtesan? Yes. I was." She stood and walked slowly across the room, sweeping her skirt along behind her. Her shoulders pulled into a straight, hard line.

Alexander got up. "Cosima," he said softly, "don't you trust me? After all your kindness to me, do you think I'd wish any ill upon you?"

"What better occupation for a woman who never gets old, never loses her beauty," her voice came harshly. She did not turn her head. "My father took my family into the city when I was eleven years old, hoping for a better life. But he perished in an accident when I was fourteen." She took a slow breath through her nose. Her fingers clenched tight in her skirts. "We all had to work to live, all of us, but I was pretty. A madame recruited me from a street corner and taught me to make my living on my back. God help me, I did well at it."

"You are very beautiful," Alexander said.

She turned and looked sharply at him.

Heat suffused his cheeks. "Forgive me. I... I..."

Cosima let out a long sigh, and her face softened. She turned around slowly and let her hands sag at her sides. "And so," she said in a gentler voice, "I gained the patronage of wealthy men and climbed in society." She ran her tongue over her top lip. "I left that life more than fifteen years ago, Alexander. I suppose that doesn't seem like a long time in the breadth of your life, but-but I'd hoped that in an immortal lifespan it could be forgiven of me."

Alexander reached out, took her limp hands in his and rubbed his finger over her knuckles.

"I suppose that is why Giovanni and I are such good friends," she continued without looking at him, "he and I have little cause to judge each other, and neither expect the other to put on a pious front. The only difference is that I reject my old ways, which is another reason why we are friends. Giovanni has no interest in me for my body, only as a person and a friend."

Alexander stared down at their joined hands. "I cannot work out what to say to you, Cosima. I grieve for you. I—"

Cosima lifted his hands and pressed her lips to his knuckles, then disentangled her fingers from his. "It is enough." She turned around again. "But I understand if you feel you cannot associate with me. I can leave in the morning."

"No! No, Cosima." Alexander dug one hand into his hair. "I want—I want—you." He grasped her shoulder and turned her toward him. "I care for you."

"And I you, Alexander." Two tears left shiny tracks down her face.

He felt his heart might stop for happiness.

"Where is Zoran?" she whispered, her face only a few inches from his.

"I threw him out because of what he said." He felt a pinch in his stomach.

"Then he cannot be angry at me for this." Cosima stood on her tiptoes and pressed her mouth to his.

Warmth spread through Alexander's belly, like a spring thaw after a long winter. He cupped her face in his palm and returned the kiss.

Later that night, Alexander walked into Zoran's room. The bed covers were thrown hither-thither. The wardrobe doors hung open, carelessly emptied. Alexander shoved one gently shut. A piece of parchment hung on the front of the door, skewered in place by a pin.

He pulled out the pin and took the paper in his hand. It was a genealogy. Adolf's name was at the top, followed by his children, and then thin, tree-root lines connecting every single generation from Adolf down to Cosima.

Alexander flipped it over.

His name was drawn in thick dark strokes at the top, the names of his children, his wife, and a large gap. At the bottom, Sophia, her parents, a handful of other names. Zoran had written his own name about in the middle, and the names of his parents.

Zoran had scrawled across it, in letters practically cut into the paper, "Don't you want to know if we are your children?"

Alexander stood, holding the paper, for a long time.

CHAPTER 19
Winnipeg, Present Day

Jack stumbled down the stairs at about ten the next morning, shielding his eyes against the bright winter sun. The knife didn't leave a headache like the gun did. This was the pure sort of headache borne of a short night. Sleep, even when he'd finally lain down at two in the morning, hadn't come easy.

"Jack?" Alannah's gentle voice came from the kitchen.

Jack turned on the balls of his feet and took one step toward the door. He paused. *Are you ready?*

He rounded the corner. A man sat at the table, leaned against the back of the chair with one ankle resting on his knee. He had skin the color of black coffee. He wore a black suit, black shirt, no tie. Either he was bald, or his hair was so close-cut that Jack couldn't see it.

The man smiled, flashing bright white teeth. "Good morning, Mr. Krause." He had a genteel, British accent. It startled Jack.

Jack paused in the doorway. "Hello?"

"I'm Cyrus, a lawkeeper under Alexander's employ." Cyrus fingered the rim of the coffee cup in front of him. "You are accompanying me to Dresden, I hear?"

"I guess I am."

"Excellent," Cyrus said and smiled again. "Then I won't have to use... unsavory methods of transporting you."

Jack flinched. Was the man joking? He was going to Dresden, he didn't need to be forced.

"Are we leaving right now, or can I have a cup of coffee?" Jack walked toward the stove and the carafe of coffee sitting on the counter. He reached up into the cupboard for a mug, his back turned to Cyrus.

"No, no, by all means. Our flight departs at two."

Jack didn't reply. He just filled his cup and took a few gulps.

This is it. I'm cut loose, Mary Rose.

"Are your papers in order? If not, I have a set prepared for you," Cyrus said.

Jack turned with the mug in his hand. "What?"

"Papers. ID."

"I've been going under Jack Gerhardt. It's my middle name." Jack set down the mug and dipped the spoon into the sugar bowl. "I haven't been Jack Krause on paper for about twenty years."

"Yes, twenty years should be long enough. You can resurrect Jack Krause, as long as you don't draw any undue suspicion to yourself." Cyrus leaned forward. "I've looked into your history. None of your aliases have criminal records. According to the government of Canada, you are a choirboy."

"The hell I raise, I raise in private." Jack's eyes skittered toward Alannah. "Mostly in private. I'm not a criminal, I just got around a lot."

"It's a good beginning," said Cyrus.

"My ID is outdated. I'll take the new stuff," Jack said.

"Certainly." Cyrus folded his hands.

"Uh..." Jack set down his coffee on the table. "I might have to get a few things, or it'll look like you're hauling a bum through the airport."

"Oh, uh..." Alannah glanced at the clock. "We might have time to go to the store. I—" She grimaced, as if taking Jack shopping was a truly unbearable thought.

She wouldn't be wrong, and Jack was tired enough to not care if he had to travel in his shabby clothes.

Jack ended up wearing the same suit he'd worn to Mary Rose's funeral, since he had no other proper clothes, and since Cyrus was already suited and booted likewise. He made all sorts of execution and funeral jokes to himself as he carried his light suitcase down the stairs, but he kept them to himself. Alannah wouldn't find them funny. And while Cyrus might have the sense humor to find them funny, Jack wasn't taking chances.

"Why the suit?" he said to Cyrus as they stood at the door. Cyrus's rental car was running at the curb, pouring white exhaust from the tailpipe. It must have been about negative thirty degrees.

Cyrus tugged on his leather driving gloves. "First, because according to my papers I am an international business man. Second, because it doesn't draw attention."

Jack grunted.

"Here," Alannah said as she pattered down the stairs carrying a grey, wool bundle. She shook it out, revealing a mid-length wool coat. "It will go much better with your suit than that—" she pointed to Jack's snowmobiling jacket.

"Figure it'll fit?" Jack unzipped his jacket and shrugged out of it.

Alannah handed it over. Jack pulled it on over his suit. The sleeves were a little short, but the wool was soft and heavy. The shoulders fit him perfectly. "Not bad for an oil worker," he said, glancing at Alannah.

She gave him a little grin.

"I'll pay him for it," he said.

"That's a five or six hundred dollar coat, Jack." She put her hand over her mouth to hide her smirk.

Jack's mouth twisted wryly. "He'll be in Dresden. I'll return it."

Jack eyed Cyrus's black wool coat and burgundy scarf. If all immortal men were such dandies, he'd soon blow through his bankroll trying to keep up.

"Well..." Cyrus sighed. "I suppose this is goodbye, Alannah."

Alannah crossed the entry and Cyrus gave her a quick embrace. As they parted, she turned to Jack. Her arms dropped, awkwardly, to her sides. "Call me from Dresden?" she said softly, "perhaps that fancy video chat that Alexander is always trying to get me to use?"

Jack smiled weakly. "If I can figure it out."

She ducked toward him like she might hug him too, but seemed to change her mind. "Good bye, Jack. Good luck."

He glanced back once, pausing by the door of Cyrus's car. She stood framed by the doorway, her arms wrapped tightly around herself, and a forlorn expression on her face.

Two hours later, as the plane reached cruising speed over western Ontario, Cyrus turned to Jack. "I was so sorry to hear about your wife."

"Yeah," Jack said. He didn't take his eyes off the little TV screen in front of him.

"If Idina would die, I'd go bat-shit crazy."

Jack swung his head back toward Cyrus.

"Not that I think you're crazy," Cyrus said, holding up his hands. Jack caught a glimpse of a gnarled tree tattooed on the inside of Cyrus's wrist.

"You married?" Jack asked, narrowing his eyes.

"Just passed my hundred and twenty-first wedding anniversary." Cyrus laughed under his breath. "Spent it alone."

"Huh." He knew what that felt like. "So, you lawmen, or whatever, travel around all the time?" he asked in a hushed voice, with a glance around the cabin.

"Yes," Cyrus said. He leaned back and laced his fingers behind his head. "We spend about nine months out of every year travelling within the jurisdictions of our Lord, which is Alexander of course."

"What do you do?"

Cyrus smiled wryly. "We enforce the laws of our society and protect our own—help them stay invisible, and such."

"I was hoping for something more of a ninja assassin," Jack said sarcastically.

Cyrus guffawed. "So was I."

"Why is it so important that you stay invisible?"

"Because…" Cyrus paused and rubbed his chin. "Do you recall the original fountain of youth myth?"

"Not... exactly."

"Suffice to say, people have been longing for eternal youth for as long as the earth is old. If they knew it truly existed, what would they stop at to find it? What experiments would they perform on us to find the cause of our eternal invincibility?" He pointed at Jack's arm. "If simply rebounding from death has the ability to cure all hurts, than it is a small price to pay, especially if the manner of death is painless."

Jack grimaced. The last death he had rebounded from had been agony. "I get the picture."

"You and I both know that immortality is more of a curse than a blessing," Cyrus said softly. "By keeping our society a secret, we protect them from themselves."

"How old are you, Cyrus?" Jack asked.

Cyrus glanced to the side, then at Jack. "Two hundred and thirty-two. You?"

"Fifty-two."

Cyrus grinned. "Practically a kid. You're the youngest immortal I know of."

"I doubt that's a compliment." Jack sank against his seat and rubbed at his chin, clean-shaven again. He pictured wearing a monkey suit and flying around, playing a hybrid of spy and mother to a few hundred immortals. "They pay you to do this?"

"Handsomely."

Well, damn. "You carry a piece?"

Cyrus looked at him. "Why would I carry a firearm?"

"Well..."

"Actually yes," he said softly, "if I think I'll need it. Stopping power is worth something, after all. Most of us prefer hand to hand, however, Krav Maga and the like. It doesn't leave a mess."

Jack laughed. "What, you actually fight?"

He shook his head, and smiled wryly. "It sounds exciting, but I'm an overqualified paper pusher most days. I just travel—a lot."

They arrived at two-thirty pm, Dresden time. Jack's eyes were heavy, his head drooped with fatigue, but Cyrus seemed perfectly unaffected by the long flight. He efficiently collected their luggage, and called a cab while Jack guarded the baggage. People milled past him, speaking perfect gibberish. It made Jack's head spin even more than it already was.

A forty minute cab drive later, Cyrus paid the driver and began to wheel his suitcase up the walk toward the square, two-story house. The fading afternoon light reflected off the windows. Jack rubbed his bleary eyes and surveyed the small, tidy yard, the high, peaked roof of the house, and the three rows of windows, two high.

"Nice house," he said.

"It belongs to Alexander," Cyrus said over his shoulder. "I own a flat in London, but I spend most of the year living here, if I live anywhere." There are a few apartments up at Schwalenburg, but like Alexander, I find it easier to leave my work behind if I live elsewhere. He suggested you stay here."

"Hmm..." Jack tugged at his six hundred dollar coat. It seemed to him that Alexander could afford to give it to him as a charitable donation. "Is the old man at home?"

"He is likely still at Schwalenburg. At this time of day, the afternoon session of the Lords is just coming to a close..." The last word stretched out into a gaping yawn. "I've already notified him that we are here. He said he'd arrive home around ten—" he yawned again. He led Jack to a side door, which led into a dark, narrow hall. Cyrus shoved his coat into a closet, and Jack did likewise. The house was cool inside, dimly lit by the wide windows, and silent as a tomb.

"Oh dear," Cyrus said. "Staying awake will be difficult, but it has to be done. Coffee?"

"I hope you make it strong."

Cyrus ditched his suitcase in a sitting area with a little fireplace and three wingback chairs. He pointed down the hall. "There is the loo. You can use any of the empty rooms upstairs. I'd suggest the one with the in-suite bath. My room is on ground floor..." his mouth gaped in another yawn. "Need any more clothes?"

Jack glanced at his suitcase. It contained his underwear, his socks, and a few pictures of him and Mary Rose on their wedding day, one with baby Clarissa, and another a few days before he'd engineered his own death, on the beach. He had pictures Mary Rose had sent him of Clarissa through the years. In some way, that bag contained his whole life.

And in other ways, his life was back in Winnipeg. Like he'd left it sitting beside the gun, where ever Alannah had left it.

"Yeah," Jack said, "I could use a few more options."

"Just a moment." Cyrus walked down the hall, and returned a few minutes later with a stack of clothes.

Jack eyed him. Cyrus had taken off his suit jacket. There was just enough definition under his black dress-shirt for Jack to know that Cyrus had spent more time in the gym than he had.

"Thanks," he said.

"Yeah," Cyrus said. "I'll have coffee in ten minutes."

Jack stumbled up the recessed staircase. It opened up into a wide, bright landing and a broad hall with four doors on either side. Jack poked his head into the first. The bed was all made up, perfectly flat. A tiny door to the side suggested this was the recommended room.

Jack grimaced at the borrowed clothes, and began to unbutton his shirt. He pulled his phone out of his bag and tossed it down on the bed. It was off. How much would it cost to use it? He wanted to call Alannah.

He returned to the kitchen. "Hey, Cyrus."

"There is coffee," Cyrus replied from the table by the window. He was texting with one hand and holding a coffee cup in the other. His thumb flew over the touchscreen. "You will find mugs up there." He pointed.

"What sort of contract do you have on your phone?" Jack asked as he pulled down a mug. "Can you use it anywhere?"

"The provider is owned by a fellow immortal." Cyrus waved the device. "There is an agreement. But there is wireless Internet here. If you connect your mobile to it, I believe you can use some functions without being charged fees."

Jack pulled his phone out of his pocket. "Do you know how to video chat?"

"With Alannah?"

"Yeah."

"Let me see it." Cyrus held out his hand, and Jack put his phone in it. "Oh, that's easy. This initiates a video call. I'll connect the internet." As he flipped through screens, he said, "Tomorrow, if it is acceptable to you, we will go to Schwalenburg and begin your initiation."

"What the heck does that mean?" Jack muttered, picturing college hazing rituals and singing Celine Dion songs in the middle of a crowded shopping center. He smirked and snorted.

Cyrus glanced up from the phone. "They will likely begin by interviewing you, and tracing your lineage back to our genealogies."

"How?"

"By interview, and by blood sample. The purpose is to determine which Lord you fall under, and see if you have any close relatives."

Damned scientific of them. "What, do I come from a long line of immortal Krauses?"

"Hardly," Cyrus said without looking up from the device in his hands. "Ah, here we are. I'd test call her, but she's at work."

"What, you follow her every move?"

"It's midmorning in Winnipeg—on a weekday. Call her at midnight."

With luck, he'd be asleep. Jack took the phone and slipped it into the pocket of his borrowed jeans.

He wasn't. At midnight, Jack was wandering around the silent house in just his borrowed jeans, opening every door and poking into cupboards.

"You can tell this is a bachelor pad," he muttered as he stood staring into the fridge. The cold air wafted out over his bare chest. "No food." There was a cupboard with two or three half-full liquor bottles. Jack opened one that said 'Ostler' on the side and sniffed it. "Hmm. Peaches." He poured an inch and took a mouthful. It was sweet and strong.

"Good stuff." He jumped up onto the counter and took another sip.

His phone dinged in his pocket. Jack slipped back onto the floor and fished it out. It was Alannah.

"How was the flight?"

"Long," he texted back. "What time is it?"

"5:30. I just got home."

"No wonder I can't sleep."

"Are you going to Schwalenburg tomorrow?"

Jack grimaced. "You've been initiated. Do they do anything funny to you?"

Moments later, "They already knew who my parents were."

Jack raised an eyebrow, poured himself another two fingers of Schnapps and poised to answer.

"They will ask you all kinds of invasive questions," she said before he could finish his reply, "and I hear they do DNA testing now. I escaped that."

"I hate needles," he texted.

"No needles."

He sipped the liquor. "Urine sample?"

He could imagine her laugh.

"Shut up," she replied.

Jack laughed and returned, "Do you think Alexander will mind if I drink all his booze?"

"You found his liquor cabinet already?"

"Cabinet? Where?" Jack texted. He shook the bottle. Almost gone.

"In that case, I'm not telling you." Seconds later, "You nervous?"

"No."

Yes.

He typed out, "It's just that I've always been alone," and paused, his thumb hovering over the send button. He sighed heavily.

The phone buzzed, and another message popped up. "Oh, that's good."

He could imagine the ring of sarcasm. He tapped 'send' on his message. He leaned against the counter and sipped the sweet peach Schnapps. Alannah didn't reply for a minute.

"I'm alone too," finally popped onto his screen, "it's hard to trust people. I get that. You can trust Alexander. You can trust Cyrus. It'll be okay."

It was nice of her to say that. He swirled the last bit of liquor and tossed it back. *How do you go from keeping everyone at an arm's length, to letting people watch over you—heck, tell you what to do?*

CHAPTER 20

"Is that yours?" Jack pointed to the shiny, black motorcycle as Cyrus unlocked the Mercedes hatchback parked beside it. It was a sleek, speedy looking bike. Beyond it was parked another motorcycle against the wall of the small garage—a silver BMW bike, a few years old.

"That it is. Can you drive one?" Cyrus asked as he slid into the driver's seat of the Mercedes.

"Yes." It had been about ten years ago though, and a Harley Davidson.

"I should have asked sooner." Cyrus looked down at the key in his hand. "I would have preferred that. I guess you'd fit Alexander's gear." He narrowed his eyes at Jack. "You know, to heck with this car. Let's do it. It will be a little bit cold, but after Winnipeg it feels like June. There's no snow. The road is dry."

Well damn. With his luck, he was liable to tip the damn thing and shred his borrowed britches.

Cyrus bounded back into the house.

Snow or not, the wind had a heck of a bite to it as Jack screamed down the road. He bent low over the handlebars of the silver bike as evergreen trees, and wide, brown fields whipped by.

Cyrus zipped through villages full of houses with high, peaked gables and red roofs, and whizzed fearlessly around tiny cars. Jack gritted his teeth, following as close to Cyrus as he dared.

Cyrus slowed, and skidded around a corner onto a narrow, paved country lane. As he straightened, he accelerated hard again. The trees' bare arms blurred by. They ascended a hill. Beyond it, Jack saw the tip of a tower rising over the trees. As they rounded a wide, sloping corner, the river came into view. There was no ice. The water was black, and running swiftly. On the rocky edge of the opposite bank, stood Schwalenburg Castle.

Jack frowned at it, barely noticing as they skimmed across a bridge. The Castle was mostly a beefy, stone house five stories high, with a steep, slate roof. A few, shorter roofs peeked above the trees. One high tower, with a crenelated top rose above it all.

The lane skirted them around the castle. Upon it's rocky base, its stone walls loomed over them. Cyrus led Jack up to a gate. The ancient portcullis hung above as they drove through into a courtyard, paved with flagstones. Three dark cars parked in a line against the wall. The yard was deserted.

Jack swung off the bike and reached to undo his helmet. Cyrus hung his on his handlebar, and Jack did likewise. Cyrus pointed to another gate, leading into the massive stone manor house. "The main entrance is this way."

"Cyrus," Jack began as he trotted after the lawkeeper, "you can't hide a castle. How do you keep your society a secret if you operate out of a damn castle?"

"Pass it down from father to son," Cyrus said over his shoulder. "Which is truthfully the same Frederick von Schwalenburg who has lived here since the medieval age. But if he updates his appearance, and if he rarely appears in public and maintains a reputation for eccentricity and being a recluse, perhaps he can get away with it."

"Really?"

"Legally we now maintain it under a family trust."

They stood before the great, oaken doors of the manor house. Cyrus pulled a chain, and Jack heard a bell ring out in the interior. Moments later, one of the two doors swung open. A young woman with blond hair and startling blue eyes greeted them both with a smile.

"Cyrus! You have returned," she said with a light French accent.

Cyrus clasped her hands and kissed her on both cheeks. "Hello, Anastasie."

"It is good to have you back in these halls." She touched Cyrus's shoulder lightly and glanced at Jack.

"This is Jack Krause—the youngest of us, I believe," Cyrus said.

She turned the full force of her blue gaze upon him. "Welcome, Jack." She clasped his hand, and as she did, Jack saw the same tattoo of a tree on her wrist.

"Alexander made no mention of you coming," she said softly to Cyrus. "Shall I call him and let him know you're here?"

"That would be lovely," Cyrus said. He gave a significant nod in Jack's direction. "Is Alexander in his office? Does he have appointments? He came and went while I was asleep, and I had no chance to speak to him."

"Lord Alexander is a man of boundless energy." She tipped her chin to the left. "He is in his office, and as I came by, his door was open."

"Good," Cyrus said. "Follow me, Jack. Thank you, Anastasie." When they had passed by her, he muttered to Jack, "Four hundred years old, almost. She is on staff here, a receptionist, assistant, and historian rolled into one small, fire-breathing package."

"As a... youngster. Am I in the majority or the minority?" Jack asked as Cyrus led him through a wide door into a sweeping hallway. Their feet echoed on the flagstones. "I seem to only meet old-timers."

"You'll meet a lot of geriatrics here." Cyrus glanced back with a little grin. "As a fifty-something? Yes, you are a minority."

Jack's eyes flicked back and forth between the stone walls. Arched doorways, some leading to other halls, punctuated the hallway at odd intervals. Cyrus led him up a flight of stairs. They passed through an open section of hallway, where they could look down into a large room. A huge Persian rug dominated the floor. An oval table made of shiny, mahogany sat in the center with six high-backed chairs pulled up to it. Beyond the table was a fireplace long enough for two men to lie end-to-end in. A bright fire leapt on the hearth. Jack thought the room was deserted, but after a moment, Anastasie passed by. She looked up and waved at them.

"That is the chamber where the Lords hold counsel," Cyrus said.

"Counsel for what, exactly?" Jack peeked over the stone railing, then followed Cyrus into the enclosed rest of the hall.

"Suffice to say that the Lords have much more influence in this world than mortal men can imagine."

"Well damn," Jack muttered, "you're the Illuminati."

Cyrus snorted. They turned one more corner, and Cyrus pulled up at a door that stood slightly open. He rapped smartly on the carved wood.

"Cyrus, sind sie das?"

Cyrus pushed the door open. "Apologies, Alexander. I cannot speak Deutsch, because Jack speaks no Deutsch."

"Ah hah." Alexander stood up from behind a gigantic oak desk. He was backlit by the early afternoon sun, but as he walked around the desk he came into focus. He was informally dressed in slim jeans and a white, button up shirt with rolled sleeves. A fire crackled in a small hearth beyond the desk. "Welcome to Germany, Jack. I won't force you to speak German." He shook Jack's hand with a firm grasp.

"I'm here to be initiated," Jack said, "I trust your hazing rituals aren't too humiliating."

Alexander and Cyrus glanced at each other. "I don't know what you mean by humiliating," Alexander said.

"Like forcing someone to speak only German?" Cyrus smirked and rolled his eyes toward Jack.

"Good heavens, Cyrus. Your German is quite passable." Alexander waved his hand toward two upholstered chairs. "And have a seat, Jack. I need to ask you questions about your family."

"Shall I take notes?" Cyrus asked.

Alexander laughed. "Heavens no. I can't read your writing."

"I don't know my family really well," Jack said.

Alexander pulled a small, flat case over and unfolded a tablet computer and a keyboard. "Tell me whatever you remember. DNA will do the rest."

Two hours later, Jack stood in the library of Schwalenburg staring at a six foot by six-foot parchment that had the entire family tree of the immortals inscribed upon it. It loomed over him, hung up on the stone interior wall of the room, lit up by the pale winter sun which streamed from three high, narrow windows. To Jack, it looked like a spider-web—a lot of scritch-scratch. It was only half filled out. The branching lines only took up half the parchment.

And just above him, was his own lineage. He stared up at the name that represented his great, great, great, great grandfather: an immortal like him. Hildebrand Gottshalk Krause: 1798-present.

"What can you tell us about him, Cyrus?" A sweet, feminine voice said, from over Jack's shoulder.

Anastasie slipped in, pushing a rolling ladder made of shiny, golden wood.

Cyrus laughed. "He's a crotchety old man who looks about thirty. He lives in Sweden, where he currently runs a bank. He is married to her—" He slid his finger over the paper to the name 'Anna Sophia Krause, nee. Schweng.' "Otherwise, I can say little to his character, other than that the temperament must run in the family."

"Humph," said Jack, still staring at the lines branching from it. "Does no one have kids, then? I guess I understand why it's unpopular."

"Not just unpopular," Cyrus said, "it's illegal for a member of our society to conceive."

Jack's mouth opened, then shut, then opened to say, "Well damn."

"We'll discuss it further, yet," Cyrus said, grimacing a little.

Jack smirked. "I'm not about to get busy."

"That's good," Anastasie said sweetly.

Jack felt a twinge of heat in his cheeks.

Anastasie climbed up on the ladder and gazed at the genealogy like it was an old friend. She began writing the names he had given in light pencil. She filled in his father's name, 'Gerhardt Krause' as he watched, and then 'Jakob Gerhardt Krause, born 1964.' She tipped her head and chewed the pencil for a moment, and then smiled. "I'll use proper ink when you've officially been received into our number, Jack. Or rather," she paused and glanced over her shoulder at Alexander, "when Alexander receives you." She slid her fingers over the lines, up toward 'Alexander Leopold Karlstan von Katlenburg. 1289-present.' Alexander was his Lord—would be. Alexander was his ancestor.

Holy shit, he's old.

And then, as Jack's eyes skimmed over the names, he realized that one branch of the tree, about halfway down, stopped at a dead end. The name, Joseph Nils Oswald, said 1770-1902 beside it.

Jack stared at it. Every other name for as far as he could see had only the birth date, except for the small names of the non-immortals which had no dates at all, but this one had a beginning and an end.

"Cy..." Jack glanced over his shoulder. But Cyrus had turned away and had walked into the shelves of books.

Anastasie floated down the ladder and stood beside him. "There you are. You're on the immortal map."

"May I take a look?" Jack asked.

"Certainly. Daniel just texted me from downstairs. Back in a moment."

Jack climbed the ladder and perched on the top, directly below his own name. He squinted at Oswald's name, scanned the roots of the family tree, taking a moment to read each name. He was about to climb back down when his eyes skimmed over a familiar name.

Jurgen Zeigler, 1901-1974.

He remembered the slender young man in the snap shot, and Alannah saying, "He's dead."

"He was immortal?" Jack said. *What about this Oswald? He was immortal? Is he dead too?*

"Jack?" Cyrus's voice came from the base of the ladder, "Do you want to see more of the castle?"

"Yeah..." Jack tipped his head down and almost asked Cyrus about Jurgen and Oswald, but the words wouldn't come out. So he just climbed down, and followed Cyrus through the shadow of the bookshelves, past a circle of reading desks and a fireplace. The room passed into another, a long narrow room with a red rug running down the middle like a causeway. He could ask about Jurgen and Oswald later.

Paintings hung on either side. Cyrus had paused beside a grid of paintings, each about fourteen inches tall, by twelve inches across. Cyrus pointed to one of the paintings. A black man, whose face contrasted sharply against his old fashioned white neckerchief, stared back at them. His face was solemn, but his eyes, even captured in paint, twinkled.

"Hah! It's you," Jack said.

"Upon my reception into the Lawkeepers' Guild," Cyrus said in a put-on, pretentious tone. He laughed. He swept his hand across three paintings to another, in a gold frame. The portrait was that of a woman with flashing green eyes and striking red hair, which was twisted into an elaborate style. She seemed to be laughing, but it was a defiant, warlike laugh. "And this is my Idina. A hundred and twenty-one years of marriage, and they've yet to hang our portraits next to each other. Things don't move quickly around here."

"Wow," Jack said.

"My Jacobite queen, a fighter since she was a youngster."

"Who has been in the law business longer?" Jack scanned up and down the rows of paintings.

"She has. Actually, she assimilated me into our society." Cyrus gazed thoughtfully at his wife's portrait. "She accidentally killed me, only to discover I couldn't be killed. I hadn't known it myself."

Jack chuckled, confused. "An accident, you say?"

"It was a highway robbery, gone awry. I was driving the coach, and she was my passenger—actually, I was her servant at the time."

"O...kay."

"I already knew my mistress was an odd woman, but I didn't know she'd be armed. She fought them, first with a pistol, and then with a dagger when one gained the interior of the coach. Unfortunately, she also shot me in the melee."

Jack raised an eyebrow. "Shit."

"Yes," Cyrus smiled wryly, "she and the footmen killed two robbers and chased off the other two. Then they tossed me into the coach—this from her account, for I was well gone—and she drove it back to town herself." He grinned at Jack. "She was never good at playing the helpless female. But to the point of the story— I rebounded inside the coach, and when she arrived home she found her servant alive and very confused. Thereafter, she saw me rather differently."

"Just like that, eh?"

Cyrus elbowed him. "She introduced me to her society, and I began accompanying her, for though I didn't know it, she was already a lawkeeper among the immortal community in England. We were married, some seventy years later."

"Why did you wait so long?"

Cyrus took a few steps down the gallery. His forehead creased as he frowned. "Think of the times, Jack. She's a white woman. I am a black man, born to a slave, just before the abolishment of the slave trade. Thirty years later, I was not technically enslaved to Idina, but according to societal mores, I might as well have been."

He laughed, then sighed. "In days past, immortals were less given to marriage, and she was older than I was, and..." he shrugged.

"How much older?"

"Seventy-nine years."

"I'd call that cradle robbery, but what do I know." He folded his arms and stared back at the portraits of the lawkeepers. "Are all these people still in the law business?"

"A few have retired." Cyrus pointed up to a few solemn faces in the top rows.

Jack rubbed his chin absently and gazed over the rows and rows of proud, stern faces. "So, one of these codgers is going to watch my daughter?"

Cyrus ran his teeth over his bottom lip. "It will be me, likely. But if you have any problem with it, tell me. She's your daughter."

Jack scrutinized his serious face. He nodded. "Let's give it some time."

Muffled footfalls came down the red carpet aisle toward them. "Cyrus," Alexander called from the far end of the room, "what sort of lies are you telling the man?"

Cyrus turned. "We're just viewing the portraits."

Alexander turned to look at the other wall of the gallery. "There I am," he said, pointing to a much larger portrait in a gilt frame. He smirked. "The one and only painting I have ever posed for." He walked over to it and gazed up at his own image. "Thank God for the invention of photography."

Jack eyed the image of Alexander and grinned at the sight of the old guy in some sort of red brocade cloak, with a sword at his side. He sported loose, long hair and a curled blond moustache.

"I think you should bring that moustache back," he said.

"Ah, the sixteenth century." Alexander's mouth twisted wryly. "No doubt in another hundred years or so, the fashion should come back."

"I'm all for swords becoming stylish again," Cyrus said, "I never got to wear one."

"I'm a scholar. That was just for the painting," Alexander said. "Would you like a tour of the castle, Jack?" He tipped his head to the other end of the gallery, where a set of double oak doors beckoned.

"Yes." Jack stepped double time to catch up as Alexander led the two of them down the gallery. "There's a dungeon here somewhere, right?"

Alexander lifted an eyebrow. "Yes."

"Will we see it?"

"I'll lock you in it for an hour, if you're so keen," Cyrus said behind them.

Alexander led them back upstairs, which contained only offices and apartments.

"There is a staff of four that lives here year round," Alexander said as they trotted past the rows of doors. "At the moment, Lord Hardwin lives in the main residence here. Lord von Schwalenburg makes his residence in Rio de Janeiro. A change of scenery."

"Indeed," Jack said.

They paused in the counsel hall, which had been the great hall of the castle in days past. From the mezzanine, Jack had not been able to see the high, stained glass windows, which filtered purple, red and blue light down upon the flagstone floor. He looked up and saw shields and the tapestries that adorned the walls. The silver shields were emblazoned with the same spreading oak tree that was stamped upon the wrists of Cyrus and Alexander.

They descended down a spiral staircase, out of the varicolored light and into sudden artificial, cold light. The stone walls were painted white, and so was the floor. The air was close, but not the dank, stale stench Jack had imagined. Cyrus held up a keycard. There was a beep, and a red light flashed, and a door slid open. They walked past an office station, where a man looked up from a computer.

"Cyrus," he said.

Cyrus nodded toward the door. "Sorry Jack, this is as close to the dungeon as you get. You need clearance to get in there."

"Actually, all I need to do is knock someone up, or so I heard," Jack said.

Cyrus just looked at him.

Jack peered through the window. All he saw was an aisle with five metal doors on either side. They had small, tempered glass windows in them. "This is rather modern."

"It seemed like a good idea to us to make the facility more hospitable," Alexander said with a ring of amusement in his voice. "The inmates are serving rather long sentences."

"How long?" Jack turned back, but as he did, he caught sight of a face in one of the barred windows. It was wreathed in shadows, but he met inky black eyes for a moment.

The man smiled, a flash of white teeth in the shade. And for some reason, Jack shivered.

"For some, hundreds of years," Alexander answered. He had not observed the interchange. He turned them around and led them back up the stairs.

CHAPTER 21

Night had already fallen when they returned to Dresden and parked their motorcycles back in the garage. Alexander had said he was taking dinner at Schwalenburg, but would return 'for coffee'.

"There's a pub two streets over," Cyrus said as he hung up his helmet. "Let's get dinner there." He replaced his helmet with a toque, and plunged back out into the neighborhood, and the orange glow of the streetlights. As they walked, the lightest of snow fell. Jack would have paid it no mind if Cyrus hadn't said, "Ah, the snow followed us from Canada."

"Sorry, Dresden," Jack said.

The restaurant was built into the bottom of a three-story building. The door faced the street at an angle, protected from the snow by the overhanging balcony of the apartment above. As Jack reached to push the door open, he realized the name inscribed in bronze letters was 'Duncan's'. "Cyrus, is this an Irish pub?"

"Yes sir." Cyrus grinned and held the door open. "I'm an Englishman, Jack. It's the closest thing I can get to home around here."

"My first beer in Germany, and an Irish one at that."

There were only a few patrons in the pub, scattered around the fringes of the small, dark room. Jack and Cyrus sidled up to the bar and sat down facing the wall of bottles. "Cyrus, hello!" A young woman with a thick, brunette braid slung over one shoulder, planted her hands opposite them on the bar and grinned. "When did you get back?" She spoke English, with only a light accent.

"Yesterday." Cyrus tipped his head. "This is Jack, from Canada. Jack, this is Lia. She's one of us."

Lia tipped her arm toward Jack, and he saw the same tree tattoo on her wrist that Cyrus had. Things clicked. The tattoo identified immortals to one another. He held out his hands. He had no tattoo.

She narrowed her eyes. "Cyrus, when you say 'us'..."

"He's in the midst of his initiation," Cyrus said softly, "we traced him into Lord Alexander's clan today."

"Oh." Her face relaxed, and she looked him up and down. Her eyes sparkled. "Let me get you drinks, and I'll come chat in a bit. The usual, Cy?"

"Yes, please."

"You, Jack?"

"I dunno, what's the usua-a-ahhh?" Jack's eyes squeezed shut and his jaws cracked as he yawned.

"Shepherd's pie and a pint of stout. I trust that will be palatable to you," Cyrus replied.

Jack nodded as Lia returned. She glanced from Cyrus to Jack, and smiled in his direction as she put down the beers. She gazed at him from under her lashes for a moment before she turned away. He was fresh immortal meat, Jack guessed.

As she walked back toward the other end of the bar, Jack flicked his gaze over her. She was pretty thin, nice legs. Her face had a good, traditional beauty, but it lacked the keen intelligence of Alannah's with her high, dark brows, or the gentleness.

But what the heck was he doing thinking about that? A pit of guilt settled in his stomach.

Jack picked up the pint and took a tentative sip. At least the bitter stout didn't bring back any of the same memories as whiskey. He took a long gulp and relished its deep, acrid taste. "That hits the spot."

"It surely does," Cyrus said.

"So, tomorrow…" Jack began.

"Yes?"

"What is next for my so-called initiation? Do I swear a blood oath, sacrifice a cat, and kiss Alexander's ring?"

Cyrus threw his head back and laughed. "Good heavens, Jack. Our rituals are hardly so dark as that. Once Alexander has verified your bloodline, you will be received by the Immortal Lords. You will be read your charter of rights and responsibilities, to which you will either agree or disagree. If you agree, Alexander will extend his hand to you in fellowship."

"And then I'm in."

"Yes sir."

Jack tipped his head back for a drink, and then turned to look at Cyrus. "Do I get the tattoo?"

"Yes sir, you do. They'll likely have it done right after the session." Cyrus tugged his jacket sleeve and ran his finger over the oak tree. "It's from Schwalenburg's heraldry." Cyrus's phone buzzed on top of the bar. Cyrus glanced at it idly, and his whole face lit up. "I have to take this. Excuse me." He got up and hurried away from the bar as Lia came and set plates in front of their places.

"Where is he off to?" she asked.

"He's taking a call." Jack stared at the steaming mound of meat, onion, peas, carrots and mashed potatoes. The savory steam wafted up to him and set his mouth watering.

"Eat up," she said. She caught Jack's eye and winked before she swung to speak to another patron. He snapped his gaze away.

Cyrus came back in a few minutes, as Jack was halfway into his Shepherd's pie and glancing at Cyrus's piece from the corner of his eye as he took another forkful. Cyrus's dark eyes were all lit up. He pumped his fist and sat down with a thump. "She's coming home!"

"Who?" Jack said through a mouthful of mashed potatoes.

"Idina. She'll arrive in eight hours!" For a moment the big man looked like a little boy on Christmas Eve.

Jack swallowed and asked, "How long has it been?"

"Three months."

Jack felt his stomach tighten. Mary Rose had been alive three months ago.

Cyrus was oblivious to his discomfiture. "Well, Alexander will have to take you up to Schwalenburg himself because I am taking the day off tomorrow. Thank *God*."

Jack did his best to hide the bitter jealousy that had risen like bile in the back of his throat. He knew exactly what it was to miss your wife for months on end, and to ache for her, and to hear her voice on the phone and burn because you couldn't be together. But Idina was alive. He'd never hold Mary Rose again.

Cyrus pushed his shepherd's pie around with his fork for a moment and shoved it away, barely eaten. "You done? Let's go home."

Alexander was home when they walked through the door, ensconced in an armchair in the sitting room. The small fireplace blazed cheerfully. He smiled when Cyrus told him that Idina would return, and said he'd be happy to take care of Jack.

"I'm only going up at noon. There's no reason why I should be there early." Alexander yawned and reached for his coffee cup. "I think I'll go for a longer run in the morning, which means I'd better go to sleep early."

"What time is it in Winnipeg?" Jack asked.

Alexander pulled out his phone, and after flipping through a few screens, said, "Twelve-eleven. Alannah is on lunch break, if that is your question." He glanced up at Jack. His eyes twinkled with amusement. "Cyrus, I've discovered this application on my phone that tracks my mileage as I run..." Alexander trailed off and tipped his head as Cyrus walked out in the middle of his sentence. He grinned. "Cyrus isn't listening."

"Yeah, I wouldn't be either," Jack said.

Alexander shrugged his shoulders and smiled ruefully. "Was your genealogy everything you hoped, Jack?"

"I'd hoped nothing," Jack replied. He thrust his hands into his pocket and found the cool metal of his phone. He pulled it out and flipped it over and over in his hand. "Apparently it's illegal to have children. Am I in trouble?"

Alexander's eyes opened a little wider. "No, no, you were hardly aware."

"So," Jack said and shoved his hands in his pockets, "men get vasectomies? What's common practice?"

"Married men commonly do, and the unmarried." Alexander glanced at his phone. "Not all are sexually active."

"Can't get your hand pregnant," Jack muttered. Out of the corner of his eye he thought he saw a pink flush around Alexander's collar as he reached for his coffee. He raised an eyebrow. "Or not. On that note, I'm going to call Alannah."

Alexander choked.

"Oh... That didn't sound right." Jack spun on his heel and hurried up the stairs before Alexander could reply.

Alannah answered his call instantly. Her oval face and big, dark eyes filled the screen. She smiled at him, bit her lip, and pushed her coffee-colored curls behind her ear. "Hey Jack."

"Hey." Jack settled down on the edge of the bed, and then lay back against the pillow. "How is Winnipeg?"

"Minus forty degrees," she said, "it doesn't matter how many sweaters I put on, it's cold in here. And my laptop wasn't cooperating this morning, and my favorite tech guy wasn't there to fix it with his mere presence."

Jack felt a grin break across his face. "Threaten it with my name. That should work."

She laughed and leaned away from the camera for a moment. Jack caught sight of a Starbucks cup in the corner of the screen. "Are you drinking a caramel mach three or whatever they're called? Does that mean someone died?"

"Macchiato," she said, pronouncing it with dramatic consonants. "Miles brought it." She sighed. "I can't decide if he's hitting on me or not."

"Let the man down easy," Jack said.

She smiled. "Are you initiated now?" she asked as she picked up her drink. "Are you one of us?"

"Well," Jack said, shifting in place, "they're just waiting on the DNA, of course, but they've traced my genealogy into Alexander's clan. I guess he's my grandpa. It's frickin' creepy."

Alannah giggled. "It could be worse. I could be your grandpa."

"I'm rather disappointed that Cyrus isn't my grandpa."

Alannah snorted, covered her mouth and began to cough.

"Those macchiatos are going to kill you. In fact, I think that must be Professor Corder's aim."

"Oh, shut up."

They blew out sighs in unison. Jack's arm was aching from holding the phone up, so he rolled to his side and propped the phone up on the nightstand. "Anyway, tomorrow Alexander is going to swear me in, or whatever it's called. Cyrus will be occupied with more important things. His wife is coming home sometime tonight."

"Oh!" Alannah said. Her eyes flickered.

They both stared quietly at each other.

He couldn't explain that he was practically nauseous with jealousy. Somewhere in the house, Cyrus was preparing for Idina's return like a groom for his bride. "It, uh," he said, "kind of makes you think."

"Yeah?" Her eyes softened. "Of Mary Rose?"

He pressed his trembling lips together. His throat was too tight to speak.

"Oh, Jack."

I want to die! Roared from the back of his head, but he couldn't say it.

"I'm fine," he forced out.

"Yeah?" Her eyes held his. "If you want to talk about it—"

"No!" Jack said, harsher than he meant to. He didn't want to talk to her about it anymore. He wanted to die. "I-I've got to go."

"Jack—"

"I'm sorry." He gulped. "I just—I'm sorry." He tapped the screen and hung up on her.

Jack jumped off the bed and began to pace. The only light in the room was the dim, orange lamp light. Outside, a few flakes of snow fell in drowsy paths toward the ground. Jack paused and pressed his hot face against the cold glass. He shut his eyes and imagined the white flash of light as the bullet pierced his brain, and the fall, and the descent, and the release.

Jack groaned. He had no gun.

He'd seen a block of knives in the kitchen.

Jack spun away from the window, but as his hand closed around the door handle, he paused.

Don't do this. This is your shot at a proper life. Don't fuck it up.

Jack's mouth twisted. Then what the hell was he going to do? He couldn't stay here in this bedroom. There had to be somewhere out there were he could go and raise a little hell away from prying eyes, just blow off a little bit of steam where no one would get hurt. Jack returned to the window and peered out. Not anywhere near here. He'd take a walk and see what he could find.

Jack slung on the borrowed leather motorcycle jacket. He put a wad of Euros in his pocket and carried his boots down the stairs. He paused at the bottom. Alexander had left his chair by the fire. The house was silent. Jack slipped out the front door and jammed his feet into his boots. One thing he was sure of. Cyrus wouldn't notice he was gone.

He wouldn't come home until he'd either chased away the urge to die, or thrown himself in front of a train.

Jack walked down the silent street and emerged from the residential neighborhood onto the shoulder of a large thoroughfare. Pellets of snow began to fall. "Really?" He lifted his head and looked up at the descending flakes, illuminated by the orange streetlights. He shoved his hands into his pockets and glanced back in time to see a bus whoosh by. It stopped a hundred yards ahead, and people got off.

Jack broke into a run and arrived panting as the doors were about to close.

The bus was full. Jack ended up standing beside three twenty-something girls. They glanced at him with mild interest. One of them smiled at him, and Jack smiled back. She said something in German to him. Jack shrugged. "Sorry, I don't speak German."

She flashed him a coy smile. "Where are you from?" she asked in a thick German accent.

"Canada. You, uh, you been there?"

"No." She shook her head, smiled all the while. She glanced at his boots and jacket. "Are you going to the clubs?"

"No, uh..." he said. "Which club?" *Smooth Jack, smooth.*

"We're going to M5." She tipped her head toward her friends. "You should come."

"Oh..." For a wild moment, the word 'yes' was on the tip of his tongue.

I think you're a little too old for that, Jack.

"That's alright," he said softly. "Thanks."

She shrugged, smiled and turned back to her friends. They whispered to each other in German.

Five minutes later the bus stopped, and the girls got off. Jack peered through the bus windows at the ordinary looking building, but for the lineup outside.

"If you were looking for hell to raise," he muttered, "that would have been it." And truthfully, a club would allow him the anonymity he'd wanted. He laughed to himself. He did look pretty young for an old guy, but he'd never spent any time in clubs. Dive bars were more of his thing.

At the next stop, Jack jumped off with another group of younger people and followed them to see if they were also out for a night on the town. They led him up to a big brick building. He squinted at it and followed them up to the doors. Lo and behold, it was a nightclub.

Inside, some sort of horrible band was playing music that consisted of bass and a thudding beat and some sort of garbled mix of German rap and screaming. It was perfect. He couldn't even hear himself think.

He pushed his way up to the bar and downed two shots of awful, cheap whiskey and felt a burn down his throat and up into his nose. He turned around to stare at the pulsing, sweaty bodies. There wasn't enough alcohol in him to make him dance.

Idiot. What the hell are you doing here?. You are way too old for this shit. He pushed away from the bar and turned toward the door.

"Jack!"

Jack rocketed straight up and spun around, almost midair, to see who had yelled in his ear.

A brunette in a tight, sparkling dress grinned at him. Her bright white teeth turned purple and pink with the strobe lights. The flashes off her sequined dress blinded Jack for a moment. When his vision cleared, Jack realized it was the girl from the bar.

"Lia?"

"Yes, it's me." She leaned in close, and he smelled sweet, floral perfume and alcohol on her breath. "We're two immortal souls in this club. Care to dance?"

"I don't dance." He had to yell to even hear himself. The band had launched into its' next track. "And what the hell is this music?"

She threw back her head and her laughter was sucked away by the noise of the club. Jack felt a grin break across his face. "Buy me a drink," she shouted near his ear, "and I'll see if I can get you in the mood."

"What's good? The stuff I had tasted like ass."

She giggled without sound and said, "Never mind. I'll order." A couple moments later the bartender put four tall, narrow shot glasses in front of them. The booze inside was clear as water.

"Rubbing alcohol?" Jack asked.

"Patron." She took one and downed it in one gulp. "Bottoms up, Jack."

Jack took one between his thumb and forefinger, sniffed it, and then shot it back. It was sweet, and stung in his throat. He took the next. She grinned and picked up the other. In unison, they threw them back. A hot flush came over Jack.

"Better?"

"Well," Jack said loudly, "that band still sounds like shit."

She threw back her head and laughed. "More tequila for you, my good sir. What are you doing here, anyway?"

"I was bored," Jack said, "and Cyrus and Alexander are a couple of old men."

She giggled again. "Don't let it happen to you, Jack. You won't get old if you don't let yourself."

"I take it you've stayed young?"

Lia leaned up against him as she laughed. Her warm curves pressed against his arm. "Don't *you* want to know?"

Jack pressed his face into her hair and said in her ear, "I do."

She smiled. "Keep buying me drinks and we'll see what happens." She pulled away and tugged at his arm. "Come dance with me!" she shouted. Jack followed her into the milling crowd, but in spite of his artificially light head and heart, all he did was stand awkwardly until she grabbed his hands and wrapped them around her waist. Her swaying body pulled him into a rhythm.

"There you go!" she shouted. The beat pounded around them. Jack loosened her grasp on him and began rocking his body in time to the bass. Lia's loose hair swung in a silky cloud around him. She turned to see what he was doing and laughed at his gyrations.

"Not bad for an old guy?" he yelled.

"You look like an idiot, Jack!"

"That's a fact!"

"What?"

"Never mind!" He slipped his hands back around her waist. She smiled at him, and they moved with the music, inches apart. He could feel the heat coming off of her, and smell her sweet sweat. Lia slid one hand up behind his head and sank her fingers into his damp hair. Her tree tattoo bobbed in the corner of his eye. Her hips brushed his.

∞

He had a fleeting thought that this had all been too easy. Four hours later, Jack had Lia pressed up against the inside of her door. She wrapped her long, thin legs around him. Her short dress was all hiked up around her waist. She gripped his shoulder and neck and sighed against his mouth as he let his free hand wander.

And then, Jack felt her let go with one hand. Her mouth paused in its wrestling match with his. He felt a sharp prick in his neck, and an instant later, he was falling, falling, falling.

CHAPTER 22
Schwalenburg, 1630

Alexander walked from his bedroom in Schwalenburg Castle, rubbing his crusty eyes, and attempting to marshal his sleepy thoughts.

"Good morning."

Alexander clapped his hand to his chest. "Oh dear God."

Zoran sat at Alexander's wide oak desk, slouched low in the chair with his hands crossed behind his head. A fire crackled on the hearth behind him. The shades were flung back, and morning light gave Zoran's mass of dark curls a silver halo.

"How now, good sir?" Zoran grinned at him.

"Where...?" Alexander took the three steps it took to cross the room, and grabbed Zoran's hand. He stared at Zoran's face, taking in the dark circles under his eyes, the prominence of his cheekbones.

"Around." Zoran shrugged. He pulled his hand away and jumped out of the chair. "I've asked the servants to bring food."

"But where were you?" Out of the corner of his eye he saw two servants enter, carrying trays.

Zoran pointed to an overflowing leather portfolio, sitting on the desk. "I went to Prague."

"And?"

"I was right. I am your relative, of your daughter Konstanze."

"Oh." What did that mean, then? Zoran had been gone over a year. Alexander had long since given up thinking of his theories.

"Sit down." Zoran swept his hand toward the table, where the servants were laying out dishes of steaming food. "Where are the Hardwins? Where is von Schwalenburg?"

Alexander pulled out a chair, sat and tucked a napkin into the loose collar of his shirt. "Frederick went with Adolf and Sophia to Rome."

"Rome! Good Lutherans in Rome?" Zoran rubbed his eyes with both hands. "I'll borrow your bed if you are done with it, Alexander."

"We can get a room outfitted for you! If I'd known you were coming, but I haven't heard—"

Zoran cut him off with a wave of his hand. "I know." He shoveled fried eggs onto his plate as he spoke. "I was on the scent, like a hunting dog. Most of your family hasn't moved a hundred miles from Katlenburg—"

"You went to Katlenburg! But you said you went to Prague."

"No, no I did not go to Katlenburg," Zoran said with annoyance, "I only skirted around the towns nearby—after I went to Prague. It was not difficult to find most them. But as it turns out, a sixth grandson of your youngest daughter travelled to England."

"You haven't been to England?"

"Not yet." Zoran's eyes gleamed. "But I shall."

"And you were looking for...?" Alexander stared at his eggs, feeling highly disconcerted.

"Rumors," Zoran said breathlessly, "and I found them! I circulated the story, merely as a folk tale, that I'd heard about a man from Katlenburg who'd ceased to age, and in fact, never died."

Prickles danced down Alexander's neck. He shoved away from his plate, unable to even think about eating, torn between dread and excitement. "And?"

"I found no one here, but I crossed over into France, where at least one of your descendants married into French family. In Nancy, they told me a story about a woman who'd died and come back to life, right in that neighborhood, but when I looked for her, she'd gone. I finally found her across the city working as a maid, and it took a bit of convincing but she told me the story. That was forty-some years ago that she died. She's now nearly sixty years old, and as fresh faced as a maid in her prime!"

Alexander slapped his palm on the table. "Dear God, another. Where is she now?"

"She's come with me, which is why I ask after Hardwin. I'd hoped to put her into Sophia's care, but I met good Ardovinni and he has called for Miss Di Gaspare to come care for the lady."

"What is her name?"

"Anastasie Bourg."

"Anastasie."

"Resurrection." Zoran smiled. He leaned forward. "I'm quite certain this has been passed all along your line."

A sinking feeling came upon him. Alexander blinked down at the congealing eggs in front of him. Then he would need to find those immortals, if they existed.

"I'm nearly positive that you are the father of several generations of immortals!" Zoran gazed, bright-eyed, at him, like he had just been the bearer of the happiest news.

"Good God! You haven't proven that she is of my line?" Alexander pressed his hand to his mouth.

"No, no not yet. I shall have to go back to the records in Nancy." Zoran stared intently at a distant point across the room. "A whole race of us. How marvelous."

Alexander rubbed his eyes, suddenly weary, suddenly electrified, all at once, confused. He stood up with such rapidity that the chair toppled and clattered against the stone floor. "Is Miss Bourg here?"

Zoran raised an eyebrow. "Indeed she is. Shall I introduce you?"

"Yes."

"Get dressed, then."

Instead of calling a servant, Alexander dressed himself and Zoran helped him with his coat and tied his cravat.

They descended together. At the foot of the stair, leading into the main entry of the manor house, Cosima appeared, holding her dripping hat and laughing. Ardovinni came along behind shaking out his coat. His clothes were soaked with rain.

"What a gentleman!" Cosima held out her hands to Alexander and tilted her cheek for a kiss. "Giovanni holds up his coat so I don't get wet between here and the carriage. He didn't succeed, but..." she shrugged and trailed off as her eyes met his, peered into him, sensing his angst.

He smiled weakly at her, then said, over her head, "Once again I must thank Master Ardovinni for his good care of you."

Ardovinni nodded, but kept his stoic expression. His brown doe-eyes glanced between Alexander and Cosima.

"Zoran, where is the lady?" Cosima clapped her hands and swung her gaze around the room, as if Zoran were hiding Miss Bourg somewhere. "What, have you left her all alone somewhere?" She slapped him on the shoulder with her hat, but smiled good-naturedly.

"No, no, Miss Di Gaspare, she is in the care of the servants. Come, come." Zoran held out his elbow for Cosima to take. "Allow me to introduce you."

Alexander followed after.

Anastasie Bourg sat in a little sitting room off a guest bedroom. She rose as soon as Zoran opened the door. She had a heart-shaped, serious face with luminous blue eyes that gazed at him serenely. "Bonjour, Sir Alexander." she held out her hand.

Despite truly wishing he was not meeting another immortal, Alexander put a smile on his face as he took her soft hand. "Miss Bourg, you are truly welcome."

Two hours later, Alexander was finally able to pull Cosima aside, alone in a little half-dark alcove. She slipped her hands into his and pulled him toward her. Alexander dropped a kiss on her lips, then leaned his forehead against hers. He slid his hands up her arms. "What am I going to do? Sophia is my relative, now Miss Bourg is my relative. How many immortal relatives do I have?"

"At least I am not your relative," she whispered in his ear.

Alexander laughed. "No, Cosima, I—"

"Forgive me. Forgive my giddiness." She tapped her finger against his lips. "I like her. You have lovely relatives."

"She is lovely." He took her hand. "Zoran is beside himself with excitement. I fear I shall now have to traipse all over Europe, searching for any other relatives I have bestowed this *gift* upon. If Zoran is correct, it is now a family trait."

She stood quietly with downcast eyes, in contemplation.

"Perhaps a Hardwin family trait also?" she said after a moment, "What shall Hardwin do about that? What about von Schwalenburg?"

"Before we know it, we could be an entire society of immortals." Alexander sighed. "We need only to find them."

"Zoran would like that a great deal."

"Zoran and I are of quite different minds," Alexander said ruefully. He disentangled himself from her and paced the three steps it took to cross the alcove, three steps back, three steps across again. "I don't want a society of immortals, Cosima. I wouldn't wish this life on anyone. But if there are others like me in this wide world, I cannot let them wander alone, not if they carry my blood in their veins."

"Alexander..."

"Therefore, I must receive a full report from Zoran, and join him in his search. If tracing my bloodline reveals more and more immortals, then it cannot be mistaken. It is a family trait, and the others must begin searching likewise."

"There is something else that this means," Cosima said while his back was turned. There was a note of mysterious emotion in her voice, "it means that any children we—I mean, any one of us—should conceive, should only further this family trait, no?"

Alexander, back still turned, nodded.

Cosima didn't answer. He sensed her behind him. She encircled his waist with her arms and leaned against him for a few moments. "I know without asking that Zoran lay in wait for you to emerge from your bedchamber, told you all his news, and you've neither eaten nor drunk this day yet. Come dine with me. Zoran will take care of Miss Bourg. Tell Zoran you'll speak again later in the day."

Alexander turned around and looked down into her eyes. Her brows were drawn together, her eyes downcast. He tipped her face up and kissed the corner of her mouth. He'd meant to release her but Cosima gripped the back of his neck, and nearly forced his lips to hers. Her mouth burned onto his.

Heat suffused into him, followed by a surge of panic. Alexander leaned back and broke this kiss.

Cosima groaned in protest, her face following his.

"No, no sweetheart," he whispered, "don't tempt me like this while I'm tired and hungry. Let us go eat with Zoran and Miss Bourg."

She shut her eyes and leaned against the wall of the alcove. "Forgive me."

"No." Alexander reached for her hand, but she pulled it away.

"I'm sorry," she said, not meeting his eyes, "I'm sorry, I have to—" she pushed past him and fled down the corridor.

Alexander stood, panting, his heart still pounding from her kiss. His confusion burned into anger. *Didn't she know this was a nightmare for him?* What was she playing at?

Instead of eating with Zoran and Miss Bourg, Alexander apologized profusely and escaped to his apartments.

The next day, shortly after Alexander had breakfasted and dressed, there was a firm knock on the door of his apartments. Zoran had promised to give him his full report that morning.

"You're a bit later than I—" Alexander opened the door, and instead of Zoran, Giovanni Ardovinni stood there. His usual indifferent expression was replaced with burning intensity. Without any niceties, he slipped past Alexander into the room.

"Ardovinni..." Alexander turned around.

Giovanni stood in the center of the room with his arms firmly crossed. He surveyed Alexander silently. His forehead creased with the look of a man who'd rushed in foolishly. He squared his shoulders.

"What can I do for you?" Alexander said hesitantly.

Giovanni met his gaze. "Sir," he said, "as you know, Cosima is like a sister to me, the only family I have. So, you will answer my questions truthfully."

"A-alright." Alexander planted his feet and mirrored Ardovinni's crossed-arm stance.

Giovanni tipped his head to the side. His doe-eyes grew dark. "You have courted Cosima for a year now. When do you intend to make good?" He paused, and when he spoke again his voice gained momentum and volume. "You must know how she cares for you, how she pines for you when you are gone. She is a beautiful and fine woman, good, and intelligent."

"You don't have to recommend her to me." His throat constricted, like a noose had dropped around it. "I know."

"Do you love her?"

"I—"

Giovanni's eyes narrowed.

"Yes! Yes, I love her!"

"Then what are you waiting for?" Giovanni said with menacing softness, "Listen to me. Sure, you are immortal and a year is not long to you, but Cosima has spent her whole life as the plaything of men and it has left many marks on her soul." He took a step toward Alexander, and said, close to his ear, "So, marry her, or leave her be. Continue to treat her as you do now, and I will make you pay."

"Ardovinni—"

Giovanni took a step back and smiled. "I know what you think of me, Sir. You think I'm an effeminate, unnatural sinner and you are the holy man." He shook his head, "But do not forget that I am an immortal. I have a long time to pay you back for your misdeeds. I do not forget."

Alexander blinked. A long, silent moment passed. "Ardovinni," he said slowly, "I do want to marry her, I just—"

Ardovinni held up his hand. "Yes, Zoran. Zoran wants you traipsing all over Europe like a mendicant monk, searching for more immortals. Indeed. You have reasons. Surely you have enough reasons to make up your mind." He fixed Alexander with a stare, paused, and slipped past him into the hall. The door slammed behind him.

An instant later it popped back open. "Good lord," Zoran said, sweeping off his wide-brimmed had, "what demon has taken hold of Ardovinni? Why did he come here? Did he declare his undying love?"

"Quiet!" Alexander shouted. His heart thumped uncontrollably. "No," Alexander said softly, "forgive me. He came to speak to me on Cosima's behalf." He clapped his hands to his forehead. "Good heavens, Zoran. If you are right, how can I marry Cosima? How can I gamble that perhaps we might produce offspring, and scatter even more of my cursed seed?"

"Ardovinni demands that you marry her?"

"Or leave her for good."

"But those are Ardovinni's words," Zoran said as if it were obvious, "Miss Di Gaspare has said before—she is her own woman. Talk to her." He paused and said with a bit more hesitance, "But I agree with Ardovinni. You've as much as promised by your actions that you mean to marry her, or at very least make her your mistress, and I know damn well you won't do that."

Alexander clutched his hair and paced slowly across the room. "You are right, of course. I should. I must." He blew out his breath. "But what of this? We shall have to investigate your findings, and who knows where that might lead? I shall have to leave home for a long time. I cannot marry her now!"

Zoran gazed at him with solemn black eyes and said nothing.

Alexander turned. *I'm on my own then.*

"Will you go to Katlenburg now?"

"Why—" Alexander spun on his heel. He lunged toward Zoran, stopped inches from his face, "If you think I'm going to Katlenburg to confirm some sort of sick fantasy about your immortal race—"

"No." Zoran's obsidian eyes went hard, flat black. "You'll go to Katlenburg because you need to know. You have to know if immortality is the foremost of your family traits. This isn't about me. This is about the truth."

"And then, you think we'll know the truth?" Alexander said through his teeth. "I am made immortal by a spring of water, a spring of water! I am trapped in this body by water!"

"I would like to see that fountain if I could," Zoran said with no reaction to Alexander's outburst.

"No!"

"You are overwrought." Zoran backed toward the door. "I will leave you."

"You're right, I must go," Alexander said, quieter, "but I must speak to Cosima first."

Zoran raised a brow, as if to say, "You'd better", then shut the door.

"And what shall you say to her, fool?" Alexander hissed. He slumped into a chair. "Curse you Zoran."

CHAPTER 23

Winnipeg, Present Day

Alannah sat in the library with the house silent as the tomb it was. She had her laptop on her knees, her lecture notes ignored for the last twenty minutes. Jack's pistol sat on the little table beside her, and every now and then she'd pick it up, turn it over, and set it back down. She'd popped the magazine out once, by accident. There was but one bullet left.

But at least it was in her hands.

She had to admit, she was still deeply disconcerted by their video conversation, despite her attempts to tell herself it was all fine, and that Alexander would take care of him.

What also made her squirm was that when his face had appeared on the screen she'd felt her heart melt—strangely, illogically. There he was, with his head obviously lying on the pillow, his face shadowy from the dim light. His eyes were hooded and sleepy, and his mouth quirked into a slightly snarky smile.

And as usual, the darkness in his eyes belied his smirk.

"Oh, Jack." Alannah sighed then picked up the pistol and wrapped her fingers around the polymer grip. She sucked in a deep breath and put it to her temple. The rim of the short barrel cooled her hot skin. She put it down again.

She got up and set the laptop gently on the hardwood floor beside the armchair. She picked up the pistol gingerly, and carried it back to her bedroom where she placed it on the nightstand. That was where she'd taken to keeping it.

As Alannah reached into her dresser drawer to pull out her pajamas, she thought she heard a faint creak, like a floorboard moving under the pressure of a footfall. Alannah froze, every fiber of her straining to hear. She could detect no sound. She picked up the pistol again and held it behind her back as she padded back into the hall. She paused, and heard the distinct clunk of a car door closing.

Alannah sucked in a breath, but as she glanced to the left, she saw the neighbor walking toward his house.. He reached out, the car honked as it locked, and he walked inside.

Her breath shuddered back out. "There's nothing to be afraid of. Nothing. He can't have you. Alexander won't let him. He won't..." She started to shiver and wrapped one arm around herself. "You could have gone with Cyrus, you know. He would have taken you in a heartbeat." It felt like once again she was willfully alone, willfully without protection, shut off from those who longed to protect her.

She remembered the day she realized Daniel was following her. Jurgen spotted him outside Zoran's apartment, one night.

∞   ∞   ∞

"Isn't that your ex?" Jurgen drew the drape and pointed. A man stood just outside the light of the lamppost. The yellow street light sent glints off his blond hair, and lit up every puff of cigarette smoke. A motorcycle stood at the curb. It was Daniel's.

"Damn!" she breathed.

What would he do? Would he come bursting in, thinking Zoran had her there against her will? At that very moment, Zoran sat at the head of his little dining table, folding leaflets outlining their newly written charter. The bold, black heading proclaimed, "Live

Free, or Not at All." Zoran meant to begin distributing them at the common council meeting the next morning.

"What should I do?" She hissed to Jurgen, her eyes on Zoran's long fingers, creasing the paper in sharp folds.

"No use hiding that you're here. He obviously knows. You're your own person, aren't you? You're doing nothing wrong. He can't stop you."

Alannah threw on her coat and marched down the narrow stairwell. She'd trembled, not exactly with anger, not with fear either. There was a tiny part of her secretly relieved to see him.

"Daniel," her voice trembled as she crossed the cobblestone street.

His face lifted, still wreathed in shadow. "Alannah," he said wearily, "what are you doing? Don't you know who that man is?"

"He's my father."

"Ernst Krueger was your father. That man up there is dangerous." Daniel gripped her hands before she could evade him. "Please, Alannah, I've known him for three hundred years."

"You haven't known him like I do!" Daniel hadn't seen the way Zoran would draw her to him, possessively, and gaze tenderly at her like she was his greatest treasure. She *was* his greatest treasure, his jewel of promise, he'd said.

"That man has broken every law of our society, Alannah."

"Some are meant to be broken!"

Daniel bent to look into her eyes. His grey gaze was steely, angry. "I don't know what the hell he is planning, but it won't be good for you. He chewed up your mother and spit her out once he'd got what he wanted. He's a bad man."

"Don't say that!" she wrenched free. "Leave me alone, Daniel. I didn't ask you to keep an eye on me. I can take care of myself."

"I'm not so sure!" he shouted.

Alannah was stunned silent for a moment. Daniel had never raised his voice to her.

"I'm afraid for you, Alannah, can't you let me care for you?"

"No," she whispered. She clenched her icy fingers. "Go away, Daniel."

He stood looking at her, motionless for a minute. "Alright."

Then he got on his motorcycle and left.

"Bravo, Alannah," Jurgen said when she'd stumbled through the door.

"D-did you watch the whole thing?" she clutched her coat shut, shivering.

"I hope it's alright. I just wanted to make sure you were okay."

"He wouldn't hurt me. He's a good man, only misguided."

Later that evening, as she prepared to leave, Zoran pulled her aside.

"Alannah, I have a favor to ask of you."

"What is it, Papa?" Her eyelids were drooping, vision blurry. It was nearly midnight.

"When you assisted Alexander, did you ever see where he kept trial evidence?"

The question was so unexpected. She stood dumbstruck, staring at his shadowed face, backlit by the incandescent light within the apartment. "Well, yes."

Zoran dug in his pocket, and withdrew a scrap of paper. He handed it to her, and she unfolded it revealing a pencil drawing. It was a sketch of a bottle of some kind on a silver chain. It had a long, narrow shape, almost like a canine tooth, but it was encircled with penciled wisps resembling vines. "Have you ever seen this before?"

She squinted through burning eyes at it. "I'm not sure."

"It was evidence in my last trial," Zoran said. He closed her fingers around it. "Tomorrow, when we begin handing out our literature, Alexander's people will concentrate themselves where we are. Will you go to where the evidence is stored and look for me? It is most essential to our cause."

"I suppose, but what's it for?"

"Find it, and I can explain all." Zoran smiled, tightly, and light kindled in the recesses of his murky eyes. "If it is still as it was, it contains the power to sway many to our side."

"Alright. I'll look."

Was it because she was tired, still distraught from her encounter with Daniel, that she did not ask more questions?

CHAPTER 24

Dresden, Present Day

Buzzzzzzz. Buzzzzzz.

Jack's eyes flickered. A dark ceiling hovered over him. He was so cold.

Buzzzzzz.... Right by his ear.

"Ahh!" Jack flung himself into a sitting position. Something hot bit into his scalp. He felt blood spill down his cheek and ear.

A woman swore in German, then said in English. "Lie down, Jack."

He recognized that bitterly cold voice. He did not lie down. He swung around and saw Lia. As he did, realized his hands were bound together. He tasted blood on his lips. He recoiled away from Lia, but from behind him, hands clamped onto his shoulder.

"She said lie down," said a man with a thick Germanic accent. "So lie down."

Jack twisted his shoulders. A fist bashed into his ear. Buzzing filled his skull. Dizzy, Jack was forced back onto the frigid cement floor to look up into Lia's angular face.

She laughed at him and brandished the electric razor. "You look so sexy with your head shaved. I rather regret that our evening progressed no further."

"Bitch!" Still woozy, he wrenched at the hands that held him. He caught a glimpse of triumphant blue eyes in a scruffy blond face.

"Now, now, that isn't very original." Lia pressed the cool tip of the razor against his head. The buzzing resumed.

"What the hell do you want from me? If you want ransom, I suppose you'll get it."

"Oh? From whom, Jack?" Lia swiped up his blood with one fingertip.

Alexander would pay to get me back, I think...

Shit, how will they ever find me?

Lia laughed, breathily, "I want exactly what you've offered me: your body. I just want it for slightly different purposes." She raked the razor over the top of his head.

Jack jerked against the restraining hands. The blade bit into his skin again, and let out a fresh, hot trickle of blood, and searing pain. That wasn't anything compared to the stab of guilt through his heart for what he'd done, or nearly done with Lia.

"Jordan said he wouldn't wake up that fast." The man's face hovered above his. He licked his teeth.

"He's really young. Maybe he rebounds faster. I gave him a good dose."

"I didn't die," Jack said. He would have known. He wished he had died.

"Oh, he didn't," the man said, "try a little more next time. I promise you, Jack, it is a nice way to die."

"My idea of nice." Jack bucked against his hands. "May be different than yours."

"We'll see. Are you done, Lia?"

"Yes."

"Good. We'll see how Jack likes to die." The man yanked at his shoulders. "Get up."

Die?

Jack tasted the remnants of metallic blood on his lips as he staggered to his feet. His quickened breath shuddered as he swung his head around, trying to take in the room, trying to figure out where he was. All he saw were bare white walls, bare cement floor, a blanket where he'd been lying, and another in the corner. The grey wool was splotched with dark stains. Blood.

"I'm not afraid to die," he said. "I've tried everything. It doesn't work."

The man shoved him through a doorway into a wide hall with the same cement floors, and metal doors painted grey, on either side. He yanked another open and pushed Jack inside. The light inside was blinding white. A man in a blood-splattered white coat looked up from a table. A fluorescent light dangled by a chain over him, making his round, slightly chubby face glow with a pale luminescence. Brown eyes darted behind round, wire-rimmed glasses. There was a body on the table, with electrodes stuck to his head and chest. Two greyish, bare feet stuck up at the end of the table.

A tremor went through Jack.

Nothing that you haven't seen before. Nothing you haven't seen before.

"He just rebounded again," the man said. His accent was American. "It took about three minutes longer this time."

"Okay, continue," his captor said. Lia slipped in behind them and bent over the body on the bed. She brushed her hand over the shaven head.

"Still with us, Marcus?" she said softly, "another day together."

The man didn't stir.

Jack's eyes skittered to an empty table, across the room. Beside him, like an array of tools in a garage, hung a variety of knives. Each blade shone in the blinding white of the light over the table. Machines and monitors stood on a stainless-steel table.

"What the heck do you think you can do to me?" He jerked against the hand that restrained one of his shoulders. "Are you even an immortal?"

Lia smiled at him and stroked the cheek of the comatose man. "Haven't you heard? Immortals aren't indestructible. They're just not easily killed."

Jack's chest clamped with a feeling that he couldn't identify. A thought had returned to him: the words in black ink upon the parchment family tree, *Jurgen Zeigler, 1901-1974.* "How?" he tried to force his words to come out strongly. They trembled.

Lia bent down and brushed her lips across the cheek of the unconscious man before her. "There are only three people who know: Alexander von Katlenburg, Adolf Hardwin, and Frederick von Schwalenburg. They hold the power of death over all of us." Her eyes lit from within, a strange, eerie light, "And so, we have no choice but to find it ourselves. Get him on the table, Peter."

Peter shoved Jack toward the table, but Jack planted his feet. There was such a wild, unpredictable look in Lia's eyes. He didn't even recognize her from the woman he'd met in the Irish pub. Her hand whipped out, brandishing a syringe. Jack shied from it, panting suddenly.

"Get on the table," she said gently, "after all, if you've tried everything, what is there to be afraid of?"

The room was silent, but for Jack's jagged breaths. He walked to the table, his feet weighted, as if by lead cuffs. He sat down awkwardly, hampered by his tied hands.

The American carried a handful of wires and electrodes toward him. "Take off his shirt, Lia," he said.

"Oh certainly." Lia took a big pair of shears and cut the long-sleeved shirt from Jack's torso. The blades of the scissors were icy cold against his skin. Jack couldn't help but stare at them as they snipped up his chest.

The American stuck the gel pads to his chest and his bare scalp. "Lie down."

Jack lay down. The American threw wide belts across his chest and clamped him to the table.

"Lovely."

Jack lay, silent and shivering. He looked away from the light reflected in the knives on the wall, and at the pale form on the table. The man was almost naked, dressed only in grey boxers. Two silicone tubes snaked out from between his legs into a white pail on the floor. The tubes were stained deep crimson and there was a dark shadow in the pail. "Shit," he breathed.

"Are you ready for your turn?" the American said. There was a glint in his dark eyes. "We will begin with a baseline." The American held up a syringe. "This is a lethal dose of morphine."

"Just bypass that shit." Jack jerked away from the needle. "I've shot myself. I've cut myself. I've drowned. If you're going to torture me, just get on with it."

"This is science," he said calmly, "I need a baseline." The American pinned his head down, and before Jack could yank away, jammed the needle into his neck. Jack felt a burn and then a creeping numbness. Black crept into his vision, and he fell toward the familiar darkness.

∞

"Hey Jacky, long time no see."

"Dad." Jack stared into Gerhardt Krause's blank eyes. He lay on the grass by the white clapboard wall of his childhood house. What was hot? What was sticky? Blood spilled in a narrow stream toward him. His father's limp hand was flung up over Jack's head. His blue lips pulled into a smile.

Then Jack was spiraling up, up, up. He saw light.

∞

He was on the table, with the American bending over him, and Lia stared down at him with a smile on her face.

"Excellent," said the American, "now we can begin." He turned and pulled a bowie knife off the pegboard.

"Oh hell no!" Jack bucked. The whole table tilted, the straps cut into his arms, sending pain through his tingling nerves.

"Sedate him, Lia!" The American said.

Jack tried to kick out as she approached with a syringe, but his legs were held down by restraints. His gaze on her, he didn't see the American's elbow until it bashed into his nose. Jack's eyes watered, his vision went white, then black, then cleared. Hot blood trickled onto his lips.

"No time to mess around," the American said, "be still and take the sedative. I assure you, you will want it."

Jack pressed himself, rigid, against the table. His limbs shook on their own accord. The needle slipped into his arm with only a slight bite. It took only a few seconds for Jack to begin feeling sleepy.

It will wear off the instant I rebound, he thought, *the whiskey always did.*

It felt like he came to life in the next instant. There had been no blackness, no release. Jack's eyes shot open, and if not for the restraints he would have sat up. His mouth opened, and air rushed out like he was screaming, but no sound emitted from his lips.

The American's fat face flashed above him. Jack felt the bite of the needle. He could feel his whole world slipping away. His head fell back, and the room vanished.

He woke again for just a second. He saw a knife flash down. He felt a red hot rod through his heart. His whole chest spasmed. His head dropped back, and burning black dark fell over him again.

"...rebounding strongly. About five minutes longer than the first, but a minute faster than last time. There's no pattern to it." Lia's voice, suffused with irritation.

"Good Lord, we could harvest organs off of him!" The American said, "If I had the supplies to pack them—"

Jack swam back to the surface, to light and life. He gasped with the fiery pain and this time his head lifted when he commanded it. In the second before a cold, rough hand pushed him back.

"Sedate him quickly! He's waking up."

The needle pierced his skin.

A high whine screamed right beside his ear and he saw a rotary blade swing down. Jack cried out, and fell back into the waiting arms of death.

Jack would never remember how many times he resurrected, awake and conscious in that cold, concrete room. The final time, he sensed that he was no longer watched. Far away, voices murmured unintelligible babble. His body was numb. Jack forced every bit of energy down toward his hand, but it wouldn't move. He couldn't feel the zip-ties that had bound him. He clenched his teeth. They began to chatter and Jack realized he was just cold, not paralyzed. His head cleared. He lay on a stretcher with a light blanket over him. The pads for the electrodes were still attached to his chest, but every bit of him seemed whole. Had it even happened? He turned his head, and saw the table. Blood soaked the slick metal surface, and dribbled in dark, dried stalactites from the edges.

"Oh shit," Jack breathed. He'd done sick things to himself on his dark, manic nights. This was something else entirely. He slid his cold fingers down his abdomen. There was a new seam there, straight down the middle of his chest, but healed and insensitive as if he'd had it for years. That would fade too, yet. He traced the length of it, down to his navel and then up into a 'y' across his chest. He'd been split open like a cadaver, like an autopsy. "What did they do?"

Jack raised his head and looked away from the table.

There was another man on a table, across the room. Jack remembered him, through a thick mental fog, blood draining from his veins. The hoses were gone now. The other man lay covered with a white sheet, face white as the fabric. His bare arm hung down like it had no bones, and his foot jutted out of the cover. His toes were grey, as if he were dead.

"Hey," Jack whispered. He tried to lift himself up and look for the American, or Lia. But the effort made him exhausted within a few seconds, and he fell back. "Hey!"

No answer.

Jack's heart jolted. *He's dead.*

No, he's not dead. His chest his moving.

Jack's stretcher shook as the American grabbed it and began to push it forward. Jack jerked into a half sit. "Oh shit!"

"Hey, hey," the American said as he pushed him back down, "you can run laps, do calisthenics, kung fu, whatever you'd like. Just wait until I put you into your room." His face was taut.

"Fuck you," Jack said.

He could feel the American's hot breath on his face. It smelled of onions and stale coffee, and Jack wondered absently when the American had a chance to drink coffee. Had the man cut him open with a cup of coffee in one hand?

The gurney rattled forward. The other man, who he'd seen before, opened a wide, metal door. The stretcher rattled through.

"Get off." The American said.

Jack struggled to sit. "Untie me, you son of a bitch."

The American's face twitched nervously. "Peter?"

The other man brandished pair of side-cutters, snapping the zip-ties. He shoved Jack off the stretcher, onto the floor, before his weak body could respond. Jack sprawled on the icy concrete.

A minute later, the American returned with the second stretcher. It slammed into Jack's side. Jack groaned and rose up on his knees.

"Stay there." The American pointed at Jack.

Jack's head swirled too persistently for him to move.

The American rolled the stretcher a little farther, and tipped it, dumping his victim like a sack of potatoes on a ragged pallet bed. Clothes came flying through the air from an unseen hand, landing in a swath across the floor. The American pushed. The door closed with a harsh 'chung!"

Jack lifted his head. A pile of blankets slouched against one wall. His cut-up shirt lay on the concrete in front of him along with a pair of blood-stained jeans and a mottled t-shirt that must have been his cell mate's.

"Get up," he said to himself. He pushed himself up on his hands and knees. He paused, wobbling. No, he couldn't get up. Not yet. Instead, he crawled toward the pallet and slumped down onto it.

Jack leaned his back against the wall and looked down at his chest. He'd been swabbed clean. The scar down the center of his chest had faded since last he'd seen it. He was perfectly whole, and whatever they'd done was no more successful than what he'd done himself. But he was so weak!

A soft moan brought Jack's gaze up. The other man had rolled onto his side and opened his eyes.

"Hey—" The word died on Jack's lips. There was no light at all in the man's brown eyes. They were perfectly dull and vacant.

"Hey," Jack tried again, weakly, "you okay?" Not a twitch, not a change of expression to say the man heard him. "Hey!" Jack said, louder. Nothing. "Oh boy," he whispered. The room was utterly silent.

Jack slid down and tried to pull the blanket over him. His whole body trembled with cold. Deep, heavy loneliness descended over him and crushed him against the cold floor.

Jack clenched his chattering teeth together and whispered through them, "So, They going to kill you?"

They don't know how.

Sure can do damage trying.

Jurgen's name, birthdate and death date swam in front of his eyes. There was Oswald too, whoever that was.

Is that what you want?

Not like this.

Jack glanced at the man across the room. He didn't want to end up like that zombie creature either. The man's glassy eyes were still open, focused on nothing. He had a narrow, delicate-looking face; pale as death. His head was shaven, but coated with a grey shadow of stubble.

"I've got to get out," he said in the man's direction, "I've got to get help for you. We can worry about dying later."

Jack conjured the image of the concrete floor and the metal doors, and the cinder-block walls. He turned slowly and took in the white-washed concrete walls of the bare, rectangular room. It was a narrow room. Above them, air ducts and pipes ran right and left. The floor had dark, scuff marks as if shelves had stood in it. And the walls had lines where the paint had been scraped off by the passing of carts, or pallets. They were in a storage room, maybe, and this was some sort of industrial building.

"Where are we? Do you know?" he said, as if his cellmate might answer.

A soft whistle of breath was his only answer.

What had the experiment room been like? Warmer, definitely, less concrete. Had there been more than one door? He couldn't remember. He'd been too panicked to get a good look.

Jack swallowed hard and licked his dry lips. Tomorrow they'd do this all over again. How would he keep his head together enough to find a way to escape?

CHAPTER 25
Dresden, 1630

"Is Master Ardovinni in?" Alexander stood back from the door, almost in line with the stone lions that guarded the entry from the street. Behind his back, one hand clutched his hat, and the other quivered.

The servant bowed slightly. "No sir, but Miss Ardovinni is in."

"If I may trouble her...?" His hands shook harder. He wanted to bolt past the slim young man, run up the stairs, fall at Cosima's feet and beg her to understand him. Instead, he entered the house, gave up his hat to the servant, and sat in the drawing room still, upright and dignified. He was keeping his word to Zoran. He would speak to Cosima, seek to both: make things right with her, and excuse himself to seek the truth about his bloodline.

Cosima swept into the drawing room a few minutes later. Her shoes clacked against the tile floor, far too loud and harsh in the still house. Her mouth was drawn into a thin, closely controlled line. Occasionally it would twitch, as if some word had rammed itself against the boundary of her lips.

She gazed at him without speaking. Her ebony eyes bored into his, barely blinking. She drew in a breath through her nose, and said, "Hello Alexander. I've heard that Giovanni spoke to you."

"I..."

"That man!" her nostrils flared. She turned quickly away. "I know very well that—" her voice broke.

Alexander found his voice, and his spine. He jumped up. "Cosima, I need to explain myself to you."

"Yes," she said in a small voice.

He crossed his arms and hunched his shoulders, his eyes on Cosima's back. He could see her shoulder blades through her fitted dress, quivering with every breath. "You've been frank about your past life, but I have not honored you with equal frankness."

"No." She did not turn around.

"Cosima, please," Alexander said softly. He took her elbow and turned her around. "Sit down. I mean to make my heart bare before you, if I can."

Her clenched jaw relaxed, though her body remained rigid. She allowed him to sit her down. Alexander sat, and withdrew a sheet of paper from his satchel and the stub of a pencil. He pulled a little side table toward them. It rocked on its spindly legs, nearly toppling in his haste.

Alexander began to draw. Dark eyes emerged on the page, a button nose, rosebud mouth, and a braid that in real life was deep chestnut in color and wound in an elaborate coil around her head. Her expression was soft and sensual. "My wife, Idonia," he said in a low voice.

Cosima's breath caught.

He put the pencil to paper again. His rapid strokes formed a mop of light colored hair, slightly protruding ears, a square chin much like his own. It was a young man, with flashing eyes and a winning smile. "Augustus, my son." He drew two more faces, young, apple-cheeked maidens with braids in coils around their heads. They had the same pert, turned-up noses as their mother.

"Annette and Konstanze." Alexander swallowed hard and laid down the pencil. "When I realized what I had become, I knew that I could not stay with them forever. Idonia and I agonized over it for months. My children were young—my girls ten and nine, my boy, fourteen. I already looked far too young to be their father, and the rumors of some sort of unnatural doings had spread about the countryside."

Alexander stroked a curve around Idonia's pencil portrait. "Finally it was decided that I must disappear. We would make it appear as if I had died in a hunting accident, or an animal attack." He squeezed his eyes shut. "We parted, as we thought, forever. I left Idonia in our bed, and rode out into the forest where I and Adolf Harwin had agreed to meet and go into hiding together."

He could see it all so clearly, Idonia clinging to him, tears mingling in their garments with the sweat of their final night together.

"If I had known I should lose you like this," she'd sobbed, "I should have loved you sooner." Their marriage had been arranged, one of pure utility for many years until deep affection had blossomed.

"I'm so sorry," Cosima said in a small voice.

"I saw her one more time after that," Alexander opened his eyes and looked her full in the face. Pain spread through his jaw as he fought not to cry. "It was three years later. By then, my children had ceased to mourn me. Augustus was a man, running the estate at Katlenburg. I met Idonia in secret, and she told me of their many tears, how Augustus had shouldered the burden of manhood at his tender age and vowed to care for her and his-his..." He pressed his lips together, drawing in deep breaths through his nose. "It shattered my heart," he said. He could hardly see Cosima through the blur of unshed tears. "They needed me—Augustus needed me. I hadn't yet imparted everything a young man needed to know. He was alone, to figure out all things on his own. How could I have done this to him? But it was too late to turn back, for I was dead to them."

He met Cosima's eyes. Tears shimmered there, on the rim of her eyelids.

"It's been three hundred years, Cosima," he whispered. He drew the page over and held it up in front of him. "Three hundred years and I mourn them still. I can recall their faces in an instant. I can remember whole conversations with Idonia, late at night. I've dreamed of them for years, which is the true source of my insomnia. I've forgotten so many things over hundreds of years but not them. I—I fear—" he dropped the page on the table and pressed his fingertips together. Cosima stared at him intently.

"I fear I cannot be a true, whole husband for you," the agony returned to his jaw, and the tears behind his eyelids. He blinked, angry at their presence. "For fear of the partings that may come."

"But why should we ever be parted?" she said gently.

"With you, no, but children—what about children? And there is now this theory Zoran has, that perhaps immortality is passing from descendant to descendant, waiting to spring forth again. It has been three hundred years. I must have a thousand descendants by now. I cannot produce more!"

Her small hand caught his clenched fist. Alexander fell silent and dropped his head. Her fingers pried his and stroked them until they relaxed open. She flipped his hand over and stroked a circle in his palm. "So you mean to make the both of us martyrs for the sake of our theoretical children?" she said it tenderly, without bitterness or condemnation. "Dear Alexander, what of me? Shall we be unhappy all of our long lives?"

"Surely not." His eyes were fixed on their joined hands. His blurred eyes longed to shut, and just focus on her tender ministrations. "God shall... shall be enough for us."

"Won't God be enough for us if we produce mortal children?" She reached across the little table and tipped his chin up so his eyes had to meet hers. "Won't he?"

"Yes," he had to say.

Somewhere in the house, a servant dropped something with a loud crash. They started, then smiled at each other. The spell was broken. Alexander's shoulders dropped. He rubbed his eyes, "Cosima, I must have answers. If I could I would marry you tomorrow—"

"If I could, I would have you tonight," she said.

He swallowed hard and avoided her gaze.

She laughed gently, bashfully. "Forgive me. Dear Alexander. There is something else you are forgetting in your dear, good thoughts of me. I was a whore. There were many years that I avoided pregnancy. Many years."

Alexander looked up, feeling far, far too much hope.

She touched his cheek. "Find your answers, and hasten back to me. I love you. I shall wait, whatever Giovanni Ardovinni may say."

∞

"There is something I want you to see." Alexander said to Zoran.

The horses stood saddled, bags slung over their backs. Zoran stood with his back turned, adjusting a strap here, tucking in a fold of a pack there. He turned, and as he did the early winter wind blew his hood up over his face. He tugged it away, shook his head, and laughed.

"There's something I want you to see," Alexander said again. He turned and nodded to Adolf and Sophia, who stood huddled in the doorway. He swung up onto the horse. "We shall make a small side trip. Are you ready?"

"Indeed." Zoran jammed his boot into the stirrup and hoisted himself up. "Tell me it isn't to say one last tearful goodbye to dear Miss Cosima?"

Alexander smiled into the folds of his cloak and remembered the heat of their parting kiss, juxtaposed with the cool ring on her finger, pressed against the back of his neck. "No, unfortunately." Instead of leading Zoran down the road out of Schwalenburg, he led him a short way down the promontory the castle sat on, and halted. He dismounted, and with a bemused expression so did Zoran.

Beside the stony road, the ground dropped steeply away. Alexander clung to the saplings and undergrowth to keep his footing on the slick, half-frozen grass. He heard Zoran crashing along behind him.

"Where—? Woah!" Zoran suddenly slid past him on his backside until he skidded to a halt. He got up, laughed, and brushed himself off. "Where are we going?" he asked with a trace of laughter still in his voice.

"Have you explored these woods?" Alexander paused, panting lightly, as Zoran collected himself.

Zoran shook his head. His eyes gleamed with curiosity.

"There is a cave below the castle," Alexander said, picking a solid footing and moving on. He jumped down a series of small, rocky ledges, and climbed over a tree. The faint rush of a river met his ears. It was the Elbe, flowing well out of sight in the woods. "The Castle was built over it, in fact."

"A cave. Why...? Oh." Zoran seemed to sense Alexander's intent. He caught up and hiked right behind Alexander. Their footsteps beat upon the rocks in unison.

Alexander frowned to himself as he picked his way down the slope. They would have never come down here—He, Adolf and Frederick. But they'd wounded a stag, and Frederick had seen it plunge down this very slope. They'd stood upon the hill where Schwalenburg now sat, and seen the tiny figure of the deer, in its death agonies on the forest floor.

Alexander leapt off a small crag and landed lightly upon the very bottom of the slope. "The original Castle Schwalenburg was up river, about a league. Frederick built this one." They were on level with the river now, though it was two or three hundred yards away, through thick undergrowth. He led Zoran around the circumference of the oblong hill. In a few minutes, he caught sight of bare rock through the trees. He cut a straight path for it.

The mouth of the cave was blocked off by boulders, placed there centuries ago. Yet Alexander climbed over them, slightly up the slope. He hoisted himself up onto a ledge and rolled aside a single, flat rock. It exposed a jagged hole, just large enough for them to drop through, into the cave. Alexander poked first one leg in, then the other, then let himself fall. He landed hard, and fell to his knees. He'd only just rolled aside, when Zoran jumped down beside him.

Alexander made no explanation. Zoran had already seen the daylight, in a solid stream through the hole, flashing in a reflection off the back wall of the cave, a small trickle of water.

"The fountain," he breathed.

They approached it. Alexander knelt beside it and plunged one hand into the icy stream. It flowed, endlessly, from a crack in the ceiling. "And here, the source of our lives as we know them."

Zoran breathed heavily. Was it from the hike, or from excitement? He trailed his fingers through the basin of the fountain, only about as wide as a wagon-wheel, and flowing not out into the world, but into some unseen crevice below.

Zoran looked up. "What should happen if I would drink now?"

"Nothing."

Zoran cupped his hands in the water and held them, filled and dripping, to his mouth. He drank and licked his lips thoughtfully.

"Water. This is what should undo us?" He drank again.

"It is difficult to believe that anyone else should access this water, but who can say where it flows to?"

"Deep into the earth—or perhaps, to nowhere! It is, surely, an enchanted fountain."

"Surely," Alexander said with faint amusement. "Meanwhile, I have asked Frederick to seal up even this opening. So perhaps this is the only time you shall see it in your long life."

"Not permanently sealed! Why should you destroy it?"

"I don't know that we can destroy it." Alexander ran his tongue over his teeth. "But, I'd not have anyone stumble upon it as we did."

Zoran rocked back and forth on his heels. His eyes stared, unfocused, at a spot somewhere beyond Alexander.

Alexander swished his hand through the water again and stood. "I just wanted you to see it."

Zoran reached into his jacket and began to pull a silver chain from his collar. A little silver vial, the shape of a lily petal and all surrounded by silver vines, emerged.

"Zoran, what are you doing?"

"I want to take some."

"No," Alexander said, "this is a secret place. You cannot take water from the fountain. What shall you do with it?"

"Examine it." Zoran said as if this were the most obvious thing ever.

"Please, do not."

Zoran's lip curled, but he stuffed the vial back into his blouse. "How will we get out of here?"

Alexander turned to the cave wall and jammed one foot onto a ledge in the wall and began to scale the wall. Behind him, Zoran laughed. Alexander hoisted himself out of the hole. When he glanced down, Zoran was out of sight in the dark hole. A ripple of unease went through him, but a moment later Zoran's face appeared. He gripped the same hand-holds as Alexander had and soon emerged into the sunlight.

"Thank you for showing me this," he said, brushing off his clothes. His forehead creased. "You will make me swear to secrecy, I suppose?"

Alexander nodded. "Zoran I would not show you if I didn't trust you."

Zoran nodded solemnly. "My lips are sealed."

They travelled together as far as the outskirts of Dresden, then parted ways. Zoran was bound for Prague, to research his own bloodline. Alexander was bound for his ancestral lands at Katlenburg.

∞

The castle of Katlenburg loomed over the town of the same name. He came upon it, almost before he knew he was there. It had spread down the hillside to the bank of the river. In his day, the town perched upon the crown of the hill. Alexander halted his horse on the outskirt of the town and gazed up at the distant crag where the old fortress loomed over the town..

He laughed, almost a sob. "The conquering king returneth."

He nudged the horse back into motion along the gravel street. Three hundred years ago, the town had consisted of wattle and daub huts with thatched roofs and there were, yet, a few of these on the outskirt with small fences and animals in their yards. After a minute, he rode among two and three-story brick houses, packed tightly together and rimming the street like spectators in a victor's parade.

Though, if he were the victor, this was a dismal parade. Riding alone, following a farmer's oxcart.

At the top of the hill, Alexander emerged into a square and was forced nearly to a halt by the crowd. The square was packed with people milling hither thither between vendors, who hawked produce from carts on the edges of the rectangular grounds. Alexander waded his horse through the melee and paused at the opposite end, a few yards from where the road exited the square.

He squinted up at the spire of a church he didn't recognize. It was new, sure, but not that new. Perhaps only a hundred years old by the stocky, rectangular tower, with a parapet and a small cone-shaped spire.

He rode out of the town again, up the winding road toward the castle, pausing every now and again to scrutinize the castle as he circled the hill. He could make out the original, square castle keep standing head and shoulders above the rest of the castle. At some point, a stocky, round tower had been built onto a corner. A section of wall jutted out over the crag. He didn't recognize it, but the patina of the stones, and the thick vine growth made him think it had been there a while.

He rode through the open portcullis, unchallenged. As he jumped from the saddle, he could imagine the footman running to take the horse by the bridle and lead it away to brush it down and bed it in the stables, and his old steward greeting him at the door while Idonia looked down from the high windows of the keep.

Alexander lifted his head toward the windows. They were empty.

He scanned the tops of the walls, then the small bailey he stood in. Thus far no one had taken notice of him, though people milled here and there between the walls. A farmer with a small cart, loaded with bags of grain, had entered the bailey behind him. He dragged the cart past, toward the castle granaries. A man walked by, toward the keep, with a haunch of meat wrapped in cloth on his shoulder and a wicked hunting knife thrust in his belt.

"Good day," Alexander said forcefully as he passed.

His head lifted, revealing a young but weathered face, and sun-bleached blond hair. "Good day sir," The young man nodded to him, took a step, then glanced back with an odd expression in his blue eyes.

"Is the Lord at home?" Alexander asked.

"Yes, Sir," the man's answer was strangely strangled.

"Thank you, my good fellow."

The huntsman walked on, adjusting his burden as he went. Alexander spotted a rail he could tie his horse to, and after he'd secured his beast, fished through his bag for the letter of introduction he'd prepared. He walked up to the manor house door—the double oaken doors through which he'd passed every day of his mortal life—with a sick feeling in his stomach. He blew out a sigh and squared his shoulders. He spotted a thin chain hanging beside the door and pulled it. Within the house, a bell sounded.

A young man answered. "Good day?"

"Good day," Alexander said, "my name is Alexander Karlstan." He held out the rolled letter, secured with a string. "I am a distant relative of your masters."

The servant took the letter. "Please come in. His lordship shall be alerted."

After half an hour, Lord von Katlenburg received him in the very room where Alexander had received guests. While Alexander waited for him, he glanced around the room at the plush settees and the ornately carved side-tables. Good, there must still be money in the family.

He perched on the edge of the settee, rigid. He felt very much like he was sneaking into Katlenburg, like he was up to shady business. It was ludicrous. No one would say, "Aren't you Alexander von Katlenburg from three hundred years ago?"

Alexander laughed, almost a giggle, just as the door opened. He leapt up.

"Good day, Sir." a middle aged man stepped into the room, looked around, smiling, and spotted him.

Instantly he started. "Good Lord."

"Sir?" Alexander took a step toward him. "My name is Alexander Karlstan, of Dresden?"

"Yes. Yes, I read your letter." Lord von Katlenburg gave his head a little shake and smiled again. "Forgive me, but you bear a very striking resemblance to my late nephew. Very striking." He took a step closer and surveyed him. Alexander mirrored his scrutiny. His successor was tall, slim, even gangly, despite his age, with a cheerful, well-lined, face and salt-and-pepper brown hair, tied back in a queue.

"Striking, but not identical," Katlenburg said. He sighed, as if this were a great relief. "None-the-less, like receiving a ghost. You don't have to convince me you are my relative. You have the family face as much as I do not." He crossed the room and held out his hand. "I am Lord Georg von Katlenburg."

Alexander grasped the proffered hand.

"I admit I had no idea I had relatives in Dresden," Lord Georg said.

"My sister and myself may be all. My parents are deceased." He used Sophia's parents' names in the letter. Ignatius and Maria Karlstan's noble blood was so well diluted, he was not surprised Lord Georg hadn't heard of them. In fact, he'd counted on it.

"Ahh..." Lord Georg sighed. He paused a moment, then slapped one hand on his knee. "What can I do for you, master Karlstan?"

"I hope this shall be a simple request with little inconvenience for yourself." Alexander leaned forward and presented the carefully crafted falsehood Zoran had given him, "There are great gaps in my family's genealogical records, which we hope to fill."

"Why?" Lord Georg said, a hint of terse suspicion in his voice.

Alexander glanced up. "My sister and I are orphans from youth. We simply seek to gain as much information as we can and form a family history. That is all."

Georg nodded, in apparent acceptance. His smile returned, but faint hardness remained around his eyes.

Alexander reached into the satchel, at his feet, and withdrew a rolled piece of parchment. On it, Zoran had crafted the beginnings of a family tree, starting with his name: Alexander Leopold Karlstan von Katlenburg, his marriage to Idonia, and their children. He'd fleshed it out with the names he knew—his grandchildren and great grandchildren. He had, also, Sophia's family near the bottom of the page, with his name scratched in as her older brother. Zoran had given him as much information as he'd gathered, mostly that from his daughter Annette's family, which had led him to Miss Bourg in the past.

"Quite spotty indeed," Lord Georg agreed. "You would like to see our records, then."

"If I might."

"Certainly, certainly." His host rubbed his chin with one hand. His other hand twitched on his knee. "Indeed we have good records. We are most proud of our private archives." A note of hesitance had come into his voice. The joviality struggled to stay on his face. "In fact, my late nephew took a great interest in them. They were his pet project. Yes," his host said finally. He stood up. "I will have someone help you. But first, let me make you comfortable. It will take hours, even days to do your research. Do you have lodging in the town?"

"Not yet—"

"No, certainly, we will prepare a room for you. You are family."

Alexander found himself put up in a luxuriously decorated apartment, far finer than the one he'd inhabited at Schwalenburg. He was told to come dine with the family, and shown the room where the ancestral records were kept. He had no time to begin reading them; he had to dress for dinner.

He was escorted to the drawing room, in a wing of the castle that had been added on in his absence.

"Master Alexander!" Lord Georg held out his hand as a servant announced his name at the door of the family apartments, and ushered him in.

"Have you had time to delve into the archives yet?" Lord Georg asked.

"Enough to get my bearings, Sir," Alexander said. "They are... most extensive."

"Good, good." Lord Georg escorted him across the reception room. The longest wall was all hung with portraits—a tall, gangly young man who must have been a youthful Lord Georg, a portrait of two young women. "My Hilda and Annaliese," Lord Georg pointed to them, "my son's portrait is not yet made. This—" He pointed to another, "is Albert, my nephew. You can see how I might have been taken aback by your appearance."

Alexander leaned toward the gilded frame, and the portrait of the man, perhaps twenty years old. He recognized the keen blue eyes, the square jaw and high forehead as very much his own. "Good heavens, I do not blame you in the least."

"I raised him. We were all... heartbroken when he passed of a severe illness, about six months ago..." Lord Georg paused, gazing at the floor for a moment.

"I'm very sorry," Alexander said toward his feet.

Lord Georg said nothing. He led Alexander into the dining room.

Lord Georg's family was already seated, along with two couples, likely guests like himself. Alexander heard a soft intake of breath but did not turn his head as he bowed to the lady of the house.

"My son, Leopold."

Alexander turned and bowed to the young man. He looked up. Young Leopold had his father's gangly frame, dark, tousled hair, high cheekbones. Both cheekbones were flushed red, like someone had touched them with a paintbrush.

Poor lad. I am the ghost of his cousin.

He shifted uncomfortably, and turned aside.

On the whole, once they were seated, dinner was a placid affair. Lady von Katlenburg was a pleasantly talkative woman, pumping him with questions about Sophia, and Dresden, most of which he was able to answer truthfully. The other couples, lesser nobles from nearby estates, were amiable but bland. He didn't know the people and events they referenced to each other.

It was only when he became comfortable, fortified with the Spanish wine, that he fed them Zoran's legend. "There is a legend I have heard in my travels that may amuse you."

Leopold also seemed comfortable now. He leaned in, his eyes bright. He pulled his goblet toward him.

Alexander continued, "There is a tale of a von Katlenburg who was impervious to death and never aged."

Leopold spat out his wine. His face turned nearly as crimson and the beverage. He swore and clapped his hands to his stained shirt.

"I have never heard such a thing," Lady von Katlenburg said with a laugh. "Leo, go and change your shirt. Where did you hear about this, Master Karlstan?

Alexander attempted a laugh that came out too high and pinched. "I attended a school in Bohemia for a time. A friend told me that tale. We are a more interesting family than I knew."

"Indeed," Lord Georg said. And just like that, the conversation moved on. A few minutes later, Leopold returned, his shirt and his spirit's restored. Still, as Alexander kept up cheerful conversation, he had the uncanny sensation that Leopold's eyes were on him.

∞

Alexander stretched his arms back into the rectangle of sunlight behind him and rubbed his neck. The pages before him had begun to blur in front of him. His fingers were stained with ink, but the entirely of the direct male line was copied onto the page in front of him, from him through Augustus, and down to Georg von Katlenburg, his host.

It was the second day of his stay in Katlenburg. It shouldn't have taken so long to copy down the genealogy, but for the little notes written in the margins of the births, deaths, and marriage records, all the same scribbling, cramped hand. Were they the late Albert's notations?

Beside his son's marriage record: *during the ceremony, the bride's dress catches on a candelabra and nearly upsets it before the groom catches it.*

He'd laughed outright, then choked up.

A few generations later he came across this note beside a baptism record: *two days later, the baby died.* He dug through the records, but found nothing. Perhaps the record had been lost, but it was a provoking thought. What if the baby did not die?

No, it was horrifying to think about it.

He picked up a sheaf of papers that he'd kept near since he'd found them. His finger traced down the birth records of his grandchildren: Alexander, Ambrose, Stephan, Viktoria, Isolde, and Ludwig. So many precious souls he'd never laid eyes on. He lingered on each name, dying to see their faces.

Bitterness roiled up in him. He pushed away from the desk, crossed his arms tight over his chest. An ache had sprung up below his sternum. "Dear God! Why have you done this to me? What did I do? What was my offense?"

The room was silent.

"Why?" he cried out.

Something thumped nearby. The door had just shut. Someone had been there.

Alexander stood, panting, in the center of the room. "Sit down, fool," he said to himself. The faster he read, the faster he could leave this house of ghosts.

Young Albert von Katlenburg's notations became more frequent the more modern the records were—about his grandfather, sheets of paper full of stories. Albert had known his grandfather well, a kindly man but—Albert had noted in a fairly self-conscious way—given to drink. Alexander read every one of the stories and began to feel kinship with Albert. Humor sparkled in each of his stories, along with keen moral observations.

He found nothing to suggest immortality in any of his descendants. Perhaps there were none. Alexander hoped against hope.

There was something else that caused Alexander the briefest of pauses. Georg von Katlenburg was the second of two sons. Albert's father, Maximillian von Katlenburg, died when Albert was a youngster. His mother died a few years later, and Katlenburg had been given to Georg's care, until Albert was of age. But Albert, according to the record, had died within months of receiving his rightful inheritance.

My family would find this disgraceful, but I suspect it shall be helpful for further generations. Perhaps, at very least, they shall understand themselves a great deal better. My father struggled with melancholy. Sometimes he was truly not himself, and said hurtful things.

Alexander flinched and turned the page.

I am told my grandfather experienced the same malady. It has caused me to read as many of the old stories as I can. There are hints that my ancestors have suffered thus.

He swallowed against the lump in his throat. Was that also a family trait he'd passed down?

Ever since he'd stepped foot in Katlenburg's walls, darkness had slowly fallen over his mind like a black curtain. He lay awake at night staring at the high stone ceiling and his mind spun in circles. He relived conversations with Idonia, with his children, with the old steward over what wine to import.

Why would he relive that? But he did.

Alexander got up and walked, shoulders hunched and arms crossed tightly, around the small, rectangular room. He sat down, palmed his face, and took a deep breath.

There was one more line on the page. Alexander squinted at it and pushed it into a bright spot of sunlight on the desk, for Albert's hand had become scratchy with hesitation.

My cousin Leopold is the same.

Alexander leaned back in the chair. A prickle skittered down his spine. After his anecdote about the immortal, Katlenburg, Leopold had left the dining table and not returned. The next time they'd crossed paths, Leopold flattened himself against the wall to let Alexander pass. The young man's dark eyes bore fiercely into him, and did not blink away long after what was polite and proper.

What has my family become?

∞

Early evening on the fourth day of his stay, Alexander realized there was not much more to glean from the records. He pushed his chair away from the desk and stretched his arms above his head. His back and buttocks ached from sitting for hours upon hours. His eyes burned from reading, from short nights, and perpetual emotion. He was so tired.

He sighed and rubbed one of the records between his fingers, the record with the names of his grandchildren.

"Rightfully isn't it mine?" he whispered.

No, no. It was but a piece of paper. He could hold their names in his heart as well as he could hold the paper in his hand.

So Alexander rose from the chair and closed his leather portfolio, with the reams of paper, copied records. He paused, inspiration lighting in his mind. He sat back down, pulled out a clean sheet of parchment and his stubby pencil. With quick, purposeful strokes, he began sketching.

He tucked the portraits of Idonia, Annette, Konstanze, and Augustus into the records. Albert would have liked them. He sighed deeply, took up his portfolio, and blew out the candles.

He paused in the quiet hallway.

For a moment it was almost possible to imagine that he'd turn to the left and return to the family apartments, where Idonia would be sitting before the fire with her embroidery in hand. Annette or Konstanze would be curled up at her feet on the hearthrug.

Alexander pressed his lips together and turned to the right and walked outside. His limbs felt heavy, but he guessed that there would be no sleep for him tonight if he did not tire himself thoroughly.

It was odd, but for all his nights in the halls of Katlenburg, he hadn't dreamt of Idonia once.

Gloom had fallen over the castle. The air was still, sultry, redolent with moisture. The sun shone through a thick haze of clouds with an almost greenish hue. Alexander lifted his face, sucked in a deep breath, and sighed. It would storm, but probably not here. The thickest clouds piled up in the eastern sky, already past Katlenburg.

A man passed him. He glanced back and nodded a curt greeting. It was the stocky blond huntsman who had greeted him the day he'd arrive. His eyes flickered, and his mouth pursed as if he wished to speak. Instead, he only nodded again and adjusted his game bag and walked on. Alexander followed after him, at a distance, so he could take the opposite path and not interfere with the man's hunting.

As his feet carried him through the gate, he passed by Leopold, astride a tall, chestnut steed. Leopold turned his head and followed him with glittering eyes.

A cold pit formed in Alexander's stomach. He broke into a lope, down the path as soon as the boy was past. After a moment he stopped, fell into a walk, and laughed sheepishly. What was he doing?

He had a mind to visit the riverbank, opposite the village, and wondered how much the terrain may have changed. From his vantage point on the raised road, he could see only a little ways into the woods. Katlenburg perched at the top of a pyramid-like promontory. The road had been cut into the shallowest side, and the river wound below the steepest. That, at very least, had not been altered by the passage of three hundred years. It was in the same place, though had worn it's way deeper into the earth.

Alexander leapt off the road and plunged into the forest.

In his day, there had been an old hut in a clearing about a third of a league into the forest, directly west as the crow flew. It was the solitary quarters of a castle huntsman. Alexander struck out in that general direction, weaving in and out among the giant evergreens, and always bracing himself slightly against the downward slope. By the time ten minutes had passed, his shirt was drenched from sweat and the humid air. Alexander peeled off his jacket and tucked it under his arm.

The muffled sunlight was growing weaker, overshadowed by thick cloud. Alexander had just thought that the entire clearing, if abandoned, could long be overgrown with mature trees, when he broke out of a thick patch of undergrowth, into a small clearing. A hut sat in the center. It wasn't the old, wattle and daub hut, with the tanned stag hide over the door. This little house was tidier, and of sturdy wood construction. A round of oak, the width of a barrel, sat beside the door with an axe embedded in it, but there was no light about the place, and no smoke from the chimney.

"But it is a hot night," Alexander said. He pursed his lips. In fact, the young huntsman he'd passed could be the inhabitant.

He skirted the house slowly, paused on the opposite side again, and looked around. As he took a step onward, a distant, sharp crack cut across the clearing. Alexander hesitated, listened, and continued toward the woods. As he entered the shadow of the trees, a droplet of rain splashed on his cheek, then his lips, then two at a time, then in earnest. The soft patter of rain on green, leafy undergrowth stifled the sound of his footfalls.

Suddenly a shout pierced the gloom, "Albert!"

Alexander halted.

"Albert!" again, closer. "I know it's you!"

Alexander stopped, straining his ears for footfalls, and his eyes for movement. Leopold. Something made him hunker down, panting, in the bushes instead of calling out to the boy.

"Albert, I know it's you!" the shout was raw-edged. Alexander heard the first crash of Leopold entering the woods, staggering footfalls. The rain pelted harder into his soaked hair and shoulders.

Alexander rose up into a crouch and crept out of his hiding place, down the slope. He would circle around and make for the castle again.

"Albert!" he heard one last call, another crash in the undergrowth, and then nothing.

After he'd snuck about a hundred yards, Alexander straightened and began to jog along the jagged curve of the hill. All the while he listened with every fiber of his being for Leopold's presence. He felt his fear must be irrational, but he was really terrified, keenly aware of his vulnerability—alone, unarmed, and without an ally, with night soon to fall.

"Stop!"

Alexander skidded and nearly fell.

Leopold stood ahead of him. His long, dark hair, fell dripping around his shoulders, plastered flat to his skull. His eyes just dark holes at that distance, wreathed in the shadows, but there was enough light for Alexander to catch the glint off a long blade in Leopold's hand.

Alexander held up both hands and began to back away. "Leopold, I am not your cousin. You're sick."

"I know what you are doing," Leopold said in a hoarse voice, advancing, "coming back to haunt me, haunt your stupid archives. I knew you'd come to Daniel's shack."

"Leopold, I am not Albert. I am Alexander of Dresden." Alexander's back collided with a tree. He gasped.

Leopold smiled, a deathly rictus. "That was a good story, about the immortal von Katlenburg." He waved his knife. "It gave me quite a turn. Well, I am going to finish what I started now. Perhaps you could survive the poison, but how will you live with your head separated from your body?" He lunged.

Alexander spun around the tree and bolted. His pumping legs carried him up the hill, his only thought to reach the hunting shack. His feet scrabbled over the mossy turf. He fought to keep his feet under him.

Leopold's ragged breath was close behind him, puffing like a wounded bear.

His toe struck a root. His arms shot out reflexively as he tumbled.

"Oof!" Alexander's chest struck a rock as he fell, driving every bit of wind from his lungs. In an instant, Leopold was on top of him. The blade swung down. "No, no!"

Steel cut through his neck. Alexander screamed with pain. He felt the hot blood flowing from him.

"You won't come back this time!" Leopold cried, "you won't—"

Something slammed into Leopold, carrying him bodily off of Alexander.

Alexander rolled, saw the broad back of the huntsman. Steel clanged on steel. Leopold swung his knife at the huntsman, who parried with his own blade in one hand, and a broad-bladed axe in the other.

Alexander grabbed for his throat, scrabbling, trying to stanch the blood. It seeped, sticky, between his fingers. Black encroached on his vision.

"Murderer!" A harsh voice called out, followed by crashing through the undergrowth.

Alexander lay, staring up at the darkening sky, the rain washing the blood from his clutching fingers in rivulets onto the ground. His dimming vision caught sight of a stern, sunburned face hovering over his.

"Sir?"

Too late. Alexander's hand slackened and fell to the damp earth, and he knew no more.

CHAPTER 26
Winnipeg, Present Day

Alannah didn't teach again until Monday, but the silent house had a habit of creaking, popping and shifting. The bitter wind howled across the chimney, voice-like sometimes in ways that made Alannah's hair stand on end. Jack did not call again, or even text, even though she sent him a few inquiring messages. She drifted into a bleak, resigned state.

She took her bag, her laptop, an electric kettle and a French press, and camped out in her cramped office at the university. Miles found her staring into space, with her laptop dead because she hadn't plugged it in, and her coffee cold. The afternoon light was fading, and the room was half dark.

"Alannah?" he asked with a confused smile on his face. He flicked on the light switch. "There's someone here to see you."

She straightened so fast that the office chair bobbed and threatened to tip her off. "Yeah?" Alannah swallowed hard and recalled the young man who had sat in on a class once. "Is he blond, with dark brown eyes?"

Miles shook his head. "Dark haired."

"Oh," she said slowly. "You're in your office, right?"

"Just down the hall if you need me." He withdrew from the doorway.

Alannah jumped up and pushed the crusty coffee mug and the press full of grinds into the corner. She put the laptop on its charger and stacked up her paper into neat pile. She straightened her cardigan, just as she heard soft footfalls, and a gentle voice saying, "Miss Krueger, thank you for seeing me."

Alannah looked up and saw a slight young man with gentle brown eyes. His black hair was pulled back in a knot, like Alexander had been wearing his. He pulled one hand out of the pocket of his grey wool coat and reached out to shake her hand. As he did, he turned his wrist and met her eyes. She looked down and saw the oak tree tattoo upon his wrist.

Alannah stiffened. She knew exactly who he was. She grasped his warm hand just long enough to shake it, then withdrew out of reach. "Mr. Ardovinni. It's been a long time."

"Indeed."

Her breath shuddered in and out but she stiffened her spine. "Would you like to have a seat?" She sat down at her desk, and nodded toward the chair she kept for the odd time that a student visited. "Please shut the door."

He did, and walked toward the desk.

"How can I help you, Mr. Ardovinni?" she asked. "We don't meet many of our people in Winnipeg." *And how the hell did you find me here?*

"I'm here on behalf of a friend." He sat down slowly and laid both hands on the table. "We had hoped to find Lord Alexander here, but since you are a close friend of his, we hope you would do us a kindness and allow us to contact him."

She injected a note of coldness into her voice. "Mr. Ardovinni, you are an immortal citizen. You have every right to walk into Schwalenburg and speak to Alexander in person."

He flinched. "The one I act on behalf of is not a citizen."

"Then surely you have a lawkeeper you can contact, if this is about assimilation into our society."

Giovanni leaned forward. "Miss Krueger, I wouldn't impose upon you if there wasn't a need for extreme delicacy."

"Go on."

"My friend is not one of us, but we know enough of his lineage to know that he is of Lord Alexander's lineage. However, he is the immortal son of immortal parents—"

Alannah gasped, and bit down on her lip. What? Twice-born? Immortal child of two immortal parents? She thought she was the only immortal of immortal parentage.

Zoran. Zoran was in this. Ardovinni certainly had the history.

How did he know she was here anyway?

"—thus he is concerned about undue scandal."

"What do you want me to do?" she said in a halting voice. "Your friend will not be faulted for who sired him."

Giovanni looked down. "But what of his parents? My friend wishes no harm to come to them—surely you would feel the same if your parents were in the same place."

My parents were in the same place. Why are you doing this? What kind of sick test is this? "They must take the consequences that are due them." Alannah stood up. She clenched her trembling hands at her sides. "I'm sorry, but I cannot aid you in circumventing the law. You know Alexander. Go to Dresden and talk to him."

He stood, and he stared into her eyes. His full lips clenched and his voice shook, nearly imperceptibly, as he said, "Miss Krueger, if you would just give a phone number..."

"Surely you have one."

"Not his private number."

"Alexander doesn't give people his private number," Alannah said forcefully.

"He might," Giovanni said gently, "if he knew who asked."

"No. Please leave." Alannah ground her fisted hands into her sides. Her knuckles popped, they were clenched so tight. She thought she saw hints of confusion, mixed with anger, in his eyes. He turned slowly, opened the door, and left. Alannah shut the door behind him and leaned against it.

Alannah's chest was constricted with iron bands. *An immortal child of immortal parents?* It was only done one way, and Zoran had been the only one to do it. He'd called it 'twice-born'. *"You're my twice born, Alannah, my miracle, my treasure."*

She stumbled to the desk and flipped open her laptop. "Alexander," she typed into a blank email, "Giovanni Ardovinni just visited me. He wanted to contact you about a friend who is a twice-born. I know what you said about Zoran, but..." She paused. Her fingers hovered over the keyboard. "Are you sure he didn't father any more children?" Her trembling finger lingered, midair, about to send the email.

Am I just being paranoid again? Am I a fool?

She choked, but no tears sprang from her burning eyes. She added, "How did he know I'm in Winnipeg?" She clicked and sent the email.

"Everything okay?" Miles said from the doorway.

Alannah jumped in her seat and swung around, clutching her chest. "Uh, I..."

"Sorry." Miles frowned and pushed up his round glasses. "You just looked a little upset."

"No, uh, it's okay." She stood up and walked around the desk to her little electric kettle. She fumbled to switch it on. "He was hoping to contact Dr. Von Katlenburg."

"Oh. Okay. Alright, well..." Miles scuffed his shoe on the linoleum floor. "I'm going. Do you want to get dinner... or something?"

She sighed and smiled wearily at him. He was sweet, and she was lonely, but now was not the time. "Some other time, Miles. Thanks."

After he left, Alannah boiled the water in the kettle again. She didn't try to bring out her lecture notes. She just drank cup after cup of black coffee and clicked 'refresh' on her inbox over and over again. Alexander did not reply.

She shut her eyes. "What are you doing, Zoran?" If he could publish writings from within his cell, could he send Ardovinni to find her?

"I may be crazy," she whispered, "but I'm not naive anymore."

She remembered the little glass vial, the one he'd asked her to steal.

∞   ∞   ∞

Alannah lingered at Schwalenburg's council room door. Frederick von Schwalenburg's voice boomed from within, "How dare you—"

Zoran, shoulder to shoulder with Jurgen and Martin Bertholet, waved a stack of his literature. "We demand that the people be allowed to hear us."

Daniel came rushing past her without a glance in her direction.

Alannah swallowed. Time to go. If he was gone, there was no one near Alexander's office.

Alexander's office door was open a crack. She knew exactly where he'd keep the vial, if he had it. He had a large safe in the corner, where he kept all kinds of things pertinent to the lawkeepers, and he'd told her where he kept the combination because sometimes when she assisted him, he'd needed things out of it. He had it written on the inside of his top, left-hand desk drawer.

Her chest ached with anxiety.

It was stupid. Alexander might not even bat an eye if he found her in there. Despite the fact that Daniel must have told him everything, Alexander still kept her as a part-time assistant. She'd manufactured an excuse about having left some of the notes she was supposed to type out.

Alannah slipped behind the wide, oak desk and tugged the top drawer open. Alexander kept that drawer packed with pens, little notebooks, business cards, and keys. She shoved them aside. Two pens spilled out and clattered on the floor. Alannah hiccupped with fright. There it was. The numbers were still there, faded into the grain of the wood.

She knelt in front of the safe and spun the dial, right, left, all the way around, right, left. There was a hair's breadth of a pause, then a click. Alannah tugged. The safe opened.

Either Daniel or Idina had organized the safe. Everything was in neatly labeled manila envelopes, filed in dated folder. Alannah found the early 1900s. There were only two folders. One, 'Joseph Nils Oswald' and the other 'Zoran Kosar'. Alannah turned the envelope over, and a silver chain slid out. A moment later, the vial followed. It was made of cloudy glass, long and narrow and pointed on the end, reinforced all about by tarnished vines of silver. As Alannah turned it over, she heard a faint 'glug'. She shook the vial. There was something in it. It had about a centimeter of liquid in it, colorless, or so it appeared through the cloudy glass.

That evening she met Zoran at a little restaurant well out of the way of his place, just in case Daniel might follow again. When she placed the vial in his hand, his eyes glowed.

"Oh, thank you Alannah." His fingers closed tightly around it. He closed his eyes and sucked his breath in through his teeth. His face was relaxed, almost euphoric.

"What will you do with it?" she asked.

He didn't answer.

"What's in it?"

Zoran pulled the chain over his head and smoothed back his dark curls. "Did you look inside?" His eyes opened.

Alannah shook her head.

He leaned in and took her hand in his warm fingers. "What is it that the Immortal Lords guard above all else, so precious that they'd keep it from their own citizens?"

She stared at him, uncomprehending. "Water? Water from the fountain?"

He laid his hand over his shirt, over the vial and smiled. "The power of immortal life, now in all our hands."

∞   ∞   ∞

When the world outside was completely dark but for the greenish streetlights, Alannah stood up and shut the laptop. She had to stop thinking about those things. Her head throbbed with worry and caffeine.

"Maybe I should take a trip—a short trip." She licked her lips. "I could go to Brandon for the weekend—maybe a little farther. Grand Forks—I could go shopping. I could use another suit."

She should leave for good, and find another place that her father's long tendrils of influence could not reach.

She drove home, convinced she could finally do it.

Wellington Crescent was still. In the silence of Alexander's big house, Alannah paced around with Jack's pistol in her hand. Her suitcase lay open on the bed, but she hadn't put anything in it. Every time she opened the dresser drawers, she froze. She couldn't lift out one shirt, one bra, one pair of socks.

"You should do like Jack and get a bottle of booze," she said aloud. Her voice echoed down the long, hardwood hall. *If booze gives him the courage to kill himself, maybe you could at least pack your bags?*

Her hand hovered over the phone on the bed. She wished she could call Jack again, just to hear a voice, but Jack hadn't responded to any of her texts, a fact that only compounded the ache of anxiety in her chest.. She opened up her laptop on the bedside table and knelt in front of it. She refreshed her emails. There was a newsletter and one of those advertisements from a clothing store where she'd signed up to get a discount. Nothing else. She checked the email to make sure it had sent. It had.

She texted Alexander, "Please call me."

Alexander would never ignore her. He had already moved heaven and earth for her safety. He would never abandon her, would he?

CHAPTER 27

Dresden, Present Day

The room was still black when Jack woke up. He groped around in the dark, trying to figure out where he was. As soon as he knocked over the empty water jar, he remembered. It rolled into the middle of the cold, dark room. Marcus stirred and sighed.

Jack planted both hands and pushed himself up. He heard a muffled rattle, the door. The door clanked and groaned, and Jack felt a draft. The light flicked on, blinding him.

"Good morning," said the American's mild voice as his round face blocked the light, "if you need to relieve yourself, you may do that now." Peter stood behind him with a fistful of zip-ties.

Jack glared at him as he stepped forward. "Will brunch be served after that?"

"Hands behind your back, Jack," he said. His lips curled into a sardonic grin.

Jack glared at him, but in keeping with his plan, turned around and let his wrists go slack so Peter could cuff them easily. Peter yanked the tie until it sliced into Jack's skin. "No need to whale on it," Jack grunted, "I'm not going anywhere."

The American spun the cuffed Marcus around and made him march in front of him. Peter shoved Jack along behind.

"How am I supposed to piss with my hands tied?" Jack asked with a sneer. "You gonna get your hands dirty?"

"Lia will be glad to assist you," Peter growled in his ear.

"I'm sure she would."

He was untied and shoved through a flimsy metal door into a white, tiled room with three rust-stained urinals and a toilet that had no partition around it. "You take too long, and we'll send her in after you," Peter said.

Jack emptied his painfully full bladder. For a moment he stood staring around the bathroom, searching for anything that might be useful. All he saw were the same white-painted, cinder block walls. There were two, industrial sinks. They were stained orange with mineral deposits. Rust streaked down the walls underneath them, mingled with something of a dark burgundy. There were three blue metal lockers in the far corner.

"What is this place?" Jack breathed. He took a step toward the lockers.

"Hey asshole!" Peter pounded on the door. "You have two minutes."

Jack glanced at the door. He pulled each locker open as quietly as he could, but each one contained nothing but dust. He washed his hands and splashed the icy water on his face and glanced at the door.

"You could bust out right now," he whispered. "Come flying out of the door." But Marcus was cuffed, and Jack had no weapon. He walked back out, and submitted to being restrained again.

They marched him down to the room with the tables and the tools. Lia was already there. She sat complacently on one of the tables, drinking from a paper coffee cup. The blood had all been scrubbed away. The stainless steel tables gleamed with menacing sterility under the white lights.

"Good day," she said. She set down the cup and jumped off the table. She had her phone clutched in one hand. "We have an exciting day planned out for you. Hey, smile!"

Jack looked at her in time to see her lift her phone and click off a picture. "Son of a—"

"Ransom photo," she said. She winked. "If I need it."

Jack bit his lip until he tasted blood, but he let Peter shove him toward the same table as the day before. *Look. Look around.*

Out of the corner of his eye, he surveyed the board. The bowie knife winked at him, mid board. It hung by a leather strap. It's keen edge shone silver in the white, fluorescent light.

He sat down on the cold metal table and tried to catch Marcus' eye across the room. Marcus wasn't looking. Lia was bent over him, laughing softly as the American fiddled with the plastic straps.

He caught a glimpse of her phone, sitting on the counter where she'd been sitting. Jack drew a breath and thought, *If I can get to that...*

"Get down," Peter said, "turn around. Don't move."

Peter's rough fingers fiddled with the cuffs. Jack felt a tiny release, and then his trembling hands were free.

Look around!

Jack's brain spun, trying to take it all in, fighting rising panic. Two doors, there were two doors at the end of the room. There was a microscope on a table against the wall, and what looked like lab equipment, a computer.

"Lie down!" Peter's fist cracked into his cheek.

Jack kicked at him, catching him in the inner thigh. Peter gasped, swore, swung his doubled fist. Jack's nose imploded. He cried out as spots danced in front of his eyes. Peter shoved him back and yanked the restraints over him.

Blood was flooding down into Jack's mouth. He coughed and gasped, turning his head, trying to clear his throat.

"Drown in it," Peter growled.

"Smile!" Lia said. Her phone appeared over Jack, and clicked.

Before she could turn away, Jack spat. Blood, mingled with saliva splattered on her phone and hands.

"Oh, that is *it.*" Lia tossed her phone onto the table. She rubbed her hand on Jack's split t-shirt, smearing it mostly on his skin. "It is too bad we're done with electrocution experiments. I suppose I'll have to settle." She picked a needle out of a tray on the table.

Jack shied away.

"Uh-uh, be a good boy," she grunted as she pressed the tip against a vein in his arm. "I think you want to be asleep when you go into the freezer."

Jack bucked against the restraints. The gurney he lay on shuddered and nearly tipped.

"Peter!" Lia's hand squeezed his arm.

Peter put his forearm against Jack's neck and bore down. Jack coughed, struggled against the blood in his mouth and the weight across his throat. He felt the needle pierce his skin. Warmth flushed him in an instant. He went limp, his eyes drooped, and shut.

He was in deep water, over his head, sinking, sinking. Far above he could see the light of the sun, but he couldn't move his arms or legs. He couldn't swim toward it. He had to fall, and fall, into the abyss without a bottom. Jack's eyes shut. He surrendered.

He never felt a release that told him he'd died. All Jack knew was plunging back to life. His eyes opened. By reflex he jerked to sit, but his body failed him. A spasm of shivers wracked his body. He lay under a bright light, covered with a sheet. He couldn't move.

Lia's face loomed over him. "Hey, the iceman cometh."

What? Had he been frozen? Was he still frozen? Jack channeled all of his energy toward his fingers. Finally, he felt them twitch. He wasn't restrained, he realized. He was weak, paralyzed by cold.

"I can't say I'm happy about it," she said, "but I'm not surprised." The stretcher lurched and began to move the opposite way that Jack was facing. He realized that the American was pushing it. They rumbled down the same wide hall they'd come up before, and then the stretcher was shoved into the holding room so hard that it toppled, and Jack plummeted toward the floor. His arm shot out reflexively. His palm pounded against the cement, and his body followed. He heard a snap as his shoulder hit the floor, and blinding pain coursed through him. "Ahh, shit! Shit!"

The American didn't even look behind him. Jack rolled on the floor, clutching at his broken wrist. The metal door slammed, and rattled. A bolt slid into place.

He lay in a heap. Blackness encroached on his vision, but oddly enough, a thought cut through the pain: he could move again. A few minutes passed. He could move his head without feeling faint. "Get up," he said.

Staggering to his feet took every bit of strength he possessed. His vision flashed around the edges, pulse throbbing in his face. "C'mon, c'mon," he hissed through his teeth. Sitting down on his pallet was a little easier. He could brace his back against the wall and slide down. A few seconds with his eyes shut, and his head felt on straight again.

Jack looked down. The broken wrist had begun to swell and bruise deep purple. He leaned his head back and panned the room with his gaze: concrete walls, once painted white, now flaked off and stained with rust. Two heavy, metal doors without latches on the inside. Certainly nothing to splint his wrist with.

Jack looked down at his cut-up shirt. If he could get it off and rip it up, he could bind the wrist tightly, but managing with one hand would be impossible. He wriggled his good arm from the sleeve inch by inch, each movement causing a fresh wash of pain. Once he had the sleeve off, he settled with wrapping the whole arm, using his good hand and his teeth. The effort left him coated in a thin film of sweat, but the pain began to dull to a low thrum.

He glanced over at Marcus's bed. He was there, lying on his side, facing the wall.

"I survived," Jack said to him in a small voice. Marcus didn't move.

Jack hunkered down and pulled his blanket over him the best he could. He'd begun to shake with cold again. He had to marshal his thoughts. He needed a plan.

Think! Think!

What if tomorrow I grabbed a knife off the board?

Jack visualized swinging the bowie knife at Lia and watching it slice into her abdomen.

Maybe it would give him enough time to bolt for the door. Which door? He didn't know. He just had to pick one and hope for the best. Somehow he had to get away.

He blew a long breath out through pursed lips. And Marcus? He glanced over at the inert form of his cellmate. Perhaps the best he could do was get away, and find help.

With a broken wrist?

He blinked. It would heal as soon as he rebounded, but he needed it whole now.

"Right." Jack got to his knees and staggered to his feet. He limped to the door and slammed his fist against it. "Hey! Hey!" He pounded against the unyielding metal until the whole room thundered with the vibrations. "Hey!"

From the corner of his eye, he saw Marcus lift his head.

A few minutes passed. Jack kicked the door and yelled again.

"Shut up!" Lia's voice echoed, guttural, on the other side.

"Lia," he shouted, "do you have a gun?"

There was a long pause. "Why?"

"Because your jackass American friend broke my arm. If you'd at least do the courtesy of shooting me, it would be healed when I wake up."

Lia cackled.

That instant the door swung open in his face. He saw a metallic tube and a flash of white light.

∞

Jack.

Jack caught a glimpse of limpid blue eyes, blond curls, pink lips. *Jack.*

"Mary Rose!" He flailed out, trying to find her. His hand struck something cold and solid. Jack's eyes flew open. He was awake, on the floor by the door in the cement-walled room and something was blocking the light.

"Holy shit!" Jack said.

Marcus knelt in front of him, head cocked a little to the side—sane, though goggle-eyed. He panted lightly, his hands were tightly fisted on his knees.

Jack pushed himself with both hands, and realized that his wrist was whole again. He was tired and weak from the rebound, but warmer and stronger than before. "Yeah, I'm okay, dude. Back off."

Marcus said something in German and swiped his hand across his forehead. He said the same thing again.

"Yeah, I still don't speak German."

Marcus's face had taken on a faint blush of color. Somehow the color made the dark smudges under his eyes more prominent and set off the red webbing of veins within them. He pointed to the spray of gore around them.

"Sorry about that," Jack said wryly. He flexed his wrist and tried to make motions to indicate that it was broken and now it was well, but this only garnered him an inquisitive stare. Jack sighed.

Marcus pointed past him. Jack turned his head and saw a plate sitting by the wall, beside the door with a pint-jar of water beside it. Jack sprang toward it, but paused to sniff it. The blue plastic plate had a dried out pile of potatoes on it, with peas and meatloaf. All cold. Jack took a tentative sip of the water. "Just eat it," he muttered, "unless now you're afraid of dying." He took a bite of the cold meatloaf. It tasted mostly of garlic, but Jack wolfed it down and drank the water without stopping. His companion knelt beside him the entire time without saying a word. His eyes skittered after every movement.

Jack eyed him. If only there were a way to tell him about his plan to escape. How long had Marcus been there? Every rebound had erased the previous day's scars, marks and sickness. His t-shirt hung loose off his angular shoulders. It was greyish, yellow under the armpits.

"How long have you been here?" he asked.

Marcus shook his head and palmed his face. His lips twitched as if he was trying to smile. "Ahh... yah," Marcus said softly. He sank back on his heels and glanced, awkwardly away.

Jack's body sagged. A headache had crept up his neck into the base of his skull. He could barely concentrate, and he needed to think. Jack swished around the last bit of water in the pint jar, threw it back, and set it down beside the empty plate. "Excuse me," he said to Marcus. He dropped onto his pallet bed and stared up at the pipes on the ceiling. Marcus shuffled back to his own bed.

After twenty or thirty minutes, the lights switched off. Someone slapped the outside of the door. "Sweet dreams," said Lia's muffled voice.

"Bitch," Jack said. He rolled himself up in the blanket, pillowed his head with his arm and tried to ignore the cold of the cement floor. He lay there, imagining the knife biting into her flesh.

CHAPTER 28
Katlenburg, 1631

A soft groan escaped Alexander's lips. He rolled over, pulling the rough, woolen blanket closer

"Oh God!" He sat up, suddenly sensible. "Oh dear God, where am I?" He sat up and clutched at his neck. It was whole, there was nothing wrong with him. Alexander swallowed hard. Death had spat him out, but where?

"Be easy, Sir." Hands gripped his shoulders gently and lowered him back to the pillow. A face hovered above his, the workman's weathered but noble visage, and a halo of shaggy blond hair. Alexander looked up at the ceiling, the bare wooden rafters and thatch poking through.

"Where am I?" Alexander asked again.

"In my hut, in the clearing."

The cabin. "Who are you?"

"Daniel," the workman said roughly. He lifted a wooden cup of water to Alexander's lips.

"I'm fine. I'm fine." Alexander took it from him. "I'm perfectly fine."

"Yes, I see that." Daniel leaned back on his haunches beside the pallet bed. Lantern light backlit his face, and sun-bleached blond hair. "Who are you, Sir? You who look so much like my deceased young master?"

"I am who I say I am," Alexander's voice trembled. How would he extricate himself now? "I am Alexander of Dresden. W-where is Leopold?"

"He ran off." Darkness came over Daniel's face. His lip curled. "You'll get no justice from Lord Georg. He knew very well that Leopold killed Albert."

This statement nearly bounced off of Alexander. There was a much greater fear on his mind. "Does Leopold know I am still alive?"

"You were well on your way to death when I pulled him off of you."

Alexander tried again to sit up. Daniel supported him for a moment until he got his bearings. He was wobbly, weak from resurrecting.

"You cannot stay here, Sir, and you cannot return there."

Alexander groaned. "The notes, the research."

Daniel squinted at him. "Your things? You have a horse. I may be able to get them for you, in the morning. But I too shall have to be gone." He trailed off and scrubbed at his scruffy jawline with his palm. "Albert was a good friend," he said, low but matter of fact. "Leopold poisoned him out of jealousy, for Albert was to inherit the estate. I had hoped one day... well." He slapped his knees. "Vengeance is God's." He stood up. He fixed Alexander with an intent gaze. "May I come with you?"

"Yes," Alexander said, taken aback, "I know not what I can offer you, Sir, but I will you repay you for my life if I can."

Daniel raised one bushy eyebrow. "I did not save your life, Master Alexander of Dresden. You did die, and death spat you out. I know, for I have done the same."

Alexander sucked in a breath and choked.

Daniel handed him the water and continued to eye him with the same placid expression. "Is this your first resurrection?"

"Are there more of your kind around here?" Alexander asked, wiping his mouth. His heart beat double-time.

Daniel shrugged. "You."

"How old are you, Daniel?"

"Fifty-seven." He looked thirty, perhaps younger if the weathering of many hours manual labor was accounted for.

"But you're not a member of the family." *Surely not. Tell me not.*

Daniel blinked. "But I am. Lord Georg's father impregnated a scullery maid, and here I am."

∞

Alexander lingered between the stone lions outside Ardovinni's house as the sunlight waned over the rooftops of Dresden. His cold fingers clutched at his clamping chest, for no speech he'd rehearsed could come close to expressing what was raging in his heart.

"Alexander," her voice came softly from the door.

He raised his head. Cosima stood in the doorway, wrapped against the cool air in a deep crimson shawl. Her hair fell in ringlets around her pale face. "Dear Alexander, aren't you going to come in?"

"I—" he said stupidly and walked forward.

In the entry, she brushed her fingertips across his jaw, and cupped his cheek. "So, you have returned." She slid her hand around the back of his neck and tipped his face down to hers. They met, forehead to forehead.

Alexander drew in a deep breath of her, earthy lavender and spice. He dug his fingers into her silky curls. "Cosima," he choked, "I found another, and he is my relative, and so I suppose I am to be the patriarch of an immortal nation after all."

"I see," she said. Her fingers moved in slow spirals in the nape of his neck. "What shall happen? What have Adolf and Frederick said?"

He said, with trembling lips, "They'll begin searching also, but how could we ever find every one of our offspring? They are like dandelions, sending a profusion of cursed seed with every puff of wind."

"Cursed seed," she breathed. Her eyes became downcast.

"Dear God, you know what I fear more than the hunt? Zoran shall arrive in Dresden, and our little society shall already have decided. Adolf and Frederick have already set it in their mind that they shall not have children. Sophia—she lost a child while I was gone. If I were Adolf—"

"I know," Cosima murmured.

"Zoran shall rage against it, him with his dreams of a great immortal society. He shall rage against me, I know it!"

Cosima met his eyes again, nose against nose, cheek against cheek. "And you? What have you set in your mind?" she asked calmly.

"I don't—I can't—I fear... dear God, Cosima!" he reared back, away from her, "I fear what I have created. I fear the children not yet born, who one day will be torn from their wives, children, families, who will linger in a life more like twilight than day, and curse me!"

Her lips pressed together until a white rim formed around them. She leaned back against the wall, wrapped her shawl more tightly around her, and stared a distant corner of the room.

Alexander clenched his fingers in coat collar, fighting the urge to rend the coat in two.

"Well," Cosima said slowly. She fixed her wet eyes on him and smiled weakly. "We are immortals, my love. It is clear we cannot be together now, but we are immortals. Who knows what shall transpire in a hundred years?" She stepped forward and took his hands. "There will be a way, my love. There will be a way." Their mouths met, first with gentle regret, then hungrily, memorizing one another, the taste, the smell, the feel. Her hands were on him, and his on her. Finally he had to break away, and leave her standing, like Idonia three hundred years before.

∞

"You sent her away!"

Alexander pressed his fingers to his throbbing temples. He bent over his desk, his back to Zoran in the doorway. "No, she left."

"So this is it, then. Hardwin, you, von Schwalenburg shall shut up all of us like a lot of nuns and monks, is that it?"

Alexander could hear Zoran's spittle fly with every clenched syllable.

"Answer me!" Zoran's hands gripped him like claws and turned him around.

"It's only for a time," Alexander said lamely, the same phrase he'd repeated every second moment from the time he'd heard Cosima was leaving Dresden. "Who knows what the future shall hold?"

"Who will ever know?" Zoran's face twisted up, eyes burning bright like he might burst into passionate tears. "Because you'll all be shut up in this fortress until you turn into Egyptian mummies." He released Alexander and stepped back. He pointed one slender finger. "But I won't. You're a damned coward, Alexander, and I won't be like you. You, who have the power to grant anyone everlasting life! You who will live until the end of the age, and you're afraid to do anything with what you're given!" His lip trembled then. He spun around toward the door.

"Zoran, please, don't go. What about the immortals... the immortals out there?" Alexander cried.

Zoran didn't look back.

"Do you think that I'm happy about this?" Alexander shouted at his back. "Do you think that I like what I have to do?"

CHAPTER 29

Dresden, Present Day

In the morning, Peter came for Jack and left Marcus behind.

Jack went with Peter quietly, without looking him in the eye. Fear pulsed through Jack. It was all he could do to control his thoughts and keep them moving in order. He repeated it to himself like a mantra: get the knife, get to the door, get the knife, get to the door.

Lia grinned at him when Peter marched him in. The American was nowhere to be seen. She had her phone in one hand and a pistol in the other. She shoved the pistol into her waistband. "You look remarkably good this morning, Jack," she said, "wanna see what you look like after you've been shot in the head?"

Jack just stared at her.

"No?" Lia winked at Peter and set the phone down.

Peter marched him past. Jack stared at the cell phone.

Grab it.

He heard Lia cross the room, out of arms reach, as he sat down on the gurney. Peter had the side cutters. An instant later, he felt his hand release.

Now!

He swung his elbow and caught Peter in the gut. Peter doubled over. Jack leapt over the table and snatched up the bowie knife. Peter straightened up and lurched for him. Jack swung the knife and felt it bite into flesh and bone. Peter howled.

The phone!

Jack snatched it from the table.

Lia spun around. Jack saw a gun in her hand. He shoved Peter and ducked as the shot exploded. Peter screamed. Jack's ears rang, and for a moment he couldn't get his bearings. He crashed into the table holding the monitors and machines. They toppled with a shattering of glass and plastic as he lunged for the door. The gun blasted again. Jack's face stung as chips of concrete bit into his cheek and temple. His hand was on the door handle. It opened, and he plunged through. He heard a body slam against it. Who? He couldn't afford to look back. He ran down the hall, another wide hall with doors like the other. He swung around a corner. He was in a big concrete room with nothing but hooks hanging from the ceiling. Rows and rows of hooks on rails, and bare concrete walls. The room was as cold as a winter morning.

A meat cooler.

Jack charged across it, aiming for a set of double doors at the far end. He heard the crack of a gunshot. He was deafened and thrown off balance. Hooks to his left gyrated wildly and clanked all the way down the rail. He veered to the right. Blam! Another shot went off, this time right at his heels. Jack grasped at the door and shoved. They wouldn't yield. He dropped the bowie knife and pulled, and they swung open.

Lia's high-pitched swearing echoed behind him, then muffled as the door slammed shut.

Jack skidded to a halt and swung his head side to side, searching for another door. He'd found the source of the spreader hooks: a chain lift at the base of a conveyor. Knives and scrapers hung on the wall beside the conveyor. The whole room stank of metal, stale blood and death.

Beyond the conveyor and two wide, stainless steel tables, gaped a narrow livestock chute. Jack bolted for it. Something squished under his feet. He skidded through the opening. The ground shot out from under him. He dropped straight onto his feet with jarring pain, ankle deep in snow at the bottom of a loading dock.

The air was frigid, and heavy with rain and fog, but despite being clad in only jeans and boots, Jack didn't notice for the pounding of his heart and the charging of the blood in his veins. He clawed his way out of the dock and dashed between two semi-trailers. He paused, straining to hear footfalls. The slaughterhouse yard was silent. Jack swiped the trickling blood from his eyes.

Now, how did he get out of this yard? Chain-link fence barred him front and back. He inched his way along and peeked around the end of the trailer. Twenty or thirty feet away, across the bare yard, there was a fence, balanced on rubber wheels. It stood open, about a foot, and he thought he saw a street beyond that. Jack swung to look back toward the brick slaughterhouse. There was no movement in the yawning black loading dock.

"Make a run for it," he whispered. "Come on. You can do this."

He sprinted, every second expecting to hear Lia's pistol blast and feel the searing pain of the bullet. He slipped and skidded through the opening. He fell to his knees, got up, and ran. He was in a narrow back street, loading docks and industrial buildings in every direction. He ran, arms pumping, across the road and through the complex of one of them. Far ahead, he thought he saw a person.

'Hey!" he screamed. "Help me!"

The figure came into focus. It was just an electrical box on a post. He veered into an empty parking lot. Jack put on all the speed he could muster, his boots pounding the slippery pavement. He rounded a corner. A semi roared past, just a couple feet away.

"Hey!" Jack shouted. He saw the driver look back in the mirror. The man's eyes widened. The truck belched black smoke and accelerated. "Stop!" Jack ran after it. "You have to help me!" The truck rounded a corner, behind a building. Jack's feet flew out from under him and he went down hard. He staggered back to his feet, swiping at his blurry eyes. Only then did he remember the phone, clutched in his hand.

Who should he call? He didn't know Cyrus's number, or Alexander's.

Alannah. She could call them.

He punched in the numbers and held the phone to his ear. It shook in his hand.

It rang, and rang again.

C'mon, c'mon!

"Hello?" Alannah's voice, quiet and hesitant, filled his ear.

"Alannah!" Jack hissed, "it's me, Jack."

"Jack? What—?"

"Listen, listen. You've got to call Cyrus. I'm in trouble—" he stopped, his chest heaving, "Lia's got me, Alannah."

"What?" panic tinged her voice, "where are you?"

"I-I don't know." Jack swung his head around. "I think it's a meat-packer's. I-I don't see any street signs, I—"

He broke off. He had no idea where he was.

Alannah was panting on the other end. "Okay, okay, I'll call Cyrus. He'll-he'll—"

"Hey, Jack!"

Jack gasped. The phone dropped from his hand.

He turned, in time to see a red hole punch through his bare chest. He didn't hear the shot. He didn't even see who'd shot him. His feet went one way, his arms the other. The earth tilted and he fell back. His eyes didn't leave the streaming hole.

No, no.

His head slammed into the pavement. The world rang shrilly and sparks exploded in his vision.

Get up.

Jack rolled over and pushed himself with superhuman effort. He got one foot under him. The gunshot rang out right above him, and he crashed back down.

"Get him back inside," the American said, above him.

Lia swore. "*You* get him inside, before someone comes looking. Idiot."

Rough hands clamped onto Jack's ankles. Jack's head slid and bounced as the American began to drag him. His bare skin scraped and tore away. Jack stared dully at the trail of blood on the grey pavement. Why hadn't he died yet?

"Shoot me," he said thickly.

The American paused.

"Are you crazy?" Lia asked. Her foot collided with Jack's side. "You stupid—" she kicked him again, in the softness under his ribs.

Jack screamed. He curled, instinctively, into a ball.

"As if I'm going to let you rebound, heal, and try this whole stunt over again. Bloody fool." Her small hands clamped on his trailing wrists. "You idiot. We can't drag him. Carry him over your shoulder."

She flipped him. Jack cried out from the movement. Black spots wobbled, larger and larger in front of his eyes.

I've failed. They're going to cut me open again. I'm never going free.

"Actually kill me this time," he groaned. "Kill me, bitch."

"I'd be happy to," Lia grunted. "Take his shoulders, Jordan. I'll take his feet."

Jack dropped. He heard his own voice bawl out, and then, mercifully, he lost consciousness.

Icy water in a torrent over his face brought him back to consciousness and searing pain. He howled in agony and rage. Lia's face hovered over him, distorted monstrously by the water in his eyes. The point of a scalpel rested on his chest, right below his chin. As he watched, she pressed on it. A thin line of dark blood appeared under the shining blade.

Jack's limbs began to shake of their own accord. His tongue felt thick and unyielding. "What are you..." He couldn't get enough breath to finish.

The scalpel bit harder into his skin. He felt the blade slice through every layer of skin, down into muscle. Jack screamed. "No! No, what are you doing?"

"What?" she drew back. Her eyes mocked him. "You are actually afraid?" She leaned in, spitting with every syllable, "You would appreciate this, if you were even a hundred years older—not having to live on while the world dies around you. You don't know what it's like to see your child die!" She jerked the scalpel down.

Jack arched his back and shrieked against the blinding agony. "No! No! No! I don't want to die!" Some reserve of strength opened up and he shot up on the table. He wasn't even restrained. He threw himself at her, even as blood spurted from his open chest and abdomen. The room tipped sideways.

Lia screamed. She fell back.

Jack toppled off the table and slammed face first on the floor. For an instant the whole world went white, then black.

Lia shrieked like a wild animal. Her nails raked into Jack's skin as she flipped him over. She had a rotary saw in her hand. It whined higher and higher as the blade whirled. "You crazy son of a bitch. I will kill you! I will cut out your heart!" The saw swung down.

An inhuman cry tore out of Jack as it bit into bone and tissue. His whole vision went red, then he plummeted toward death like being sucked underwater.

Jack.

The voice was so sweet, so gentle to Jack's brutalized mind.

Jack.

He swam toward it.

He was hovering above himself. He could see the whole lab room—and empty bed where Marcus had lain, Jordan bursting in through one of the doors, and his own pale, half naked body in a puddle of cardinal blood. His whole chest was peeled open. Lia knelt over him.

But as he stared the image blurred. Once again, he was in darkness.

Jack. Sweetheart.

Mary Rose. He fought to open his eyes. *Mary Rose.*

I'm here.

His eyes fluttered open. He was lying on cloud-like cushions. A soft sheet covered his skin. All the pain was gone.

"Jack."

It was her sweet velvety voice and her floral perfume. He wanted to turn his head but he was paralyzed. "Mary Rose, they've done it. They cut my heart out."

Her rose-petal lips brushed across his cheekbone. Her baby blue eyes came into focus above him and her pink lips pulled into a bow-like smile.

Jack felt peace wash over him and he smiled back. "Mary Rose," he whispered.

She wasn't the frail, fragile woman with the dark bags under her eyes. She was Mary Rose as she'd been on their wedding night, twenty-two years old, in a white satin nightgown. Her pale blond ringlets cascaded around him, surrounding him with her scent. Her dimples appeared in her full, peaches-and-cream cheeks. He reached out for her, but as far as he reached, he couldn't touch her silken skin.

"I'm sorry," he rasped.

"Why are you sorry?"

"I promised I would take care of myself and I haven't."

"Sweetheart, I wanted you to be happy." Her mouth hovered close. "I wanted you to be happy."

"I was going to join the society. I was going to start a new life..." He trailed off as he looked up into her blue eyes.

"It's okay," she whispered, "I'm glad for you. Make a new life, make it without me."

"I failed you. I hurt myself again."

"You didn't fail me," she breathed, "I always knew you loved me, and you were doing your best."

"I want to be with you, but I'm... I'm not ready to die."

"I know. Jack. You need to go." Her outline shimmered and her skin took on a gossamer sheen.

"Are you leaving me?"

"You need to go back, sweetheart. You're on the edge of a new life." A diamond tear hung in the corner of her eye and fell out to glisten on her cheek. "You will be happy again, Jack." Her laugh was like a summer breeze, brushing over him warm and soft. "I believe in you. I always have."

"Mary Rose." He reached out again. His fingers passed right through her translucent form. She smiled and was gone. In her place a light like a summer sun grew brighter and brighter.

Jack sucked in a deep breath and rose up into the light like he was breaking above the surface of the water.

CHAPTER 30
Winnipeg, Present Day

Alannah sat on her bedroom floor with her phone clutched in her hands. The only light was the glow of the screen. Two hours had passed since Jack had called her, and her heart rate had yet to return to normal.

She'd awoken from a deep sleep, and answered the phone before it could even register that the number was European.

Jack's terrified voice on the line sent a shot of adrenaline through her.

"I'm in trouble! Lia's got me."

And then, from somewhere beyond the phone, "Hey, Jack!" A sharp crack, a gasp from Jack and then garbled voices as she listened, unable to hang up.

Finally she'd managed to hang up. She sat against the headboard of the bed, willing her fingers to punch in Cyrus's number. It took him only seconds to answer.

"Alannah?"

"C-c-cyrus, Jack's in trouble!"

"I know," he soothed, "we're working to find him—"

"No, he called me!"

"From where?" Cyrus's tone went from near patronizing to stern in an instant.

"He-he didn't know. He thought it was a meat packers."

Cyrus said, in German, to someone in the background, "Is there an abandoned abattoir nearby?" Then, to her, "Did he say anything else?"

"Lia has him." Tears burned behind her eyes. "She must have found him again, 'cause he—"

"There's an abandoned slaughterhouse in Freital," a voice said in the background.

Cyrus had hung up, with a promise to call her when they found Jack. That had been about two in the morning. It was four now. The battery of Alannah's phone was draining steadily from constantly waking the screen over and over.

She was so helpless, and Jack was an ocean away. Was he dying?

He's not dying.

But what if he was?

∞   ∞   ∞

"How do I answer to this without sounding like a brute?" Alexander's voice, within his office, was scratchy, n's pronounced almost like d's through a stuffed nose. "I want to be the one to answer. Frederick will come out blasting like a canon, and Adolf will ignore it as nonsense." Alannah, outside the door, pressed against the wall, heard the flap of paper, the pamphlet.

"He has them all wrapped up," Daniel's voice was thick with bitterness, "all dancing on the end of his string."

Fire burned in Alannah's belly, but not bright enough a flame to make her charge in and defend her father's honor. Daniel would scoff her back out of the room.

"It's not the idea I'd counter—" Alexander began to cough, a deep, hacking cough. A glass slid across a table. "Thank you," Alexander squeaked, "ahh... my God! It's not the idea. It's that they demand to know the secrets of life and death. Zoran knows every secret, he knows far more than I do. If that's what they want, why

301

aren't they blasting their way toward the Fountain? Hasn't he told them? God, I wish I never brought him there." He coughed again, and fell silent. Daniel was silent. In the quiet, Alannah could hear Alexander wheezing.

She pressed her fingers into her sweaty palms until her nails bit into the skin, little crescents of pain. She blinked. But why the Fountain?

Oh...

"The water," she whispered, "the water is the secret." Alannah took a step backward, then another. Her breathing quickened. She spun and bolted down the corridor, down the staircase into the foyer.

"Alannah?" Anastasie's ethereal voice came from over her shoulder, but Alannah did not look back.

'If Zoran succeeds, we won't go on accumulating these pains forever,' Jurgen's voice in her head.

'The power to sway many to our side'—Zoran, his eye glazed with heady triumph.

Power, but not for life—for death.

Thirty minutes later, Alannah stood on Zoran's landing, slamming her fist against the door. Her whole body shook with adrenaline, mingled with panic. "Zoran!" Pain jarred through her knuckles. "Zoran! Let me in. Zoran!" she bawled.

One flight of stairs down, a door opened. "Everything alright?" A woman called up, sternly, she'd been disturbed from her tea, or soap operas.

"Yeah!" Her voice cracked, but the door shut. As it did, the apartment door creaked open.

Zoran stood in front of her. His white button-up shirt was soaked through, showing the tones of his skin.

"What did you do?" she bleated.

"Quiet!" Zoran grabbed her wrist and dragged her through the door. His dark curls were full of water droplets.

302

"What did you do!?" Alannah wrenched her wrist from his hand and plunged toward the hallway. He let her pass. She slid on water into the bathroom and fell to her knees, face to face with Jurgen.

He lay, like a body prepared for burial, on the tile floor. He was fully dressed in a drenched wool sweater and light chino pants, barefoot. His face was nearly as pale as the grey tile, lips bluish.

"Jurgen!" She began slapping his face, sobbing in hiccups, "Jurgen! What did you do?"

"He's dead," Zoran said behind her. His voice was oddly cold, devoid of emotion. "Don't be distressed Alannah, it is what he wanted."

"Come back!" Every strike against his cheek only warmed her own hand. "Jurgen, come back! Come baaaaack—"

Zoran's hand pressed over her mouth, squelching her cry. His wet clothes dampened her back as he restrained her. "Alannah, you must be quiet."

She squeaked against his hand and struggled.

"Alannah! Alannah, this is our proof! Proof, Alannah! Hope! Do you know how many there are of us who wish for death? All this time, the method has been in front of us, guarded by those men. Jurgen went willingly!"

"You're lying!"

Her words, garbled though they were, must have registered with Zoran. He gripped her so tight it bruised her cheeks.

"Let me go!" she screamed into his hand. She thrashed with all the strength she had. "Jurgen! Jurgen!"

He hit her so suddenly, drove his fist into her gut so hard it knocked all the breath from her lungs. She doubled over, wheezing, eyes popped wide open.

"Quiet!" he hissed, his teeth right in her face. "Do you want the neighbors to call the police? If they take this body, I'll have to kill you too. Mark my words."

She went limp, slumping over next to Jurgen's serene, cold face.

Zoran bent down so he could look her in the eye. "Life and death, right in my hand." He held up the vial. There was, yet, water in it. "Did your dear Alexander ever tell you that this has been done before? Probably not. He covered it all up last time, and let everyone go on believing that they were trapped in these undying bodies for all eternity."

Hot tears spilled down her face. Bile burned in her throat. She wanted to vomit.

"Tonight we'll bring Jurgen to Schwalenburg. Tomorrow, Alexander won't be able to deny the existence of immortal death."

He smiled, an expression of pure happiness that would visit Alannah in her dreams for decades.

Zoran locked her in the windowless room, to curl up on the wet floor beside Jurgen's body. She lay on her side with his icy fingers in hers. "Wake up, Jurgen," she whimpered, "wake up, please. Please, Jurgen.

∞   ∞   ∞

Alannah shook herself, like she could shake off the memory. Of course she couldn't. She couldn't stop herself from imagining Jack's face, cold and grey like Jurgen's.

She pulled her knees to her chest, overcome with a deep feeling of isolation. She'd give anything to hear a friendly voice, Cyrus— Alexander would be even better. But they'd be busy, she hoped, with Jack.

You should go to Dresden.

I can't.

She got up and put on her housecoat. She stumbled down the stairs into the kitchen. She sat at the table, drinking coffee and staring at her dark cell phone.

You should go.

I can't.

Seven in the morning, the weak, bluish rays of the morning sun mingled with the light over the dining table. Alannah lifted her head, and pushed away the cup. She had to go on, if she could. She had class to teach. She had to shower, get dressed. Alannah got up and twisted the nob, switching on the element under the still-warm kettle. She pulled open the fridge, sniffed at the milk and pushed it aside to grab the container of yogurt and the sandwich she'd made the night before.

She pushed aside the curtain long enough to reveal the pale pink glow of the sun peeking through the trees on Wellington Crescent. It would be a clear day, and very cold, and she was cold, even in her fleece robe.

Behind her, the kettle began to whistle. As it reached the peak of its shrill whistling, Alannah thought she heard a distant chime. She grabbed the kettle off the element. The steam blasted her wrist as the whistle petered away.

The chime sounded again. Alannah's mouth dropped ajar. It was the doorbell.

Jack!

Idiot, of course not.

Her heart began to hammer.

She pulled her robe tighter around herself, opened the little drawer nearest the kitchen door, and withdrew Jack's pistol. She slipped it into the pocket of her robe, beside her phone. Its weight tugged the whole garment down and strained the belt. She padded in her bare feet to the door. She opened it a crack, and found herself staring into the eyes of Giovanni Ardovinni. She gasped.

"Miss Krueger, may we speak to you?" he asked softly.

We? Alannah lifted her gaze and realized that the blond man with the deep brown doe-eyes stood beside him. She opened the door another couple inches. "Talk."

Giovanni glanced back at the other man, who then stepped closer. Alannah stared at him, and the blond man stared back. He had a hard face: a straight nose, square jaw, chiseled mouth. His form, even cloaked under a black coat, bore signs of muscle.

Alannah felt a quiver go through her and she nearly slammed the door, until she looked up into his eyes. They were the deepest brown, sensitive, hesitant.

"Miss Krueger," he said, looking furtively back at his companion, "we came to plead with you one last time. I need to speak to Lord Alexander most urgently."

"Who are you, anyway?" Alannah shivered and curled her bare toes against the frigid draft. "Do you think I give Alexander's contact information to people at random?"

"My name is Alexei." His voice had a muddy, confused accent. She couldn't place it at all.

"Who are your parents?"

Alexei flinched. "That's what I need to talk to Alexander about."

Alannah steeled her spine. She slipped her hand into the pocket of her robe and closed her fingers around the grip of the pistol. "Look," she said, "I don't know why you're coming to me, and I don't know how you found my house. But if you think that I'm just going to swallow your story about being twice-born and go along with your scheme, you are sorely mistaken."

The earnest emotion vanished from his eyes, and black walls slammed down in their depths. "Why must you be unreasonable? Have you no feeling, no heart for your fellow immortals?" He took a step forward.

Alannah shrank back, and tugged the door shut. His hand snaked around and yanked it back open. Her hand flew from her pocket. She shoved the pistol in his face.

He drew back and his face froze into a shocked rictus.

"M-miss Krueger," Giovanni said behind Alexei.

Alannah waved the pistol in Alexei's face. "You go back and tell him... you tell Zoran that-that I won't come back. I won't be his, ever!"

"Miss Krueger..."

"Go away!"

"Please." Giovanni tried to tug Alexei away from the door and step in front of him, but Alexei resisted and stood his ground. "Miss Krueger, we mean no harm—"

"Go away!" Alannah wound up to slam the door shut, but before she could, Alexei spun around and grabbed Giovanni by the arm.

"Leave her," he said. His jaw bunched taut. His eyes burned black. He yanked Giovanni down the sidewalk toward the road. His voice softened with resignation. "There must be some other way."

They were halfway down the hallway when Alannah had a flash of an idea. She grabbed her phone from her pocket. "Hey!" she yelled after them.

They both turned back. Alannah raised the phone and snapped a picture, freezing their shocked expressions on the screen. Alexei's face went as white as the snowdrifts around him. He pulled Giovanni toward a dark SUV. The Italian's face was still pleading.

Alannah slammed the door and bolted it. She leaned against it, panting. Slowly she lowered the gun to her side and slipped the phone back in her pocket. Alexander knew whom all of Zoran's people were, right? Maybe Alexei was known to him, somehow.

She punched in Alexander's number and let it ring eight times. She swallowed hard, and texted him: *Alexander please call me when you can.*

"I can't stay here," she groaned. "I don't know what kind of sick game this is he's playing, but I'm not going to cooperate. I have to go." Alannah stumbled back into the kitchen. She didn't want coffee anymore. She tossed the sandwich back into the fridge. She had to go now. No going to work. She'd call in sick and she'd skip town.

I can't!

She slumped down against the wall, underneath the light switches by the kitchen door. In the pocket of her robe, her phone clunked against the gun. Alannah gasped, and pulled the pistol from the pocket and laid it beside her on the floor. She wrapped her arms around herself, shivering, despite the robe, in her tank top and flannel pajama pants. Alannah unwrapped one arm from her body, held up her hand in front of her face and watched it tremble.

Any help was hours, maybe days away.

That fateful day, curled up in a ball beside Jurgen, frozen to her core, weeping broken sobs, she hadn't known that Daniel had heard her by Alexander's door and followed her, watched her drive out of Schwalenburg's gates like the hounds of hell pursued her, and gone after her. The moment Zoran flicked off the light and left her in the dark with her dead friend was the moment before Daniel kicked in the apartment door.

Not this time. This time she was truly alone.

"I'm so tired of this," she said hoarsely.

Her bottom lip began to quiver. "Why won't you call, Cyrus? Haven't you found him? Why isn't Alexander answering?"

Leave.

"Noooo…" she groaned. She fought to keep back the panic forming a fist of pain in her chest. "No, I can't. I can't."

Alexander, she texted again, *I need to talk to you. Please call me.*

She called her superior at the University. "I can't come in. I'm… I'm really not feeling well." Her voice was trembling sufficiently that she hoped to be convincing. She really wasn't feeling well. It was no lie.

"O…kay. But you teach in an hour and a half. What should I do?" She could hear his computer keys clacking on the other end of the line.

"Cancel it, put up a notice… I don't know. I'm sorry. I'm…"

"It's okay. I'll figure it out."

Move. Alannah clenched her jaw. *You've got to move.*

She stood frozen for a moment.

Cyrus and Idina have a flat in London.

You can do this.

Alannah took a deep breath, and ran up the stairs to her room. She stuffed her photos into one big rolling suitcase and padded it with all her socks and underwear and her wool dress coat. She put all the clothes she cared to keep in her rolling carry on. She'd take the laptop bag, and leave the purse. She walked through the library and stared at the books that were hers. All of them were too heavy to pack. Still, she grabbed the tattered, leather bound Bible that had belonged to her mortal father, the good man who'd raised her. She'd wear the wool coat and leave her parka. As soon as they lifted off from Winnipeg she wouldn't need it any more.

She stuffed Jack's handgun into the depths of the kitchen garbage, under the eggshells and the coffee grinds, and tossed the whole thing out for garbage pickup. When she'd done that, she leaned heavily against the counter. A small stack of photos sat there, in front of the toaster.

She stood over her suitcase, flipping through the small stack of photos. She barely glanced at them, she knew them so well. The crushing loneliness overtook her, and tears dropped onto the photos. She swiped them dry against her pants. She stared into Zoran's eyes.

Zoran had the strangest eyes, and they had always unnerved her, even when she had trusted him. They were black, obsidian chips in his face. They pierced her like razors, as if even from the page he could see every chink in her armor.

"You are mine, my twice-born immortal, my miracle."

He'd done it again, somehow. Here was Alexei. Zoran was reaching beyond the bars of his jail, still proving he knew the secrets of immortal life and death.

Alannah squared her shoulders. Not this time, not to her.

Her phone jangled on the counter. Alannah leapt out of the chair to snatch it up. "Hello?"

"Alannah," Alexander's voice was breathless and terse. "What's wrong?"

"Jack? What about Jack?"

"We found him. They're on their way back right now."

Alannah burst into tears.

"It's alright, Alannah, he's okay." Alexander's voice wobbled a little, "It's alright."

"Alexander, he's found me," she sobbed, "I'm leaving Winnipeg."

"What? Who?" Alexander growled, "where are you, Alannah? Are you in danger right now?"

"I-I'm at home. I'm going to leave. I can't stay here." Her chest convulsed and fresh tears spilled down her face. "He has another twice-born."

"What?"

"Ardovinni came to my door with this other man. His name was Alexei—"

"Alexei," Alexander whispered to himself.

"—and he pleaded with me to put you in contact with him. When I said no, he was very angry. Alexander, Zoran had another child! Ardovinni told me Alexei is twice born!"

Alexander paused for nearly a minute. Finally he said, slowly, "Come to Dresden, Alannah."

"No! No." Alannah took a deep breath. "I'm going to London. Can Cyrus call me when-when he can?"

"It might be a little while," Alexander said gently, "can you stay in a hotel when you get there?"

"O-okay," she quavered.

"Text me all the details of your flight, your hotel, everything. As soon as I can, I'll get Cyrus to call you. I just don't think it will be today."

"O-okay."

"Alannah," Alexander said softly, "I won't let him hurt you again. As far as it depends on me, Zoran won't even look on your face again."

"I'll..." Alannah brushed the tears from her eyes, "I'll text you when I get a flight."

"Text me often."

"Okay."

"Keep your eyes and ears wide open."

"I will."

"You'll be alright, Alannah. You're a brave woman." Alexander hung up.

"Brave woman." Alannah sniffled. She stood up on wobbly legs. The thin stack of photos still sat on the counter, Zoran face up. Alannah picked them up and slid his picture under the stack revealing Jurgen's face. He smiled, but there was darkness in his eyes.

Jack's alright. He's not dead, like you.

Tears spilled over.

"This too gets easier, as does living." Jurgen's words came back.

"When?" she said to the picture, "when, Jurgen?"

It didn't matter. She had to lock up the house that had been her den of safety for forty years, and get on a plane. She had to leave it behind now. She had to leave Jurgen too.

Alannah let out a shaky breath. She had one thing left to do.

Five minutes later, she stood in the dark kitchen in her parka. Her car chugged in the garage, warming against the bitter cold. Alannah lay the pictures of Jurgen side by side in the stainless steel sink and pinched a match between the folds of the matchbook. The cardboard match flared to life, reflecting in the faucet and the scuffed sink.

Alannah dropped the match onto the photos and watched the flame lick at the papers. For a moment, Jurgen's deep, dark eyes were alight with fire, then his face dissolved. He was gone forever.

CHAPTER 31
Winnipeg, Present Day

Alannah sat in a padded plastic chair in the boarding gate. Outside the giant, plate glass window, the shiny white nose of the plane gleamed in the blinding tarmac lights. Fifteen minutes, and she'd be on it, bound for London.

She was so tired, exhausted just from driving to the airport and lugging her suitcases to the desk. Reluctantly, she'd let her suitcase containing her precious photo collection be checked and stowed under the plane.

Her eyes flicked around the waiting area. It was nearly full, almost impossible to see everyone there. But she didn't see any familiar faces, nor Alexei's probing ebony eyes.

Those eyes haunted her. They were so full, with all the joy and pain that his face could not show. They weren't Zoran's flinty, shark eyes.

She reached into her purse and pulled out her makeup compact. She stared at her own face, slightly distorted in the tiny mirror, until her bloodshot, chocolate brown eyes came into focus.

Alexei didn't have her eyes either.

Alexei had seemed genuinely hurt, but then... Alannah bit her lip and remembered Zoran's pleading gaze as she'd backed away from his cell, deep in the bowels of Schwalenburg.

"You are my family." His hand extended to her. *"My own blood. Alannah, my sweet daughter, I never meant to hurt you."*

Alannah shook her head and blinked away the tears that had sprang up. She shoved the compact into her purse and pulled out her phone.

Alexander had replied to her last message, "Good to hear. Text me when you land."

Alannah crinkled her nose. She should send him the picture of the two men. In her haste to get out of Winnipeg, she had forgotten that she had taken it. Alexander had a remarkable mind for faces. If he'd seen them, he would know them. She'd have him show them to Daniel as well. Daniel might recognize them.

She tapped on the screen and brought up the picture. She squinted at their shocked, frozen faces. As Alannah ran her eyes down the line of Alexei's jaw and his linear nose, something triggered, deep in her memory. Something was strange about his face, so familiar that she wondered why she had never thought of it.

She swiped back into her archived photos. The images glided across the screen in blurs of motion until she reached a picture of Alexander. It had always been one of her favorites, for the memory it contained.

He'd been reading in the library of his home, and she had been playing with her brand new smart phone.

Hey Alex!

He swung around, mouth slightly agape.

She snapped the picture and giggled at his expression. His face slackened, and he chuckled. "Alas, I am besieged by paparazzi."

Alannah stared at the image, then returned to the photo taken that morning.

"Oh God," she said.

Why hadn't she seen it before? In that expression, the two men were mirror images. Goosebumps popped up under her coat sleeves. She stared at Alexei's deep, brown eyes and traced the outline of his face with her gaze.

But if he has Alexander's face... Are those Cosima's eyes?

"Who are you, Alexei?" she whispered.

Dresden, Present Day

"Cy, he's waking up." It was a woman's voice.

"'Lannah?" Jack said through numb lips. His lids were heavy and his eyes burned with tears.

"Come on then, love. Open your eyes. You can do it." It wasn't Alannah. She had a thick Scottish accent.

The warm surface his head lay on shifted. Jack's eyes flickered open and he looked up into cheerful but tired green eyes of a woman. His head lay on her knee and his body was arranged on the backseat of a car, covered by a wool coat. The car rocked gently as it turned a corner.

"Well hello." She smiled down at him.

"Where am I?"

"You're on your way to Schwalenburg, Jack."

"Are..." He licked his parched lips. "Are you Idina?"

"Yes. We found you."

Jack shut his eyes and sagged back down. Under the coat, he reached his trembling hand toward his heart. He pressed his cold fingers to his sternum and felt a thin indentation of new skin where Lia's knife had split him open. His fingers travelled upward and pressed against his carotid artery. Blood throbbed there, as strong and regular as ever.

He lay perfectly still, with his pulse beating under his fingertips. For a moment, he believed he could still smell Mary Rose's perfume and feel the brush of her breath against his cheek.

"I'm alive," he said.

ABOUT THE AUTHOR

Geralyn Wichers writes from the Canadian prairies, where she moonlights as a manufacturing operator at a large factory. When she's not wearing a respirator and handling hazardous chemicals, Geralyn is either writing about the impending zombie apocalypse, or training to survive it by running long distances.

Geralyn is a marathoner, a foodie, and a coffee addict. She is the author of *We are the Living*, an apocalyptic story of love and hope in the midst of destruction, and *Sons of Earth*, the story of a clone finding his humanity in a dystopian near-future.

Follow her on Twitter @geralynwichers and check out her website geralynwichers.com.